HER BRIDEGROOM LIST

RAKES & REBELS: THE ST. BRIAC FAMILY, BOOK 5

CYNTHIA WRIGHT

OLIVERHEBERBOOKS

PRAISE FOR CYNTHIA WRIGHT

"Her Bridegroom List is Cynthia Wright at her most delightful! A defiant, independent heroine, and an irresistible libertine of a hero. A blend of passion and adventure, Emeline & Hart's story made me fall in love with historical romance all over again!"

— USA TODAY BESTSELLING AUTHOR KIMBERLY CATES

"Another brilliant masterpiece by Ms. Wright! Experience the excitement of archeological finds and the romance of a captivating love story that draws you in."

— TG, AMAZON READER

"An Absolute Triumph! Cynthia Wright does it again."

— LS, AMAZON READER

"A lively, determined young woman and a charismatic, sardonic aristocrat unearth treasure, love, and passion in Her Bridegroom List!"

— MSM, AMAZON READER

"It was just like every Cynthia Wright book I have read: one sentence and I was lost in the story. I laughed with the spirited Emeline, I felt for Hart as he struggled to love. I reunited with amazing characters from other books again. It felt like coming home and staying with family."

— HC, AMAZON READER

"Cynthia, you have a winner!! I loved everything about this book. It has been a LONG time since I have been so invested in a romance!"

— NCL, AMAZON READER

"An engrossing read with a Victorian archaeological twist, Her Bridegroom List delivers a story of stubbornness, passion, and characters who defy convention. Highly recommend!"

— SSF, AMAZON READER

For Lynne Shear and Heike Conrad, treasured friends and faithful readers. Here's to our next reunion in a new part of the world!

PROLOGUE

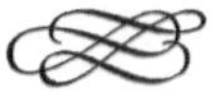

LONDON, ENGLAND, APRIL 1840

*L*ord Jasper Hartcliffe, widely known as Hart the Heartless, reclined against a pillar in the magnificent ballroom of Riven Court. Under hooded lids, he surveyed the throng of glittering guests and closed his fingers around a small, folded note.

The hostess of this predictably dull Spring Ball, Susanna, Countess of Riven, had pressed the paper into his hand just minutes before.

Hart's blood pulsed as he thought of her brazen invitation to rendezvous with her at two o'clock in the morning. *I yearn for you. I will be waiting in the bedchamber at the top of the stairs.* Although the ball would be winding down by then, Susanna's overbearing husband would still be occupied in the library, deep in his usual game of whist. Lord Riven cared far more for cards than the ample charms of his countess.

Still, Hart mused, it would be mad to cuckold the man under his own roof.

Wouldn't it? The edges of his hard mouth flickered as he considered this.

"Scanning the crowd for your next conquest, I surmise," a voice murmured just behind Hart's left shoulder.

No need to look back, for the speaker was his brother, Austell, 9th Duke of Caversham.

"Envious, Your Grace?" Hart taunted lightly.

"Envious?" Austell repeated, pausing for effect. "Far from it."

"Ah." This finally drew a brief glance from Hart. "That's right, you are still besotted with your duchess. Or is it simply that we agree that all of these young beauties are as monotonous as an array of porcelain dolls with painted smiles?"

This was one reason Hart rarely attended formal gatherings among the haut ton. He could not be bothered to play their tedious social games, especially because they usually involved yet another insipid female in her first Season, angling for a titled husband. In truth, he'd really come tonight to see how his brother was getting on.

"Even if I were not devoted to Margaret," replied Austell, "I would have the good sense to realize that, at one-and-thirty, you and I are too old for this sort of marriage mart."

Too old? Hart narrowed his eyes. "Speak for yourself." The jest was rapier-sharp, for they were fraternal twins, sharing a birthday and yet opposites in both looks and personality.

"I may be older by a few minutes, but hard living has left its mark on you," Austell persisted, gesturing toward the silver hairs glinting liberally throughout Hart's dark locks. "And it's not only your age…" He seemed to consider whether to go on, but put up his chin and finished, "You are an infamous libertine. No respectable mama who loves her daughter would dream of handing her over to the likes of you."

"That's just as well." Hart lifted a dark brow. "I have no interest in respectable females."

If Austell hadn't been born just minutes ahead of him, Hart would have been the one to assume the dukedom when their father died two years ago. Ever since Papa had brought the fraternal twin brothers, on their fifth birthday, into the drawing room and announced that Austell was first born and thus would one day be the duke, Hart had felt a bittersweet mixture of rejection and relief.

Thank God he'd come to realize that, in truth, *he* was the fortunate one. Each morning, he awoke to a surge of freedom that his tradition-bound brother would never know. He could do as he damned well pleased, with no concern for society's censure.

He turned now and met Austell's soft brown gaze, the opposite of his own crisp midnight-blue eyes. In a nearby mirrored wall, Hart glimpsed their reflections. He was tall, lean, some said imposing, with chiseled features and cropped black hair heavily salted with silver. Austell was slighter, paler, his chestnut curls thinning. No wonder people were doubtful upon hearing that they were twins.

"Clearly, you do not envy me my debauched libertine's existence." Hart endeavored to keep the cynical edge from his voice as he added, "And why would you? You have achieved your life's dreams. You're a duke, after all, and you are smitten with your duchess."

His brother looked oddly nervous, even as he nodded. "You're quite right, of course. I am terribly fortunate."

What lingered in the air, unspoken, was the reality that Austell and Margaret had yet to produce an heir after five years of marriage. And Hart suspected something more lurked behind his brother's tense expression. Did he really want to learn what it was? God, no.

Hart glanced away before reluctantly asking, "Have you found that investment you were seeking?"

"I believe so! In the shipping sector!" Austell's eyes were a bit too bright. "You have no doubt heard there are brilliant new *steamships* being built, driven by propellers rather than paddle wheels." Austell's voice rose with excitement. "Iron and steel replacing wood."

Hart knew a pang of relief that he had no ties to the family fortune. Austell wanted the title and all that went with it, and he was damned welcome to it.

Yet it was disorienting to realize that Austell had actually replaced their shrewd father overseeing the vast holdings of Caversham Castle. The old duke had been conservative with the estate funds, avoiding risk. However, two years into Austell's dukedom, Hart suspected that his brother might be running up debts, and not the sort that came about from improvements to the estates. When Hart had last visited Hartcliffe House in London, the duke, after a few brandies, had very casually inquired if Hart knew of any splendid investments.

"You are acquainted with a lot of those cits, aren't you?" Austell had pressed. "The vulgar fellows who are building rail-roads and factories?"

"I have an aversion to vulgar fellows," Hart had replied drily, sidestepping the question. In the next moment, his sister-in-law, Margaret, had appeared in the doorway, ending the awkward conversation.

Now, Hart suppressed a sigh. "I hope the new steamships make you very rich."

"Yes, I believe they are bound to do so," Austell replied. "*Very* rich."

Sensing the gray cloud that continued to hover over his brother, Hart wished he could walk away and leave him to it. This was what Austell had dreamed of his entire life: the duke-dom, the estates, the title, an exalted position in Society. Hart hoped His Grace could simply occupy himself taking care of it all, as their father had done, and Hart could continue to go off and seek his own forms of pleasure.

Across the ballroom, illuminated by an array of new gas-lit, crystal chandeliers, elegantly clad guests were taking their places for the next dance. Hart turned his head as the musicians began to play Chopin's latest waltz, an appealingly lively piece. His gaze followed the pairs of dancers as they dipped and turned, stopping abruptly on one arresting female.

"Who is that beauty with old Lord Fulham? I've never seen her before."

Austell craned his neck and blinked. "Never seen her? Why, that's Emeline St. Briac. They call her the Exquisite." He paused, then added, "Her father's a pirate, you know. One of those notorious corsairs from St. Malo. Retired now, but rich as Croesus." He paused for a long moment, staring at the girl. "She's enchanting, but they say she goes against the current."

"Does she indeed?" Intrigued, Hart leaned negligently against the pillar but continued to follow the movements of the spirited brunette. Radiant in a simple, elegant gown of amethyst silk, her ebony locks smoothed into a chignon at the base of her neck and decorated with a single white English rose, the girl was enchanting. She was nothing like the others, with their schooled, polite expressions. On the contrary, her countenance displayed her thoughts and feelings for all to see, whether she realized it or not.

The chit didn't want to be here anymore than he did.

"She is on the husband hunt?" Hart wondered in an offhand tone.

"More like the other way round! By Jupiter, man, you have been absent from polite society longer than I realized."

"It would seem that I am sadly ignorant."

"Emeline St. Briac came out nearly two years ago," Austell reported. "Margaret says she's had many excellent offers and turned them all down for one reason or another. It's rumored that she means to run out the clock so her papa will surrender and allow her to go off and live independently."

"How very…unexpected," Hart murmured. "What do you think she means to do?"

His brother snorted. "Search for *fossils*, or so they say."

Fossils! Hart decided he could not have heard Austell correctly. However, before he could question him further, Margaret,

Duchess of Caversham, motioned from across the room with a subtle movement of her silk fan.

"I must go. My bride beckons." Austell straightened his cuffs.

Hart looked at him. "I'm leaving for Italy next week."

"Are you indeed! You only appeared tonight to say goodbye?"

Discovering his glass on a nearby side table, Hart drank down the champagne and nodded. "I wanted to see you before I go. I mean, in case you should need me for any reason."

"And what if I did?"

He had a point. "We are brothers, after all…"

Austell gave him a half-smile as he turned to go. "So we are."

A moment later, the clock struck two. The note in Hart's pocket seemed to catch fire, urging him on to the forbidden assignation with his hostess, Lady Riven.

It was mad. Licentious. Reckless!

Just the sort of thing Hart badly needed to feel alive.

* * *

LORD FULHAM WAS LOOMING SO close to Emeline, she caught a whiff of his breath, a mixture of cigar and port. She would have been annoyed if not for his air of menace.

"Sir, it is good of you to ask me, but I cannot possibly stand up with you for another waltz," Emeline said firmly. "My slippers have begun to pinch."

"Can't hear a word over the din in this room," came his shouted reply. He caught her arm and began to lead her toward the doorway. "Do come this way for just a moment."

Should she try to wrest her arm from his? Emeline looked around and saw that no one was paying the least bit of attention to them. Fulham, with his thick graying side-whiskers, was a powerful, respected figure in Parliament, after all, and heir to a fortune. No one would challenge him. Newly widowed at forty, he was sought after on the marriage mart in spite of his age.

When they came into the wide, dimly lit corridor, Emeline saw that they were completely alone. Her heart kicked up, even as she scolded herself for being frightened of this man. Of any man!

He was smiling down at her. No, *leering*. Emeline tried to free her arm, but he held her fast and attempted to force her against the wall.

"I must ask that you release me, sir," she said.

"Ask away." Fulham leaned closer, staring at her mouth.

Emeline's palms began to sweat. "Let me go."

"You cannot have any notion how desirable you are, my sweet." He came closer, and she glimpsed the bulge in his trousers.

"You must be mad. Do you imagine I am some doxie that you can accost at will?" She attempted to twist free, and Lord Fulham scowled.

"You've been teasing every gentleman in London for the past two Seasons, my girl. It seems that you are begging to be taught a good *lesson!*"

Even as he spoke, Emeline reached with her free hand to lift her gown and petticoats. Fulham glanced down in confusion just as she brought one knee up and struck, hard, at his groin. Eyes protruding, he emitted a howl of pain, grabbed himself with both hands, and staggered back.

Without a second glance, Emeline turned and sped away. Down the corridor, up the broad staircase, past a startled young footman on the landing. From the top step, she spied a closed door. There was no time to think about the risks of her actions. Grasping the brass knob, Emeline twisted and pushed it open. To her immense relief, she found herself in a silent, darkened room.

Alone.

Heart pounding in her ears, she closed herself inside. Surely Fulham must be following her. She felt for a key in the lock, to no avail. Hide! She felt her way across the room, moving through a sea of inky darkness, until she encountered a waist-high obstacle.

A bed! Just as Emeline was wondering if she might conceal herself under it, a low, male voice spoke.

"I'd begun to think you were not coming."

She froze and stopped breathing. Was this real? The voice was husky, seductive, tinged with amusement. To Emeline's surprise, her primal self took notice. Good sense told her to go the other way, that this stranger was probably worse than Fulham, yet she felt paralyzed. From the shadows, powerful arms reached out to enfold her, lifting her up onto the high bed.

"We are very bad," he murmured. His hands, strong and warm, lightly caressed her bare arms, grazed the curves of her breasts that swelled above her silk bodice, and she knew a shock of pleasure.

Emeline felt drugged as the stranger drew her down on the bed. Dimly, she made out a sculpted face, saw the glimmer of his eyes as he bent over her.

"It's been too long." His mouth scorched a trail along the tender line of her throat, her neck. "Sweet. God, so sweet."

Emeline felt herself tremble helplessly. This was utter madness! Madness on a grand scale. Just as she was about to speak, to protest, the stranger began to kiss her. She'd been kissed before, but this was something completely different... He used the tip of his tongue to coax her lips to part for him. He tasted her slowly as if she were the most delicious morsel in the world, and she felt compelled to brush his questing tongue with her own. A tantalizing heat spread over her entire body, a kind of *wanting*, and her nipples ached. Her hands fluttered, not daring to touch his broad, bare chest, to feel his heartbeat.

A moan rose in her throat.

At that, the stranger drew back in the shadows. He was staring at her as moonlight stole between the bed draperies. His face remained in dark silhouette above her, but Emeline realized that he doubtless could see now that she was the wrong woman.

"What the devil…?"

Emeline's face flamed. "Unhand me, sir," she managed to croak in tones of mortified outrage. Scrambling off the bed, she made for the door.

Just as she turned the knob, a low laugh reached her ears. "Methinks the lady doth protest too much," taunted the stranger.

This is the last straw, she vowed. *If I never come near another man, it will be too soon!*

CHAPTER 1

LYME REGIS, ENGLAND, SEPTEMBER 1842

The sky was leaden as Emeline trudged along the rocky beach beside her cousin, Louise, back to their cottage in Lyme Regis. The wind from the English Channel stung her eyes. She was hungry, wet and, she admitted privately, discouraged.

"How many days have we been doing just the same thing?" Emeline heard herself ask under her breath. Mary Anning, the great fossilist, was walking a short distance ahead of them, and certainly *she* would never ask such a question. Her passion for hunting and excavating fossils was far stronger than any selfish notions about drudgery.

Louise, pale and bedraggled, glanced over and gave a rueful laugh. "I could not possibly begin to count them." She reached out to touch Emeline's hand. "Do I detect a seed of doubt?"

"Doubt?" Their skirts were tied up, their heavy shoes were wet and muddy, and Emeline wondered if she would ever be able to get the smell of salt water and dead sea animals out of her pores. She held up a silencing hand to her cousin. "I'll tell you when we've eaten. By then I may have changed my mind."

Mary Anning turned and brandished her bucket of fossils:

ammonites, devil's toes, bullet-shaped belemnites, and vertebrae from the immense plesiosaur, who had lived in this place thousands of years ago. "It were a good day!" she exclaimed. "But I must get home to look after Mam. She's poorly." The plain woman, now in her fifth decade, took a few more steps before adding over one sloping shoulder, "Louise, ye are going to discover your own great plessie soon. I feel it."

Emeline and Louise watched as their mentor trudged off, limping slightly, toward the home she shared with her mother above Anning's Fossil Depot. Mary's workshop was there as well, where she labored over her discoveries by candlelight, assembling the fragments and sketching her progress. It was certainly true that fossils of every size took precedence over furnishings or the comforts of home.

For an instant, Emeline felt a sharp pang of longing for her own family home, filled with the laughter of loved ones, the fragrances of delicious food, music, treasured books, and beautiful furniture.

Louise glanced over, seeming to sense Emeline's mood. "There will be soup for us tonight," she said as they began to climb up Broad Street, past the empty market stalls, the Three Cups Inn, and the Assembly Rooms. Her slender hand reached out to touch Emeline's back. "Tell me what you are thinking."

"Oh… I am only pondering Mary's life here in Lyme," Emeline said as a wave of melancholy swept over her. "Of course she has made tremendous discoveries, but it seems she has sacrificed her own happiness for the fossils. Not just a husband and children…but also a wide circle of friends and the pleasures of concerts, lectures, museums…" Her voice trailed off as a flock of sheep interrupted their progress up the hill. "Louise, when you came here, years ago, to work alongside Mary Anning, did you mean to stay forever?"

Her cousin's cheeks went pink.

"I didn't make a plan," Louise confessed. "I wasn't certain what might happen, only that I felt comfortable and fulfilled here in Lyme, helping Mary and learning so much. It's true that the days do run together, but when there is a magnificent, rare discovery, nothing can compare with the thrilling sense of having been part of a miracle."

They had reached the door of their tiny, whitewashed cottage perched high above the sea.

"Yes, that's true. A miracle." Emeline thought back to her very first visit to Lyme Regis, when she was ten years old. Even the discovery of an ammonite fossil, a perfectly spiraled work of art, had felt like a magic trick. She couldn't wait to recreate that thrill. In later years, when she watched Mary Anning uncover the first pieces of a prehistoric ichthyosaur and daily helped to assemble the entire fossilized creature, Emeline had glowed with the wonder of it all.

A high-pitched, plaintive *mee-oww* broke into her reverie. Louise opened the cottage door to reveal their new soot-gray kitten, Bartholomew, poised to spring. When he had appeared one day in their garden, wet and pitiful, the two women immediately adopted him. Bartholomew was the closest thing either of them had to a child. Now the kitten fairly leaped into Louise's arms, and Emeline joined in the reunion, laughing and kissing Bartholomew's tiny head.

"Ow, he bit me!" exclaimed Louise. "His teeth are sharp as razors!" Setting the kitten down on the threadbare rug, she shook a finger at him. "You should be more grateful to have a home, rascal."

"Such as it is," Emeline parried with a rueful laugh as she surveyed the cramped cottage with its low ceilings and unremitting smell of damp. The proceeds from their fossil sales paid the modest rent, but Emeline had begun to consider the limits of their future in the small coastal town. Glancing over, she saw that Louise was watching her.

"I shall warm our supper and then we'll talk," Louise said in a solemn voice.

Emeline nodded and went off to wash up in the dim bedchamber she shared with her cousin. In one corner there was a table she used for sketching, and on top of her supplies lay the most recent letter from her father. Her heart squeezed at the sight of it. With a sigh, Emeline dried her face on a linen towel, slipped the letter into the pocket of her skirt, and went to join Louise.

* * *

THE KITCHEN FELT cozy yet confined, Emeline thought as they finished the last of their vegetable soup. The stove provided warmth against the cold evening, and the company was very fine, but when she considered the prospect of continuing in this situation for the rest of her life, she felt a sudden chill.

"Something is weighing on you," Louise said. She dabbed at her mouth with a napkin and sat up straight. "You promised to say more after we had eaten." Pushing a small dish of rice pudding across to her, she added, "Out with it."

Emeline did not eat the pudding. Instead, she brought the folded paper out of her skirt pocket and opened it. "I've had a letter from Papa. As you well know, he can be rather…"

"Charmingly dictatorial?" Louise supplied sweetly. "Uncle Justin is one of my favorite people, but he can find it difficult to stand by and allow others to make their own choices."

She nodded. "It isn't easy to be his daughter, but as Mama always reminds me, I am also a Raveneau. I *must* chart my own course in life, no matter what Papa says."

"Indeed, you have ever been fearless!" Louise proclaimed admiringly. "That is the reason you abandoned London during your second Season and came here to work alongside Mary

Anning and me. We don't care a button for the haut ton…or men!"

"Very true." Emeline flushed slightly as a memory of the night of Lord and Lady Riven's Spring Ball reared up inside her. "I couldn't remain there another day," she agreed.

Glad for a distraction, Emeline dipped her spoon into the rice pudding and tasted it, reflecting again that perhaps her sweet cousin had another reason to turn her back on men. For years, Louise had quietly carried a torch for Charles, Emeline's half-brother from Mama's earlier marriage to Sir Harry Brandreth, Baronet. Charles could be insufferably pompous, but quiet Louise had always perceived other qualities in him. When his attempt to marry into the aristocracy failed, Charles had studied architecture and departed for Rome. During the intervening decade, Louise had scarcely set foot outside of Lyme Regis, devoting herself to her work with Mary Anning.

"What about you?" Emeline asked for the second time that day. "Do you intend to spend the rest of your life like this? You may as well be in a nunnery." She paused as Bartholomew leaped up onto her lap, then forced herself to add, "I cannot imagine that you want to end like Mary Anning."

The sight of Louise's delicate face turning pink in the candle-light was answer enough.

"You are a brilliant fossilist," Emeline went on, "and you have made many excellent discoveries, but there has to be more to life than this."

"I gather that my Uncle Justin has written to inform us what that might be," her cousin murmured dryly.

"At first, I dismissed his letter out of hand, but I found myself thinking about it all day today." Her eyes stung. "Mary lives in such a small, constricted world, rather like our tiny cottage. I don't think she is truly happy, not in here." Emeline touched the center of her chest. "And more and more of late, she seems worn down."

Louise slowly nodded. "I don't think she has been the same since Tray was killed in a sudden landslip. That dog was her constant, loyal companion through all the long days of fossil hunting." The corners of her mouth turned down.

"Oh, yes, it was the most terrible day, especially since Mary narrowly escaped being buried herself!" Emeline's gaze held Louise's. "Have you ever considered that her closest companions were her dog Tray and her mother?" She let this sink in before adding quietly, "I think you and I deserve fuller lives."

"What exactly do you mean? Have you changed your mind about men and marriage?"

Emeline gave a short laugh. "Not a bit! But together, we can chart a different, *unconventional* course." Excitement infected her voice. "What if we take lodgings together, in London?"

Her cousin's soup spoon was suspended in mid-air. "And how would we fund such an endeavor?"

"As it happens, Papa has written to me on this very subject." Leaning forward, she spread open the single sheet, covered with Justin St. Briac's bold writing. "It is as if he read my mind. He wrote that winter is coming, and they believe I should return to London. Papa knows of an aristocrat who requires that someone do research for him. The man is willing to remunerate us very generously."

Louise blinked. "What sort of research?"

"Some sort of antiquity, I believe," Emeline replied with a negligent wave.

"Hmm. How very fortuitous!"

"I can see that you are skeptical…"

"I know my Uncle Justin very well," Louise murmured, "and he has been known, let us say, to shape events and people to his will."

"But listen, cousin! Papa knows that we wish for our independence, and he suggests that we might live on our own. He even knows of a small townhouse near my family in Grosvenor

Square. Because you are thirty years of age, there will be no question of impropriety if we two females share a home." Emeline heard the excitement in her own voice and suddenly felt more alive than she had in a very long time. "We shall chart our own course! We will earn our own way in the world without resorting to such demeaning occupations as seamstress, serving maid, milliner, or governess."

In the lamplight, a telling flush spread over Louise's cheeks. "It sounds…too good to be true."

"Only consider, Papa is helping to make it so. He desires that we return to London, but he knows it must be under our terms." She held her breath and reached for Louise's hand. "Just imagine of all the pleasures that we can enjoy as independent women in London!"

"What sort of *pleasures* do you mean?"

"Never fear, nothing that has to do with the social games of the ton or angling to catch the latest eligible nobleman." She felt her inner glow, so long tamped down, kindle again. "Rather than succumbing to the allure of romance, we shall find fulfillment in friendships and scholarly pursuits." After a moment, Emeline dared to add softly, "I mean to be admitted to the library at the British Museum."

Her cousin closed her eyes, then opened them and smiled. "All right. I am convinced. It sounds quite mad, but perhaps at my advancing age, it's time to throw caution to the wind."

"Hurrah!" Emeline jumped to her feet, causing the dozing Bartholomew to spiral from her lap onto the rug. Quickly, she scooped the kitten back up into her arms and danced around the tiny kitchen. "Yes, let us throw caution to the wind!"

Suddenly, it seemed that the future could not come soon enough.

* * *

"I must say, darling, you are a marvel," Mouette St. Briac murmured to her husband as their carriage rolled to a stop before a modest townhouse on Chesterfield Street.

"*Eh bien*, I know that very well," came Justin's ironic, French-accented reply. "Yet did you not doubt that I would find a way to bring our wayward Emmie back to us?"

"Perhaps, for she is as stubborn as her papa." Mouette looked out at the bottle-green front door topped with a charming fanlight and shook her head. "Before we go inside to greet Emmie and Louise in their new home, do reveal the identity of the gentleman who has engaged them to do research. Who is he, and by what miracle did you find him?"

"You should know me better than that." Justin flashed a wicked smile just as a groom opened the door and put down the step. "There is no *gentleman*. Only this wealthy papa you see before you, tired of waiting for our daughter to admit how bored she has grown, digging for fossils. Emmie is too stubborn, too proud! I was forced to take matters into my own hands."

"You are shocking," Mouette accused, but of course she was not truly shocked. Her charming husband could also be outrageous, even manipulative. "Do not imagine you can conceal this ruse from her for long. What do you mean to do next?"

He winked at her with his eye that was not covered by a black patch. "*Ma belle*, when I hit on the right plan, I promise to tell you."

* * *

Emeline wore a voluminous white apron as she wielded her feather duster in the snug, pale yellow parlor of their new home. The unusually sunny London morning seemed to foretell good fortune for Emeline and Louise as they embarked on life as independent females. Just as she was brushing a few specks of dust from a pair of chairs near the bow window that overlooked Chesterfield Street, she spied her parents emerging from a dashing green landau. The sight of them made her heart soar.

No sooner had Emeline lifted the latch on the front door than the portal burst open, and her father was enfolding her in his strong embrace. How could she have endured the last two years of nearly constant separation? Justin St. Briac exuded the same sort of energy that flowed through her own veins, and once again it came to her how alike they were.

"At last," he proclaimed, lifting her off the floor as he had done when she was a little girl, "you are back where you belong, with your family."

Emeline glanced over at her mother, who watched them with a faintly wry smile.

"I'll own I am feeling quite happy to have returned to the hustle and bustle of London. Louise and I are elated to have a home of our own…and is it not providential that Papa knew of a gentleman who wishes to engage our services as research scholars?"

Louise came in at that moment, carrying a tea tray, which Justin promptly took from her and placed on a fluted table near the window.

"It's wonderful to see you both!" she exclaimed warmly. "I'll own, Uncle Justin, that you have outdone yourself with this agreeable house. We love it, though I'm not at all certain we can afford it."

He held her at arm's length and shook his head. "It is a very modest place, I think."

Emeline spoke up. "But, Papa, we are in the very heart of Mayfair. The rent must be exorbitant."

"*Pas du tout!* Not a bit. Your papa knows exactly the right people to call on when a favor is needed." As if sensing that Emeline meant to question his last words, he rushed on, "Which is not to say that you have received special treatment. I can promise you that your new employer means to remunerate you very well for your services."

As he spoke, he began to pour tea for all four of them, and soon they were facing each other on two petite sofas.

"Mouette," her father declared as soon as they had all sampled the hot tea, "no doubt you are already making plans for this humble parlor. It was convenient that this furniture was already in place, but how much better it will be when it can be changed."

Mama glanced at him, brows aloft, and replied mildly, "Really, Justin, do you think these young women want you to take charge of their home decor?"

"Who better?" he demanded, only half in jest.

"Papa, do stop," Emeline said, and wagged a finger at him. "This is why I stipulated that Louise and I must have a home of our own. I am well aware that if I lived under your roof, you would be an intolerable overlord."

"Intolerable?" One brow slanted upward. "Many have said that great *strength* is my best quality."

Her mother laughed at this and cuffed his coat sleeve. "Really, Justin, you are the outside of enough." Turning back to Emeline and Louise, she said, "If you should desire to change anything in your new home, do call on me. I love to decorate! And, more seriously, your Grandmama Raveneau means to send you a cook. Dora has been learning to manage a kitchen from old Mrs. Butter, and this seemed a perfect opportunity for her to practice her skills."

"But I don't think we really need a cook," protested Louise. "We have done without one until now! It's just the two of us, and our tastes are simple."

Papa looked shocked. "Of course you need not only a cook, but also a butler or housekeeper. But one thing at a time." He consulted his pocket watch and abruptly rose to his feet. "Ah, I have an appointment, so I regret to say I must leave..."

"But you have just arrived!" protested Emeline.

He smiled. "Never fear, your mama will stay. Helivet will wait here to take her home in the carriage. I am only going a short distance to my office. I can walk."

It came to Emeline that somehow the entire visit had been taken up with Papa leading them in conversational circles. She pointed a finger at him. "I will not let you go until you reveal the identity of our employer. Who is this aristocrat who wishes to hire *both* of us to do research for him? If he is a scholar, why doesn't he do it himself? And has it not occurred to any of you that Louise and I may not be permitted, as women, to set foot in the Reading Room of the British Museum? That is the only place in London where any proper scientific papers can be found."

To her consternation, her father tucked his watch away and drew on his gloves. "You worry too much. What does any of it matter, as long as he remunerates you two ladies handsomely?" Bending, he kissed her brow, as if she were still a little girl. "And now, I must take my leave. Au revoir!"

When the door had closed behind Justin St. Briac, Emeline turned to her mother and threw up her hands. "Oh, how very maddening he can be. Do *you* know the identity of our mysterious employer, Mama?"

"No...I do not." She sipped her tea and added with a hint of amusement, "However, I can share the latest *on dit*. I was riding in the park with Frederica yesterday when we encountered Lady Clarissa Graystone. She confided that the notorious libertine, Lord Jasper Hartcliffe, is back in London, after two full years on the Continent. Everyone is waiting to discover what he will do next." Eyes twinkling, Mouette pretended to fan herself. "They call him Hart the Heartless. I'll own, if I were younger and not wed to your papa, I should be plotting to cross paths with him myself."

"Really, Mama, you sound like a green girl in her first Season!" Emeline chided fondly. "Is this man truly so mesmerizing?"

"Well, I can only say that Lord Jasper is known to be *fatally* attractive." A dimple winked in Mouette's cheek. "No doubt his appeal is heightened because he is notoriously elusive. His lordship seems to care nothing for the ton and comes and goes from London without a care for the usual activities of the Season."

Louise sat up straight, flushing. "Yes, I remember, Hart the Heartless! I encountered him at a garden party, when I was much younger. He is an infamous rake."

Emeline pretended to yawn. "That's all very well, but we are not interested in men, are we, Louise? Especially not men known to be *fatally* attractive."

Her mother lifted both brows and glanced toward Louise, who confirmed, "Emmie is quite right. We have renounced romance in favor of intellectual pursuits."

"Indeed? Hmm." Mouette nodded, but the dimple quivered again in her cheek. "Fascinating."

CHAPTER 2

Amidst the shouts and tumult of Oxford Street traffic, Hart stepped out of a hackney cabriolet and paused before the offices of Premier Oceangoing Vessels. The building's sober façade led him to suppose that the company's founder would be dull as dust.

Consulting his watch, Hart longed to tell the driver to return in a mere half hour. If he achieved his goal quickly, he might continue on to the British Museum for a leisurely afternoon in the Reading Room, but it was impossible to know what lay in store with this legendary Frenchman.

Hart paid the driver and sent him on his way, then entered the building. A bell jingled to herald his arrival. Beyond the vestibule, he found himself in a large office richly appointed in shades of sapphire blue and burnished gold. A thin, austere young man glanced up from his desk and blinked a question behind his spectacles.

"Lord Jasper Hartcliffe," Hart supplied. "I believe I have an appointment."

"Of course, my lord." The man rose and nodded his head respectfully. "You are expected."

A moment later, a paneled inner door swung open and the tall, arresting figure of an older man appeared. In spite of the charcoal-gray silk patch covering his left eye, the man took Hart in with one sweeping glance.

"Do come in, my lord," he invited in a deep, French-accented voice, adding, "Allow me to make myself known to you. I am Justin St. Briac."

Hart's memory flickered. Could this man, the owner of Premier Oceangoing Vessels, also be the French pirate Austell had spoken of at the Spring Ball two years ago?

"I am very pleased to know you, sir," Hart said. They entered a spacious, handsomely furnished office that felt more like a welcoming study in a manor house. "I have heard about you from my brother, the duke, and I am surprised we have never met."

"I agree it is odd, but I understand you have been abroad for some time."

"Yes. I have traveled widely but resided mainly in Florence and Paris these past two years."

St. Briac poured coffee for them both, gesturing toward a pair of handsome armchairs near the window. When they were seated, he inquired, "Did you come here today simply to make my acquaintance?"

Hart leaned back against the leather upholstery and sipped the excellent coffee. "I wish that were the only reason." He met the Frenchman's gaze. "After returning to London, I visited my brother and found him in very low spirits. I soon perceived that his problem may stem from an investment he made in your steamship company."

"I tried to dissuade him," St. Briac said bluntly. "Last year, His Grace made clear his wish to buy a stake in my new enterprise. He approached me at White's and declared that he was sailing on the River Tick…if you take my meaning."

Hart wanted to cringe. "I understand."

"The duke begged me to advance the funds, convinced that soon enough he would recoup enough to clear the loan and much more. If it had been any other man but the Duke of Caversham, I would have refused outright..." He paused. "I had to wonder what had become of the old duke's fortune? Your father notoriously guarded his purse."

"I believe my brother desired to make several improvements to Caversham Castle, and one thing led to another." Hart lifted his cup, wishing it were filled with cognac instead of coffee, and drew a harsh breath. "Pray allow me to speak frankly, sir. I arrived from the Continent last week to find Austell in a state of agitation. Although I have not been much of a brother, I could not turn away from the sight of him, pale as death. After a good deal of brandy, he divulged that he had squandered much of Pa's fortune at the gaming tables...but he was holding out hope for his investment in your steamship company, sir." Hart's gut twisted. "Now I learn that even that supposed source of income is encumbered by a *loan*."

"Worse than that, I fear. Allow me to offer you something stronger." Justin rose and poured two small portions of cognac. Standing over Hart, he held out the glass. "I just had word that our newest ship, the *Helena*, suffered a fire in the smokestack and sank off the coast of Ireland. The crew survived, but there will be no profit for any of us this year." He shrugged lightly. "My past adventures at sea have provided me with enough wealth to weather any setback. However, His Grace's loan continues to increase, at a time when he expected to have the means to pay it off."

"Bloody hell." Hart closed his eyes to block out reality. His mind raced, recalling Austell's dark, shaky state during their last meeting. If Hart tried to intercede, his brother would be humiliated. After a long moment, Hart looked at St. Briac. "What do you mean to do?"

The Frenchman prowled over to a tall window and stared out at the crowds and traffic on Oxford Street. "Naturally, I must arrange a meeting and give him the news."

It felt to Hart like a gut punch, yet what else could the man do? Before he could offer an argument, St. Briac spoke again, his tone thoughtful.

"His Grace doubtless has options. He could sell land or pieces of art from his vast collection—that is if he hasn't already sold it all." St. Briac glanced back at Hart. "One thing is clear. The duke is a man of honor. He will insist on doing the right thing."

"Yes, of course." Hart was surprised by the depth of his desire to protect Austell from this cruel blow. "I agree on all counts. However, my brother's state of mind is...precarious. He has gotten himself into a very deep hole." He stopped himself from revealing more, adding simply, "I would ask that you spare him the blow of this news."

"*Sangdieu.*" St. Briac blinked. "What can you possibly mean?"

Hart put up a hand in surrender. "You will be repaid, sir. I shall settle his debts instead."

"You!" This brought St. Briac back to perch on the edge of his chair, facing Hart.

"Indeed. My brother need never know about this catastrophe. Allow him to go on believing he is getting closer to financial solvency."

"But how could you have the means to do this? Are you not the second son?"

"I am. Because the dukedom was entailed to Austell, my mother found a way to bequeath her modest private inheritance to me, including Woodcroft Priory, her family estate in Suffolk." A caustic smile touched his mouth as he continued, "I was wild in my youth—many would say I still am. People assume that I've come by my fortune at the gaming tables, but that is only partially true. Unlike my brother, each year I have made careful investments, and there is also income from tenants at the estate."

"Fascinating." St. Briac sat back in his chair, watchful. "Tell me more about yourself."

"There is little to tell." Hart kept his tone offhand. "I am, as you have noted, the second son. Because my brother and I are twins, I escaped the dukedom by mere minutes."

"Escaped?" The Frenchman cocked his head. "Do you mean to say you wouldn't choose to be Duke of Caversham if your birth order were reversed?"

"God, no. He is much better suited to the smothering constraints of that title." Hart hoped St. Briac couldn't hear the tense undercurrent in his voice. "Austell was always the good brother, obedient and devoted to our parents, while I was restless. Wayward. Didn't fit in. I craved travel, adventure, and knowledge. I still do. I'm easily bored." He raked a hand through his silver-flecked hair. "I have no patience for deuced *propriety*."

St. Briac looked thoughtful. "That explains why I have not seen or heard much of you here in London."

"I might say the same for you, sir."

"*C'est vrai*," he allowed wryly. "It is true, I have other homes, in France and Cornwall. And I find the *beau monde* a dead bore. Thankfully, their consequence has faded, along with the assemblies at Almack's." St. Briac paused before adding, "However, we do spend a portion of the year in London, and I tolerate some social events because it gratifies my wife. Madame also maintains that our daughter, who is now a young woman, must have the opportunity to meet the...right people."

"Understandable, I suppose." Hart's tone was polite, even as he wondered where the devil this Frenchman meant to take this conversation.

"But we were speaking of you, my lord. You have come here offering to pay the duke's considerable debt to me, to protect him from a painful financial shock." St. Briac paused, as if pondering the situation. "I had heard that you are a reprobate, enjoying a licentious existence on the Continent, but clearly there is more to your story."

"If you imagine that I am concealing a devoted wife and family on my estate in Suffolk, you would be quite wrong." Hart gave a low laugh. "On the contrary, the rumors you have heard are true. I am an unrepentant libertine."

"Yet you must care a great deal for your brother, the duke." The Frenchman lifted a brow above his eyepatch. "I pursue this line of conversation for a reason. *Voyons*, I will not take your coin, Hartcliffe, but I would strike a bargain with you. I will forgive the duke's considerable debt in return for your assistance with a…personal matter."

Hart stiffened. *What the devil?* He wanted to flatly decline and take his leave, but the memory of Austell's pale countenance rose up before him. What was his brother capable of if his transgressions were exposed to all of London society? Last night, Hart had dreamed that he'd come upon Austell lying in their father's library, dead, a smoking pistol in one limp hand.

The vision had been too horrifying, too *real* to now dismiss in the light of day.

"Go on, then. I will hear you out."

"My daughter is unique. Although she is quite lovely, she would declare that she does not 'care a button' for the London ton." As he spoke, St. Briac crossed to a shelf near his desk, picked up a framed miniature, and returned to show it to Hart. "Emmie is more interested in cursed *fossils* than socializing with people her own age. She turned her back on her second London Season and fled to Lyme Regis, where she has been digging for ancient bones with her spinster cousin ever since."

A young beauty who preferred to hunt for fossils? Hart wondered where he had heard something of this sort before. Then he glanced down at the miniature and felt a prickle at the back of his neck. Memories awoke. Of course! *Emeline St. Briac.*

He had seen this very woman at the Earl of Riven's Spring Ball two years ago! The pieces came together in Hart's mind then. Once again, he heard his brother's voice, explaining that the beauty cared nothing for society, that she was merely pretending to accommodate her father's wishes so that, at Season's end, she might escape London and dig for fossils.

Endeavoring to keep the spark of interest from his voice, Hart asked, "I surmise that the personal matter you mentioned has to do with your daughter?"

"Correct." He coughed. "I managed to persuade Emmie and her older, unmarried cousin, Louise, to return to London. Can you blame me, as a father, for wishing my only daughter to give up the solitary, sterile life of a scientist? No, it could not continue!" St. Briac avoided Hart's gaze by pouring more cognac into their glasses. "But my Emmie is very proud. I had to convince the two women that they could live together in this city independently. Of course, they protested that they had no means of support...and so I claimed to know a scholar who wished to employ them to do research."

Good God, thought Hart, torn between incredulity and amusement. *He has deceived his own daughter.*

"I can see that you are shocked by this." St. Briac protested, "Yet, what sort of father would I be to simply leave my beloved Emmie to live out her days digging on the cold, rocky beach of Lyme Regis? She is already dangerously near the verge of spinsterhood, but she cares nothing for that."

"You surmise that she does not know what is best for her," Hart said.

"What other conclusion can logically be drawn?" declared the Frenchman. "And if her own papa does not intervene, who will?"

"I see what you mean." He wanted to laugh aloud at this outrageous man. "What does any of this have to do with me, sir?"

St. Briac paced across the office, then back to the desk. "Emeline and Louise are asking questions. I imagined that I could simply allude to their benefactor and quietly pay their bills, but they demand to know who he is and exactly what work they will do for him."

"And there is no such person." Hart had the uneasy suspicion he knew where this was going.

"Until now, perhaps. However, if *you* help me, I will forgive the Duke of Caversham's debt to me." He paused. "All of it... and your brother need never know."

"This entire scheme sounds quite mad."

"*Oui.* Perhaps so!" St. Briac appeared to reconsider all that he had said. "I see your point. What was I thinking? This plan needs a confident person who can easily converse with my daughter and niece on a range of scholarly subjects." He let out a harsh breath. "I will find someone else."

Austell's panicky face swam in front of Hart's eyes. It seemed that St. Briac's absurd plan offered the only escape. Stifling a groan, he asserted, "No. I can do this. As it happens, I privately hold a ticket to the museum's Reading Room, where I have lately passed long hours among the rare volumes."

"To what purpose?"

It seemed he must divulge more. "Woodcroft Priory, my estate in Suffolk, retains an ancient relic that only recently came to light. To my surprise, I have become very invested in discovering exactly what it means, and how it came to be there."

St. Briac sat up straighter, his hard countenance alight with interest. "What sort of ancient relic?"

"I would rather not say, sir." Hart narrowed his eyes. "The point is, I can engage in scholarly conversations as well as any man."

"Ah, then, very well! You have convinced me, my lord." The Frenchman's grin was triumphant. "When you have satisfied our agreement, I will burn all the papers that record your brother's debt to me. Now then, let us discuss the plan for you to play the role of Emeline's employer."

It came to Hart that St. Briac was weaving a web. He meant to entrap not only his daughter, but Hart as well. His mouth hardened as they shook hands to seal their bargain.

Silently, Hart replied, *You don't know it yet, St. Briac, but you have met your match.*

CHAPTER 3

"*W*ouldn't the dowagers faint at the sight of what we are doing?" Emeline asked, laughing as she tucked a stray black curl back under the scarf wrapped round her head.

On the other side of the dining room, Louise paused in the midst of arranging various artifacts on a shelf that was meant to display fine china. Her customary reserve gave way to a giggle. "Indeed! It's quite shocking."

The two women were in the process of transforming the formal dining room into a study that they could both use. All six mahogany leaves had been inserted into the Chippendale table, stretching it to its full nine-foot length, and Emeline and Louise had each created makeshift desks at opposite ends.

As she positioned her inkstand and letter holder on the worn, burgundy leather blotter, Emeline looked around for Bartholomew. The kitten, who grew larger by the day, lay curled up on one of the dining chairs, pretending to sleep.

She affected a stern tone. "I am quite aware that you are only waiting for your chance to leap up on this table and disrupt the items we have so carefully arranged. Be warned, if you should do so, there will be no sardines for your supper." Glancing across at Louise, she whispered, "Heaven help us if he tips over an inkpot."

Bartholomew had opened one eye, just a fraction.

"I believe we can trust him," Louise asserted as she came close enough to survey the kitten. "Isn't that so, Mew?"

This made Emeline laugh out loud. "I fear we may become eccentric spinsters, raising a cat together instead of marrying and having real children."

"Perhaps it's just as well. What husband would tolerate *this*?" Louise swept a slim hand through the air, indicating the stacks of books, the sideboard given over to cases of fossils, and walls hung with Emeline's framed sketches of everything from ammonites to Mary Anning's faithful spaniel, Tray.

"That's right. *He* would be demanding to know where he could expect to enjoy his feast!" laughed Emeline.

Louise's eyes danced as she rejoined, "And his port!"

For a moment, they leaned against one another, laughing. Emeline imagined a conventional scene wherein she was clad in a proper gown, her hair neatly arranged, and a sober man was seated at the table, waiting for his breakfast to be served. He would be obscured behind the newspaper, barely aware of his wife.

She couldn't even begin to imagine small children in this tableau. Of course, if they were messy eaters, their father would not permit them to sit at the same table with him. Emeline suppressed a small shudder. Thank heavens she had gotten away from the London Season when she had the chance, two years ago!

"I could never do it," she declared to Louise. "I mean, be a *wife*."

To her surprise, her cousin gave a wistful shrug. "I suppose it might seem more appealing with the right man."

She is thinking of Charles, Emeline realized with a pang.

"Ah-hem!" came an uncertain cough.

Dora, their new cook, peeked around the doorframe.

"Oh, hello, Dora." Emeline tried to look more serious. "What is it?"

The petite young woman, sent to them by Grandmama Raveneau, blushed to the roots of her coppery hair. "I thought to cook breakfast for you, my ladies."

"That's very nice," said Louise, though Emeline suspected her cousin wasn't any hungrier than she was. Who could think of food when they were in the midst of creating their wonderful new study? As if reading her mind, Louise added, "We are expecting a visitor in less than an hour, and I suspect we shall need to fortify ourselves."

"That is a very good point." Gesturing to the cook to come closer, Emeline said, "If you were expecting us to behave as conventional women, Dora, I fear you must be disappointed. However, we do like to have fun, and our needs are modest. Will that suit you?"

The girl's freckled face broke into a relieved smile. "That suits me fine, miss! I have been in the Raveneaus' home since I was fifteen, so I am accustomed to folk with eccentric ways—though they do use the dining table for meals."

"Yes, my grandparents are more civilized than I am," Emeline said, amused. "Perhaps you can bring us coffee and something very light."

"Toast with fruit compote?" Dora suggested brightly.

"Delicious!"

When the cook scurried off, beaming, Emeline turned to Louise. "Until you mentioned our new employer, I had almost forgotten that he is coming to meet us this morning! I look a fright." She glanced down at her simple sky-blue gown, one that had served her well when she spent her days either searching for fossils or piecing them together over a worktable with Mary Anning. Her long hair, twisted into a chignon, was mostly concealed under a scarf. "Do you think I ought to change my clothes before the men arrive?"

"How funny you are." Louise patted Emeline's cheek. "Just last night you declared that our employer was doubtless a fat old man with jowls who is too lazy to waddle to the Reading Room and do his own research. Do you now desire to impress him with your beauty?"

"You make a splendid point, dear cousin." Emeline happily turned back to arranging her books. "I shall be exceedingly content if I don't have to leave this room all day."

* * *

WHEN IN LONDON, it was Hart's custom to take rooms at the Pulteney Hotel. The location overlooking Piccadilly and the Green Park was ideal, and the establishment was impeccably managed. There was even a staff of footmen, waiting to do errands for the guests.

Hart had a tastefully appointed suite of rooms for himself and a second apartment for Mrs. Peachey, his housekeeper, and her younger brother, William. Assigned to the young Lord Jasper first as groom and later as manservant, William was more like a plainspoken uncle than a servant.

Mrs. Peachey, meanwhile, had overseen the kitchen staff at Caversham Castle for two decades. Thus, when Hart left university, it had come as a shock to the old duke to hear Mrs. Peachey firmly declare that she meant to manage "young Lord Jasper's household," and she and William would reside with him. His Grace had barked that Peachey and William had both taken leave of their senses, but they went all the same.

Was she motivated by pity for him, bumped down not only from the dukedom, but even a title of any consequence? Perhaps. Yet the tiny, determined housekeeper quietly followed wherever Hart traveled, if he allowed it. It really made no sense at all.

"Will you permit me to tie your neckcloth?" William inquired now as they both stared at Hart's reflection in the mirror.

"Not today," Hart replied, as he had nearly every day for all of his adult life. He sent William a crooked smile. "No offense, old man."

"None taken, my lord."

There were many things Hart did that made William and his sister blink. Hart couldn't count the number of times Mrs. Peachey had asked why he didn't purchase a "proper home" in London rather than return to the Pulteney. How could he explain that he didn't want to remain long enough in London to draw comparisons with his brother, the Duke of Caversham? Ever since that life-altering day when their father had summoned the little boys and proclaimed that Austell was the first born and would succeed him as duke, Hart had striven to find his own, clearly separate path.

What did it matter if he traveled the Continent, took mistresses, and flirted with danger? It suited Hart to keep the beau monde in a state of uncertainty about his nature. When he lived a rake's existence by night, no one would expect him to have finer interests by day.

William held up the charcoal-gray wool coat Hart had chosen, and he slipped into it. It was the most sober piece of clothing he owned, and it lent him a properly distinguished look. He then picked up a brush and, as his valet watched in evident surprise, tamed his usually disheveled hair into a more conventional style.

"I perceive you have noticed my altered appearance," Hart remarked dryly. "Never fear, I have not reformed. I merely have a part to play this morning."

The older man pressed his lips together as if to suppress further comment. Instead, he extended Hart's finest black silk hat and cane, just as a knock sounded in the parlor next to them. He heard Mrs. Peachey's voice, then a deep, French-accented reply.

Hart went out to greet Justin St. Briac, enjoying not only the promise of a new adventure, but also the satisfaction of knowing he was resolving Austell's thorny problem. Perhaps his brother need never know how dire the situation had become.

"Good morning," he greeted St. Briac, pausing to don a pair of spectacles. "Do you think I look scholarly enough?" Even from a distance, he felt Peachey's curious gaze.

The Frenchman laughed. "*Oui!* Well done, m'sieur." He laughed but gestured to the spectacles. "There's really no need for those. Your age and white hairs will be enough to convince them that you're a scholar."

Hart shrugged and removed the spectacles before opening the door to the hotel corridor. Turning back, he spoke to William and Mrs. Peachey, who stood side by side. He seldom told them where he was going or when he would return but rarely omitted words of parting. "You two are at liberty to enjoy the city in my absence."

"Yes, Lord Jasper," came Mrs. Peachey's reply. After a brief moment, she added, "Do take care."

It was a fine day, the sun peeking out intermittently, and Hart walked beside Justin St. Briac the short distance to Chesterfield Street. After a bit, the older man inclined his head toward a narrow, three-story townhouse with a delicate fanlight above the bottle-green front door. "My daughter and niece live there. Just remember our plan, my lord. Invent a plausible subject for them to research and leave them to it. As long as the women are being properly remunerated, they will have no reason to question you."

Hart nodded yet determined to keep as close to the truth as possible. The reason for this morning's meeting with the two women might be an elaborate ruse, but Hart had decided to go by his own name, and he'd even contrived a real subject for the two women to research.

As they stepped back to avoid a curricle speeding recklessly down the sloping lane, Hart inquired, "You are not concerned about me visiting your daughter on my own in the future?"

"Because you are known to be a libertine?" St. Briac gave a snort of laughter. "I can assure you, my lord, even if you should dare to make romantic overtures to my daughter, she would have none of it."

Hart sent him a sidelong glance. What the devil did *that* mean?

St. Briac shook his head as if reading Hart's thoughts. "You are far too old for my Emmie. Not her type in the least."

"Ah. I see." Had he been insulted?

"In any event," continued St. Briac, "you are merely a figure-head, on hand to reassure the girls that they are not living here on my charity." He paused to send Hart a conspiratorial look and added, "Which they are, of course, but they must not know that."

They had reached the front door, and Hart was having serious doubts about the entire scheme. Instead of lifting the brass knocker, St. Briac reached for the door handle.

"Emeline and Louise have refused to have servants, so there is no butler or housemaid," he explained with furrowed brow. "Nevertheless, I insisted on a cook. And eventually, I will see to it that they have a decent staff."

"I don't doubt that," Hart returned with a trace of irony.

"Emeline has a lot of ideas of her own."

"I see." Clearly the man wished to manage his daughter, and Hart's own role in this drama was proof of that. "Did you not tell me that Miss St. Briac is three-and-twenty?"

The Frenchman frowned. "She may be, but that does not mean she knows what is good for her." In the next moment, an expression of wry amusement played over his face. "If my wife were here, she would delight in reminding me that Emeline takes after me. We are both stubborn and ungovernable."

"Fortunately, it will not be my place to govern your daughter," Hart reminded him, wondering yet again what he was getting into.

"*Pas du tout!*" St. Briac gave him a sharp glance, then, without knocking, turned the doorknob. "Come in but wait in the entryway until I summon you. I must smooth the way."

Hart nodded and followed him into the small vestibule. It was no wonder Emeline St. Briac rebelled against her controlling papa, Hart mused. He stood in the shadows, near the door, and waited as the Frenchman looked first into the parlor, then crossed into what must be a dining room. Female voices were engaged in conversation, but they broke off as St. Briac entered. From his vantage point, Hart glimpsed shelved cabinets built into the corners, but instead of dishes, they were filled with books and artifacts of some sort.

"Papa! Louise and I have forgotten the time," cried a voice that must belong to Emeline. "We have been so happily occupied, we aren't properly dressed."

"It's fine," replied the Frenchman's deep voice. "Lord Jasper Hartcliffe is a serious scholar, and as such is not concerned with such matters."

This announcement was met with a feminine cry of astonishment. "Papa, are you saying that our employer is...Lord Jasper Hartcliffe, the notorious rake? We have heard shocking stories about him. Perhaps he is hoaxing you."

An odd, unsettled feeling came over Hart, and his body grew taut, almost as if the chit was mocking him.

There were muffled voices as Justin St. Briac seemed to chide his daughter, and then he appeared in the doorway and gestured to Hart.

"The ladies are here," he said. "Come this way."

Suddenly, Hart was possessed by a strong urge to turn and leave. The feeling was tinged with something like foreboding. He had no idea what these people might do or say next. Yet even as he glanced back toward the exit, he thought of Austell.

Bloody hell. There was nothing for it.

* * *

EMELINE STOOD close to Louise and waited, wondering what an infamous rake who turned female heads all over London would look like. Satan, perhaps…

However, the tall man who entered appeared, at first glance, unexpectedly sober. He wore a plain, dark suit, but Emeline perceived the outline of the lean, hard physique beneath his clothing. When her gaze traveled to Hartcliffe's face, her heart began to race. Sculpted features, a slightly crooked nose, astute deep-blue eyes with golden depths. His skin was tanned, as if he spent more time outdoors than in a library. When he smiled, she caught the quick flash of white teeth.

As he removed his hat, Emeline was surprised to realize that his lordship's raven hair was liberally salted with silver. Even more than Papa's—but surely this man couldn't be *that* old?

"Ladies, it is a pleasure to meet you," he said, smiling politely at Louise, then letting his gaze travel to Emeline.

She stared back at him, shockingly aware of his well-cut, sensual mouth. Her tongue felt thick. Fortunately, Louise intervened and shook Hartcliffe's hand.

"My cousin and I are very pleased to assist with your research, my lord, and are eager to learn more. As you might know, we have years of experience in the field of paleontology."

"Yes," he replied smoothly. "Your fine reputations precede you."

Emeline at last found her voice. "We are serious scholars ourselves, my lord." She stared before taking the strong, masculine hand he had extended, shocked by the warmth and pressure of his fingers. It was nothing like the clammy handshake of most aristocrats she had met. "We are eager to know more of your assignment for us."

"Let us not stand on ceremony, ladies. Since we shall be working together, I suggest that you use my given name." With a dry smile, he continued, "I am known as Hart."

CHAPTER 4

"*H*art…oh my goodness, that's right!" Louise exclaimed, then looked surprised, as if she hadn't meant to give voice to her thoughts. "I mean, I remember hearing a story about your name some years ago, when I visited London with my parents."

"Did you indeed?" Hart watched her, waiting, smiling slightly.

"Yes. You were at a garden party I attended. A friend pointed you out and said…" She fell silent and bit her lip.

Emeline St. Briac nudged her with an elbow and prompted, "Yes?"

"My friend said Lord Jasper Hartcliffe was ironically known as Hart because he is a libertine who *lacks* a heart!" Louise tilted her chin, adding, "Perhaps it is rude of me to say so."

"Rude?" Hart gave a caustic laugh. "Not a bit. I am well aware that I've been called Hart the Heartless, with good reason."

Justin St. Briac, who had been watching the scene unfold from a distance, stepped forward now. "Yet, look at you today, my lord. Clearly, you have grown wiser with age. You have spent most of the past few years on the Continent and have gained respect as a man of letters."

The Frenchman's intent look warned Hart to remember the role he had agreed to play. Suddenly, Hart wished he hadn't tried to pretend to be anyone other than his true self.

He forced himself to turn to Louise St. Briac. "One can change with time."

Just then, a swinging door opened on the far wall, and a petite, freckled girl with fiery red hair appeared. She pushed a teacart, the odor of burnt toast following her into the room.

"Beg pardon, m'ladies, but I had a bit of a problem with the toast," the girl confessed, cheeks aflame.

"Oh, dear. We are so sorry, Dora," soothed Louise.

As Dora began to set dishes on an empty stretch of the table, Emeline St. Briac turned to her father. "Papa, you must not stay. I know you are very busy, and we are quite capable of talking to Lord Hartcliffe about his assignment for us. No doubt you would find it all terribly dull."

Hart admired her brisk manner and noted the slight tension between daughter and father. He fully expected the Frenchman to refuse to go, but before he could speak, a small furry object sprang out from one of the dining chairs and flung itself at St. Briac.

"What the devil?" St. Briac shouted, even as the feline attacker hooked its claws to the front of his tailored coat and emitted an earsplitting yowl. "*Sangdieu*, there is a wild animal in this house!"

"Oh, Papa, must you be so dramatic?" laughed Emeline. With one slim hand, she caught the kitten around its middle and dislodged it from her father's coat. "This is Bartholomew. I'm quite certain you two have already met."

"I no doubt tried to put the little beast from my mind."

Cuddling the gray kitten until it began to purr loudly, Emeline shook her head. "Little Mew probably can sense that you don't like him, and he feels threatened by your presence. He is highly intelligent."

St. Briac glanced heavenward. "I fear that you females have

been living alone too long. You treat the cat as if he were your babe."

As the two cousins lovingly stroked the kitten's small head, Emeline said, "Why should we not? Mew is doubtless as close as either of us will come to a child. As you know, we plan to make our own way in the world, unburdened by husbands."

Hart choked on a laugh. In spite of his growing opinion that the St. Briac family was eccentric, he was rather beguiled by this outspoken—and quite ravishing—daughter.

"I trust you don't really mean that," St. Briac said, reaching out to pat her cheek.

"But I do! And well you know it, Papa."

"*Eh bien*, Emmie. I surrender." He smiled and threw up his hands. "I will be on my way, for your beautiful *maman* is expecting me to share a delicious luncheon with her in St. James's Park." Turning, he sent Hart a pointed look. "I hope your discussions go well, my lord."

"Why wouldn't they?" Emeline parried and led him to the door.

Louise, the older cousin, poured coffee into three cups and set out the plate of buttered, scorched toast with a tiny bowl of orange marmalade. When Emeline returned, she glanced toward Hart, and he felt another magnetic jolt as their eyes met for an instant.

This is not good, he thought with an inner groan. It was one thing to seduce experienced women and even to engage in harmless flirtations with females who hung after him at balls and routs, but this was different. If Hart crossed the line with Emeline St. Briac, it would ruin everything.

"I do hope you aren't put off by our sadly unconventional ways," Emeline was saying to him as she grouped three chairs on one side of the table. "But you are looking for someone to carry out an assignment, are you not? One hopes propriety is not a central qualification."

Before Hart could reply, Louise gestured toward a chair for him and seated herself in the middle, as if she sensed the invisible sparks flying between Hart and Emeline. "My cousin is quite right, my lord. We may not aspire to entertain well, but that is because our interests lie in science. It would be a sad waste of this room if we used it for dining instead of study."

Hart nodded, bemused. "I understand completely." Out of the corner of one eye, he noticed that Emeline was scanning her reflection in a small oval mirror that hung nearby. Perhaps she was wishing she had dressed more carefully for this meeting? The predatory rake in him bit back a smile. He wanted to tell her that she looked enchanting in her worn blue gown that was tantalizingly snug. Her expressive face was radiant, without artifice, her lips utterly kissable, her violet eyes edged with thick black lashes. Hart couldn't help himself. He imagined having Emeline alone, removing the scarf that haphazardly concealed her raven curls, unfastening the gown that she seemed to have outgrown, revealing…

"My lord?"

He blinked, returning to the present. Both women were looking at him. In the next instant, Hart realized that his momentary fantasy had physical consequences. *Good God.* Deftly, he adjusted the edge of his coat to conceal his arousal.

This has to stop. Immediately.

"Will you describe the duties you expect us to carry out?" Louise inquired. "We are told it is research of some sort."

"Yes, Papa has been quite mysterious!" Emeline swallowed the last bite of toast and waved her free hand to indicate the room they had filled with books, geological artifacts, and framed nature sketches.

"As you see, my lord, we have been laboring to create a study where we can work," Louise interjected.

"I fear we cannot wait another moment," Emeline said firmly. "Pray enlighten us."

Returning his cup to its saucer, Hart angled his chair toward the two women. Emeline perched on the edge of her seat, back straight, unaware of how charming she looked.

He didn't plan to reveal much about his small archaeological project at Woodcroft Priory. Hart preferred to keep the details to himself, to continue spending hours at the Reading Room at the British Museum, searching through the books for bits of information that might enlighten him about the sword and its origins. It wasn't so much a secret as something meaningful that belonged to him alone.

"A few artifacts have been discovered, buried on the grounds of my estate in Suffolk." He paused, keeping his tone even despite the familiar rush of energy he felt whenever he thought of the sword. "Mainly a sword. Very old. Viking, perhaps."

Emeline's eyes were sparkling. "How thrilling! Have you brought it to be analyzed?"

"No. It is in a fragile state, and I don't want to move it. I came back to London to do some research and discover what might be known about a relic of this sort."

Justin St. Briac had cautioned against offering too many details about the sword. *Draw out this endeavor as long as possible. All that matters is that the girls trust their employment is legitimate.*

"What else can you tell us?" coaxed Emeline.

Hart hesitated, then took a deep breath and drew a folded paper from his inside pocket. "I did bring a rough sketch." Opening the paper on the flat surface of the table, he pointed. "Of course, the iron blade is corroded, and some pieces are broken or missing, but the sword itself is nearly three feet long. The hilt is very impressive, silver and gilt, and the pommel is inlaid with a row of garnet cloisonné."

Louise looked awestruck. "How did you discover this sword, and where is it now?"

"I confess it was my gardener who recently unearthed it while digging a new garden near the old priory ruins, while I was still in Florence. The gamekeeper helped to bring out the pieces, and then they realized they should not disturb the rest of the area."

"We find this utterly compelling, having spent years with Mary Anning, painstakingly uncovering and cataloguing fossils," Louise said thoughtfully. "However, our experience lies in the science of paleontology. You will doubtless want to consult with an archaeologist. Perhaps we can help you locate one."

Hart nodded, thinking that task would keep them occupied for a while. "That is an excellent plan."

"But surely we can be of more use than that!" protested Emeline. She leaned forward to study the drawing. "Are there not similarities between the two sciences? Even many of our tools and methods are the same. And geologists, like William Buckland, have accidentally made archaeological discoveries while searching for fossils!" She turned to look at Hart, glowing. "I surmise that you wish us to discover the provenance of your ancient sword. I mean to read every bit of documentation the British Museum's Reading Room has to offer about Viking-era swords and other similar archaeological finds!"

Louise looked doubtful. "That would require a ticket to use the Reading Room, and as you well know, women aren't supposed to apply." She paused. "I mean, it's almost unheard of."

"*Supposed?* Such a flimsy word," scoffed Emeline. "Since we know the books can only be studied inside the Reading Room, there is nothing for it. We *shall* obtain tickets. I will ask my brother Anthony to write a recommendation for us."

Hart casually plucked the paper from the table, folding it again, and returning it to his inside pocket. "Your brother Anthony?"

"Yes! He is a respected naturalist. Not only was Anthony aboard the Beagle with Charles Darwin, but he also knows Mr. Panizzi, librarian at the British Museum." She gave a little snap of her fingers. "Never fear, my lord, we shall soon be spending hours in the Reading Room, earning our wages."

Even as Hart wondered what Justin St. Briac would think of these new developments, he shook the thought away. Had he ever met a more refreshing female? With her beauty and intelligence, Emeline could have been the toast of London society, but instead she had embarked upon another path entirely.

An odd feeling stole over him as he remembered her words: *unburdened by husbands.* For a moment, Hart wondered if she might prefer the company of women to that of men, but then he remembered the intensity he'd felt when their gazes locked...and he knew damned well she'd felt it, too.

Emeline's voice broke into his thoughts. "There is no time to waste. I must contact Anthony as soon as possible to acquire our tickets!" Looking at the clock on the mantel, she added, "Therefore, if our discussion is concluded..."

Hart bit back a smile as he realized he had been summarily dismissed. Although it wasn't at all the way he'd expected this meeting to end, he found himself more intrigued than ever by the unconventional Miss St. Briac.

* * *

WHEN EMELINE KNOCKED at the door of her brother's charming home in Charles Street, she was greeted by Rafael, the Brazilian-born manservant who, as a boy, had stowed away and attached himself to Anthony during his voyage home from South America. Rafael was now eighteen years old and like a member not only of this family, but also of Emeline's cousin Camille Hawke's family in Cornwall, where he helped to manage their bird sanctuary.

"It's lovely to see you, Rafael," she said warmly. "And how handsome you have grown."

"You are too kind, miss." He gave her a raffish smile. "It my pleasure to meet you again."

In the background, Emeline glimpsed Mrs. Bell, the white-haired housekeeper who had come to Anthony with Frederica, who was now his wife. The old woman approached with a slower step.

"Hello, Mrs. Bell!" Emeline greeted her.

"I was just about to bring the carriage around," said Rafael, bowing slightly as he turned to go. "I should take my leave."

Alone with Mrs. Bell, Emeline asked for her brother. The housekeeper shook her head. "They are all about to travel to Mr. Darwin's home for a gathering. Little Oliver is going as well," she added, referring to Emeline's three-year-old nephew. "I don't believe—"

"Is that my sister's voice I hear?" It was Anthony, descending the stairs with Oliver, who clung to his father's hand. Her heart leaped at the sight of her brother, always so dashing. Anthony was ten years her senior, and she adored him. Now he came into sight, smiling, and little Oliver rushed into her arms.

"Auntie!" cried the boy.

"Freddie is just tying the ribbons of her bonnet," Anthony said. "We are off to Darwin's for a small farewell luncheon. He and his growing family are moving house to Kent, where they will live in an old vicarage called Down House."

"How you will miss him here in London!" exclaimed Emeline.

"I will, but I think this change is for the best. My friend has had health struggles since the voyage of the Beagle." Anthony held her away from him. "Forgive me, Emmie, but the carriage is just drawing up. Will you allow us to postpone your visit?"

"Of course! I should never have appeared uninvited." She knew she should let him go gracefully but couldn't resist catching his sleeve and adding, "Anthony, do you think it would be possible to obtain tickets for Louise and me to study in the Reading Room at the British Museum?"

Frederica had just joined them, and Rafael jumped down from the box to assist the family.

"Tickets…to the Reading Room?" Anthony cocked his head, as if he thought she had misspoken.

"Yes! I know it isn't the usual practice for women—"

He gave a snort of agreement. "Far from it!"

"Yet long overdue," interjected Freddie with a wide smile. "Good for you, Emmie!"

With that, her sister-in-law kissed Emeline's cheek and led Oliver down to the waiting carriage.

"I will come by tomorrow to learn more about this," Anthony told Emeline as he took up his hat and gloves. "Honestly, chit, you never cease to surprise me."

* * *

THAT EVENING, Emeline and Louise ate their supper on the tea table in a cozy corner of the parlor. Dora served their meal looking rather shamefaced. The roast chicken was dry, the potatoes needed seasoning, and the green beans were cold, but the cousins were in good spirits all the same.

When Dora had left them, Emeline put down her fork and mused, "I must ask my grandmother if she really believed Dora was skilled enough to leave the Raveneau kitchen and manage a kitchen of her own."

Louise smiled. "Perhaps Devon merely thought that, for the two of us, any cook was better than none." She raised her glass of wine. "I think we should celebrate the many new developments in our lives. Whenever I ponder Lord Hartcliffe's visit, I feel excited. To think that he is actually going to *pay* us to gather pertinent information regarding his ancient artifacts... Oh, it is quite thrilling!"

Flames danced in the nearby grate, enhancing the festive mood. Emeline lifted her own glass and touched it to her cousin's. As she sipped the wine, warmth spread through her body. She, too, was exhilarated by the challenge his lordship had set before them. Yet Emeline was also keenly aware of other, confusing feelings, an intoxicating, physical tug that she hadn't felt since the long-ago night at the Spring Ball when she had stumbled into a stranger's bed. It was a memory she had labored to bury, yet today that unsettling part of her had awakened when Lord Hartcliffe pinned her under his blue gaze.

Beware, Emeline warned herself.

At length she replied, "I too am most anxious to gain access to the Reading Room. Surely there are papers there regarding recent archaeological digs here in England. Perhaps some were conducted in Suffolk, near Woodcroft Priory!"

"Yes," agreed Louise, "and we can gather information about artifacts like those unearthed at his lordship's estate."

"I confess I find archaeology utterly fascinating! It brings a human aspect that doesn't exist with fossils," Emeline said. "Who owned the sword discovered at Woodcroft Priory, and what was his story?"

Louise sipped more of her wine, cheeks pinkening. "Do you really think Anthony will be able to obtain our tickets to the Reading Room? When I first came to London everyone said that ladies ought to use circulating libraries so that we might read shut away in the confines of our homes. It was considered very improper for a female to spend hours among the men in the Reading Room, and I daresay that is still the case."

"Men enjoy making lot of ridiculous rules for *ladies*," Emeline proclaimed. "That is why I turned my back on the London ton. As for the Reading Room, I have heard that Harriet Martineau studied there within the last few years. Although we shall doubtless invite a lot of stares and whispers, I shall relish the opportunity to look down my nose at those odious men!"

Her cousin leaned forward then and waggled her brows in a way that suggested she was feeling the wine. "Speaking of men… Will you also relish Lord Jasper Hartcliffe's future visits?"

"Louise!" Heat flooded Emeline's face.

"Ah, I see I have struck a nerve." Sitting back, she nodded

triumphantly. "I may be a spinster, but I am not oblivious to the signs of…" Her voice trailed off.

"Of *what?*" challenged Emeline.

"Well, nothing so obvious as a flirtation, but I did perceive a certain *current* in the air. I suppose it's attraction, though I am no expert on that subject." Louise paused to drink the last drops of wine in her glass before adding plainly, "I saw the way he looked at you."

"You said yourself that he is a renowned libertine. I have no doubt that he attempts to charm every eligible female he encounters." Emeline drew a shaky breath. "Besides, his lordship has more white hairs than Papa! No doubt he is quite old."

"Do you really think he is so advanced in years?" She shook her head. "Look closer next time you meet—if you dare."

As Louise's words sank in, Emeline became conscious of a tingling warmth that spread over her body and settled in her intimate core.

"I am not used to hearing you talk this way," she said, glad to turn the conversation away from her own reactions to Hartcliffe. "And I thought we had agreed to pursue lives free of the distractions of men. Especially wicked libertines!"

Louise averted her eyes. "Yes, I know. We did agree about that." A telltale flush crept over her cheeks.

Emeline's heart sped up. "I hope…you are not attracted to Lord Hartcliffe yourself?"

"What?" Her cousin glanced over in surprise. "Oh no, not that. Not that at all."

She knew a sinking feeling. *Charles.* Of course! Louise was still secretly pining for Sir Charles Brandreth, who had been living in Italy for years. Even though Charles was Emeline's half-brother, she strongly felt that Louise was too good for him. Charles had always cared most for his own well-being and forming connections with powerful, wealthy aristocrats. Perhaps there was no point in saying any of this aloud, Emeline thought with a sigh, and yet she loved her cousin too much to continue pretending she did not see the truth.

"Is it Charles?" she asked gently.

Louise blinked nervously. "Why do you say that?"

"I know I am considerably younger than either of you, but I am not blind. I think all the family could see the way you always changed in his presence. You glowed whenever Charles came into the room." Emeline paused, noting her cousin's dismayed expression. "It would be just fine except that Charles doesn't deserve so fine and lovely a woman as you!"

"You don't understand." Louise shook her head, blinking back tears. "There has always been a…special understanding between us. I am his friend! I feel that I can see inside his mind and heart in a way that others cannot." She paused. "I've always felt that Charles was scarred by his childhood and, thus, wary of giving his whole heart to a woman. Perhaps, when he next returns to London, he will be a wiser, stronger person."

Emeline wanted to exclaim that Louise was a fool to nurse such dreams, but she forced back the words, realizing that such a speech would only cause pain. Instead, she nodded. "Perhaps so. Anything is possible."

For her own part, Emeline hoped that Charles would remain in Italy until the torch Louise carried finally burned out.

Setting down her empty goblet, she proclaimed, "Let us end this talk of men. For my part, I plan to spend so much time at the British Museum, studying in the Reading Room, that there won't be time to fret about any member of the male species, especially Lord Jasper Hartcliffe!"

CHAPTER 5

For once, Hart didn't know how to fill his day. When in London, he generally did as he pleased, either riding or driving in Hyde Park, visiting his club, or walking to the British Museum to search through historical and archeological papers in the Reading Room. Nights were often spent at the theatre or pursuing more decadent pleasures: drinking, gaming, or bedding a woman of experience and discretion.

On occasion, all three.

When, inevitably, Hart began to feel a sense of connection or obligation, especially to a female, he would announce to Mrs. Peachey and William that it was time to return to the Continent. They were expert at packing up Hart's temporary household and moving on.

However, this morning felt oddly different. Drinking his coffee at the dining table, Hart found himself thinking of Emeline St. Briac. Her irrepressible laughter echoed in his memory, and he saw again the militant sparkle in her violet eyes. Hart set down his newspaper and frowned. There was no good reason for this. He had done his duty, as spelled out by the girl's manipulative father, and now Emeline would be indefinitely occupied with the challenge of obtaining a special ticket to the Reading Room.

True, Hart had agreed to continue to play the role of the cousins' employer, but that should require only very occasional meetings. Brief, formal appearances.

And at the end of six weeks, he would go. Far away.

Just then, a loud knock at the outside door broke into his thoughts. Mrs. Peachey went to open it, and moments later, Justin St. Briac was striding toward Hart.

"*Bonjour,*" greeted the Frenchman, barely smiling.

Hart rose and they shook hands. "Good morning. Pardon my appearance." He gestured toward the tailored, charcoal gray coat that he'd slung over a chairback. "I must have forgotten our appointment."

"There was no appointment." There was a note of irony in St. Briac's deep voice. "However, I was sent away from Emmie's yesterday, and I am impatient to discover what happened in my absence."

Hart gave a short laugh and indicated that the older man should take a chair. "Do join me."

Mrs. Peachey appeared with a fresh pot of coffee and a plate of her special blackberry scones. St. Briac selected one, cocked an eyebrow at it, took one tentative bite, and drew back with a smile. "It is surprisingly good," he pronounced, adding, "we French are born with discerning palates."

"I'm relieved that you approve, sir." Hart folded his copy of the Times and set it aside. "Perhaps you will be comforted to know that it wasn't long before your daughter sent *me* away yesterday as well."

"She is not suspicious of us, I hope."

"No. I don't believe so. In fact, the two women appear to be very intrigued by my project. However, when your daughter discovered that one or two women have managed to set foot in the museum's Reading Room, she became determined to obtain special tickets."

Justin St. Briac gave a low chuckle. "That should keep my Emmie occupied for a very long time."

"My thoughts exactly, sir. I should not need to intervene again for several days. Weeks, possibly."

"So it would seem." St. Briac looked thoughtful. "Yet, it could be a mistake to underestimate my daughter. She is not like other females. Emeline has a way of surprising everyone."

Just then, William burst into the room, out of breath. "My lord, excuse the interruption, but as I was returning from your tailor, I saw the duke emerging from a carriage in front of the hotel! I ran all the way up to tell you—" He stared at Justin St. Briac. "That is, I mean to say…"

"I know!" Hart interrupted. Standing, he turned to his visitor. "Given Austell's dealings with you, m'sieur, he must not know that we are acquainted, much less arranging plans together."

Before he could decide what to do, another knock sounded. Hart felt a surge of panic even as he thanked Providence for the small alcove that separated the parlor from the entry door.

"William," he whispered roughly, "greet His Grace and tell him that I have gone out. You don't know when I will return."

Quickly, he drew Justin St. Briac into the bedroom and closed the door. The two of them stood together, rigid, waiting until the two, muffled male voices died away.

A soft tap came at the bedroom door and Hart opened it. Will stood before him, looking troubled. "Well?"

"Although I do not care to engage in outright deception, I did as you bade and told the duke that you were out. His Grace replied that he simply happened to be passing and was not surprised to find you away from your rooms. He asked me to give you this."

As Hart accepted the small envelope sealed with the Caversham ducal crest, he sensed the curious gaze of Justin St. Briac.

Gesturing for the others to precede him back into the drawing room, he waited for the two men to turn, then broke the seal and scanned the brief note.

My dear brother,

I have been called away unexpectedly to Caversham. Seems there has been a fire in the kitchen and I fear I must assess the damage.

Yours, etc. A.

Standing alone, Hart closed his eyes and drew a sharp breath, wondering how Austell, who lacked both inner strength and monetary resources, would cope with this crisis. Then, exhaling, he put it from his mind.

Emerging into the drawing room, Hart joined St. Briac. "My brother's appearance here this morning was a warning, I think," he said. "I may reside in a hotel, but people will notice who comes and goes, nonetheless."

With one eye shielded by a silk eye patch, St. Briac was inscrutable. "I take your meaning. I will not arrive again unannounced."

Hart nodded. "When you wish to see me, simply send word."

They walked together to the door. No sooner had the Frenchman crossed the threshold than he turned back. "I am trusting you to fulfill our bargain, my lord. Do not forget about Emeline."

The man must be in jest, Hart thought sardonically. It was impossible to forget Emeline St. Briac, for she invaded his consciousness from every direction.

"I will not forget," he said, "but I have an added stipulation. I must leave London in six weeks, so my obligation to you will end at that time." Hart already breathed a bit easier knowing there was an escape route on the horizon.

The Frenchman furrowed his brow. "I suppose I must agree."

"No doubt, six weeks will be more than enough time. Is it not my role to merely, uh, delude the young ladies into believing their income is being fairly earned? Perhaps the less they see of me, the better."

"Perhaps."

Watching St. Briac disappear down the hotel corridor, Hart wondered where he could go for a respite from this drama.

* * *

"I COULDN'T BEAR to be confined inside that house another moment," Emeline said as she and Anthony walked toward Berkeley Square. "Your visit was just the excuse I needed to escape."

Her brother looked smart as always in his riding clothes. "I understand that feeling," he acknowledged.

They came into the green square, strolling under the spreading branches of great plane trees, and Emeline breathed deeply. "Oh, lovely. The air is so fresh and sweet, a welcome change from my own house." She glanced up at Anthony. "Our darling grandmother has sent us a very sweet cook who, unfortunately, cannot cook at all. In the kitchen, Dora burns or scorches nearly everything she touches, and the smell does linger."

"I suspect Grandpère had a hand in placing Dora with you," Anthony laughed. "No doubt he had little patience for such shortcomings."

Emeline nodded even as she remembered the reason for their meeting. "Enough of this polite conversation," she declared. Stopping on the footpath that bisected Berkeley Square, she reached for Anthony's hands. "Tell me, have you brought me our tickets to the Reading Room?"

"Brought them...*today*?" He blinked. "Such a miracle cannot be achieved overnight."

"Whyever not?" She felt outraged. "Why must everything I want to do be so difficult? It should be a very simple thing for you, as a respected member of the Geological Society, to obtain cards of admission for your esteemed sister and cousin."

"Emmie, surely you know by now that London society does not operate according to your wishes." She recognized all too well his dry, faintly mocking tone. "I did all I could. The rules clearly require a *written* application. However, given your urgent plea, I went to the Reading Room this morning and spoke to Antonio Panizzi myself."

Emeline knew a sense of dread. Everything she needed to do hinged on this simple ticket. If she and Louise were *men*, it would be provided to them without question, the moment Anthony submitted his recommendations.

"Is it possible that Mr. Panizzi has refused?" she asked in a softer voice.

Her brother put an arm around her. "It's just that...he was resistant. The Reading Room is crowded with *men*, all doing research around long tables and engaging in sober discussions. I know it's a lot of nonsense, but they say that it goes against etiquette to mix females into such a place." He paused, then added, "And of course, you made a name for yourself during your two London Seasons. Lord Fulham, who was standing nearby, spoke up to wonder why the Exquisite would want to mix with serious male scholars."

"Fulham!" Her face grew hot as she remembered how the viscount had tried to force himself on her at the Spring Ball, two years ago. "He is insufferable."

"Even before Lord Fulham spoke up, Panizzi was circumspect. He advised that you and Louise seek out one of the ladies' reading rooms, where you will be more comfortable."

"Anthony St. Briac, do not tell me that you believe such fustian!" In frustration, she made a little fist and struck his chest.

"I am but the messenger," he replied, lifting both hands in surrender.

"Oh, how could Mr. Panizzi be so…backward?" she cried, shocked. "Is that his final word?"

"Perhaps not. I suggest that you give it time, Emmie. Allow me to submit the written application for your tickets, as the rules dictate. Perhaps he will unbend in the meantime." Anthony drew her off to one side of the path and put an arm around her rigid shoulders. "You cannot force change, especially on an institution like the British Museum."

"Given all the injustice toward women that you have witnessed during the past few years, I can hardly believe my ears. You know very well that our own Miss Anning was forced to remain outside Somerset House while a lot of titled *men* presented her fossilized pterosaur to the Geological Society. And to this day, women are still not allowed among its ranks!"

Anthony held her away from him with a bemused yet somewhat impatient smile. "See here, why are you angry with me? You asked me to apply for two tickets to the Reading Room, not storm the gates of the British Museum. I have done my best! It would be a mistake for me to try to coerce Antonio Panizzi or anyone else."

"All right. Yes! I see what you mean." Fuming inside, Emeline set her chin in a determined line. "Clearly, I must take matters into my own hands."

* * *

A FEW SHORT HOURS LATER, Emeline sat next to a desk at one end of the British Museum's imposing library. Just through the open doorway she could see the long Reading Room. Glorious shelves of books rose to a balcony that encircled the entire perimeter of the room, and above that soared another ten feet of bookshelves. There seemed to be more volumes in that space than Emeline had ever seen or even imagined. She ached for the freedom to peruse them, like the scores of men who now occupied the tables crowding the vast floor of the Reading Room.

Emeline tapped her neatly shod foot, waiting for Antonio Panizzi, the Keeper of Printed Books, to appear.

She couldn't remember the last time she had dressed with such care. Her unembellished gown of amethyst moiré was a shade darker than her eyes, and a crisp white collar attached to her chemisette peeped primly above the gown's neckline. Even Emeline's raven locks were concealed beneath a simple silk bonnet stiffened with cane hoops.

"Do you think that anyone will recognize me as the so-called Exquisite?" she had asked Louise as they surveyed her reflection in the cheval mirror.

"Not a bit," her cousin had laughed. "Rather, I should suppose you were a bluestocking, or a very strict governess."

Emeline smiled to herself at the memory but quickly turned serious as a middle-aged man with thick dark hair, heavy eyebrows, and side whiskers came into the room. She held her breath as he set down a sheaf of papers and turned to speak to her.

"What brings you to my desk, miss?" His tone was distracted.

She heard his Italian accent and knew this must be Panizzi. Her brother had told her that the Keeper of Printed Books had come to England as a young man to avoid arrest as a revolutionary in Italy. As a librarian at the museum, he helped to reorganize the collection and plan for its expansion. This year, Panizzi had begun enforcing the 1842 Copyright Act, which required publishers to give the British Library a copy of every new book published.

Emeline had a dozen questions for this man, but all of them would have to wait. Instead, she rose, gathered her wits, and approached him.

* * *

AT THE FIRST table in the Reading Room, Hart leaned back in his chair and watched the scene unfolding in front of Panizzi's desk. When it seemed that Emeline might glance his way, he lifted an open book to block part of his face. It was impossible not to stare at the chit. She might look very proper in her stiff moiré gown, but there was no disguising her radiant beauty or the fire of her intelligence. It was not a surprise that she had come to face Panizzi, to plead her case in person, but Hart guessed that the rigid Keeper of Printed Books would not be so easily swayed.

And of course, that was exactly what Hart—and Justin St. Briac—were counting on. The more barriers impeding the details of her employment, the better.

"Allow me to make myself known to you, sir," she was saying to Panizzi. "My name is Emeline St. Briac. This morning, I believe you had a visit from my brother regarding tickets of admission to the Reading Room for me and my cousin, Louise? Anthony tells me that you declined our request. Could it be because we are female?" Did Hart detect a slight quaver in her voice? *Brave girl.* "I have come to personally appeal to you. Perhaps you suspect that we are not serious scholars—"

Panizzi cut her off with a shake of his head. "I must set limits, Miss St. Briac. You see for yourself that there are already more readers at the tables than space comfortably allows." He lowered his voice. "It is my duty to oversee all that transpires in the Reading Room, and in my experience, females present an unwelcome distraction. That is why there are lending libraries where *ladies* may borrow books to read in the privacy of their homes."

Behind his open book, Hart allowed himself a sardonic smile. He couldn't have written Panizzi's lines better himself.

"Mr. Panizzi, this is outrageous." Emeline paused, lifting her chin. "My cousin and I are very serious women! And as you can see, there is nothing distracting about my garb."

The librarian reached for the papers on his desk, signaling an end to their interview. "My good lady, if you must persist in this course of action, follow the rules like everyone else. Go home and have your brother submit a *written* application on your behalf."

Her face fell. "But how long would it be before a decision is reached?"

"It is impossible to say. These things take time, and as you can see, I am a very busy man." Stepping behind his desk, he added, "And now, I must bid you good day. I have a great deal of work to do."

Hart nodded to himself, ignoring the odd pang in his chest. *Yes, good!* Now she could leave and wait for the interminable process to play out, and he could go on with his life.

However, instead of retreating in surrender, Emeline took a step closer to Panizzi.

"Sir, I implore you," she began more softly. "It is vitally important that I be granted access to the volumes inside these rooms." Raising one gloved hand, Emeline gestured longingly toward the book-lined walls.

Something in her voice tugged at what might have been his heart, if he had one. Hart slowly lowered his book, closed it, and set it aside. To his own surprise, he found himself rising to his feet. As if guided by an unseen hand, he walked under the arch that separated the Reading Room from Panizzi's office area.

"Pardon the interruption." Hart approached the pair and stopped next to Emeline. "I feel compelled to intervene."

Emeline looked up, surprise and confusion mingling in on her face. Her very pretty mouth made an O.

"Lord Hartcliffe," Panizzi's tone was now deferential. "I do beg your pardon. No doubt you have been disturbed in your studies." He sent a quick, accusatory glance toward Emeline.

"No, not a bit," Hart assured him languidly. "In fact, I was delighted to notice that my esteemed colleague, Miss St. Briac, had arrived, no doubt to collect her special ticket? As it happens,

I have engaged the ladies to do some very important scientific research on my behalf."

"Important…research?" Antonio Panizzi flushed under his side-whiskers, but after a brief, skeptical pause he nodded. "I see, my lord. Of course. With your strong recommendation, I shall issue the cards for Miss St. Briac and her cousin at once."

"Excellent. Just bring them along to my table when they are ready." Hart offered his arm to Emeline and gave her a faint, knowing smile. "There is something special I've been waiting to show you."

As he led her away, into the exclusive Reading Room with its tables of men, Hart thought, *Mad! I've gone utterly mad.*

CHAPTER 6

$\mathcal{A}$s Lord Jasper Hartcliffe led Emeline toward his table, she was acutely aware that every male in sight seemed to be staring at her. A murmur of whispers followed their progress. It was a relief to be able to take the chair he drew out for her and, she hoped, become less conspicuous.

"My lord," Emeline began when he was sitting next to her.

"Not *my lord*," he whispered, leaning very close.

"Lord Jasper, then…"

"No. Only my family address me as Jasper, and I have never cared for it." He flashed a smile. "Call me Hart."

She liked that. "I agree that titles are very stuffy. Yes, all right…I will call you Hart."

Emeline suddenly noticed that he smelled very good. His essence was appealingly male, a mixture of clean linen, citrus, and something indefinable yet arousing. A memory flickered in a deep corner of her subconscious, causing her to lean away to a safer distance.

"Do you give me leave to address you as Emeline?" he asked in an undertone.

She nodded, wondering why she found him so striking today. It came to her then that Hart's clothing was more impeccably elegant than when he came to Chesterfield Street. In contrast, his hair was now rather windblown. Attractively so. Perhaps Louise was right… Hart was not so old after all. When one paired silver-flecked hair with his arresting cobalt-blue eyes, the man's appeal was potent.

"I do not understand why *you* are here," she said, gathering her wits. "I thought you had hired Louise and me to labor in the Reading Room because you could not do it yourself."

"Ah, yes." His eyes glinted when he smiled. "That is a very logical question."

"I am glad you approve. Do, kindly, reply."

Two of the young men at their table lifted their heads and leveled disapproving stares at them. A third, elderly gentleman with a withered countenance paused in the midst of writing notes to make a stern *shh*-ing sound. Hart rose, took Emeline's arm, and led her to the nearest wall of books.

"You find me here because…I wasn't certain how long it might be until you and your cousin were possessed of your own cards of admission," he explained smoothly. "In the meantime, I thought I would peruse the various books that will be available."

"Oh, I see. It sounds as if you just walked into the library today, yet Mr. Panizzi seems to be well acquainted with you," Emeline pressed. "As if you have been here often."

Hart smiled. "Perhaps I have made a strong impression on him."

"No doubt." Emeline's mind was spinning as she tried to remember the things he had said just yesterday when the three of them discussed the Reading Room. "However, I must say, I am a bit confused. If you have a special ticket yourself, why didn't *you* apply to Mr. Panizzi on behalf of Louise and me? I was under the impression that you had no real knowledge of this process, and we must seek another person to help us gain access."

"I suppose I didn't think of it." Before Emeline could press him further, Hart pointed to a book on the nearest shelf. "Look at this. It seems to deal with Viking artifacts!" Turning, he motioned to one of the library aides, then informed the young man that he wished to read that particular volume.

Hart reminded her then that none of these books or manuscripts could be removed from the Reading Room. When she and Louise came here in the future, one of the library aides would procure whatever titles they needed. They were permitted to study them at one of the tables and, when they finished, must summon an aide to return them to the shelves. This was the reason so many people spent entire days here, reading, writing, or simply searching for obscure information.

"Various British archaeologists, including William Wylie, have begun writing papers about their discoveries. Some of them are working here at the Reading Room," Hart murmured as they waited for the aide to bring the book.

Emeline felt excited. "Oh yes, I was saying that very thing to Louise last evening! I am very anxious to begin searching for those works."

"I will give you a list of names, and you and your cousin can begin by asking for those."

The pale young man approached them again, empty-handed. "I beg your pardon, my lord, but a previous request for that particular volume was made just minutes ago."

Emeline then watched as another aide, stocky and balding, removed the book from the shelf. She and Hart watched as he trundled across to a distant table and presented it to a lean, fair-haired man who had the look of a university student.

"It's Peyton," muttered Hart, eyes narrowed. "One of the more self-important antiquarians."

"Do you mean Sir Giles Peyton? I believe I met him briefly during my last Season." She recalled that Sir Giles had been quite friendly, but she had given him no encouragement. "If he is an antiquarian, perhaps he could shed light on the artifacts you have discovered?"

This innocent suggestion was met with a dark frown. "Absolutely not."

From the table where they had been sitting, the withered man swiveled in his chair and again hissed, "Shh!"

"Perhaps I should go," whispered Emeline.

Antonio Panizzi was approaching at that moment, holding the special cards for Emeline and Louise in one hand.

"When you return with your cousin, Miss St. Briac," he said in accented English, "kindly apply to me at my desk. I will explain the code of conduct for our Reading Room."

"Of course, sir. Thank you so much," Emeline replied as she put the cards in her reticule and started toward the door.

To her surprise, Hart was walking next to her. Emeline waited to address him again until they had come into the wide corridor of the museum's new north wing.

"There is no need for you to accompany me, my lord."

"It's Hart, remember?" A smile touched his mouth. "And I will see you safely home. I assume that you came by hackney cab? Alone, no doubt, with a disreputable driver."

"Indeed, no. I walked." Emeline quickened her steps. "And I am quite capable of walking home again."

He easily kept pace beside her, gesturing as they walked toward the gallery that featured Egyptian antiquities. "Everything is being changed, as you can see," Hart indicated a tall window overlooking the courtyard. Outside, construction of the new wings of the museum continued, and a wall blocked the view of passersby on Great Russell Street. "I think Panizzi has plans for a grander, larger Reading Room as well."

"One that welcomes females?"

"I wouldn't bet on that." His tone was laced with irony. "And yet, now that you have arrived, Emeline, anything may be possible."

* * *

Outside the museum, Hart fell into step beside Emeline, pointing out the improvements the museum was undergoing, and to his surprise, she made no protest when he continued on with her in the direction of Chesterfield Street. In fact, she chatted with him in an unaffected manner about everything from her impressions of Antonio Panizzi to the "shocking" treatment of the hackney cab horses lined up across from the museum.

"It is outrageous!" she fumed. "I never had to witness such cruelty when I was in Lyme Regis, or if I did, it was on a much smaller scale. No doubt the horses must stand in their own waste, in rain and cold, often deprived of food and water…"

"First oppressed females and now ill-used animals," Hart reflected when she paused for breath. "I perceive that you mean to be a crusader. Never fear, you will find plenty of causes here in London."

Emeline looked up at him. "No doubt a rather…dispassionate man like you finds me tiresome." Pausing, she stared at the hackney cabs, as if tempted to cross the busy street and give the drivers a piece of her mind. "Yet I cannot ignore cruelty."

"Tiresome? Not at all." Hart had to suppress a desire to tell her it was just the opposite.

"Try as I might to be circumspect, I cannot help saying just what I'm thinking."

"But do you indeed try?" he queried dryly. "I doubt that. But never mind. Your candor is charming."

She set her chin. "I will not apologize for caring about the oppressed."

"Nor should you." As they turned onto Oxford Street, Hart added, "Perhaps your work for me, in the Reading Room, will keep you so well occupied you won't have time to search out the injustices that plague London."

She seemed to make a decision not to reply to this. They

walked in silence for a minute before Emeline inquired, "And where is your home, my lord?"

"My—home?"

"Yes." She sent him a curious glance. "Where in London do you live?"

"I don't have a home." Suddenly, he felt unsettled. "I mean, I don't *care* to have a home. When I am in London, I reside at the Pulteney Hotel."

"At a hotel? But you are an aristocrat. You must have a home."

"I thought you didn't care for the rules of conduct imposed by the ton. I can assure you, neither do I. I do as I please. I come and go, so I have no need for a home."

"You have no family here in London?"

After a moment, Hart said, "I do have a brother."

"A brother?" she prompted gently.

"His Grace, the Duke of Caversham. I simply choose not to partake in the pretensions of the beau monde. Austell sees to that for both of us."

"Oh yes." Emeline glanced over as if measuring her words. "I perceive that you prefer to hold yourself…at a distance."

Oddly stung, he replied, "First you refer to me as *dispassionate*, and now I am distant. How did you come by these powers of perception?"

She merely smiled enigmatically, not looking his way. "I am a woman, my lord. I was endowed with them at birth."

Almost without warning, Hart realized that they had reached Chesterfield Street and then Emeline was pausing outside the trim three-story house she shared with her cousin. He waited for her to invite him inside for tea, but she only extended her slim, gloved hand.

"I know how very busy you are, my lord, and I thank you for finding the time to see me home."

His instincts urged him to bring her hand to his lips and insist again that she call him Hart, but he restrained himself. "Think nothing of it."

"I thank you also for procuring our cards for the Reading Room." Her eyes shone. "Now Louise and I can truly begin our work, and you will be free to pursue your other pleasures."

"Yes." He took a step backward. "Just so."

Emeline turned and walked lightly toward the house, pausing only to wave and send him another fetching smile before she disappeared inside.

Hart stood there for a long moment, staring at the green front door. Now, he wondered, what the devil was he to do for the rest of the day?

* * *

HAVING JUST LEFT Anthony's home, Justin St. Briac paused with Mouette on the corner of Charles Street and witnessed the scene of parting between Emeline and Hartcliffe.

"Oh, look!" Mouette tugged at Justin's sleeve. "Who is that man with Emmie?"

They both stared as their daughter extended her hand and the man held it for a moment too long.

"Shh." He sensed that Mouette might start forward. "Wait."

A sixth sense Justin didn't fully understand compelled him to remain on the corner, watching until Emmie went into the house and Lord Hartcliffe turned away and started south toward Piccadilly.

"That was Lord Jasper Hartcliffe, the fellow I told you about," Justin told Mouette. "The one who is...employing the girls."

"My goodness." She seemed to be having a great many thoughts as she gazed after his lordship's tall, broad-shouldered figure. "Is their employment genuine?"

If there was one thing Justin dreaded, it was being caught in a bit of subterfuge by his exceedingly clever wife. "Of course. I told you, it was a stroke of luck, encountering Hartcliffe at the very time he desired someone to do research for him."

"Oh yes. How fortuitous for you, darling. You didn't have to deceive our daughter after all!" She was watching him, but he pretended not to notice.

He nodded. *"C'est vrai!"*

Before Mouette could press him further, Justin took her arm, and they started toward Chesterfield Street.

"I didn't realize his lordship was so handsome," she said after a few moments. "Don't you think so? He has a very compelling air about him."

Justin gave a harsh laugh. "Handsome? Compelling? That is a great deal to observe from such a distance."

"I now recall that we have met in the past. His eyes…that hair. Very striking." She lifted her brows, as if on the verge of a sigh.

"Are you trying to incite me to quarrel with you, madame?"

"Of course not." Her blue eyes danced up at him. "But I am still a woman, still breathing. Do you never appreciate a beautiful female?"

"I might." He wanted to take her in his arms at that very moment and kiss her in a way that would burn away thoughts of anyone else! However, because it was broad daylight and they were approaching Emeline's pretty green door, Justin refrained. And even as he lifted the knocker, he realized that the small contretemps with Mouette had served to distract her from his hidden scheme for Hartcliffe's "employment" of the two young women.

* * *

When Emeline heard her parents' voices downstairs, she hurried to finish changing out of the stiff moiré gown and into a soft day dress patterned with sky-blue stripes. Without pausing to secure a few loosened curls, she went down to join her family.

Louise was already pouring tea for her parents who sat framed by the pale light streaming through the bow window. Emeline rushed over to embrace them and perched on the window seat, between their two chairs.

"We were just coming from Anthony's," Mouette explained. "Oliver is at the most delightful age, and we can't resist popping in often to say hello. Since we were so close, we thought we would just stop here as well..."

"You have come at exactly the right moment!" Emeline exclaimed. "I haven't even told Louise the news yet." Reaching into the pocket of her skirt, she withdrew the two prized vouchers to the Reading Room and brandished them in the air. "Behold! I have acquired the tickets we need to continue our research."

Louise gasped. "Are you roasting us, Em? Can they truly be real?"

"Yes, yes, I have achieved the impossible!" She couldn't help laughing and waving the cards under her father's nose. "Can you believe it, Papa? Even Anthony failed in his quest for the tickets today, and he told me it might be impossible because we are female."

Justin looked rather stunned. "I congratulate you, *ma petite*. But...how?"

Another irrepressible laugh escaped from Emeline. "I went to the British Museum today to appeal personally to Mr. Panizzi, the Keeper of the Printed Books—but to no avail. He was utterly set against the idea of two women being admitted to the all-male Reading Room, even though a few women have managed to breach its hallowed walls in the past."

"I suspect none of them were as distractingly beautiful as you, love," murmured Mouette.

Emeline threw her a smile before continuing, "To my own astonishment, Hart came to my rescue today when he saw that I was going to be unfairly turned away!"

Her father arched a brow above his eyepatch. "Did you say… *Hart*?"

"Yes, Papa! Lord Hartcliffe insists that we address him as Hart, and after all, it is so much nicer than 'my lord,' don't you agree?"

Mouette blinked. "How did he happen to be present? Did he accompany you to the museum?"

"No, no, nothing like that! In fact, I was quite shocked to see him sitting at one of the tables in the Reading Room when I was speaking to Mr. Panizzi." Turning toward Louise, who was listening with wide-eyed interest, Emeline added, "When Hart engaged us to do research for him, I surmised he didn't know the first thing about the Reading Room, but that isn't the case at all!"

Looking a bit uncomfortable, her father spoke up. "As I understand it, his lordship has other pressing duties to attend to."

Emeline shrugged. "Perhaps that's so. In any event, when he saw that I was being turned away, he walked over and very firmly explained the situation to Mr. Panizzi. Minutes, later, I had these in my possession!" Once again, she triumphantly waggled them in the air.

"His lordship is quite a compelling character," her mother said rather cryptically.

Justin, meanwhile, was frowning. "Well, now that you have the tickets, we won't be seeing much of him in the future. He has passed the baton, as it were." He paused. "Incidentally, Hartcliffe will only be here in London a few short weeks. Six as I recall."

What? Emeline felt as if a stiff wind had jolted the room, taking her breath away, but she did not betray her consternation. "Indeed? Oh well, as long as Louise and I continue to receive remuneration, that is all that matters."

"Which reminds me," her father carried on without missing a beat, "you two beauties cannot shut yourselves away completely from the world. You should begin to go out in London society and meet people."

"Papa, when have you ever cared a button for such things?" Emeline exclaimed, half laughing.

Looking a trifle uneasy, Louise rose and excused herself to fetch more biscuits. No sooner had she left the room than Justin pointed a finger at Emeline.

"Do you mean to just wither away here?" he demanded. "What a waste that would be! You may be independent, but that doesn't mean you must renounce men."

"Of course not!" She couldn't resist teasing him. "Just because we are unmarried, we needn't give up all pleasure." After the briefest, strategic pause, she added, "You of all people should understand that."

"*Sangdieu*! What are you implying?" he cried in outrage. "Do you mean to take *lovers*?"

Emeline shrugged lightly, amused, but she was beginning to realize that he might be truly concerned. And when her papa focused on such concerns, a plan to control her destiny could not be far behind.

The secret, Emeline had learned over her lifetime, was to intercept him before he could go too far.

Justin had bolted to his feet and paced across the parlor. "I cannot stand by and watch you squander your future, your beauty, your loving heart! And do you intend to deprive your dear mama and me of grandchildren?"

"You have Oliver!" she protested.

Her papa waved a dismissive hand. "I mean *your* precious babes, ma petite."

From her chair near the window, Mouette shook her head. "Really, Justin, you are the outside of enough."

"I love our daughter too much to be silent at such a time." He turned to stare at Emeline. "Now that you are here in London, I intend that you should meet some worthy men, and I already have a few names in mind! You are still young enough…there is still time before you are relegated to spinsterhood." He inclined his head toward the back of the house and added in an under-tone, "Like your poor cousin."

Mouette pulled him back to sit beside her again. "For pity's sake, Justin, do stop."

Grasping control of the situation, Emeline rose and went to stand before her parents. "As it happens, I have been thinking about this very thing, Papa. In fact…I mean to compile my own list, so you needn't put yourself to any trouble."

His dark brows flew up. "A list…of *men?*"

Laughter bubbled up inside Emeline, but she pushed it down. "Exactly so." In a burst of inspiration, she added, "I call it my Bridegroom List!"

CHAPTER 7

$\mathcal{E}$meline watched a number of emotions cross her father's face before he settled on a frown. "You surprise me," he said at length, jaw clenched. "Show me this list."

"No, thank you. It is private."

"I am your papa," he pressed. "Nothing should be private from me." When Mouette, sitting at his side, gave an exasperated sniff, Justin amended, "For your own welfare, you know."

"How considerate you are," Emeline responded with a tight smile, "yet, one feels, also excessively inquisitive." Out of the corner of her eye, she saw her mother's lovely mouth twitch.

Brows lowered, he muttered, "Perhaps I have a suggestion or two of my own for this *list*."

"If so, you must make a record of your own," came her sweet reply. "You might call it your Son-in-Law List."

They locked eyes. Emeline enjoyed sparring with Papa, for there was no one else she understood quite so keenly.

"We must go," Mouette said. "But first, I wanted to tell you that your Raveneau grandparents are having a small party to celebrate Grandpère's birthday. He, of course, scoffs at such a plan, but the rest of us insist." Her expression was wistful. "How many more birthdays will he enjoy, after all?"

Emeline's heart stung at the realization that she hadn't even visited her grandparents since returning to London. True, it had only been a few days, but she had meant to go to them immediately. "A party is a splendid notion! When will it be?"

"This Saturday. You and Louise must both come."

Louise and Emeline were cousins through Papa's brother, Gabriel, but that didn't matter to the Raveneaus. Louise and her sister, Camille, had always been welcomed as part of Mama's family.

With that, Emeline hastened to see her parents on their way, just as Louise reappeared with a plate of biscuits.

"Oh, how lovely." Emeline put a biscuit in her father's hand. "Eat this on your way home so you don't become peckish and get into a tiff with Mama."

No sooner had the door closed, than Emeline caught Louise's arm and drew her back into the parlor. Their eyes met and they both began to laugh at the same time.

"I can't wait to hear every detail," Louise exclaimed. "And what about Lord Hartcliffe? You are now calling him *Hart*?" She tilted her head suggestively. "It seems that you two are becoming quite...familiar!"

Emeline was dismayed to feel her cheeks grow warm. "You're being ridiculous. Besides, as Papa said, he is leaving London very soon." She tried to sound very serious. "What is truly important is our new ability to spend our days in the Reading Room! Oh, you cannot imagine the books they have! And there are aides to wait on us, bringing us any volume we desire..." Remembering the young archaeologist who had requested the Viking book, just moments ahead of Hart, Emeline amended, "That is, unless someone else has already claimed it."

At that moment, her excited speech was interrupted by a

shriek from the kitchen at the back of the house. "No, no, get *out!*" cried Dora.

Emeline lifted her skirts and rushed toward the kitchen with Louise mere steps behind, just in time to hear a series of feline warning screeches. Entering the room, she beheld Bartholomew, tiny back arched and all his fur on end, confronting a dirty, shaggy, short-legged little beast that vaguely resembled a dog. The animal cowered in the doorway to the garden, holding one front paw in the air.

Dora came at the intruder with a raised broom. "Out, get out, mongrel!"

Bartholomew chimed in with a long, low, threatening growl that sounded as if he were possessed by a demon.

The scruffy animal retreated a step or two.

"What is happening here?" exclaimed Emeline, lifting her hand to signal that Dora should put down the broom.

"This filthy cur has been lurking outside the kitchen door all day," Dora cried. "I shooed it off, but it comes back. Doubtless it has some horrible disease!" She was trembling with emotion. "I won't have it in my kitchen!"

As if to corroborate this speech, Bartholomew strained to arch his back higher, hissing for good measure.

Emeline regarded the intruder, whose eyes were obscured by long, dirty tangles of fur. Was it a dog? After a moment, it lifted its face in her direction and whimpered softly. Bartholomew began to growl again.

"That is quite enough, Mew." She went forward, crouching down, and firmly moved the cat to one side. Bartholomew narrowed his green eyes at her but stayed put.

"I'll deal with this little tyrant." Louise knelt to join her and held their cat on her lap. Emeline noticed she was holding a long towel, just in case Mew's claws came out.

Extending her hand to the little dog, Emeline said softly, "Hello there, young sir. Are you hurt?"

To her surprise, it lifted its right front paw a little higher.

"What a clever dog you are! Will you let me touch you?" When she received no reply, Emeline reached out, first running a gentle hand over his filthy, furry back, then slowly gathering him closer. She lifted the tufts that hid his eyes, and he gazed back at her. Tears sprang to her eyes. "Oh, he understands!"

"Mistress!" There was a scolding edge to Dora's voice. "Do you wish to have *fleas*? The house will be infested soon enough!"

"What would you have me do?" Emeline spoke softly, as if hoping the dog would not understand their conversation. "This poor creature needs our help."

"London is beset with stray curs on every block. Would you save them all?"

"Perhaps, if it were possible, I would try! However, we must begin with this one injured, helpless dog." Emeline carefully probed the animal's front leg, but he quickly jerked it away. "If nothing else, we must allow him to heal from his injury in a safe environment."

"I'll help you," said Louise, pushing her spectacles back into place as she straightened. "I think he must have a bath straightaway."

Soon, they had filled a basin with warm water and some strong-smelling soap. After banishing Bartholomew to the garden and donning long aprons, the cousins lifted the dog into bath. Emeline expected him to resist, but instead he softened his small form and seemed to sigh as they lathered and rinsed him thoroughly. When he was wet, she felt the sharp outline of his ribs and nearly sobbed aloud.

"Poor little man! He is starving." Looking around for Dora, Emeline commanded, "Kindly prepare a meal for our guest. Do you have chicken or fish? I think it should not be anything too rich since he may not have eaten properly for a long time."

"Chicken or fish! For that mongrel?" exclaimed Dora.

"Yes, indeed! A generous portion, if you please."

Soon enough, she and Louise had cradled the dog in a warm towel. They combed out his mats, clipping the worst of them away, and trimmed his overgrown fur until his black eyes were visible and there was a bit of shape to his frizzled, tan coat. When they were finished, Emeline stared.

"Oh, my, look at his ear." The dog's right ear stood up to a point, but the left one was missing its top half. It almost looked as if it had been bitten off long ago and healed. Her throat thickened with emotion.

"How sad! At least, whatever happened to him, seems to be in his past. It's a badge of honor," pronounced Louise, standing back to survey the little dog. "I think he is some sort of terrier, don't you agree?"

Emeline nodded. "One of our neighbors in Grosvenor Square had a Dandie Dinmont terrier. I think this fellow might be a smaller cousin." As the dog continued to gaze up at her, she added, "I would like to call him Monte. Do you approve?"

Louise pushed a damp chestnut curl back from her brow and nodded. "It's perfect, I think."

"Hello, Monte," Emeline said warmly to the dog. "You are looking so much better, but what about your leg?" Tentatively, she reached for his paw, and he allowed her to look at it for a few moments before once again pulling free. "I don't see anything like an imbedded thorn, so it doesn't seem to be your paw. We shall endeavor to discover the nature of your injury, but in the meantime, you must stay indoors and rest."

She carried him into the parlor and set him down on another towel. Louise looked on with a dubious smile as Monte gobbled up the dish of giblets Dora had grudgingly prepared.

At length, Louise wrinkled her nose and ventured, "What about Bartholomew?"

"Well, I suppose we must move Monte to a bedroom."

"I don't think Mew will stand for this dog being in his house. Cats are very territorial, you know."

"Perhaps he will surprise us," Emeline said hopefully.

She carried Monte up to her bedroom and folded a blanket to make a little bed for him on the rug. However, when she suggested he might like to lie down, he came and stood against her skirts. There was a knock at the door, followed by Louise's voice.

"I have brought Monte a small bowl of water." She paused. "Bartholomew is creating quite a ruckus, howling in the garden. I will bring him into the house and see what happens."

Emeline cringed a little but nodded. "All right." She took the water and offered it to him, but he was not interested.

A very short time later, a scratching commenced at Emeline's door. Monte hurried over to investigate. A soot-gray cat's paw appeared under the door, claws unsheathed, followed by a series of now-familiar low growls.

"Bother," muttered Emeline, even as Monte began to yip at the threatening paw.

After a few minutes of this, Louise spoke from the other side of the door. "Emmie, I don't think this is going to work out." She paused. "How can you ever bring Monte out of this room? Or risk leaving a door open? I have no doubt that Mew would not hesitate to attack poor Monte, and how could he defend himself against those claws and sharp teeth, especially given the injury to his leg?"

Suddenly, Emeline remembered the sweet little robin Bartholomew had murdered when they lived in Lyme Regis. She heaved a sigh. "What shall we do?"

"Can you take Monte to Anthony and Frederica?"

"No! All three of them have gone to help the Darwins unpack and get settled in Down House, their new country home. I don't know when they will return."

"I don't suppose Uncle Justin would..."

Emeline cut her off. "No! I can't imagine Monte living there, and I would never hear the end of it from Papa. And don't suggest my Raveneau grandparents. They already have a dog, Daisy, and that is more than enough for Grandpère, who is getting on in years."

There was a scuffling sound as Bartholomew began to bump against the door and Monte's yips grew louder. A desperate feeling swept over Emeline as she remembered all the work that she and Louise needed to do at the British Museum. If Monte lived here, how could they ever leave the house?

"What do you suggest?" came Louise's voice from the other side of the door.

Emeline heaved a sigh. "If only we could send Monte on the stagecoach to Cornwall, where he could happily live in the walled garden at Elysium with your parents."

"That is a very nice dream," her cousin replied tartly. "Meanwhile, you find yourself trapped in your bedroom."

"All right. I take your meaning." She leaned her forehead against the door for a long moment. Her heartbeat accelerated as Monte dashed back and forth, barking at Mew's outstretched paw. "I will think of something…"

* * *

"IF I MAY INQUIRE, MY LORD…" William cleared his throat. "Do you know the approximate hour of your return?"

Standing in front of the mirror, Hart cast one last appraising glance at his expertly tied cravat before turning toward his valet. "I have a…late engagement tonight. I may not return until morning."

"Ah, I see."

"You must not wait for me. Carry on as if I had gone away for a day." He thought he saw William draw a rather wistful breath, as if he might wish that he too could partake in a "late engagement." It seemed that his manservant had given up a private life, not only to follow Hart on his adventures, but also to stay by his spinster sister's side. Mrs. Peachey had already taken a risk in life by leaving her secure position at Caversham Castle to become housekeeper to Hart, the family's black sheep. It was necessary that someone else, like her brother William, be there with her as well. And although Hart was not disposed to form attachments, the three of them did feel rather like a family.

Hart turned back to the mirror and scanned his midnight-blue frock coat, pleated white shirt, gray waistcoat, and snug trousers. "You're doing an excellent job with my clothing, William. Not even a hint of a wrinkle or speck of dust."

This elicited one of the valet's ready grins. "If I may say so, my lord, it is a pleasure to tend the clothing of a man who wears them so well."

"My tailors thank you."

Smiling, William gathered Hart's hat and walking stick, and they went out into the parlor where Mrs. Peachey was waiting.

"Are you *quite* certain you don't want supper before you go?" she asked for the third time in an hour.

"Did you imagine I would change my mind?" Hart paused to fondly pat her rounded shoulder. "I shall dine at my club." *Unless I go immediately to Valencia's to attend to my...other appetites.*

In part to counter any sightings of him studying at the British Museum, Hart had planned to visit his club to indulge in supper and a few reckless hours of hazard and whist. The last thing he wanted was a reputation for serious intellectual pursuits, or anything that would cause London to compare him to his brother. Not that he cared, of course, but Austell was the bloody duke, and Hart preferred to be known as the family black sheep.

Perhaps he really *would* dine at Boodles and wait before visiting the recently widowed Lady Valencia Brook at home in Wigmore Street. He certainly didn't need to engage in hours of intimate conversation before bedding her. She would be quite pleased to have him at any hour, as long as he didn't leave too soon.

Hart felt a disquieting pang as he realized that, in many ways, Valencia resembled Emeline St. Briac. Both were brunettes, with fine bones, inviting mouths, and small waists. And as he recalled, Valencia even had a hint of the militant gleam in her eyes that he found so appealing in Emeline.

Later tonight, when the lamps were doused and Valencia was naked, perhaps he might imagine the unattainable Emeline was in his arms, yielding to him, returning his kisses—

From a distance, Hart became dimly aware of Mrs. Peachey's soft voice.

"… and I do worry that you won't have a proper meal…"

He blinked. *Thank God one's wicked thoughts cannot be overheard.* He aimed a smile at the housekeeper. "You have been saying that to me since I was a boy, Peachey. What would I do without you?"

"Well, as it happens, that is just why I'm here!" Spots of color appeared on her cheeks. Then, after looking him up and down through her spectacles, she added, "May I say, you look quite handsome tonight, Lord Jasper? It makes me proud."

Hart bent to put an arm around her small frame. "You are an exceptionally good woman, ma'am."

William glanced meaningfully toward the clock on the mantelpiece. "I left instructions that one of the footmen downstairs should order your carriage at nine o'clock," he hinted.

"Ah, yes. I will go now." Drawing on his gloves, Hart took up his walking stick and black beaver hat. However, he had taken no more than two steps when a knock sounded at the door.

"Who can it be at this hour?" Hart held up a gloved hand when William started forward. "No, I will see who it is. Hopefully it's just a footman with a message."

Even as he started forward, the knock sounded again, this time with greater urgency.

Faintly annoyed, Hart threw open the door and was stunned to discover Emeline St. Briac standing in the broad corridor.

"Good evening," she said with forced brightness. "No doubt you are surprised to see me."

"I am indeed," he agreed dryly. Remembering the fantasy he had enjoyed just minutes earlier, Hart wondered if she might be a mirage.

Emeline took in the sight of him, hat and walking stick in hand, and her chin went up a notch. "You are clearly going out. However I have come on a matter of grave importance."

He swept her with his gaze. Emeline wore a hat with a concealing brim, a warm blue mantelet, and in her arms she clasped a rather large basket covered by a knitted blanket. When something moved inside the basket, he stared.

A muffled sound emerged from under the blanket. "Woof!"

Hart glanced right and left in the corridor before he reached out and drew her inside. "I can spare a few moments." His tone verged on a warning. "What can you be thinking, my girl, coming here alone at this hour—and what the devil do you have in that basket?"

CHAPTER 8

Moments later, Hart and Emeline stood in the lamplit entry alcove, and he looked down into her face. He couldn't help thinking how radiantly lovely she was, even holding what appeared to be a basket filled with laundry.

"I did not come alone," she assured him. "Louise is downstairs. I knew it wouldn't do to send a card up first, so I persuaded her to offer one of the footmen a guinea to discover the location of your rooms and then to look the other way while I hurried upstairs with Monte."

Hart cocked his head as if attempting to translate a foreign language. "I have no idea what the deuce you are on about."

Emeline seemed to assess the situation. Watching her gaze sweep over his tall form and impeccable evening clothes, he bit back a smile. *She is impressed. Even...attracted.*

She shifted the unwieldy basket in her arms, undeterred. "You see, my lord, after your kind assistance this morning at the Reading Room, it came to me that you were just the person to help my poor Monte."

"My patience wears thin," he said tersely. "Who or what is—"

"Lord Jasper," came Mrs. Peachey's gentle voice from the adjacent sitting room. "Will you invite your guest to come into the parlor?"

Trapped like a hawk in a snare, Hart froze. He must have been mad, telling Emeline that he lived at the Pulteney! Next, she would be mixing with Peachey and William, effortlessly charming them. But now, what bloody choice did he have? Sweeping an arm forward in a faintly mocking gesture, he ground out, "After you, Miss St. Briac."

Just as she started forward, something squirmed under the knitted blanket and whimpered. Emeline quickly glanced up, and he knew that her heart had skipped a beat.

Taking the basket from her before she could resist, Hart said, "Allow me to carry that for you."

"But—"

"Oh, no, I insist."

Emeline was clearly too preoccupied with the live creature in the basket to wonder whom she would meet in the sitting room. However, when they entered and Peachey came forward, radiating kindness, Emeline beamed as if they were old friends.

"Miss St. Briac," Hart said, feeling uneasy, "this is Mrs. Peachey, my housekeeper." Seeing William enter from the bedroom, he added, "Her brother, William, is my valet."

Mrs. Peachey's smile widened. "My brother and I look after Lord Jasper as much as he'll let us."

"I am pleased to know you both," Emeline said as cordially as if they were nobles.

"Welcome, Miss St. Briac," Mrs. Peachey rejoined. "What have you brought us in your basket?"

Hart set the basket down on a garnet-striped sofa and eyed it dubiously. Almost immediately, an animal poked its head out, blinking, and emitted an uncertain "Woof?"

Emeline was there in an instant. "Oh, Monte, you needn't worry," she exclaimed, hurrying to perch beside the basket and smooth frizzled tufts back from the mongrel's face. "You are safe from Bartholomew here."

"My logical mind tells me that this entire scene must be a bizarre dream, yet I fear it is real," muttered Hart. "Pray explain, Miss St. Briac."

"Well, as you may readily perceive, this little dog was living on the streets of London. He appeared at our kitchen door, begging for scraps, in the most deplorable state imaginable." Her eyes were bright with tears. "Dora, our cook, even attempted to hit him with a broom!"

"Shocking," Hart remarked in a sardonic undertone, wishing he could send Peachey and William to their own apartment so they wouldn't witness this scene.

"Indeed," Emeline rejoined, as if he had spoken from his heart. "So terribly shocking! However, we gave him a thorough bath, combed and trimmed away his mats, and fed him. Louise and I call him Monte."

To Hart's dismay, the dog turned to stare at him, then managed to clamber out of the basket and went closer, pushing his damp nose against Hart's elegant, spotless trousers.

"Oh ho, it seems the little fellow likes a challenge," William offered, amused.

Hart pointed a warning finger at the dog. "Do not touch my clothing."

"Monte, do be a good boy and come to me," Emeline coaxed, but the dog would have none of it. Instead, it reached a paw toward Hart's hand. She gave a little laugh. "Goodness, my lord, he has taken to you!"

Conscious that all three of them were watching, Hart patted Monte's head, just once. "It is of no consequence. You and this dog are only visiting, correct?"

Even as he spoke, Mrs. Peachey hurried out of the room and returned moments later with a dish of water and a few morsels of ham on a plate. "Poor little thing," she said, in the voice he recognized from his own childhood, and set the dishes down on the carpet. Emeline hastened to lift Monte down from the settee.

"He cannot jump, you see," she explained as the terrier ate the ham and licked the plate. "He has injured his leg, and he won't allow anyone to touch it. That is the reason I had to bring him to *you*, my lord."

"Indeed." He narrowed his eyes. "I must be very obtuse. I cannot see any clear connection between this dog's injury and my residence."

"You have met Bartholomew, our cat, have you not?" Emeline did not wait for a reply. "Mew has taken a strong dislike to Monte, I'm afraid. I cannot even keep Monte in my own bedroom without Bartholomew lying in wait outside the door, howling. And worse." As she spoke, she watched Mrs. Peachey stroke the dog's head.

So cozy, Hart thought. *Just as I feared.*

"Whatever will you do, Miss St. Briac?" Mrs. Peachey wondered aloud as she returned to stand beside William.

"My own family members are either away from London or quite ineligible to house Monte while his leg heals." Emeline sighed. "That is why I came here."

"What makes you suppose *I* am not ineligible?" queried Hart, one dark brow arched. He continued to stand a short distance away, waiting for a chance to take his leave.

"May I be frank?" Emeline turned her expressive violet eyes on him. It was bad enough that the chit was enchanting, but worse was his apparent inability to resist. Hart's chest tightened as she continued, "At the moment when I was forced to make a decision about Monte, I remembered how you stepped in to assist at the Reading Room. In fact, my lord, ever since Louise and I came to London, you have quietly intervened to improve our lives."

Mrs. Peachey and William both looked on, wide-eyed, and Hart glared back at them. "I simply provided employment for the two women! They are doing research for me about Viking burial sites."

"Ah, of course," William nodded.

"None of that speaks to the situation at hand," Mrs. Peachey said. "This sweet dog needs a refuge, and we can provide it." Straightening, she looked at Hart. "If you don't wish to have Monte here, Lord Jasper, William and I will shelter him in our rooms."

"You are very kind," Emeline said with feeling, and for a moment Hart feared she might embrace Peachey. Instead, she seemed to remember that the housekeeper was not the decision maker. Stretching out her slim hands, she implored, "Your lordship, will you agree? Only until Monte's leg is healed, of course."

"How good of you to consult me." His tone was tinged with sarcasm, but Emeline did not look away. Then, as she stood before him, inviting him to take her hands, something shifted inside Hart. It was like the moment in the Reading Room when he suddenly felt compelled to intervene with Panizzi. Feeling almost queasy, he closed his eyes and drew a deep breath.

"I know your stay in London will end in a few short weeks," Emeline went on. "I promise, I will endeavor to find Monte a new home long before then."

"Yes," he heard himself say. "All right, he can stay." In the distance, he heard Mrs. Peachey gasp softly and he turned toward the two servants who had known him all his life. "Did you think I was such a selfish brute that I would consign the dog to a life on the streets?"

As if he understood every word, Monte limped over to Hart's side and gazed up at him adoringly.

Emeline clapped her hands together. "I knew I could depend on you, my lord."

"That is the last thing I am known for," he said dryly. "And I am very busy. I certainly cannot be this mongrel's nursemaid, but he can stay here as long as he behaves himself. Mrs. Peachey clearly intends to look after him."

Monte tentatively rested his injured right paw on Hart's expensive leather shoe in a clear demonstration of preference. But before Hart could give the animal a set-down, Peachey hurried to the rescue and lifted him into her arms.

"You must come with me to our rooms, little man," she told Monte on the way to the door that separated their two apartments. "William and I shall make you a lovely bed…"

Emeline followed along and pressed a kiss to the dog's head before he disappeared inside, and the door closed. When she returned to Hart's side, he saw that tears misted her eyes.

"I think he was beginning to fall asleep, and no wonder," she said. "So sweet! I am very grateful to you for helping us."

Keenly aware that he and Emeline were alone, Hart felt his gut tighten. What the devil ailed him?

"In truth, I find it difficult to refuse you," he confessed with wry honesty.

She smiled. "That is fortunate for Monte!" A lovely flush stained her cheeks, yet she took a step toward the door and added, "But I am keeping you from your evening plans. No doubt someone is expecting you."

"Not really." He considered offering her wine. *And, perhaps, locking the connecting door.* But he said, "Of course, you should not be here, alone with me. If your father could see us, he would call me out."

"Nonsense," Emeline laughed. "You must be aware by now that I live an independent life. Papa has no authority over me! And as you know, Louise and I make our own way in the world."

A sharp pang of guilt caught him off-guard. What would she say if she knew the truth, not only about Justin St. Briac's manipulations, but also Hart's role in the deception?

"Is it possible that you care nothing for social conventions?"

"I made a choice to go my own way, after suffering through

two interminable Seasons. During that time, I became convinced that I am not designed to be a wife." She lifted her delicate, stubborn chin. "I made up my mind to do what I feel is right for me, not what society dictates. And I believe, in spite of everything, my parents understand. They did just the same thing when they were young."

"I see." He lifted both brows, enjoying every word she spoke.

"However in the meantime, Papa has gotten it into his head that I should not be alone, and he should act as my matchmaker. I know he does this out of concern, but he forgets that I am every bit as shrewd as he is."

Hart wanted to laugh. *Delightful.* "You have a plan of your own?"

"I do! When Papa began talking today about suitors for me, I told him I had begun a list of my own. A Bridegroom List!" An artless smile lit her face. "Isn't it inspired?"

"Brilliant," he agreed. "Who are the lucky candidates?"

"Well, it will all be a sham," Emeline told him cheerfully. "To throw Papa off the scent, you see. But I shall have to put a few names down in case I am forced to show it to him." Pausing, she stepped closer and laid a confiding hand on his arm. "I was hoping you might know some eligible young men of the town I could use as decoys."

Cynically, Hart thought that none of the libertines he fraternized with would pass muster with her father. And although Hart had claimed he didn't want to be entangled any further with Emeline, when the moment came to detach, it seemed he couldn't do it.

"I will think about it." He felt his mouth twist in a smile. Good God, did she regard him as some sort of uncle or older brother? Even as he had this thought, he felt the delicate pressure of her hand on his forearm and breathed in her fresh, lavender scent. The temptation to take her in his arms was almost unbearable.

"Oh my, I have just had an idea!" Emeline said, glowing.

"There will be a small party at my grandparents' home in Grosvenor Square this Saturday. I shall invite you, and perhaps *you* might bring along a possible candidate for the Bridegroom List! Someone you socialize with at White's or Tattersalls, or some such place."

"What?" He blinked. "No, I don't think so. That is, we should not imply to your father that I have any involvement in your list." Hart cleared his throat, mentally casting about for a plausible excuse. "That is, I already have a sort of business relationship with St. Briac. And since I am employing you and your cousin, I don't think he would appreciate me, uh, meddling in your private life."

She looked unconvinced. "All right."

"However, between us, I will think about a name you might privately add to your list."

"That's a good plan." Emeline nodded. "And now, I really must go. Louise is waiting for me and if I don't appear soon, she will begin to worry."

When her hand slipped from his arm, he nearly reached out to bring it back. "I will watch you go down the corridor, but I cannot accompany you. It wouldn't do for anyone to see us and think you were here, alone, in my rooms."

Emeline nodded again and went ahead of him into the entry alcove. Then, as Hart reached to open the door, she turned, rose up on her toes, and impulsively embraced him. "Oh, Hart, I can never thank you properly for what you are doing for Monte." She kissed his cheek, her sweet lips brushing his rough jaw. "And for me."

Closing his eyes, he turned his face a mere inch, until his mouth grazed hers and he heard the soft intake of her breath. Desire overtook him as if he were a green youth, flooding his hard body with urgent need. For one burning instant, he tasted her mouth and knew it had to stop, or he would be doomed in more ways than one.

He straightened and set her from him. "I am glad to be of assistance." His voice was hoarse.

Emeline gazed up, eyes searching. He saw something in them... Could it be desire? *Shock, more likely.* Did it mean anything that she had murmured "Hart" when she embraced him? *She was merely thanking you, idiot! And you had to twist it into something carnal.*

Emeline was speaking, he realized.

"Goodbye, then." Color rose in her cheeks as she opened the door. "I do thank you."

Hart wanted to take her hand again, to let her see that he knew he had erred. Instead he merely nodded and watched as she disappeared down the corridor.

* * *

BACK INSIDE HIS ROOMS, Hart felt oddly disoriented. At the sight of his own reflection in a gilded mirror, he shook his head slightly. Clad in evening dress, tailored to emphasize the lean, powerful lines of his physique, he was the picture of a libertine... which of course was exactly the role he had meant to play that night.

Until Emeline appeared with her ridiculous vagrant dog.

Other women, like Valencia, spared no expense to achieve beauty, yet Emeline possessed a radiance that was priceless. Furthermore, she seemed quite unconcerned with the latest modes of fashion. His attraction to her felt different as well...

Hart had just stripped off his tailcoat when a quiet voice spoke from a distance.

"Lord Jasper?"

It was William, standing in the doorway that connected their rooms, watching him in a way that grated on his nerves.

"What do you want?" he snapped.

"Well…if you are no longer going out, perhaps I might assist you in your…undressing."

"I am perfectly capable of taking off my own clothes." He tugged a bit too hard at his neckcloth. He knew damned well that William was wondering why he had decided against his planned night of debauchery. "After that drama with Miss St. Briac and the dog, I have lost my desire for…gaming."

"Perfectly understandable, my lord." William nodded.

Why are you explaining to him? Hart silently demanded of himself. "Where the devil have you put the brandy?"

William entered the parlor then, carefully expressionless. No sooner had he produced the decanter of brandy and poured a liberal amount into a glass than a furry mongrel peered around the doorframe. The instant the dog clapped eyes on Hart, he engaged in frenzy of barking and hobbled, limping on three legs, across the fine carpet.

"Quiet!" commanded Hart.

To his surprise, the dog not only fell silent, but also sat down and waited, blinking his black eyes.

William offered a tentative comment. "He's missed you, my lord."

"Don't say that. Besides, he went away quite willingly with you and Peachey. I have no doubt that the little beast will grow very attached to both of you."

This prediction caused Monte to close the distance between himself and Hart. He sat down again, this time lifting his injured paw and gazing up at his would-be master.

"It would help if we could discover the true nature of Monte's injury," said William, "but Miss St. Briac said that the little fellow won't allow anyone to touch his leg." As William spoke, Mrs. Peachey came through the doorway and stopped next to her brother, watching.

"Curse it," muttered Hart. The mongrel might well be hoaxing them, faking this supposed injury, but he'd seem a villain if he said this aloud. Instead he crouched down and met the dog's black eyes. "I am going to see what's wrong with your leg. Do not dare to bite me, understood?"

"His name is Monte," Mrs. Peachey called helpfully.

Hart sent her a tight smile. "Thank you."

As he reached for the dog's left front leg, he heard Peachey draw a worried breath. For an instant, Monte started to pull away but seemed to think better of it. Slowly and carefully, Hart felt along the stubby canine limb, checking for evidence of a fracture.

"There is swelling at the shoulder joint," he pronounced, "but as far as I can tell, nothing is broken. A little rest and our vagrant guest should be perfectly well. William, take him with you. Perhaps you should visit one of the large potted palms on the terrace before you retire for the night?"

William obeyed, lifting Monte into his arms and starting off. Hart tried not to notice the way the dog craned his neck to look back at him until the moment they disappeared around the doorway.

Hart was swept by a renewed urge to seek distraction after all, at the faro tables or in Valencia's bed. He was looking around for his discarded coat and neckcloth when Mrs. Peachey silently appeared at his side.

"It's a fine thing you are doing, Lord Jasper," she murmured.

"What?" He shrugged, pretending not to understand, even though he knew damned well she could see through all of that. "Oh—are you referring to that stray?"

Mrs. Peachey nodded. "Yes. Monte. I have to tell you, just between us, that I am reminded of the little dog you loved as a child. He must have been abandoned, and you found him on the road. You chose his name yourself." Her voice was soft, like a dream. "Do you remember?"

Hart wished he could make her stop. "Vaguely." An image of the scrawny, aged dog, with his white muzzle and pleading eyes, sprang up, unbidden, in his memory. "I called him Felix. God only knows how I settled on *that* name."

Peachey lifted a wisp of linen and dabbed at her eyes. "Yes, that's right. Dear little Felix."

He willed her to relent, to no avail.

"I could never forget that day," she went on. "After the duke announced that Lord Austell was to be his heir, you didn't speak for a full year. Not a word! So when you opened your mouth and uttered *Felix*, Her Grace...your dear mama, was over the moon."

"Of course." His gut clenched painfully. "Very touching, yet I don't think we should attempt to draw any parallels between poor old Felix and this brazen interloper."

"No? If I may say so, Lord Jasper, I suspect you understand it more than you wish to admit." Mrs. Peachey patted his white shirt sleeve. "That's enough for one night."

Hart sent her a narrowed gaze. "Suddenly I am tired."

"Yes, my lord. You do have a great deal to consider." She started toward the door to the rooms she shared with her brother. Midway, she turned back to add casually, "It was lovely to meet Miss St. Briac. So natural and unaffected. Charming, I thought."

Peachey's timing had always been impeccable, Hart thought ruefully as she took her leave. After the connecting door closed, he heard Monte woof several times, but then there was quiet.

Hart stood in the middle of the parlor, alone. At a loss. When he drew a deep breath, it seemed that an unseen force was squeezing his ribs.

He glanced around for the abandoned glass of brandy and drank it down.

Devil take it. There was nothing for it, it seemed, except to go to bed. Perhaps he could elude the chit in his dreams.

CHAPTER 9

Emeline sat beside Louise in the dimly lit Reading Room.
Although rare books with engravings of Viking
weapons were open before them on the table, her mind
wandered.

"What's wrong?" whispered Louise.

"Wrong?" She spoke as softly as possible, all too conscious of
the stodgy old men who made free to converse among themselves but sent scolding glances whenever a female so much as
cleared her throat. "Whatever can you mean?"

"You haven't turned a single page since the aide brought you
that book!" Louise lifted a delicate brow.

Casting about for a plausible reply, Emeline murmured, "I
think we need more detailed information from Hart about the
artifact he has discovered. It's one thing to say that the sword is
Viking, but what proof does he have?"

"I think he hopes that *we* will uncover that proof." Louise
smiled wryly. "I suppose we might discover something in these
old tomes when we least expect it."

"Yet we may be wasting our time. How can that possibly
benefit him?"

Louise shrugged. "As long as his lordship continues to remunerate us, I'll keep poring over these books."

"Hmm. Yes." Emeline couldn't tell her cousin that she was plagued with distinctly unscientific thoughts of Hart. Ever since last night, when they parted at his hotel suite, she'd felt dazed, even as her nerves tingled with new sensations.

Later, how long had she lain awake in bed, her senses spinning, confused yet excited in a way that was completely new? Alone in the dark, she still felt the shock of Hart's mouth on hers, burning, arousing…although the kiss, if it could be called that, had lasted only an instant. Perhaps he hadn't even intended to kiss her at all, yet secret parts of her body were alive again…for the first time since she had wandered into a stranger's bed at Riven Court. If Emeline didn't know better, she would imagine he had given her some sort of potion.

Louise broke into her thoughts, murmuring, "Suddenly I am very hungry."

At this, two of the men at their table sent them pinched glances. "Shh!"

The cousins exchanged nods and gathered their things. Minutes later, they had emerged onto the museum's bustling, noisy courtyard. They had taken only a few steps when a familiar female voice called out to them.

"Darlings! Do my eyes deceive me?"

Emeline focused on the elegant older couple coming toward them. "Oh my, it's my grandparents!"

She rushed toward them, her joy tinged with shame that she had not found time to visit since returning to London. Her petite grandmother seemed ageless, and her grandfather wore his nine decades with the same careless assurance he'd once exhibited on the quarterdeck of his privateer, the Black Eagle. One scarcely noticed that Grandmama held his arm, more for his support than her own.

"Oh my goodness, hello! What a surprise," cried Emeline.

"We have come to view the new exhibit of Greek antiquities," Devon Raveneau explained. "We did not expect to see you girls here, of all places. I began to think you had forgotten about us," she scolded gently, blue eyes twinkling as they embraced.

For a moment, Emeline clung to her, breathing in her familiar scent. "I am so sorry! I don't know where the days have gone. Forgive me." She looked toward her grandfather. "Both of you, please?"

André Raveneau leaned slightly on his ebony cane and flashed a smile. "Ma petite, do not let your grandmother tease you. We are only glad that you and your cousin have come back to London."

"That's right," beamed her grandmother. "You must enjoy other pleasures besides visiting *us*. Perhaps some dashing young men will appear on the scene?" Before Emeline could challenge this notion, Devon turned to Louise and embraced her. "How wonderful that the two of you are making a home together. Independent females! I want to hear everything. You will both come to our party for André's birthday on Saturday?"

"Yes, we are coming. In fact—" At that moment, Emeline was interrupted by a rather nasal male voice calling out to her.

"Ah, Miss St. Briac. We meet again!"

As they all turned, Emeline beheld a tall, lean young man with gold-rimmed spectacles and an earnest expression striding toward them. He carried an umbrella and, reaching her side, doffed his tall hat to reveal thick golden locks that fell over his brow as he bowed slightly. Emeline realized it was the antiquarian from the Reading Room whom she had seen yesterday.

For a terrible moment, she couldn't remember the fellow's name, but he intervened. Bowing to her grandparents and cousin, he pronounced, "Allow me to present myself! Sir Giles Peyton, at your service."

After introductions were completed, he turned to Emeline. "Unpardonably rude of me to push in this way, Miss St. Briac, but when I saw you, I could not resist." To the Raveneaus, Peyton added, "I was fortunate to meet this beautiful young lady during her last Season, but then she disappeared from London. Imagine my surprise upon observing Miss St. Briac yesterday, in the Reading Room! Quite a rare feat for her to gain entrance there, among all the male scholars, you know. Couldn't help being impressed!" His hazel eyes fixed on her face. "Be pleased to assist in any way, Miss St. Briac. I am not only a member of the Antiquarian Society but fancy myself an archaeologist as well. My true passion. Oversaw a very fine dig in Surrey just this past summer!"

Louise nudged Emeline and said, "We may indeed turn to you for assistance, Sir Giles. The work we are doing in the Reading Room is related to archaeology."

Seeing his eyes light up, Emeline interjected, "But we are not at liberty to discuss it at this time."

Devon Raveneau, watching with interest, now addressed the young man. "Sir Giles, clearly my granddaughter and her cousin would like an opportunity to know you better. We are having an informal gathering at our home in Grosvenor Square on Saturday afternoon...a garden party to celebrate my husband's birthday. It would be delightful if you could join us."

"B'honored, madame! Very kind of you. Will you give me the particulars?" When this was accomplished, Peyton bowed again, bade them all farewell, and headed off toward the museum entrance.

"What a nice young man," Devon said a bit too casually. "And you have interests in common!"

Emeline had felt her grandmother watching her during the interlude with Sir Giles, but she suppressed the urge to protest. She wanted to ask why, if Grandmama preferred *nice young men,* she herself had chosen a notorious libertine for her own mate?

Instead, she agreed, "Sir Giles indeed seems to be a fine fellow."

"This *intimate* gathering for my cursed birthday is growing larger by the day," Grandpère said ironically. He shifted his weight to indicate that he was ready to continue on to the museum.

Emeline was sorely tempted to ask if she might invite Hart as well but managed to restrain herself. If she made such a suggestion, she'd never hear the end of it from Louise.

In any case, it would be wise to keep her distance from him as much as possible. Hadn't she already been inappropriate enough, throwing herself into his arms and kissing his cheek? The expression on Hart's face when he drew back had been a warning she should heed.

"We are looking forward to having you girls with us on Saturday," Devon was saying. "Goodbye until then."

Her grandparents continued on their way while Emeline and Louise started toward Great Russell Street.

"I had the distinct impression that you were going to invite Lord Jasper to the party," Louise said after a few moments.

Emeline hoped her cheeks weren't turning pink. Really, there was no fooling Louise. "Clearly you were wrong!"

"I still find it difficult to believe that you convinced his lordship to keep Monte."

"He did agree, for now, at least. He employs an exceptionally kind housekeeper, Mrs. Peachey, who was quite taken with Monte and pleaded his case. I suspect Hart did not want to seem a curmudgeon in her eyes." She quickened her step, Louise keeping pace at her side as they emerged onto the bustling thoroughfare. "Mrs. Peachey's brother, William, is Hart's valet, and it seems that they have been with him since he was a boy."

"Do you mean that they left the old duke's employ to remain with Hart...the scapegrace second son?" Louise sighed. "Very heartwarming."

"It is pure speculation on my part," Emeline confessed, smiling. "In any case, Hart agreed, under some pressure from the rest of us, to let Monte stay until his leg heals. He said Mrs. Peachey can look after him in her and William's own rooms." Amusement infected her tone as she continued, "However, Monte may have other ideas. He is very taken with Hart."

Louise laughed. "I certainly had my doubts when you went up to his lordship's suite with that basket, but I should know by now not to underestimate you, my dear cousin."

"Very true!" Then, impetuously, she said, "I must admit, I am yearning to see Monte and discover how he fares. Let us stop at the Pulteney Hotel for a few minutes! If you are with me, it will be perfectly acceptable."

They climbed into the broken-down hack and Emeline leaned forward to give the hotel's address to the driver. But before she could speak, Louise put a hand on her arm. "I am going to advise that we go home instead, where you may consider this impulse. Of course, I am no expert on the subject of men, but I do think he might, uh, misunderstand if you turn up there again so soon."

"That's ridiculous. It's Monte I want to see!" Even as she spoke, Emeline felt her cheeks flush and knew it was no use pretending. "Oh, all right then." She gave their own address to the driver and sank back against the malodorous squabs, frowning. "How tiresome."

* * *

THREE DAYS LATER, Emeline and Louise arrived early at Raveneau House in Grosvenor Square. The autumn afternoon was unseasonably warm, and it was no surprise to find that the sun-dappled, walled garden behind the house was looking even more exquisite than usual.

Servants had covered long tables with fresh, blue-patterned cloths interspersed with bouquets of coral dahlias and purple asters. Arabella, the housekeeper, was directing maids to set out artistically arranged platters of succulent purple grapes, thinly sliced apples, ham, and a variety of cheeses. There were plates of freshly baked rolls with butter, dishes of perfect walnuts, and Arabella's own pear tarts.

Emeline's perusal of the food was interrupted by her mother, who appeared and wrapped her in a warm embrace. "Oh, Emmie, it is wonderful to have you and Louise with us today." Mouette's gaze lingered on Louise, who stood at a distance, chatting with Devon. "You know, before the guests begin to arrive, there is something I should tell you…"

She broke off at the sound of Justin's voice. "My two beauties," he murmured, inserting himself between them and addressing Emeline. "Prepare yourself, ma petite. Now that you are restored to London, all the men will be circling you like bees to honey."

"Nonsense, Papa," she scoffed. And yet she knew that she was looking especially pretty today in a gown of lilac-shot silk that set off her black-lashed eyes and raven curls. After two isolated years in Lyme Regis, digging for fossils, it felt rather pleasant to be a female again.

"Oh, look," said Mouette, apparently forgetting what she wanted to tell Emeline, "there are Lord and Lady Wraxham, such old friends of Papa. I must welcome them."

Emeline's grandparents were sitting together under an elm tree, its leaves now turned deep red. Before she could go to them, she saw her mother guiding Lord and Lady Wraxham toward their shaded bench.

"Ah," said a deep voice from behind Emeline. "There you are."

Turning back in surprise, she promptly bumped into a broad male chest and gasped. Her senses took in a slate gray waistcoat, the fresh scent of his linen shirt, strong hands clasping her arms, holding her slightly away. *Hart.*

For an instant, Emeline felt dizzy. "It's you!"

"None other." He looked down at her, his mouth quirked with wry amusement—an expression she knew well by now.

Her heart was racing. "But—what are you doing here?"

Their surroundings seemed to evaporate. Emeline fought an urge to press herself against him, to tip her head back and seek, feel, taste his mouth on hers. She wanted it badly, and from the look that passed for a brief instant over his handsome face, he seemed to want it too.

But, after one charged moment, Hart had the sense to gently set her away from him. "Your father sent a note, inviting me. He wishes to make me known to Madame St. Briac."

"I see. I was merely surprised…since you rejected the notion of attending when I mentioned it." Somehow, Emeline composed herself. "But no doubt you felt obligated to accept Papa's invitation."

"Exactly so." He sounded bemused. "I hope you have been well since our last meeting?"

"Oh, yes, Louise and I have been *quite* busy at the Reading Room." She waved a casual hand for emphasis.

"I am pleased to hear it."

What was it that seemed to be vibrating in the air between them? Could he feel it too? She licked her lips. "And what of Monte? Has he been settling in?"

He gave a short laugh, and one dark eyebrow flicked upward. "You could put it that way, I suppose."

"No doubt he is missing me. Perhaps I will visit—one day." Emeline paused. "But I daresay Monte is getting on famously with Mrs. Peachey and William."

He winced slightly. "I should tell you that he has not taken to them as I had hoped. Instead, the mongrel has attached himself to *me*."

"Oh!" She smothered a laugh. "Oh, dear."

"Indeed." Hart glanced around then. "People will whisper if you're seen with me a minute longer, and I ought to greet the rest of your family."

Emeline led him toward the bench under the elm tree where

her Raveneau grandparents were holding court while Justin and Mouette stood nearby.

"You already know Papa, of course," Emeline said. Before he could reply, Mouette lifted a hand in greeting and came toward them.

"Good afternoon, Lord Jasper." She gave him one of her most beautiful smiles. "I think we may have met before, during one of your past sojourns in London, and of course we know your brother, the duke, and his duchess. It's very good of you to join us today."

Bowing to kiss Mouette's outstretched hand, Hart flashed an equally charming smile. "I am honored." He glanced back at Emeline. "The two Misses St. Briac are helping immensely with my research."

"I'm so pleased, especially since you doubtless have other pressing concerns. Are you in London long, my lord?"

"No. Never." His tone was ironic. "In truth, I depart for Lisbon a fortnight hence."

Emeline had known this, yet hearing him say it aloud was still a shock. *It's just as well,* she admonished herself. *Time to stop being nonsensical!*

Hart was soon chatting with her grandparents, leaning against the elm tree. At length, as other guests approached the hosts, he unhurriedly returned to Emeline's side.

One of the kitchen maids approached with a tray containing goblets of sparkling wine, and Hart took two, handing one to Emeline. She had just sipped from the goblet when someone waved from the direction of the garden gate.

Hart squinted slightly. "Is that who I think it is?" He had removed his hat, and Emeline noticed how the sun glinted on his silver-flecked hair.

A tall, thin young man wearing gold-rimmed spectacles was making his way through the guests who milled about in the garden. As he drew nearer, Emeline spied fair hair poking out around the brim of his tall hat. *Sir Giles Peyton.* Good heavens, she had nearly forgotten he had been invited!

She nodded. "Yes, I believe it is Sir Giles."

"You and Peyton are friends now?" There was a decided edge to his voice.

"I wouldn't go quite that far…but Hart, do listen." She tugged lightly on his coat sleeve. "I have had the most brilliant idea. Sir Giles is a perfect candidate for my Bridegroom List!"

CHAPTER 10

*H*art cocked a brow in disbelief. "You are roasting me."

"Indeed, I am not. Papa wants me to seek out prospects, does he not? Sir Giles would seem to be ideal. Educated, established, titled, reasonably good looking, and of a proper age."

Unable to help himself, Hart demanded, "What constitutes a proper age?"

Emeline waved a hand. "I can't give you a precise number, but it cannot be an elderly roué like some who pursued me during my two Seasons." She shuddered for emphasis. "I am thinking particularly of Lord Fulham."

Hart frowned, quite certain that Fulham was scarcely forty years of age. But perhaps to someone young and fresh like Emeline, even Hart at thirty-three, was *elderly*.

"I can hardly wait to tell Papa the news."

He watched her go off, wondering what caused her to shudder at the thought of Fulham. Had the man said something improper…or tried to *touch* her? A hot poker of rage seared Hart, deep in a recess of his chest he hadn't known existed.

* * *

Emeline found her father sitting on a bench in front of a stone wall covered with climbing white roses. He balanced a plate on his lap that contained three delectable apple *tartes* and a bunch of succulent grapes.

"Papa, really, *three* tartes?" Emeline pretended to scold as she sat down beside him.

He laughed. "Do not tell your mama." Gesturing toward Daisy the corgi, who sat attentively at his feet, he fed the dog a piece of crust and added, "Daisy is to blame. She persuaded me to take three."

For a moment, Emeline leaned against her father's strong shoulder, breathing in his familiar scent. She loved him desperately, but all her life he had warned her against "men like me." Smiling, she shook her head. "You are very bad, Papa."

"Indeed." He nodded. "That's why I married your mama, so you would have at least one estimable parent as a model."

For a moment, Emeline thought of her two brothers. Anthony had been raised with Charles until the age of ten, believing their father was Sir Harry Brandreth, who died in prison, disgraced. After Mouette married Justin and Emeline was born, it came out that the couple had met long ago, during Mouette's first marriage, and Anthony was the product of a shared night of passion. The confusion the boys had felt, especially Charles who then felt isolated in the family, lingered for years.

"Oh, but you are quite estimable, Papa," Emeline assured him now.

"*Ma chère petite*, loyal as ever." He arched a brow above his slate-gray eyepatch. "Now what brings you to my secluded bench in the midst of this party?"

Emeline felt a little guilty for bending the truth, but after all, had she not learned this skill from Papa himself? "I came to tell you that I have met someone who fulfills the requirements to be on my"—she lowered her voice conspiratorially—"*Bridegroom List.*"

Immediately she saw him scan the fashionable guests who milled about the walled garden. To her surprise, he declared in a hard voice, "Above all, he must be *honorable*! I will kill the man who hurts you." Glaring into the distance, he growled, "Slowly, with my bare hands."

"Really, Papa!" She wanted to laugh. "One would think you didn't mean it when you declared you want me to marry."

He shrugged. "I meant it…but that is also why *I* want to do the choosing."

"Outrageous!" accused Emeline.

In the next moment, she spied Sir Giles Peyton walking toward them, a goblet of wine in one hand. When their eyes met, he raised it and gave Emeline a tentative smile. Doubts assailed her. It was one thing to concoct a scheme and quite another to actually carry it out, with real people.

"Papa, that is the man," she whispered. "Sir Giles Peyton."

Straightening, Justin peered at Peyton and flared his nostrils. "He looks a dull sort of fellow."

"You are the outside of enough," Emeline scolded fondly. Rising, she went forward to meet the young scholar.

"Do hope I'm not interrupting," he said, speaking in his customary rushed fashion. "'Tis a capital party. So kind of your grandparents to include me."

Justin St. Briac rose leisurely and extended a hand. When introductions had been performed, Emeline said, "Sir Giles works almost daily in the Reading Room, Papa. He is not only an antiquarian, but also an archaeologist."

"True, true," the young man agreed. To Justin he said, "Extraordinary female, your daughter, sir! Holds her own with the best of us." He quickly turned to Emeline, coloring slightly.

"Miss St. Briac, being aware of your strong interest in archaeology, I thought you might like to attend an excavation. Two days hence, newly unearthed treasures will be revealed at Amity Park, Viscount Tobias Melford's estate. A mere hour's drive west of London. Select guests will gather and a light luncheon will be served." He bowed to her. "Be honored to escort you."

Her eyes lit up. "An excavation! Oh, yes, I should adore it. How kind you are to invite me."

Behind Sir Giles, Emeline noticed that two more guests, a richly garbed couple, were making their way across the crowded garden. It came to her that she had met them both in passing, during her two Seasons. The man, slender and pale, wore side-whiskers, a monocle, and a tall silk hat, while his wife was clad in a fashionable gown of moss green, set off by a matching green hat decorated with ostrich plumes.

They were the Duke and Duchess of Caversham, Emeline realized. Many guests turned to greet the duke, but the nobleman's gaze was fixed on a tall figure near the arbor. *Hart.*

Sudden realization dawned. *This* man, the Duke of Caversham, was Hart's brother! Hart had mentioned him, but perhaps she hadn't been listening properly. A memory returned from a long-ago ball, when Frederica had pointed out the duke standing with his shockingly attractive brother. She had commented on the stark difference in their looks, adding that one wouldn't think they could be twins. "It does happen, I believe, that some twins don't look at all alike, but even so…"

Turning back to speak to her father, Emeline found him pretending to listen to Sir Giles drone on about archaeology tools. "One must use a brush, you see, like the sort our cook uses to baste the fowl!"

Even as she watched, St. Briac turned his head ever so slightly, following the progress of the Duke of Caversham as he drew closer to Hart. Her father's good eye narrowed in a way that made Emeline wish she could read his thoughts.

* * *

HART KNEW a sense of dread as he watched Austell coming toward him. Margaret seemed to be focused on their host and hostess, but Austell clearly had other priorities.

This was the reason Hart hated parties. One either felt trapped in conversation with a dead bore or forced to encounter a person to be avoided. Hart had been in both situations more times than he cared to remember. Once, at a court function following Queen Victoria's coronation, he'd been cornered by the inebriated husband of his latest paramour. The man had proven to be *both* a dead bore and a person to avoid.

It was all so much simpler for Hart to do as he pleased, ignoring social conventions, coming and going from London whenever he sensed a change of scene was in order.

Now, as Austell drew near, he wished he hadn't come today.

"Ah, what a surprise," he greeted his brother with a faint smile. "I thought you had obligations at Caversham. A kitchen fire, was it not?"

Austell seemed not to hear. "What are *you* doing here? I thought you could not be bothered to go out in society!"

Damn. Keeping his face impassive, Hart replied casually, "I am acquainted with one of the guests who shares my interest in archaeology...and I also came to pay my respects to the legendary André Raveneau." As long as he kept his association with Justin out of it, there was no reason for Austell to be suspicious. And meanwhile, Hart could deftly turn the conversation around. "But what of you? I had no notion that you and Margaret were friendly with this family."

Austell peered over at the Raveneaus. "As you say, André Raveneau is a legend. He doesn't care a jot for social status, yet everyone wants to know him, to claim friendship with him. And even though his wife, Devon, is American, she's become rather an icon here in London over the decades." He paused, considering. "As a duke, I felt obliged to attend."

Even as he spoke, Justin St. Briac came into view. The Frenchman made his way toward the Raveneaus, Emeline on his arm. Hart drew a breath and watched for his brother's reaction.

When a footman paused before them with a tray filled with champagne goblets, Austell took one and drank it a bit too quickly. "I'd forgotten that Justin St. Briac is married to the Raveneaus' daughter, Mouette," he muttered.

Hart watched, feeling tension thicken the air. "Has he offended you?"

"Not precisely." His brother flushed. "You may as well know, I have had a few…difficulties of late with my…" He turned his face away from the arbor where St. Briac stood chatting with his in-laws. "Investments."

"I see." Hart felt as if he had suddenly stepped in quicksand. "You did mention that you had some concerns about a loan from St. Briac." He wished he could tell Austell that he had mended matters for him so there was no further cause for worry, but of course his brother's pride was too fragile, and Hart's own bargain with St. Briac had not yet concluded.

"I have a bad feeling about it," Austell said as beads of sweat dotted his brow. "Do you know, I often wish that I hadn't come into this dukedom after all, that *you* might have been the first born, the heir to the title and all the bloody problems that come with it!"

Painfully aware once again of his brother's fragile state, Hart murmured, "I don't think you should worry, old fellow." Leaning a bit closer, he briefly put a hand on Austell's sleeve. "Have faith. I believe it will all come right in the end."

* * *

IT WAS no surprise that Austell found a reason to leave before long, although Margaret looked rather confused as they made their excuses to the Raveneaus.

Watching them go, Hart wondered how Monte was doing at home with Peachey and William. If the mongrel was howling, as he had done the last time Hart tried to leave, they might well be ejected from the hotel. He had just reached into his waistcoat pocket to consult his watch when he was interrupted by a familiar French-accented voice.

"That was a bit awkward, *n'est-ce pas*? Your brother's presence, I mean."

Hart glanced back over one shoulder at Justin St. Briac. The man seemed to be everywhere. "Awkward for me? Yes. He's afraid of you, I think, and I don't want him to discover that I am involved in his dealings with you." He paused. "I am glad that my bargain with you will soon be finished. I can't sail for the Continent soon enough."

St. Briac's dark brows arched upward. "But there is still work to do regarding Emmie."

"Our arrangement is simple, I believe, yet I have already gone above and beyond your requirement that I pretend to employ and pay your daughter and niece. I helped them get their tickets to use the Reading Room, which was no easy feat."

"It seems that the situation has grown a bit more complicated, and I must beg your continued assistance." Before Hart could protest, St. Briac continued, "You see, Emeline, is…headstrong. No sooner did I tell her that she is making a mistake by living like a nun, cloistered with her books and fossils, than she announced that she has a…*list*."

Hart forced himself not to smile. "A list?"

"*Voyons*, she dares to call it a Bridegroom List! And now she tells me that Peyton fellow is her first candidate. He is not a proper choice for Emmie! His handshake is that of a wet fish." St.

Briac shook his head emphatically. "She has no notion of men or what is good for her."

With difficulty, Hart suppressed a laugh. "I take it you do, sir?"

"*Bien sûr!* That is why I need your assistance. It is a very small thing, I assure you."

As Justin St. Briac detailed Peyton's plan to escort Emeline to one of the newly fashionable luncheon parties that centered around the unveiling of archaeological relics, Hart took a step backward.

"I would like you to keep an eye on them," St. Briac finished casually, as if this was a perfectly normal request.

"At the luncheon?" Hart shook his head. "Impossible. I am not invited."

"Oh, I am confident you will find a way," the older man parried. "It's being held at Amity Park, the estate of Viscount Melford. Surely you know him from the clubs?"

"I do. But allow me to protest that this was not part of our bargain, sir. You assured me that after I presented myself as your daughter's employer, I would show my face as little as possible."

"*Mais oui!*" St. Briac nodded, tightening the noose. "You need only watch Peyton and Emmie, from a distance. She will never know of your presence." After pausing for a strategic moment, the Frenchman added, "This would be a great favor…to me."

Hart closed his eyes, remembering the sheer panic emanating from Austell when Justin St. Briac appeared in the garden. And he thought of Emeline, always so certain she could fend for herself. What if Peyton dared to *touch* her? Scanning the garden, he allowed his gaze to settle briefly on Emeline's slim, animated form. She was talking to her cousin Louise, gesturing, her ebony curls agleam in the sunlight as she laughed and shook her head. Watching her, Hart felt a sharp, mysterious pain in his midsection.

"All right, damn it. I will do it," he heard himself say. "But this is the very *last* time!"

* * *

EMELINE PLUCKED one of the creamy pink roses that clambered up the garden wall, lifted it to her nose, and inhaled appreciatively. "I'll own I am looking forward to the luncheon party tomorrow at Amity Park," she said to her cousin. "I only wish you could be there too. What treasures do you suppose they have unearthed?"

"You must pay close attention for both of us," Louise said. Her delicate countenance was slightly flushed with emotion. "Perhaps you should take a notebook and pencil."

"Yes. I will," Emeline replied, only half listening. Out of the corner of one eye, she watched Hart conversing with her father. What in the world could they be discussing so intently?

"Would you really welcome Sir Giles as your suitor?" Louise asked in a softer voice.

"Oh, no. It's all a show to put Papa off. He can hardly put other men in my way if I am already being courted by someone like Sir Giles."

Louise looked dubious, but before she could reply, Emeline saw her mother approaching.

"Hello, darlings." Seemingly unaffected by the crush, Mouette brushed back a stray curl and kissed each girl on the cheek. "Louise, you are looking very lovely today! Jonquil is a perfect color for you."

Louise glanced down at her gown, simple yet fashionable with bishop sleeves and a narrow waist. "Oh, thank you, aunt," she said. "I am glad to have a chance to ask you about—"

Mouette held up a silencing finger. "First, you must hear my news. Do you remember that I mentioned it when you first arrived?"

Emeline saw that there were spots of color on her mother's cheeks, a sign that she was feeling anxious. Her own mouth felt dry. "Go on, Mama."

"Well…as it happens…" Mouette broke off and gestured toward the terrace, clearly finding it difficult to speak the words.

At that very moment, the French doors swung open, and Emeline heard Louise gasp. Emeline looked again and blinked. Was it possible? There, striding boldly out into the sunlight, was her half-brother Sir Charles Brandreth.

CHAPTER 11

"No!" Louise raised a hand to her mouth. "Can it be?"

Grateful that they were standing off to one side in the crowd of guests, Emeline put an arm around her cousin. "Steady," she whispered. "It's only Charles."

"That is just what I meant to tell you…" Mouette said, wincing slightly.

Slowly, Louise seemed to recover her senses. She stood up a bit straighter, and a hint of color returned to her cheeks. "As Emmie says, it is our own Charles, returned at last," she managed. "How lovely."

Emeline watched as her mother started forward to greet her first-born child. Charles had aged, but the years agreed with him, Emeline thought. Her half-brother was turned out in the latest style, from a gleaming black silk neckcloth to his double-breasted frock coat, popularized by the queen's husband, Prince Albert. As he strolled closer, Charles swept off his tall hat, revealing carefully brushed, wavy golden locks with side whiskers. He paused to embrace both Mouette and Emeline, and then glanced toward Louise, his smile widening.

"Ah, Louise!" he proclaimed. "Yet, I should not be surprised. Even after all these years, you have a way of turning up in England wherever I am—even here in the cosmopolitan environs of London."

Sensing the storm of emotions inside her beloved cousin, Emeline stepped between them. "But Louise and I have been in London for some time, so it is *you* who has turned up where she is." Her tone was light, almost teasing. "We have taken lodgings together and are engaged in serious scholarly endeavors at the British Museum."

He flicked a monocle from his breast pocket, lifted it to one eye, and cocked his head to one side. "Are you indeed?" Surveying Louise from head to toe, Charles added, "No surprise, I'll own. From a young age, you've always been a bluestocking at heart." He turned toward Emeline and added, "But I didn't expect it from a diamond like you, Emmie! Last I heard, Justin needed reinforcements to fend off your suitors."

"That's nonsense." She sent him a warning glance. "And Louise is the diamond, not I."

Seeming to realize that he had said the wrong thing, Charles stepped closer to Louise and gave her shoulder a brotherly pat. "Well, of course!" He smiled into her eyes. "Our Louise always was a very rare sort of female. Ah, I see my old friend Lord Marsh." He waved to a figure near the arbor. "Must go and pay my respects." Charles took two steps before glancing back at Louise, who had gone pale. "We will catch up properly later on, yes?"

"Oh...yes!" she stammered. As he turned his back and started off, she added, "It's good to see you again."

No sooner had Charles moved away from them than Emeline turned to her mother. "You knew that he had returned, I take it?"

"I did..." She managed a strained smile. "He arrived last evening, but I wasn't entirely certain he would attend this gathering since he just completed a long journey from Rome." Wincing slightly, she added, "I did try to tell you."

"I must say, Mama, you didn't try very hard," Emeline said with a trace of irony.

"I hesitated to stir up old feelings," her mother confessed with a faraway look in her eyes.

Emeline set her chin. "Meanwhile, I wonder what brings him home." Privately, she suspected that something must have happened to drive him from Italy.

Louise seemed to gather her composure. "How nice it is to see Charles again after so many years," she said.

Watching her, Mouette said gently, "You have ever been his loyal friend, even when the rest of us were out of temper with him."

"Yes…and he was *my* friend. It will be fascinating to hear more about his time away. No doubt he has become a well-regarded architect."

Across the garden, Charles was chatting with wealthy Lord Marsh's daughter. Emeline's heart ached for Louise.

"Do you know, I feel a headache coming on," Emeline said. "Louise, why don't we go home and have a nice cup of tea in our own little parlor? Little Mew is doubtless waiting to curl up, purring mightily, on your lap."

Her cousin's relief was palpable. "Oh, yes." She let out a deep breath. "That would be just the thing."

* * *

THE MORNING of the luncheon at Amity Park, Emeline awoke to see a few crimson leaves fluttering past her window. Stretching, she lingered in bed for a few more minutes, remembering that the day ahead would be filled with new sights and people. What recently discovered relics would be revealed at today's gathering, and who else would be present? Perhaps some artifacts would provide useful information for the project she and Louise had undertaken for Hart.

It was odd to anticipate spending the day with virtual strangers. After all, she barely knew Sir Giles Peyton, no matter how exuberantly she had spoken of him to her father. And she felt not a flicker of attraction for him, though that would remain her secret for now. Anything to stop Papa from conjuring up his own list of suitors for her.

Emeline reached to throw back the covers, yet paused as a thought rose, unbidden, inside her. *Where is Hart today?* She and Louise had left her grandparents' garden so precipitously, she'd had no chance to speak to him again or bid him goodbye.

Lying there in the morning quiet, Emeline closed her eyes and thought back to her last encounter with him at the garden party, when she had turned and bumped into his broad, hard chest. Hart had caught her forearms and held her against him for a few moments that had felt...oh, deliciously intimate. Her heart raced now as she let herself feel it all again.

Turning against the soft bed linens, Emeline imagined, just for an instant, what it would be like to wake and find Hart sleeping on the pillow next to her. His warm, strong hands touching her...

This fantasy was rudely interrupted by scratching at the door, followed by a demanding "Meeoow!"

Just as well, Emeline thought ruefully as she rose and went to admit her morning caller. Dreams like those could never come true, not unless she accepted a carte-blanche from Hart. He had made it clear that he would never marry...and of course, neither would she!

Two hours later, dressed in a stylish but understated promenade gown of dove gray silk set off by violet accents that brought out her eyes, Emeline waited in the parlor for Sir Giles to arrive.

Because they were traveling to Amity Park in his post-chaise, Emeline had chosen a becoming bonnet with a veil to shield her from the elements, and she carried a violet-striped reticule.

"Oh, miss, you look like a princess," proclaimed Dora as she appeared with a plate of day-old scones.

"Thank you! It is definitely a change from my usual attire," Emeline replied, smiling.

When Dora took her leave, Louise spoke up from her chair by the bow window. "I am certain it will be wonderful. You'll have to tell me everything when you return."

"Of course I will! And I hope to befriend Viscount Melford so that he may eventually know you and include us both in future invitations." She paused. "I wonder if the viscount is very old?"

Just then, a drab carriage drew up in front of their house and Sir Giles emerged, looking rather harried. "Oh, dear. What shall we talk about?" Emeline said suddenly.

"I have never known you to be at a loss for words," Louise soothed.

"I rather dread being alone with him though…" She thought suddenly of Lord Fulham, and so many other men. They had feigned respectful adoration but, once they had her alone, could think of nothing else but her female body.

A knock sounded at the door. Moments later, Dora was ushering Sir Giles into the parlor. He was proper, as always, yet clearly in a hurry. "Don't like to leave the horses standing," he explained as they bade Louise farewell.

Outside on the footpath, Sir Giles paused.

"Ought to tell you, my mother, Mrs. Peyton, is with us." He looked embarrassed. "Very keen on these sorts of things. A great friend of Cartwright, the archaeologist."

His mother? As Sir Giles handed her up into the carriage, Emeline found herself wedged in beside a stately dragon of a woman who surveyed her through her pince-nez. By the time they reached Oxford Street, Mrs. Peyton had made it clear that she came first in her son's heart, and there was no space for other females. The remainder of the rather slow journey was taken up with a dull conversation between Sir Giles and Mrs. Peyton about the need for new horses. Grateful that she didn't have to be alone with her would-be suitor, Emeline looked out at the countryside and felt a rising sense of anticipation for what lay ahead.

When, an hour later, the equipage turned up the sweeping drive to Amity Park, she sat up straight. They passed through an avenue of ancient oak trees, russet leaves gilded in the autumn sun, and soon a handsome manor house came into view.

"Not far from the Thames, you see," murmured Giles. "Cartwright, the archaeologist in charge of the dig, believes there was a village here centuries ago. Viking, even Roman? Access to the river, very important."

In the distance beyond the manor, the grounds sloped downward toward what Giles said was the excavation area. A white canvas tent had been erected nearby, and guests were already mingling on the freshly cut lawn.

Emeline felt both excited and uncertain as she was handed down from the carriage. However, just as Mrs. Peyton began to implore Giles to assist her, a male voice called out to them.

"Giles, old fellow! At last." A thickset man with broad shoulders, dark chestnut hair, and a kind face was striding up the hill, one hand raised in greeting. "I'm so glad you were able to come."

"Ah, Lord Melford," Giles replied, drawing his mother forward. "I apologize if we are tardy."

Emeline watched their host bow over Mrs. Peyton's hand. After a few moments of polite conversation, he suggested that Giles start toward the luncheon tent with his mother.

Just as Emeline wondered if she had been forgotten, the viscount turned her way, smiling warmly. He stretched out a big, ungloved hand that enveloped hers.

"You must be Miss Emeline St. Briac. Giles said that you

would be coming today, and I confess I've been looking forward to this moment." There was a twinkle in his green eyes. "You see, I danced with you more than two years ago, when you were celebrated as the Exquisite. Although I was a married man at that time, I confess that I've never forgotten that waltz." He patted his heart for emphasis.

Emeline felt her cheeks warm. "How kind you are, my lord." She paused, remembering that Giles had mentioned that the viscountess had died of a fever. "Please accept my condolences on the loss of your wife."

"Will you allow me to escort you to join the other guests? Excellent." As they started down the gentle slope, he went on, "I am grateful for your kind wishes. In truth, I wasn't certain I could ever enjoy life again after my Kitty left me, but then I discovered archaeology and now I feel positively invigorated when I awake each day. Can you imagine? Cartwright, working with antiquarians like Sir Giles, has uncovered graves that predate the Conquest." He shook his head. "Simply amazing!"

"I couldn't agree more." Briefly, Emeline told him about her years digging for ancient fossils with Mary Anning, and how she and Louise had now turned to archaeology. "One feels that new scientific discoveries are being made almost daily, and history is being rewritten. Don't you agree, my lord?"

"Yes, exactly so, Miss St. Briac!" They were approaching the tent, and Lord Melford paused to smile down at Emeline. "I despise that stuffy title, and I am not your lord. My name is Tobias."

With this friendly bear of a man, social norms felt stuffy indeed, and she heard herself reply, "And I am Emeline."

"Excellent." He looked toward the long table draped in snow-white linen and set with silver and fine china. "You will be seated between Giles and me." He winked, almost imperceptibly. "Wouldn't want to set his back up by separating you, though no doubt he is fully occupied with Mrs. Peyton."

Emeline nearly laughed aloud. "I think you may be right."

Chatting animatedly, the guests were making their way to the table.

A liveried footman drew out Emeline's chair while another poured claret into a cut-crystal goblet. The table was adorned with arrangements of wildflowers gathered from the nearby meadows, and the air was filled with the scents of autumn leaves, freshly roasted fowl, and ripe fruits. Emeline was dazzled. She looked down the table at the assembled guests: scholars, clergy, landed gentry, and a few well-dressed, noble couples from London whom she recognized. On her left, Sir Giles was whispering with his mother, seemingly still discussing the desperate need to purchase new horses. And something about a garden wall.

On Emeline's right, the viscount rose from his seat at the head of the table, smiling, and held up his glass of ruby claret. "My friends, I am grateful for your presence! Today we gather not only on my family estate, but on the soil of history itself. Thanks to the dedication of the esteemed antiquarian Leo Cartwright, we have unearthed treasures that illuminate an era long ago, centuries before Amity Park was in existence."

Mr. Cartwright, a pudgy, bespectacled man with thinning gray hair in need of a trim, pushed up from his chair and returned Lord Melford's toast. "Thank you, my lord. I would be remiss not to mention the many aspiring archaeologists who have aided in this endeavor, especially Sir Giles Peyton."

Giles stood, too, bowing for a moment while his mother led the applause, then he quickly returned to his seat.

As Cartwright concluded his brief remarks, a red-cheeked squire called out, "Rumor has it that you have discovered a jeweled scabbard! Could it have belonged to a Roman governor or other ruler?"

"Patience, sir, patience," Cartwright replied with a chuckle. "All in due course. Following our meal, you will view a fine sample of the treasures. Of course, they are priceless, but even more valuable is the history they reveal to us."

As footmen appeared to serve luncheon, the guests turned their attention to fragrant platters of roasted quail, pigeon patties with truffles, lamb chops, buttered green beans with almonds, stewed carrots, mashed potatoes, and a delicious assortment of freshly baked rolls. Tobias continued to chat with Emeline throughout the meal in a way that left her little opportunity to turn and speak to Giles or anyone else.

At last, Tobias set his fork and knife on the gold-edged plate and sat back in his chair. "Ah. This is my idea of a perfect afternoon, Emeline." Leaning in her direction, he added softly, "The company could not be more beautiful...or enchanting."

"You are very kind...Tobias," Emeline said sincerely. Yet she couldn't help wondering: was it simple kindness, or was the viscount making subtle romantic overtures to her?

At that moment, Mr. Cartwright made a sign to his host, and both men rose. Emeline felt a thrill as she realized that soon she would see the artifacts discovered on the grounds of Amity Park. Clutching a weathered notebook filled with papers, Cartwright led the way out of the tent, down the sloping hill to the excavation site.

The display table was positioned near a row of ash trees, shielded from the sunlight by spreading branches. Small yellow leaves, like bits of lace, fluttered down with the breeze to land on the men's top hats and women's bonnets. Some of the women unfurled their parasols in the sunlight, but Emeline couldn't be bothered.

Her mouth felt dry, her heart beating faster, as Cartwright opened his notebook and began to remove the velvet cloths covering the artifacts. The observers whispered, some gasping in wonder. Emeline wished she could shut them all out, that she alone could approach the table and get a better look. Oh, to be able to touch those pieces that had witnessed history beyond their imagining!

Tobias stood nearby as the archaeologist held up a round brass brooch with a knot design. At its center was a dark red gem. A garnet, Emeline guessed. "This brooch would have doubtless fastened the cloak of a person of high status."

"Already cleaned and polished," Giles murmured to her. "Assure you, terrible condition coming out of the ground! But now, treasures indeed!"

Cartwright was pointing to several pieces of beaten metal spread across a velvet cloth. "These may be fragments of a helmet," he explained, holding one up. "You can see the bits of etching and decoration that remain. We hope eventually to uncover the remaining pieces."

"Any idea who would have worn such a helmet?" called a very tall antiquarian Emeline had seen in the Reading Room. "A chieftain—or a king?"

Tobias spoke up. "We are still in the early stages of the deeper story."

More artifacts were revealed: fragments of a burial vessel, a silver belt buckle, wooden drinking vessels, and finally a broken scabbard adorned with blood-red jewels.

"Been telling them, worth a king's ransom," whispered Giles, and his mother nodded, staring at the trove.

"I assume this was a grave," said the tall antiquarian. "Viking?"

"Possibly, but again, there is more research to be done," said Cartwright.

"Wouldn't be seeing jewels or gold if it was Anglo-Saxon," stated Giles.

Everyone nodded in agreement that such advanced artistry and riches would not have been possible during Britain's Dark Ages.

"Roman?" came a guess from the red-cheeked squire.

"We will keep you all appraised as we learn more," Tobias

announced in a friendly tone. "Thank you all again for being here."

As the relics were covered once more, some of the guests began to wander back to the tent to sample the currant tart, apple puffs, and other sweets.

Near Emeline, an older man with a white goatee murmured to his companion, "Well, well! 'Twould seem that my nephew Tobias has stumbled on the means to finance that new roof he needs so desperately."

"Indeed," chuckled his companion. "It was a stroke of luck that the gardener decided to plant some trees and unearthed the first bit of treasure."

Emeline felt outraged that the two men were discussing these historical artifacts as if they were winnings at the faro table. She was about to speak up when, to her relief, Sir Giles intervened. Leaning closer, he addressed the man who seemed to be the viscount's uncle and Emeline waited for him to put the fellow in his place.

"Just so," nodded Sir Giles. "If his lordship is wise during the next steps, he may soon be wealthy beyond his dreams." He paused, spectacles agleam in the sunlight, before adding in an undertone, "Collectors...looking for ancient pieces like these. Might know of one or two."

Tobias's uncle blinked, clearly interested. "Sell 'em, you mean?"

Horrified, Emeline could not hold back. "History is not for sale!" Her cheeks grew hot as she gave vent to her deeply held feelings. "I cannot believe my ears. Sir Giles, I believed that you were a true antiquarian. You, of all people, must be aware that these relics belong to history, to scholarship—not to avaricious buyers seeking trinkets for their parlors!"

Emeline broke off as the faint sound of applause reached her ears. She felt the tiny hairs on the back of her neck tingle. Shading her eyes, she turned and looked a short distance up the hill. Under a trio of ancient oaks, a tall man reclined on a bench, one hand resting on the head of a scraggly yet adoring mongrel.

Her heart began to race as a powerful feeling swept through her body: a mixture of joy, relief, and potent attraction.

The man offered more muted applause, and Emeline could almost see the ironic yet affectionate glint of his smile. "Brava," he called, and it seemed he spoke only to her. "Brava."

CHAPTER 12

"*I* hadn't meant to do that," Hart murmured dryly, glancing toward Monte. "Now we are in for it." In response, the dog frantically wagged his stubby tail.

Hart watched as Emeline began to speak to the men around her, first that self-important puppy Sir Giles Peyton, and then Hart's Oxford classmate, Tobias. The breeze had carried Cartwright's booming speech and Emeline's outraged lecture up to him, but now their voices were muted, and he had to wait.

Sitting above the fray on a secluded bench, Hart had been content to observe the proceedings, to notice how the men, young and old, looked at Emeline. Of course, she was exquisitely beautiful, but so were many other young women. Far more arresting was the radiance Emeline exuded and the sense of passion that had bravely spilled forth just now, when she had decried the sale of priceless artifacts for profit.

Hart drew a breath. He had agreed to come here today to appease Justin St. Briac and to save Austell from the consequences of his own folly, but he concealed another motive.

For reasons he wasn't prepared to examine, Hart had wanted a look at Emeline with her supposed suitor. And after he and

Monte had arrived late and seated themselves beneath the spreading oak trees, Hart had silently watched the proceedings at the excavation site.

It quickly became apparent that it was not Sir Giles Peyton who was smitten with Emeline, but Viscount Tobias Melford.

This thought caused something unfamiliar to twist inside Hart's chest. Tobias had a great deal to offer an unconventional female like Emeline. He was respectable and titled, yet unpretentious. He was good-looking, kind, and honorable. It wasn't difficult to imagine the viscount declaring himself in the near future…even making her an offer of marriage.

Glancing over at the attentive Monte, he remarked, "I suppose you think I am getting ahead of myself? Yes, you are right. I will try to remember they just met."

Below, Emeline was extending her hand to a bemused-looking Tobias, and, it seemed, he held it a bit too long before she turned away. Hart leaned forward as she opened her parasol and gracefully started toward him, up the gentle slope.

It seemed wise for him to go and meet her. Rising, Hart tucked Monte under one arm and went forward, summoning his most irresistible smile.

* * *

EMELINE KNEW it must seem excessively odd that she was making her excuses to not only her escort but also her kind and attentive host. And of course, it was quite improper for her to leave the gathering and go off alone to speak to Hart. Fortunately, she could not be bothered with such concerns…especially after the scene of hypocrisy and greed she had just endured.

The timing of Hart's slow, almost sardonic applause had felt like deliverance. As Emeline lifted her skirts and walked toward him, her heart lifted. All day, in spite of the kindnesses of Tobias and the unveiling of treasures she had witnessed, a part of her missed Hart. How many times had she wanted to look for him, to share something, even a glance or a smile?

He was coming toward her, Monte wedged under one arm, carelessly handsome in the golden sunlight. Emeline badly wanted to rush forward and embrace them both.

"Are you very angry?" he asked.

Emeline shook her head, smiling. "Angry? Why would I be?" She rubbed Monte's furry head with both hands and bent to receive several wet licks.

"Because I made a scene in front of all your new friends. Most of them don't approve of me, and of course I interrupted your outing. Sir Giles—"

"Bother! I don't care a button for him or his horrid mother." She paused to laugh. "Oh, how lovely it is to be able to say what is really on my mind."

"I like that about you as well."

Color rose in her cheeks before she remembered their situation. "But what are you doing here?"

"Observing." He gave her a slow smile, as if hoping she would not press him further.

"Did you come because you imagined I couldn't manage on my own and I might need you?"

"*Do* you need me?"

"Of course not." Her chin went up a fraction. "I was actually managing very well on my own. I have made an excellent new friend in Lord Melford, and the display of artifacts discovered here on the estate is magnificent." A pause. "However..."

"Ah, so you *do* need me," Hart challenged, amused.

"Please don't be odious." Impulsively, she took his hand and drew him behind the tree, where the people below could not see them. "It is just that circumstances have made it unbearable for me to return to London with Sir Giles. Did you hear what they were saying just now, before you made yourself known?"

"My hearing is not *that* acute." He set Monte down on the grass and lightly clasped her two elbows. "Kindly enlighten me."

"It was so deplorable, I can scarcely believe it." Emeline leaned closer to him and the story spilled out, beginning with the goatee man who chuckled, "Now Melford can afford that new roof for the manor house," and progressing to Emeline's even greater shock when Sir Giles insinuated that he might know of a buyer for the artifacts. "*Collectors*, he called them!" She paused to shudder. "I believed Sir Giles was a true scholar, dedicated to the emerging science of archaeology. How wrong I was. And now you must see why I cannot return to London in his carriage."

"Of course." His gaze was intent.

"You do understand!" Emeline exclaimed. "There's nothing for it but for me to plead a headache and take my leave before Sir Giles begins asking a lot of questions. I've already told him and Lord Melford that I am not feeling quite the thing, so it will be just fine." She came closer, smiling up at him. "My dear Hart, you have come at just the right moment to drive me home."

* * *

HART STROLLED DOWN to the excavation site to speak to Tobias, leaving Monte behind in Emeline's care. It was fortunate, he realized, that his old classmate was well occupied conversing with a cluster of guests about the newly revealed artifacts. After waiting on the fringe for a bit, he caught Tobias's eye and lifted a hand.

"Hello," he said pleasantly.

Melford stepped away from the others, smiling. "Greetings, Hart. I see that you were able to attend after all."

"Good of you to include me. I apologize for remaining at a distance, but you see I had to bring my new…uh, dog, and I'm afraid his manners can be unpredictable."

"Yes, I noticed you lounging there under the oaks." Tobias held his gaze. Though not as tall as Hart, he still cut an imposing figure with his strong, stocky frame. "Pardon me for asking, but have you stolen Miss St. Briac? I haven't seen her since she went off in your direction."

"Stolen?" Hart gave him a lazy smile. "No, not a bit. In fact, Miss St. Briac sent me to present her regrets. She is unwell. A headache, I believe. As it happens, I am returning now to London, and she has asked me to see her home." He cleared his throat. "No need for concern. It's all quite proper. I am her... employer."

Tobias narrowed his eyes. "Proper is not a word I have ever associated with you, old fellow."

"Is Miss St. Briac under your protection? I thought not." Overcoming a mad urge to demand that Tobias stay away from Emeline, Hart drew a breath and continued more calmly, "The trouble is, Peyton has upset her, and the chit has a temper. She won't go with him now."

"I see. Yes, understandable I suppose." Nearby, a white-haired dowager trilled a question to Tobias, and he smiled tightly in her direction. With seeming reluctance, he shook Hart's hand. "I must go. Thank you for coming today."

* * *

"This is delightful," Emeline said as Hart handed her into a smart phaeton pulled by a pair of matched chestnuts. Monte sat between them, glancing back and forth as if wondering what would happen next. "I have two handsome gentlemen to escort me home."

"Monte is less an escort than chaperone, I believe," Hart said dryly.

Something in his tone sent a shiver of pleasure through her. The phaeton's top was folded back and as they drove away from Amity Park, Emeline savored the breeze on her face.

"I didn't know you owned an equipage." She paused. "Or horses."

"Why should I not?" Deftly handling the reins, Hart negotiated the corner at the foot of the avenue.

"You don't seem to have many possessions." She felt herself flush. "I mean, you live in a hotel. You travel to the Continent regularly and stay for long periods of time. You…" Emeline broke off before she could remark that he chose not to take a wife.

"Yet I must have transportation when I am in London," he replied before smoothly changing the subject. "Now tell me, what did I miss today? I was only able to hear portions of Cartwright's talk about the artifacts."

Emeline told him all about the brooch, the helmet fragments, the wooden drinking vessels, and the sword hilt, as well as the theory that they might date to Viking times. "Oh, Hart, it made me long to know more details about your own discoveries. I'm certain that would aid in our research."

"Hmm." He almost seemed not to hear her request. "Well, perhaps."

After a full minute of distant silence, Emeline said impulsively, "May I ask you a question?"

A faint smile touched the corners of his mouth. "You may."

"Why do you live as you do?" Her heart sped up. "Without any true connections to a home…or people?"

To her surprise, Hart did not make a dismissive reply but kept his eyes on the road ahead as they bowled along through the golden countryside. At length, he said, "You may know that my brother, the duke, is my twin. Scandal seems to follow me, even in the form of rumor, and I don't want that to interfere with his life—especially since he came into the dukedom. In order for me to carry on with my own…pursuits, it is simpler to remove myself from London."

Emeline regarded his harsh profile and sensed that he had drawn inward. "Perhaps it was difficult for you, deferring the dukedom to a twin who, one assumes, was born only minutes before you?"

"If you imagine that I care for any of that, you are deluded," he bit out, eyes flashing. "The more our father favored my brother and poured his energy into readying Austell to become the Duke of Caversham, the more I burned to get away. My father was a tyrant. I thank God it wasn't me! I could not have borne the oppressive rules and expectations attached to such a weighty title."

She blinked, sensing the pain simmering beneath his anger. How must it have felt as a boy, to be pushed aside in favor of his twin?

"Yet you love your brother," she murmured, remembering the scene she had witnessed between them at her grandparents' garden party. The duke had appeared at times to be pleading with his brother, and Emeline had seen Hart's brusque manner soften.

"Love?" Hart made a dismissive sound. "Of course I care about him. He is my twin! I don't want to see him botch his life now that he finally has what he spent three decades preparing for."

Each time Hart spoke, he revealed just enough to make Emeline long to ask more questions. But all her instincts told her he was done talking about the Duke of Caversham. "I understand, I think. But what about your own happiness? Don't you ever long for a family of your own? Children?"

"No more than you do, my girl," he shot back. "I have said I could not abide a settled life. And, in any event, I should make a devil of a husband." Then, as they came into a village, he slowed the horses' pace and looked over at her. "And what of you, Emeline? What has caused *you* to stray so far from the accepted path for young ladies?"

How neatly he had turned the questions back on her! Emeline gathered Monte onto her lap and stroked his bristly fur, considering.

"I don't think I have ever been like other girls," she said, more seriously than she had intended. "When I was a child, we lived in Cornwall and Brittany rather than London, and Papa went on behaving like the smuggler and corsair he had been for years before marrying Mama."

Hart sent her a sidelong glance. "He continued to engage in those pursuits?"

"No! But in Papa's heart that's who he is." Emeline smiled, remembering. "Our home in St. Malo is in the grand row of *Maisons de Corsaires*, overlooking the ramparts, and the vaulted cellar is filled with all manner of treasures." She felt Hart watching her as she spoke. "Growing up, I enjoyed every sort of outdoor adventure, searching out rare birds and fossils and shells wherever we went. At ten, I went off for several weeks to Lyme Regis with Louise, hunting for fossils with the great Mary Anning. My Aunt Isabella, an artist, taught me to paint, so I was able to sketch and paint all the discoveries we made."

"Amazing," he said, clearly impressed. "And yet, as I recall, you did not rebel when it was time for your come-out into London society."

She gave a tiny shrug. "I was curious enough to try doing it the proper way. During my first Season, I was naturally dazzled by the parties, gowns, and the attentions of young men. But eventually I realized it was all hollow and quite dull. Too many men did not care who I really was. They were usually interested only in my looks or my father's fortune, and that was quite awful. Before the end of my second Season, I had reached the end of my tether." Glancing over, she saw Hart nod. "It came to me that I could choose a different path, one that would not be controlled by men."

"I see!" He turned to look at her. "And what did your father say when you went off to dig for fossils?"

"Papa? Oh, he balked. We are too much alike, I fear. He would like to guide me..."

"Manipulate, perhaps?"

Surprised, she studied his face, but he had returned his attention to an approaching curve in the road. "Perhaps. But I know how to beat him at his own game. Hence, my counterfeit Bridegroom List."

"Indeed, very shrewd."

Warming to her topic, Emeline continued, "You know, it's not only Papa who makes me feel stifled. I confess that I was very ill-at-ease today, up to the moment I saw you under the oak tree. First, I was stuffed into a carriage with Sir Giles and his over-bearing mother, then there was that dull luncheon filled with guests who needed to puff up their own consequence. And finally, although the unveiling of the treasures was thrilling, it was nearly spoiled by those men talking of ways to profit from the sale of the artifacts." She heard her voice rising. "I realized that once again I had no control at all, because I am a female. Just like the Reading Room at the British Museum. When dealing with men, women have so few choices!"

Nodding, Hart remarked casually, "What about Lord Melford? Were you out of patience with him today as well?"

"No, not a bit! Tobias is lovely," she replied quickly. "I felt immediately at ease with him. And not only was he good enough to welcome me into a gathering among male guests who were well acquainted, but I also discovered that his interest in archae-ology is quite serious. Indeed, meeting Tobias was the best thing that happened today!" Had he stiffened at those words? "At Amity Park, I mean."

"Yes, Melford is a good fellow." His tone was cool. "We were up at Oxford at the same time."

Emeline shifted her attention to Monte. "And how is *this* good fellow? His leg seems much better!" The dog enthusiastically wagged his tail and laid his head on her lap. "Do you know, I think Monte is proof that you are not as indifferent to others as you pretend to be. Indeed, his adoption is actually evidence of your kind heart." She waited for him to remind her that he was only looking after Monte until his injured leg healed.

Instead, Hart said, "The mongrel has grown so attached to me that I would be an evil brute to put him out now." As if he understood every word, Monte stretched one paw toward his master. "However, it becomes more complicated to have this animal at the Pulteney. There have been numerous complaints about his barking." He paused. "And someone has to carry him downstairs and across to the Green Park at regular intervals."

At this, Monte gave a series of yips that seemed to have a special meaning.

"Oh, for God's sake," complained Hart. "There, you see? Now I must find a place to stop and let him out."

The horses slowed and soon, upon turning down a short lane from the road, Hart was bringing the phaeton to a stop in a grove of beech trees. In the grassy carpet beneath the treetops, Emeline beheld a profusion of wildflowers: delicate blue harebells, frilled yellow hawkbits, wild pansies, and wood anemones.

"What a lovely spot!" she exclaimed as she followed Hart and Monte down from the phaeton. "I must pick a bouquet to remind me of this day."

When Hart went to the horses' heads and spoke to them, they stood quietly, waiting. Monte began to frolic in the grass, sniffing and leaving his mark, while Emeline picked wildflowers. When she looked back at Hart, he was watching her with a gaze so intense it made her heart flutter.

"What is it? Have I done something wrong?"

He shook his head and glanced away. "No. But we shouldn't linger here."

Leaving the horses, who remained obediently still, he walked toward her. Emeline hurried to meet him, still holding the colorful bouquet, but after just two steps her slipper caught on a stone that was nearly hidden by the tall grass. It all happened in an instant. Emeline pitched forward, the wildflowers scattering in the air, and Hart immediately came forward to catch her.

She found herself in the warmth of his powerful embrace, absorbing his heartbeat, his masculine essence: intangible yet utterly intoxicating. The real world fell away. Time stopped. Reaching up, Emeline twined her slim arms about his strong neck. As their eyes met, desire flared deep inside her.

Hart began to shake his head *No,* even as he bent to cover her mouth with his, kissing her with raw, fiery urgency.

CHAPTER 13

*H*ow long had he ached to kiss her this way? Not some chaste brush of closed lips, but just this sort of hungry kiss. It was searing pleasure…feeling her mouth open to his questing tongue, tasting her, and sensing the moment when she awoke to her own passionate need.

Moaning softly, Emeline pressed her breasts against his chest in a way that made him long to strip away the layers of restrictive clothing. He felt her fingers in his hair, and her scent was an aphrodisiac. His sex, stiff, throbbing, confined in snug buff trousers, wanted only one thing.

Together, they sank down in the tall grass and wildflowers until they were lying entwined, face to face. Hart drew back for one instant and saw the warm flush in her cheeks, the storm of desire in her violet eyes. She seemed, under her gown and petticoats, to arch her hips against him. *Oh God.* He stroked one hand up her side and was about to mold it to her breast when Monte began to bark.

"Curse it," he said roughly. Turning his head, he saw the dog standing just inches away, his increasingly urgent barks now interspersed with low growls. Just that quickly, Hart fell back to earth. His heart thudded in his chest as he separated himself from Emeline and quickly helped her to her feet. Monte, now silent, looked on approvingly.

Facing Emeline, Hart tipped her chin up with one long finger until her eyes met his. "I won't even attempt to offer an excuse," he said hoarsely. "Clearly, I must have lost my mind. Can you forgive me?"

"That's not necessary, for I am quite certain I did not resist. Perhaps we both lost our heads, momentarily." Lifting both hands to her tumbled ebony curls, she added, "And I've lost my hat as well, it seems."

Hart looked back over one shoulder and spied her bonnet lying in the grass among the scattered wildflowers. Retrieving it, he watched as she donned it again and tied the ribbons firmly under her chin.

"Your flowers..." Gesturing toward the lost blossoms, he surprised himself by saying, "I will pick you some more."

"Oh, it doesn't matter." Emeline smiled, but a shadow seemed to cross her face. She seemed to search his face for a long, disquieting moment, as if hoping to read his thoughts. "No doubt they would have wilted before we reached London."

Remembering her unguarded joy when they arrived in this wooded glade just minutes before, Hart felt a stab of guilt. He had ruined it all. Indeed, perhaps now he had joined the ranks of lecherous "elderly" men who had forced themselves on Emeline during her two Seasons.

Handing Emeline up into the phaeton, he kept his tone light. "Right then. Monte will see to it that I deliver you home without any further diversions."

* * *

IN ALL HIS ADULT LIFE, Hart had never made improper advances toward an innocent, gently bred lady. That sort of entanglement was the last thing he wanted, so what the devil had possessed him? And why did Emeline continue to appear so often in his thoughts...and fantasies?

The next day, when Hart received a note from his occasional paramour, Lady Valencia Brook, he accepted her invitation to visit her that evening. Perhaps he lusted after Emeline because too many weeks had passed since a woman warmed his bed.

Yet, that night, as Hart followed Valencia's butler, Riggs, up to her ladyship's bedchamber, he was skeptical that something so simple could cure what ailed him.

Riggs knocked discreetly at her door and disappeared down the passage. Hart entered, expecting to find Valencia clad in one of her filmy Parisian negligees, either curled on the settee or reclining on her great four-poster bed.

"Oh, lovely, there you are!"

He looked around, eventually locating Valencia's shapely form bent over an open trunk. She was fully clothed, her hair pinned up into an elaborate series of black coils.

He blinked. "What are you doing?"

Valencia crossed the room, stood on tiptoe, and gave him a brief kiss. "I'm packing. Congratulate me, darling Jasper. I'm going to be married!" She leaned forward and he caught a whiff of the wine she'd been drinking. "Can you believe it? Horatio Stilton has proposed."

His brows flew up. The man was sixty if he was a day, but he was also a very wealthy tradesman, and no doubt that security meant a great deal to Valencia.

"Don't look so surprised. I like him, and he certainly seems to like *me*," Valencia declared with a saucy smile.

"Oh, I don't doubt that!"

"You needn't take that tone. It's not as if you wanted to wed me yourself!" she chided. "I *adore* sleeping with you, darling, but our tumbles in bed won't buy new gowns or pay my staff."

"Congratulations. I'm happy for you." Surprisingly, Hart felt a surge of relief that Valencia wasn't expecting him to bed her tonight. "I take it you're moving to Stilton's mansion in Berkeley Square?"

"Yes. We leave tomorrow and will marry in Paris, then return to Stilton House for Christmas." She turned back to her packing, adding with a little pout, "I couldn't go without telling you myself, darling…even though it seemed you might never visit me again."

"What about this house? Are you going to sell it?"

"Yes!" She sent him a speculative glance. "Do you want to buy it?"

Hart paused to consider. "Actually…I might."

* * *

TWO LONG DAYS passed without any word from Hart, and Emeline hardly knew what to do with her unexpected emotions. They colored her dreams and woke her in the night with vivid fantasies of Hart, his mouth on hers while every other secret part of her ached for something she scarcely understood. *What would it be like?* Her only clue lay in the long-ago night when she had stumbled into a stranger's bed at Riven Court. He had awakened her to sensual pleasure she had never before imagined, but he was a stranger. In the darkness, she couldn't even see his face.

Being kissed and touched by Hart evoked so much more than that shockingly unexpected interlude. And realizing that he would soon leave London made her heart ache for reasons she wasn't prepared to examine.

On the third afternoon following the luncheon at Amity Park, Emeline and Louise walked home from the Reading Room along Oxford Street. It was cold and foggy, which seemed to heighten the smells of coal gas and horse excrement that infused the city air.

"Do you ever miss Lyme Regis?" Emeline asked as they turned south on Davies Street.

"I think of Miss Anning every day, but now I would rather be in London, even when it's unpleasant," Louise replied, smiling to herself. She carried a leather folder emblazoned with her initials, a gift from her parents. It held their research notebooks. Glancing over now, Louise adjusted her spectacles on her delicate nose and asked, "Do *you* miss our fossil hunting days, Em? I might remind you that you were always the one who urged me to break free of our limited existence there, to embrace new adventures and new people. Have you changed your mind?"

"No, I haven't changed my mind. But I sometimes wish I had more control over the new adventures that come to me," she said wryly.

They were passing Berkeley Square when a familiar voice called out, "By Jove, is that my little sister?"

Emeline turned to see Charles standing under one of the square's great plane trees. She waved to him without enthusiasm, even as Louise's entire countenance brightened. A few moments later, he was beside them.

"You must allow me to escort you the rest of the way to Chesterfield Street," he proclaimed. Emeline noticed that his tall, pale gray hat was immaculate, and he wore a purple aster in the buttonhole of his dark coat. Turning to Louise, he doffed his hat. "Ah, Louise. How do you get on? Seeing you again is one of the great pleasures of being back in London."

Emeline watched as her cousin's cheeks pinkened. "Well, of course it is," she said. "We are the best of friends, are we not?"

"Always." He offered her his arm and reached for the leather folder. "Allow me to carry that case."

Emeline walked behind them the rest of the way to their little house, trying not to worry about Louise. When they came in the front door and had divested themselves of their cloaks, Charles addressed her before they were even seated in the parlor.

"Word has it that you were a guest at Amity Park for the unveiling of Lord Melford's artifacts. Is that true?" His tone was casual, but she knew him well enough to perceive that this was the real reason he had come with them.

Emeline sank into her favorite chair before the bow window, hoping that Dora would soon appear with tea. "Yes, I was there, but how did you hear?"

"Oh, I believe I had it from Sir Giles Peyton…" He paused as if searching his memory. "Yes, saw him at the club last night, and he told me. What was it like, Em? Peyton said Melford took such a liking to you, no other fellow could get near."

Dora entered then with the tea tray, glancing over in surprise at their handsome guest. After directing the maid where to set the tray, Louise set about making Charles's tea just the way he liked it.

"Ah, Louise," he sighed after one sip. "You know me so well."

Watching them, Emeline wished she could wave a wand and cause her besotted cousin to return to reality. Surely there was only pain in store for Louise if she continued to moon over Charles, whose self-centered ways were bound to cause her grief. Yet even as Emeline pondered this, she thought of her own tangled feelings toward Hart. Each day, the cousins seemed to stray farther from their vow to pursue independence from men.

"Now then," Charles said, turning back to Emeline, "I want to hear about the relics…and your new friend, Lord Melford."

She began to describe the various artifacts, with Charles interrupting frequently to ask about any gems and exactly what metal had been used. When Emeline spoke of the wooden drinking vessel, his attention wandered. "Yes, yes, but what about the sword? Giles said it is encrusted with precious jewels!"

"I believe only a scabbard was discovered, not a sword, but I did see some gems," she allowed.

"They haven't stopped digging, have they?"

"Really, Charles, what a lot of questions you ask! I don't think

I can tell you any more than Giles did." She frowned. "And, I must say, my opinion of him has been drastically altered. He actually suggested that Tobias might *sell* these antiquities for monetary gain!"

Charles nodded strenuously. "Yes. Shocking!" After an awkward pause, he ventured, "And yet, what if their sale could save a struggling estate?"

Before Emeline could give vent to her feelings, the knocker sounded at the door. Louise half-rose from her chair nearest the bow window and tried to peek around the curtains.

"It is a man I do not recognize," she whispered.

Dora was crossing the entry hall to answer the door, and they all waited until she appeared before them, wide-eyed, to present a calling card. Then, as if unable to stay silent, the maid said, "Viscount Tobias Melford is calling, Miss Emeline...asking for *you.*"

Emeline felt herself flush as both Charles and Louise turned to stare at her.

"How nice," she said brightly. "Do show his lordship in, Dora."

She rose as Tobias appeared in the entry hall, looking all around at his surroundings. In their rather cramped house, his sturdy frame seemed outsized. Watching as the viscount handed his gloves, hat, and a case of some sort to Dora, Emeline went forward to meet him on the threshold of the parlor.

"What an unexpected pleasure, my lord," she said warmly.

His smile was as kind as she remembered, and once again, Emeline felt at ease. After being presented to both Louise and Charles, Tobias took the chair nearest her own and accepted a cup of tea.

"I must apologize for simply appearing, unannounced," he said, before turning to look at Louise. "What a pleasure it is to meet you, Miss St. Briac. Your cousin has told me all about you. You two women are extraordinary, forming your own establishment here and making your own way in the world."

Glancing toward her brother, he added, "Don't you agree, Sir Charles?"

His brow furrowed as he seemed to consider this. "That's a nice way of putting it, my lord! My sister has always been rather...headstrong, if you take my meaning. It's fortunate that our dear Louise is here to see Emeline doesn't do something rash."

Emeline burned to call him out. How dare he? But before she could utter a word, Louise spoke up. "You are quite right, my lord. Emeline is extraordinary! She captivates everyone who meets her."

Tobias looked at Emeline. "I hope you will show me the room you described during our lunch at Amity Park." Turning to Louise, he added, "Your cousin has told me that you and she transformed your dining room into a study where you are laboring over research for Lord Jasper Hartcliffe."

Glad to be able to move away from Charles, Emeline rose and gestured toward the room on the other side of the entry hall. "We should be happy to show you, my lord."

"Tobias," he reminded her softly, smiling into her eyes.

In the study, Emeline and Louise took turns showing Tobias around the room. He appeared to be interested in every sketch and watercolor hanging on the walls, each book and fossil displayed on the shelves.

"It's quite amazing that you two ladies have spent the past two years with Miss Anning in Lyme Regis," he said. "I am a member of the Geological Society and of course, her discoveries have been presented to us with great ceremony."

"Miss Anning is a brilliant person," Louise confirmed. "It has been my honor to labor at her side for several years even before my cousin joined us."

Emeline tried to restrain herself without success. "Tobias, perhaps you are unaware that Miss Anning was barred from the meetings of your very own Geological Society when she brought her greatest fossils to London? A man presented them in her place, while she waited outside! All because of her sex."

He blanched slightly. "I can assure you, I had nothing to do with that decision! In fact, I believe I was still at university."

"That's right, Em," Louise scolded lightly. "I'm sure this kind gentleman would have supported Miss Anning, had he the chance."

As Louise continued Tobias's tour, Charles stood nearby, tapping his foot impatiently. When Louise finally came to the last piece, he spoke up.

"Fascinating, isn't it, my lord? And we have something in common. I, too, was a member of the Geological Society before I removed to Italy several years ago." When he saw that Tobias was not going to reply, he added, "I find it so original of these ladies to display these oddities in their dining room."

"It is not a dining room any longer," Emeline told him. "It is our study."

"Yes, yes." He made another effort to catch Tobias's eye before inquiring a bit too casually, "Speaking of artifacts, my lord, one cannot help wondering what you mean to do with all the treasures you have unearthed at Amity Park?"

"I haven't decided yet," replied the viscount. "We aren't quite finished with the excavations, and I would like to consult other… experts."

Emeline straightened at this. Was it possible that he might sell some of the artifacts? It was impossible to ask him any questions of that nature now, with both Charles and Louise standing by. However, perhaps there was another way.

Turning alongside the long mahogany table, Emeline faced her new friend and touched his coat sleeve. "As you know, Louise and I are doing research about relics that may be very similar to those on your estate. Would it be possible for me to return and bring my cousin with me?"

"I should like that very much!" A smile warmed his face. "Both of you ladies would be most welcome to come to my estate. You may observe the excavations, unless of course you would like to *participate?*"

* * *

WALKING TOWARD CHESTERFIELD STREET, a large, rolled-up paper tied with a ribbon held loosely in one gloved hand, Hart wondered if he should turn around. *You're not to be trusted,* warned his better self.

Since his lapse into madness on the road from Amity Park, he had continued to vacillate between a resolve to stay away from Emeline and a powerful urge to be in her presence again. Hart was a libertine, his past strewn with reckless affairs and broken hearts. Furthermore, he was in league with her father, both of them keeping secrets from her.

Emeline deserved better. Much better.

I should be halfway to Lisbon at this moment, he thought darkly. And yet, what of Austell and his problems—and Hart's bargain with Justin St. Briac? And what of Monte? It was a deuced tight corner he was in, and a timely reminder why he had never allowed himself to be constrained by anything or anyone. Sinners like him were better off alone.

I will see her just one more time, he told himself grimly as he approached the house.

One more time.

* * *

"PARTICIPATE...IN THE EXCAVATIONS?" Emeline echoed, thrilled by Tobias's invitation. "But we have no real training in archaeology."

He shrugged his big shoulders. "It is a very new science. Mr. Cartwright can teach you everything you need to know." Starting toward the entry hall, he added, "And as it happens, I have brought you a small gift that may be helpful."

Emeline watched as Tobias located the wooden case he'd left with Dora upon arrival. At first glance, it resembled a thinner version of her traveling art box. "A gift? Oh, but…"

"It is my pleasure!" Setting the case on the long table, he fished a small brass key from his pocket, put it in the lock, and opened the lid to reveal velvet-padded crevices fitted with various sized brushes, thin-bladed trowels, and tiny metal picks.

"Oh my goodness," breathed Emeline.

"These tools should give you a start," Tobias said. "You'll also need a small pickax and a shovel—"

"Emmie has those already, from our years hunting fossils!" interjected Louise.

"There, you see, you already have training in a similar endeavor. Please say you will accept these," he said warmly. Then, addressing Louise, the viscount added, "I would be honored to procure a set of tools for you as well. Perhaps this will earn me forgiveness for my Society's past transgressions toward Miss Anning."

Before Emeline could reply, a knock sounded at the front door. "Is it possible that we have yet another guest?" she said with an irrepressible laugh. "Let me see who it is."

Crossing the few steps to the entry hall, Emeline paused in front of the door, suddenly aware of a sense of anticipation. A delicious shiver ran down her slim back as she turned the carved brass knob and opened the door.

CHAPTER 14

*H*art stood before her in the doorway, so shockingly attractive that she felt breathless.

"I was expecting Dora to open the door," he said with a roguish smile. "What have you done with her?"

"Dora is busy, so I came myself," Emeline said, gathering her wits. "My brother, Charles, is visiting, as well as Lord Melford."

Once inside, Hart raised a brow as he glanced toward the voices in the dining room. "Ah. Most ill-mannered of me to arrive unannounced and uninvited. Perhaps I should go away again and do it properly?"

"Do not be nonsensical! Come with me." Out of the corner of her eye, she saw him set his hat and a long, rolled-up paper on the side table.

They entered the former dining room to find Tobias regarding an ammonite, while Louise described its discovery during her very first visit to Lyme Regis. "It has always meant more to me than any other fossil because it opened a new world."

"Fascinating," said the viscount, looking impressed.

Charles offered, "Louise has always been very studious.

Really, how many young ladies do you know who would give up pretty gowns and balls for a lot of ancient fossils?"

Noticing Hart, their conversation stopped.

Tobias seemed to stiffen, but then he chuckled and extended his hand. "Well, Hart, I daresay I've seen more of you this past week than during the entire decade since we left Oxford!"

They shook hands before Hart turned to greet Louise and Charles.

"I was just passing by," Hart explained, adding with a wry smile, "I must check in on my research staff from time to time, you know."

Charles came closer. "So, you are the mysterious employer I've heard about. By Jove, I am eager to learn more, my lord. Do you have an excavation underway at a secret location?"

"Not at all," he said flatly, turning his attention to the case of tools Tobias had brought, spread open on the long table. "Ah, what's this?" He looked at Emeline. "Perhaps you plan to expand your research, Miss St. Briac?"

Before Emeline could explain, Tobias said, "As it happens, I brought the tools to Emeline, as a gift. I hope that she may use them at Amity Park in the future." Then, smiling at Louise, he added, "I have, of course, invited *both* Misses St. Briac to participate."

As the viscount spoke, Emeline saw Hart's eyes flash when Tobias used her Christian name. Suddenly the room felt very small. Before Hart could respond, she moved to stand between the two men.

"Lord Melford, it was very generous of you to bring these tools," she said, "and we look forward to putting them to use in the near future."

"It was my pleasure." He paused to consult his pocket watch. "And now, I must take my leave. My grandmother is expecting me for tea." To Emeline he said, "Will you see me out?"

Her cheeks felt hot as Tobias bid the others goodbye. They

went into the entry hall and, when he had gathered up his hat, gloves, and walking stick, Emeline opened the front door.

"Come out with me for a moment, please?" he murmured.

She could almost feel Hart's keen eyes, following their progress through the walls. "Yes, of course."

Outside on the footpath, amidst the clatter of passing carriages, Tobias turned to face her. "I came today to ask if you will accompany me to Kew Gardens on Thursday. It's been transformed these past two years, and it would be a pleasure to see it with you before autumn passes into winter." He drew a deep breath before adding, "Would you like that, Emeline?"

When she hesitated, a shadow crossed his face, and her heart went out to him. "Yes, of course I will go with you. It sounds lovely."

He took her hand for a moment, smiling into her eyes. "Excellent. I'll call for you at eleven o'clock on Thursday morning."

* * *

WAITING for Emeline to return inside, Hart wished he had resisted the temptation to come here today. His chest felt tight with something that might be jealousy, an emotion he knew little of, and he realized this was just the sort of slippery slope he had managed to deftly avoid his entire life.

Why can't you simply stay the bloody hell away from her?

His thoughts were interrupted by Sir Charles Brandreth, musing, "Hmm. One must wonder what Melford is on about. I mean, could he seriously be wooing my sister?"

"Why should he not?" Louise replied serenely. She wrote something on a paper and, leaning a bit closer, Hart saw that it was Emeline's Bridegroom List. As he watched, incredulous, Louise carefully printed "The Viscount Tobias Melford" at the top, above a half dozen other names.

Charles continued, "Well, Emeline might be a beauty, but we

all know that otherwise she's hardly in the conventional line. I mean—"

Just then, the door opened, and Emeline appeared, her cheeks pink. Hart immediately thought of the way she blushed when she was close to *him*. Had Melford touched her? Was she attracted to him? A mysterious fiery knot twisted inside his chest.

"Goodness, what a busy day," she said lightly. Her gaze fell on the case of archaeology implements. "Wasn't it kind of Tobias to bring these for us?"

"Are you planning to use those tools in the dig at Amity Park?" Hart couldn't keep the edge from his own voice.

"Perhaps! He has invited me to do so." Emeline looked toward her cousin and added, "And, as you may have heard, Tobias has kindly invited Louise as well. How exciting it would be to move beyond our research and participate in a genuine excavation!"

Unable to stop himself, Hart flared, "Perhaps you have forgotten that I am employing you to spend your days at the Reading Room, doing research on *my* project."

He was gratified to hear Emeline gasp. On the other side of the long table, Charles coughed nervously, and Louise looked up from that cursed Bridegroom List.

"Kindly step into the parlor, my lord," Emeline said, her frigid tone belied by an undercurrent of fury. "I would have private speech with you."

* * *

EMELINE LED THE WAY, her back straight, crossing all the way to the parlor's bow window before she turned to face Hart.

"See here," he began, his tone less combative than before.

"No, *you* see here, my lord!" she flashed. "You may employ us, but that does not give you the right to dictate all our comings and goings. If there is one thing I will not tolerate, it is a man attempting to manage my life."

He towered over her, a muscle moving in his jaw. "I see. Clearly, Melford is a paragon who never puts a foot wrong!"

"Since you have mentioned it, yes!" Some devil made her fling out, "In fact, Tobias has been kind enough to invite me to drive with him to Kew Gardens on Thursday."

"Drive with him! Alone?"

His ice-blue eyes caught fire, and for one thrilling instant she thought he was going to catch her up in his arms and kiss her. Passionately. *Ruthlessly.* This vision brought with it a rush of arousal.

"Indeed, *alone*," she taunted. "I am persuaded you cannot find this shocking, since you took me up alone in your own carriage just a few days ago." Their eyes met, sparks flashing, and she knew he was thinking of how that interlude had ended, with them sinking down into the grass, kissing.

"That was different, and well you know it, my girl," Hart shot back, stepping closer.

"I assume so, for Tobias is a gentleman," came her sweet reply. "I do not imagine that he will attempt to ravish me, as *you* did, my lord."

"I see." His jaw hardened and he ground out, "I believe our business is concluded. I will bid you good day."

The abrupt end to their heated exchange left Emeline feeling off-balance. She followed him into the entry hall and watched as he reached for his things. Surely there was something she could say to best him at this crucial juncture!

"Oh, by the way," Hart said brusquely. He held out the rolled-up paper and fairly pushed it into her hands. "I didn't come here to endure a lot of set-downs from a headstrong chit. In fact, in response to your request, I brought this larger, more detailed drawing of the sword that was discovered on the grounds of my estate. You may keep it, for now. Perhaps it will help—that is if you and your cousin can find time to fulfill the terms of our agreement."

Outraged, Emeline opened her mouth to reply, but Hart had already wrenched open the door and was disappearing down the footpath.

* * *

ON THURSDAY MORNING, having taken extra pains with her attire, Emeline joined Louise in their study and waited for Tobias to arrive. Her cousin had four different books open at her end of the long table, next to the new sketch of Hart's sword, and she appeared to be immersed in her work.

"I so wish we could see this sword, rather than a sketch, no matter how detailed. It's a shame that it wasn't discovered in one piece," mused Louise. "I know we were told it might be Viking, yet I have the feeling there is more to this discovery than his lordship has divulged to us."

"Indeed!" Emeline agreed hotly. "A libertine like Hart doubtless has secrets. Our entire employment may be some sort of sham."

Under her cousin's probing gaze, Emeline could not sit still. Rising, she paced across the room and smoothed the skirts of her rose and cream promenade dress.

"The weather will be very fine for your outing," Louise offered, clearly hoping to smooth the waters. "I rather envy you, visiting the gardens now that the property has passed from the Crown to the government, and the public are able to go there freely."

"Yes," she replied absently. "It should be very pleasant."

Louise drew a breath. "Are you still thinking about your quarrel with Lord Hartcliffe?"

After a moment, Emeline managed to reply, "I'll own I didn't expect him to respond so harshly to Tobias's presence and his... gift."

"Didn't you?" Louise sent her a knowing smile. "I thought that might be your intention when you continued to use Lord Melford's Christian name, implying that you and he are on quite intimate terms."

Emeline nodded, feeling queasy. She had reimagined her quarrel with Hart with increasing frequency, especially as the days passed with no further word from him. The notion that he might be jealous seemed too farfetched to consider, yet wasn't that what Louise was really suggesting? It seemed more likely that he was just angry enough to sever all ties with her.

Just then, a knock sounded at the door. Dora bustled to open it and soon Tobias entered the room and bowed to both women.

"Ah, you are ready. Excellent. I hope you are hungry, for my cook has made us a picnic."

"Oh!" Uneasily, she imagined them reclining alone on a blanket in a hidden, sylvan glade, sipping wine and sampling an array of delicacies. "That sounds lovely, yet perhaps it is not quite..."

He raised one of his big hands to silence her. "I am fully aware that it would be improper to invite you to share a picnic with me alone." As Tobias turned to Louise, his smile widened. "That is why I would like to invite you to join us, Miss St. Briac."

She smiled back at him, then rose to her feet. "How kind. I will agree on one condition."

"Name it."

"Because Emeline and I are both called Miss St. Briac, it will be much simpler if you address me as Louise."

"With pleasure...Louise."

* * *

They drove in comfort to Kew Gardens in Lord Melford's handsome black and burgundy carriage, known as a clarence. It was the latest style, named after the king's brother, the Duke of Clarence. The three passengers fit neatly inside, while a dignified driver perched on the box.

Although the trees were swiftly losing their russet leaves, the day was mild, and the sky seemed even bluer in contrast with the burnished hues of autumn. As the carriage rolled through the sun-dappled avenues approaching Kew, Tobias explained that the place had begun nearly a century earlier as a royal garden, populated with exotic plants and seeds gathered during voyages to Tahiti and the South Seas by both Captain Cook and the HMS Bounty.

"Most recently, plants are being sent from the Falkland Islands. Kew's director, Joseph Hooker, is bringing them himself in special glazed Wardian cases. It's said to be the newest way to keep the plants alive during a long voyage." He paused, smiling as the carriage began to slow. "Now that the gardens have passed into public use, many more people will be able to enjoy the rare specimens growing here."

"Oh, it is glorious," exclaimed Louise. As she leaned forward to look through the curved front window of the clarence, the sun glinted on her delicate spectacles. "Visiting Kew Gardens is one of the advantages of living in a great city like London. I have doubtless closed myself off from the world during my years as a fossilist. Now I savor the opportunity to see new places and be with new people."

"Excellent," Tobias approved.

A liveried groom had come to let down the steps and they emerged into a world of lush greenery populated with trees of every description. Tobias pointed out some of the oldest varieties, including the Japanese pagoda tree and towering ancient oaks. They strolled for at least an hour, viewing the vast Orangery with its grand arched windows, as well as the extensive rose gardens, fading now as winter approached.

At length, Tobias returned the two women to the carriage, and they were driven slowly back down the avenue.

"There is a lovely spot with a view of the Great Pagoda where I thought we might have our picnic," he said. "I have no doubt that my chef, François, has prepared a delicious meal."

The clarence was passing a huge, partially built glass structure that promised to be quite splendid. "I believe they are calling it the Palm House," Tobias explained. "Perhaps it will be finished by the next time we visit."

Emeline thought she saw Louise sit up a bit straighter at his words. "There must be so much more to see," murmured Louise.

"After our picnic, would you like to extend our outing?" Tobias suggested, looking between the two women.

"That would be too much to ask." Louise earnestly shook her head. "No doubt you have other matters to attend to this afternoon."

"Not a bit! I should enjoy it myself. We will make a second excursion, past the Orangery. There is much to see…"

Emeline felt oddly uncomfortable. She had a great regard for Tobias, and she adored her cousin, yet this sort of polite and proper outing fit her like a tight pair of slippers. Considering this, she sighed. Her impatience with such things was one of the reasons she had left London society for a freer life in Lyme Regis.

Soon enough, the clarence drew up near a vast lawn. In the distance, between stately rows of cedar trees, the tall, striking Chinese pagoda rose into view. Tobias took them out to a secluded spot where the groom and coachman spread out a blanket and brought the woven wicker basket that contained their picnic lunch.

"I never imagined such a place existed," said Louise. "Papa would adore Kew. He is a botanist, you know. He has planted splendid gardens of every description at our home on the Cornwall coast."

"Ah. No wonder you seem to be in your element here," Tobias said, nodding. "You have other interests besides paleontology and archaeology."

"Indeed!" Emeline chimed in. She turned to their host and added, "My cousin is a true Renaissance woman."

Louise blushed. "Emeline is speaking of herself, I think." Gazing down the avenue of cedar trees, she murmured, "That pagoda is a brilliant creation. I wonder if my parents have seen it?"

"Possibly not," said Tobias. "As I mentioned, this was all royal property until recently." He helped Emeline and Louise to recline on the tartan blanket, then knelt to join them. "You may be interested to know that for some time after the pagoda was built, it was the tallest building in the world!"

As lunch was unpacked from the crisp linen-lined basket, Emeline tried to enter into the conversation, yet her mind wandered. What was Hart doing today? She knew very well that he would soon leave London for Lisbon. Had their quarrel ruined the special connection they shared? Perhaps she would never see him again.

At this thought, a cold lump of misery settled in the pit of her stomach.

Dishes were emerging from the willow basket: slices of cold roast chicken and ham, a small round of creamy Stilton, and a large cluster of succulent red grapes. There were sandwiches made with thick slices of bread: cucumber with mint butter, walnuts and cream cheese, chestnuts and butter. Off to one side waited the sweets: tiny tarts layered with paper-thin sliced apples as well as jam puffs and a carefully wrapped sponge cake.

The groom served lemonade, which tasted very refreshing to Emeline. She picked at the food on her china plate, but Louise was in high spirits.

"I love it here," her cousin proclaimed. "Oh, do you hear that sweet bird song? I believe it is a blue tit, my very favorite bird."

An instant later, she was on her feet. "Will you pardon me while I go and look? It sounds as if it is very near. I will be only a few minutes."

Before Tobias could reply, she set off in the direction of the pagoda.

Emeline suddenly found herself alone with Tobias. "Louise's sister, Camille, is quite obsessed with birds," she said, glad for something to talk about. "She has been a lifelong crusader against the feather trade for ladies' hats."

"What a unique family." He looked into her eyes. "And at least one of you is shockingly beautiful."

Emeline realized that Tobias seemed quite near, and if he leaned forward, he could kiss her. She felt a rush of panic, but just then the sound of a dog barking reached her ears. Immediately, her pulse began to race in a very different way, and she pushed up to sit straight, feeling intensely alive.

"What was that?" she heard herself ask.

"A dog, I suppose." Tobias glanced around, clearly not welcoming the distraction. "Henry, my groom, will see to it that the animal doesn't disturb our luncheon."

Emeline wanted to gather her skirts, get to her feet, and go in the direction of the barking, but how could she possibly explain? Instead, doubting her own hopeful heart, she held her breath and waited, palms damp.

The barking drew nearer, and soon a short-legged dog with patches of curly fur came bounding through the grass. A moment later, Hart appeared, illuminated by a shaft of burnished sunlight that broke through the cedar trees. Emeline's heart skipped a beat.

I must be dreaming.

But no, he was quite real. He strode toward them with his usual cool assurance, hatless in the breeze, his whip caught under one arm.

"You must forgive my dog for disturbing your peace." Hart

stopped a few feet away and gave them a brief, ironic bow before glancing toward Emeline. "Clearly, he sensed the presence of his rescuer, who will always be first in his heart."

As he spoke, Monte hurried across the pristine blanket, clambered over Tobias, and quickly settled on Emeline's lap where he promptly licked her cheek.

CHAPTER 15

At first, when Monte had perked up his torn ear and commenced barking madly, Hart had doubted him. Yet, as Hart drew the phaeton to a halt on the grassy verge bordering Kew Road, he recognized Melford's clarence standing farther away, beyond an avenue of cedar trees.

Hart held the agitated Monte back by his collar. "See here, you have a mission to complete. It's not enough just to find Emeline. Do we understand one another?" Monte stared back into his eyes and gave a low *woof* of agreement. "Very well then. Carry on."

With that, the scruffy dog leaped from the phaeton and began to run, still barking, toward a row of tall cedar trees. Hart jumped lightly down, handed the horse's reins to William, who was acting as groom, and followed Monte at a more leisurely pace.

It was a good sign, Hart knew, when the barking stopped. A moment later, he saw Emeline, sitting up on a blanket while Melford reclined nearby. Close enough to touch her, damn him. An array of delicacies surrounded them. *How romantic...*

Hart couldn't take his eyes off of Emeline, who was clad in a fetching gown of rose and cream fitted alluringly to her small waistline. The barking caused her to lift her face, searching. At

169

the first sight of Hart, her countenance was transformed from beautiful to radiant.

Unable to look away, in that moment Hart saw into her heart.

He felt at once thrilled and terrified, and again a demon taunted, *Why can you not stay away from her? You are incapable of giving her what she deserves.*

None of this inner turmoil was evident in Hart's voice when he spoke. "You must forgive my dog for disturbing your peace." He stopped a few feet away and gave Melford a faintly mocking bow. "Clearly, he sensed the presence of his rescuer, who will always be first in his heart."

Monte heard his cue and climbed onto Emeline's lap, heedless of her gown, and dared to lick her cheek. Hart bit back a laugh.

Tobias was on his feet. By the look of him, his customary patience had run out. "Hartcliffe! Why are you here? By Jove, I begin to suspect you of following me."

"I'll own it may seem that way," Hart replied smoothly, "but in truth I came to Kew to have a look at the new glass structure being built. As we were passing the Great Pagoda, this wretched dog began to bark. Apparently, he sensed that his goddess was nearby."

"Indeed?" Tobias lifted his eyebrows.

Hart addressed Emeline, who was trapped under Monte's happily squirming form. "So nice to see you again, Miss St. Briac. Kindly excuse this interruption." He pointed at Monte and ordered, "Come!"

As if they had rehearsed at length, Monte snuggled closer to Emeline. And when she gave Hart a glowing look, he could have sworn she was in on their scheme.

"Monte," she said, "you must be a good boy and obey your master." Gently, she pushed him off her lap.

The dog whimpered.

"Come here this instant," Hart commanded.

Monte's head drooped as he lifted his previously injured right paw and gave Emeline a pitiful look.

"Why, he is in pain," she exclaimed. Looking toward the incredulous Tobias, she added, "Poor little fellow. It seems he has hurt his leg again. After all, it wasn't long ago that he could not even *walk*."

"He is just fine," Hart uttered sternly.

"My lord, I am grateful to you for offering Monte a home," she said, rising gracefully from the blanket and allowing the dog to half-conceal himself in her skirts, "but can you not show more compassion?"

As this exchange went on, the viscount looked back and forth, as if undecided on the best course of action.

"Compassion?" Hart gave a derisive laugh. "Next you would have me give him a seat at my dining table!" He motioned again to Monte. "Come with me, wastrel."

The dog continued to hold his paw aloft, gazing up at Emeline, who bent to pet him. After a long moment spent gazing into Monte's stricken eyes, she straightened and extended a pleading hand toward Melford.

"I do not think this little fellow will go with his lordship unless I accompany them," she said. "I know it is very ill-mannered of me to leave you here like this, but I feel I have an obligation to poor Monte. I believe he never knew kindness until the day he appeared in our garden, and his very first real attachment was to me."

Hart felt a surge of triumph but schooled his features to remain sober. "Ordinarily, I would not agree to such a plan, but since the dog's injury does seem to be flaring up…"

Monte moved the drama along by holding his paw up even higher and looking back and forth between Hart and Emeline.

Melford drew closer to Emeline and spoke to her in a low voice. "My dear, are you quite certain this is what you want?"

"Yes. I think I must." Her answering smile was a bit too warm for Hart's liking. "In any event, Tobias, you wanted to see more of the gardens, and I find I have a little headache, so it's just as well that I go…to help with Monte."

The viscount frowned. "Something doesn't feel right about this business, but I must accede to the lady's wishes." He jabbed a forefinger at Hart, adding, "I trust you to behave as a gentleman toward Miss St. Briac!"

This proprietorial speech made Hart long to hit him, but the feeling passed as Emeline picked up her sunshade and took a step in Hart's direction.

"Perhaps you will have to carry Monte," she suggested. "I don't think he can walk."

The blasted dog seemed to nod agreement, so Hart picked him up. In spite of his short stature, he was as heavy as a sack of potatoes. Monte laid his head on Hart's shoulder and sighed.

To his dismay, Melford took Emeline's elbow and walked with her the distance to the phaeton, speaking to her in a low voice. From time to time, she nodded or made a reply that Hart couldn't hear.

Reaching the open equipage with its hooded top, Hart set Monte in the small open place behind the seat and gestured to William to ready the chestnuts.

"Thank you for coming this far, Melford." He sent the viscount a sharp look that was meant to punctuate his own victory. "Goodbye."

With that, he handed Emeline up to the seat and William took his position in back. With a flick of the reins, the equipage started forward, turning back onto Kew Road.

"I must say, you were quite rude to Tobias," Emeline pronounced as they gained more speed. She was sitting close to him, her skirts partially obscuring his hard thigh.

"Did you mind?"

"He has been very kind to me."

Hart flicked up a brow. "That's not an answer."

The road was straight with no one else in sight. Holding the reins lightly in one hand, Hart turned his head and gazed down into her thick-lashed eyes. What he saw in their violet depths made his heart clench.

"No...I didn't mind." Color stained her cheeks. "I was glad that you came."

* * *

"I ASSUMED that must be the case because you played your part in our little drama as if you had helped to write the script," Hart said with heavy irony.

"Of course I knew it was an act. Both of you were behaving outrageously!" She laughed, remembering Hart's very stern demeanor toward Monte. "But is it possible that Monte actually understood how he was meant to behave in response to your severe treatment?"

"So it seems." He cast an ironic look back to the dog's sleeping form. "The mongrel appears to harbor a secret talent. Perhaps he will leave my protection to join an acting troupe."

Emeline happily moved closer to Hart, feeling the warmth of his hard body. "It's true, Monte does have a gift for theatrics."

"And what of you?" he asked. "Weren't you enjoying your outing with Viscount Melford?"

Emeline considered her reply. "Tobias is a truly lovely man, but I don't care for a lot of ceremony and polite conversation."

"Ah, I see. It was not your desire to have liveried footmen serve a picnic lunch?"

She lightly cuffed his arm. "You are teasing me."

From the space behind their seat, Monte emitted a snoring sound, and they both laughed.

"Truly, this is what I love. Freedom!" Emeline exclaimed, happily looking around at the passing countryside, even as the outskirts of London appeared in the distance. "I prefer not knowing what might happen next."

"So do I."

She nodded. "Yes, I have sensed that about you. We are both rather misfits in London society, don't you think so?"

"I have always been so," he replied, a shadow crossing his handsome face.

Remembering their previous conversation about his disdain for a settled life or even a house of his own, Emeline dared to prod, "Is that why you will not make a home here?"

"Perhaps." They were now leaving the countryside behind, and Hart drew in on the reins enough to slow the horses' pace. His tone was casual as he continued, "However, you may be surprised to learn that I am considering the purchase of a house."

Emeline sat up straighter, thrilled by this news for reasons she couldn't quite understand. "A—*house*! Why, you said it as if it were a small matter. But surely, for you, that is not the case!"

They passed an open wagon with a large, black dog staring over the side. Suddenly Monte came awake and sent the other animal a menacing growl.

"Don't be a fool," Hart chided him. "That beast could eat you for breakfast."

"Do tell me more about this house," Emeline prompted. In a few minutes they would reach Chesterfield Street, and she would be forced to disembark.

He shrugged, his gaze fixed ahead on the crowded street. "I don't believe I have a choice. It's quite impossible to keep this mongrel at the Pulteney any longer. As I have already told you, there have been complaints about his barking, and William has threatened to leave my employ if he has to get out of his warm bed one more time to take Monte across to the Green Park."

"I see!" Was it really possible that a hardened rake like Hart was prepared to alter his entire way of life simply because of a stray dog? The notion was mind-boggling.

As if reading her mind, Hart declared, "The only remedy was a house with a garden, where Monte will not require an escort to relieve himself."

"Of course," she hastened to agree, suppressing laughter. "Where is this house?"

"Actually, we are nearby. It's in Wigmore Street, next to Cavendish Square."

"Not far from the British Museum! How lovely." The air felt heavy between them for a long minute until Emeline spoke again. "I'll own I am very curious to see this residence. Will you show it to me?"

He gave her a look that made her heart jump. "That would be even more improper than leaving your escort in the middle of Kew Gardens to return to London alone with me."

Feeling very warm, Emeline met his gaze and nodded agreement. "Indeed."

Hart made no further reply but altered his course slightly and drove them to Wigmore Street. They drew up in front of a handsome three-story townhouse of red brick, its classical doorway framed by white stone pilasters and crowned by a fanlight. Monte gave a yip of excitement and leaped, unbidden, from the phaeton.

"I think he wants you to go inside," said Hart.

"I should like that very much!" Emeline gave him her hand to step down from the equipage. "How did you learn that this house was available?"

He looked a trifle discomposed. "A...friend, a widow, lived here. She has just wed a wealthy tradesman and no longer needs this house."

"I see! How kind of her to tell you about it." She felt a stab of jealousy, even though she knew very well that Hart had doubtless had more mistresses than he could count. "But how shall we enter? I mean, the house isn't yours yet, is it?"

Hart instructed William to see to the horses and led her to the front door. His tone was offhand as he replied, "Oh, yes, it's mine."

"But you said you were *considering* it!"

"I did consider, and then I made the purchase." His hand was on the doorknob. "Time was of the essence since I shall depart for Lisbon in only a few days."

A shadow fell over her euphoric mood. "I see. Monte will stay here, then?"

His only reply was to sweep open the door, and Emeline found herself in a spacious entrance hall. Monte capered before them, leading the way into an equally large stair hall, where wide, shallow stone steps rose up to a landing.

As Emeline watched the clearly uninjured Monte, she could not resist laughing, "He was not hurt at all. How very naughty!"

"Indeed. Naughty is his byword, I believe." As Monte dashed about, Hart added, "Excuse me while I put this ruffian out in the garden, where he can explore at will. Wait here."

Emeline nodded, but no sooner did dog and master disappear down the wide corridor than she glimpsed a nearby doorway opening onto another room. Uncertainly, she approached, then peeked inside. Drapes were drawn, blocking any light from the windows at the front of the house. Three walls were covered with bookshelves of burnished wood, further darkening the space. *A library!* Emeline realized with a shiver of pleasure.

She took a few steps inside and made out the shapes of several wooden crates stacked near the empty shelves. Impulsively, she parted one set of drapes, just enough to let in some light. Then, approaching the crates, she saw that all of them bore labels announcing LORD JASPER HARTCLIFFE, Wigmore Street, London. Nearby, a small red chest with a curved lid was marked "Woodcroft Priory"—the very place where Hart had discovered the ancient sword and other artifacts. The chest's latch was secured with an iron lock.

One crate was already open, Emeline realized, and she

yearned to look at the books inside, to glean some insight into Hart's mind. Extending her hand, she had just touched an enticing, gold-embossed volume when a voice spoke.

"You are incorrigible, my girl."

"Oh!" Emeline quickly straightened and saw his tall, powerful frame silhouetted in the doorway. "You startled me. I trust you don't mind that I was drawn to your library. Won't you show me your books? And what is in that little chest from Woodcroft Priory?" Smiling, she gestured toward the locked chest. "I have been so eager to know what other relics you discovered on your property."

Crossing the room, Hart positioned himself in front of the crates and stared down at her. "I don't recall inviting you to enter this room."

She gave a nervous laugh and touched his clenched hand. "Can it be that your books are a secret?"

"Not a secret, but my private property." His voice was harsh. "You should not be here."

"I don't understand," she protested.

"No, of course you don't."

Emeline became aware of the air between them, charged not with anger but potent, sensual hunger. For someone like her, pursued in the past by men until she had come to avoid them, these feelings were both exciting and disturbing. Just as she thought he would reach for her, catch her up in his arms and kiss her, Hart turned away.

"I am damned thirsty," he muttered as he went to a low bookshelf and removed a bottle. Pouring caramel-hued liquid into a small crystal glass, he drank it down, then looked at Emeline. "My apologies, the other glasses are still packed." Without asking, he poured another small portion, returned to her side, and extended the glass. "Brandy."

Strong spirits were almost as foreign to her as lust for a man, but she boldly took the brandy and put her mouth where his had been. The first sip burned, but then heat spread through her body, heightening her arousal.

"You should not be in this dark room, alone with me," Hart said in a rough voice.

"There are so many things I shouldn't do," Emeline whispered, feeling like a wild horse finally set free. "And yet, why not?"

She looked up at him in silent invitation.

"Why not?" he repeated hoarsely. "There are a dozen reasons."

"But in this moment, do any of them matter?"

"Emeline." He caught her elbows and drew her almost roughly into his arms. "You are a bit mad."

"Like you," she whispered.

He lifted her easily off her feet and brought his mouth down over hers, searing, searching. His tongue found its way between her lips, and Emeline responded hungrily. How good he tasted! The heat of his male body against hers made her want to caress his bare skin, the contours of his hard muscles, the wild, intimate parts of him. Instinctively, she pressed closer, her breasts tingling, and he obliged by bringing one strong hand to mold itself to her bodice until her nipple strained and ached.

"Please," she gasped, longing to simply rip her gown open. Between her legs, she was wet, swollen...and thrillingly, she sensed that he was well aware of this.

Hart pressed her back against the empty bookshelves and rucked up her skirts with one deft hand. "Sorceress," he muttered.

Recklessly, Emeline opened her legs as his questing hand found its way up her stockinged thigh. As if from a distance, she heard herself making soft animal sounds. When his fingertips parted the slit in her drawers and finally *touched* her, she felt an abrupt, delicious tremor of release that only made her want more. Hart was kissing her again, his tongue moving in her mouth in a way that Emeline knew mimicked the sexual act. Helplessly, she moved her hips against his fingers, kissing him back, her breathing hot and quick. Nothing mattered except this blinding pleasure and the need that pulsed inside her.

Suddenly, through the wall, Emeline heard the front door open and close heavily, followed by footsteps crossing the entrance hall. A loud voice called, "Lord Jasper!"

For an instant, Hart seemed to go dead white. He stepped back, her skirts tumbled back into place, and Emeline sagged against the bookshelves. Tears stung her eyes. Quickly, Hart crossed to the doorway and stepped into the brightly lit stair hall.

"What is it?" he demanded.

William's urgent voice carried clearly to the library as he replied, "It is His Grace—your brother! He recognized the phaeton outside and desires to enter and speak with you."

CHAPTER 16

This was just *one* reason why Hart had never owned a home. The people who wanted to visit were all better off not having an address for him.

"You may tell the duke that I will see him in the drawing room." He reached out and caught William's arm as he turned away. "Wait. It wouldn't do for him to discover Miss St. Briac here. Find something to keep him occupied until I can see her safely away."

William nodded, and for a moment his clear gray eyes seemed to penetrate Hart's conscience. "Why not send the young lady out the garden door? I shall bring the phaeton round to the mews and drive her home while you converse with His Grace."

I deserve to burn in hell, Hart thought. "Yes, yes. Thank you, William."

The last thing he wanted to do was meet with his damned brother, who was the unknowing cause of all his problems. Reentering the darkened library, Hart told himself it would be better if he had never met Emeline. His life had been unmanageable since the day Justin St. Briac brought him to the little house on Chesterfield Street.

Emeline was coming toward him, her gown set to rights and her hat neatly replaced atop her ebony curls. She had the bearing of a queen. "I must go, Hart."

She hates me, he thought with acid satisfaction. *It's better that way.* "I'll take you through the garden and—"

"I know, I heard." She was arranging the little cape across her slim shoulders. "Don't worry, I understand completely."

"No, you do not. The truth is that William saved you from utter ruin. I tried to tell you that you should not be here, alone with me, but you refused to listen."

Even as he spoke, Hart heard his brother's voice outside on Wigmore Street.

"I find this conversation quite tiresome," Emeline said with admirable control, adding as she started toward the door, "Perhaps when next we meet, you will be saner."

He wanted to shake her, but there was no time. "Curse it, Emeline, this is who I am."

She turned back and gave him a keen look. "Is it?"

Unable to reply, Hart lightly took her arm and led her through to the drawing room, which opened onto the back garden. The elegant room held only two pieces of furniture: a newly acquired settee upholstered in royal blue velvet and Hart's cherished square piano, shrouded in a holland cover against the far wall. It was the first possession he had acquired when he left Oxford and came into some funds of his own, and it had just arrived from storage that morning.

As they passed, Emeline looked toward the covered piano, but before she could speak, Monte appeared at the French doors, barking as if he hadn't seen them for years.

"Ah, there is your devoted friend," Hart said.

He opened the glass door, but Monte bustled over to him first, rising up on his stubby back legs. "No, I didn't forget about you," he told the dog with mock severity. "Come in."

He was saved from any further conversation with Emeline by

the sight of William, who waved from the far side of the garden, near the mews.

"I shall be on my way then," she said in her usual forthright manner, and reached out to shake his hand. "It was a lovely afternoon. Thank you so much."

Hart had time only to utter a parting word or two before she started off, briskly crossing the neat garden. He thought he saw her give William a friendly smile, as if absolutely nothing untoward had happened so short a time ago.

There was nothing for it now but to go and find his brother.

"I hope you realize that this is all your fault," Hart admonished Monte as they walked together toward the front of the house. "If your behavior at the Pulteney had not been so disreputable, none of this would be happening!"

The dog jumped up and yipped, as if receiving words of high praise.

"Ah, there you are," Austell exclaimed as the pair entered the stair hall. "I hope you don't mind. Your man asked me to wait on that bench by the door, but I heard your voice and felt certain you wouldn't mind if I came forward."

As they met in the center of the empty hall, Hart noted that his brother was clad in a moss green frock coat with a velvet collar, and his black silk cravat was set off by a large pearl stickpin. However, in spite of his expensive attire, Austell appeared thinner and more worn than just a few days ago.

Hart extended his hand. "Are you well?"

"Haven't been quite myself, but no doubt it will pass. By Jove, I'd rather talk about this house! Could have knocked me over with a feather when I saw your phaeton outside. Now that Lady Valencia means to wed that wealthy cit, has she offered this house to you?"

He shrugged. "Perhaps." Gesturing toward Monte, who was exploring the perimeter of the room, he added, "I happen to have this dog, and the dog needs a garden."

"But how absurd!" Laughing, Austell seemed to relax. He looked all around the stair hall, up the steps, then into the shadowed library. "You have avoided owning a home in London for more than a decade! Do you expect me to believe that you will finally put down roots because of a *dog*?" Raising his monocle, he surveyed Monte. "Why the devil do you have this mongrel to begin with, Jasper? He don't look like much."

"You're quite right. He lacks breeding, good looks, and manners." Hart shrugged. "But I promised a friend he would not be put back out on the street."

"Promised a *friend*?" Austell echoed in disbelief. "Who the deuce could that be?"

"Never mind." Hart waved this away. "More to the point, I have just taken possession of this residence. It is empty; clearly not yet fit for guests—especially not dukes. I suggest that, unless you have a matter of importance to discuss with me, we both go on our way and meet again at a later date."

Austell was not so easily fobbed off. Looking around again, he marveled, "Nothing at all in the place? Not even a spot of brandy to quench a fellow's thirst?"

Forcing back a sigh, Hart gestured toward the broad stone stairs leading to the upper stories. "If you aren't too exalted to take a seat on those steps, I'll bring you a brandy."

With that, he went into the library, trying not to look at the place where he had ravished Emeline a short while ago. Still, her faint scent assailed him, and he couldn't suppress the memory of her in his arms, hungrily kissing him back, opening her thighs to welcome his touch…

Groaning, he grabbed the bottle and glass from the empty bookshelf and returned to his brother. "I do happen to have this brandy." Hart proffered the bottle. "And one glass."

"Capital," Austell approved, accepting the glass and taking several swallows.

Hart resisted the temptation to drink from the bottle. Instead he sat down beside his brother and looked over at him. "Was there something you wished to discuss with me?"

"Now that you mention it, I wanted to ask you about the excavation at Amity Park. Word has it that fellow Cartwright has found all manner of Viking treasures and that you were at the unveiling party! And they say you've been sighted in the Reading Room at the British Museum. What's it all about?"

"I've developed an interest in archaeology," Hart replied in an offhand tone. "So many intriguing discoveries are being made all over the world."

At this, Austell became animated. "I might have known you would be up to the mark on the latest craze, brother. You always have had the most obscure interests!"

"Thank you," Hart replied dryly. Across the stair hall, Monte was lying on his side, sound asleep on the stone floor.

"The *on dit* is that Melford has discovered some valuable treasures. Have you seen them? I wonder what he will get for them! I heard that there are collectors on the Continent willing to pay huge sums for such antiquities."

Hart decided to cut to the heart of the matter. "Do you ask because you are still on the brink of ruin? I had hoped that situation might be sorting itself out."

"I...do hope that is the case, but I fear otherwise." Growing even paler, Austell drank down the brandy.

"I hope you know, you can trust me with the truth," Hart said quietly. "We are brothers."

Sudden tears shone in Austell's brown eyes. "In spite of everything...I suppose that is still true."

"Most certainly." Unwelcome feelings stirred inside Hart as he patted his brother's arm. "Kindly enlighten me."

"It is that fellow St. Briac." Austell put a hand on his own chest as he drew a breath. "You will recall that I invested in his steamship enterprise, but I never told you I also had to *borrow* from him to raise the blunt for a proper stake. I know that must sound mad to you, but I was certain my share would quickly be returned many times over."

Hart wondered what rumors had reached Austell's ears. St. Briac had promised not to break the bad news to the duke as long as Hart helped him with Emeline, but perhaps the Frenchman couldn't be trusted after all! Calmly, he replied, "Have you heard otherwise?"

"Not precisely. But yesterday, when I encountered St. Briac at White's and asked whether I have yet seen a profit, he put me off. Made an appointment for me to come to his offices next week." Austell looked as if he might be sick. "What if there has a been a change in the company's fortunes and my debt has *increased*, instead of the other way round? He'll expect me to mortgage one of my properties! And Margaret… I vow, if she learns how I have mucked it up, she'll never allow me in her bed again—and then I shall never have an heir!"

With forced calm, Hart said, "You are too far out in front."

"I haven't slept in three days," confessed his brother.

He wanted to simply give Austell the funds to set things right, but he well knew that would only add to his brother's mental suffering. After a moment, he offered in a neutral tone, "If I can help in any way, do not hesitate to ask."

Austell had been hunched over, staring morosely down at his fine bespoke shoes, but now he lifted his head. "Do you mean it? In truth, you *could* assist with a plan I have been mulling!" He paused and bit his lower lip, as if trying to decide how much to say. "Dash it, Jasper, my valet tells me you have discovered artifacts on Mama's estate! Then, when I heard about Melford's dig, I thought, why wouldn't there be valuable relics buried at Caversham Castle as well? By selling them, I amass the funds to not only reimburse St. Briac but also finance all manner of castle renovations."

Hart felt a familiar stab of resentment when his brother referred to Woodcroft Priory as "Mama's estate," as if it didn't actually belong to Hart at all. When the duchess had died a decade ago, and her bequest to Hart was read aloud, Father had strenuously objected, insisting that he was her husband and all her worldly goods should pass to him. *And thence to Austell...*

Fortunately, their lawyer, whom the duchess had taken into her confidence, had intervened. Mr. Frith had a quiet but resolute manner, and even the imperious old duke was forced to cede control.

With an effort, Hart focused again on his brother. "You might not find a thing, but even if you did discover ancient artifacts," he explained patiently, "you can't simply *sell* them all, pocket the money, and walk away."

"Why not? They would belong to me to do with as I wish!"

Hart instantly thought of Amity Park and remembered Emeline's shock when Giles Peyton and his cronies began to talk of selling the treasures to collectors in Italy. He could still hear her voice, putting the men in their places: *These relics belong to history, to scholarship—not to avaricious buyers seeking trinkets for their parlors!*

"There is a great deal more to it, I'm afraid," Hart informed his brother. "Spend a day at the British Museum and you'll know what I mean. If everyone who uncovered antiquities hoarded them or sold them to gain wealth, the museums would be empty."

"When exactly did you acquire such a rigid moral code?" scoffed Austell.

"*Touché.*" Hart allowed himself a twisted smile. As he considered Austell's tart comment, a chill swept over him. The notion that he might have ruined everything with Emeline struck with painful force, and yearnings, buried for most of his life, awoke in his heart. Was it possible to embark on a new path, never before explored or even imagined? Perhaps, if he faced Emeline and they talked openly, he would learn the answer.

The tall-case clock in the library struck three. The afternoon was waning, and Hart needed to be on his way to Chesterfield

Street. Rising, he turned to Austell. "I know you are very busy. I won't keep you here any longer."

Taking his cue, the duke stood, and Monte silently trundled over to join them. They had taken only one step, however, when Austell stopped and put a hand on Hart's arm. "I would be neglecting my duty as a brother if I did not raise a certain matter with you."

Now what? "Go on."

Austell cleared his throat. "I must speak to you about Emeline St. Briac." His eyebrows lifted. "You know, the Exquisite."

"What about her?"

"People are talking, Jasper. She has been seen *in your company*. In your dashed phaeton! If Justin St. Briac should suspect that you have taken liberties with his daughter…"

Hart had weathered enough condemnation in his lifetime to hide his feelings, even the dark foreboding that chilled him now. It might be true that St. Briac himself had asked him to keep an eye on Emeline, but Hart had crossed a forbidden line with her long ago.

"Being seen in my company hardly means she is in my bed," he said roughly. "As it happens, Miss St. Briac shares my interest in archaeology." Realizing how flimsy that sounded, Hart hastened to add, "In any event, she is a woman grown, as she herself would tell you."

"And *you* are a notorious libertine. Even this house has come to you through one of your illicit affairs, and I can assure you all of London will soon be aware of it!" Austell took out a handkerchief and wiped his brow. "I hesitate to speak to you in so frank a manner, but it seems I must. Emeline St. Briac may be an independent woman who has set up her own establishment, but the fact remains that she is inexperienced in the ways of men like you, Jasper. Such an association might well ruin her chances for a respectable husband, and I shudder to think what her father would do in that case."

Hart's gut clenched tighter with each word Austell spoke. "Are you quite finished?"

"Oh, yes! I shall say no more on that head." The duke straightened his shoulders. "Let us part instead thinking of the future… and what may be hidden underground at Caversham Castle."

Glad for the distraction, Hart nodded. "If you should decide to conduct an excavation on the castle grounds, I will share any knowledge I have with you."

His brother was looking almost cheerful as they reached the front door. "By Jove, I think I will do it. No doubt Margaret would be quite impressed, and I rather fancy the notion of being known as the Archaeologist Duke!"

* * *

Arriving back at Chesterfield Street, Emeline longed only to go up to her room, close the door, and ponder in solitude all that had happened that day. When she removed her hat and reached up to pull a few pins from her hair, she caught the arousing scent of Hart on her bare hands. Memories came flooding back…of their intoxicating kisses, her fingers sinking into his hair and caressing his strong neck. Emeline leaned against a bedpost, lightheaded with desire. He had called her *Sorceress*, but surely it was Hart casting the spell.

Her heart was in turmoil, especially as she remembered their parting. After what they had shared today, she would hope for a tender gaze, a few intimate words, but he gave her none of that.

Instead, he had warned her away from him. What had he said? *Curse it, this is who I am.* Doubtless, she should heed those biting words, and yet the prospect of life without Hart felt bleak beyond imagining. It could not have been mere lust that drove their passionate encounter in his library. Emeline felt otherwise every moment she was in his arms, responding to his mouth, his touch, his male body. Furthermore, there had been a flame in his eyes that reflected her own deeper feelings.

Surely, once his brother was gone from the house on Wigmore Street, Hart would come to her. They had to talk. It seemed that the future, for both of them, hung in the balance.

From the stairs, Dora called, "Miss Emeline, will you have tea? I ventured to bake a seed cake today and it is still warm."

"Oh… Yes, thank you, Dora. I will be right down."

No sooner had Emeline changed into her favorite, simple blue gown than she heard voices on the street below. From her bedroom window, she saw Tobias handing Louise down from his carriage. It was just the distraction Emeline needed. One hoped Tobias would bid Louise goodbye at the door and then the cousins could sit together, drink tea, and chat about Louise's adventure at Kew Gardens.

Emeline hurried down the stairs just as the front door opened to admit both Louise and Tobias. To her consternation, the viscount deposited his hat and walking stick in the entryway, as if he were quite at home.

"Hello, Emmie," exclaimed Louise. "How lovely to find that you have also returned!"

"The fresh air has certainly done you good," Emeline told her as they embraced. "You are glowing."

At this, her cousin blushed. "It was a wonderful day, wasn't it? Oh, I see that Dora has just served tea." She turned to Tobias. "You will join us, won't you, my lord?"

"I would like that very much." He turned to smile at Emeline.

"I doubtless have bits of grass clinging to me," Louise said, and started toward the stairway. "Will you excuse me for a few minutes while I take off my hat and shake out my skirts?"

Emeline watched her go up the steps and steeled herself to be alone with Tobias. Turning, she smiled at him. "I take it that my departure did not spoil the rest of the afternoon for you and Louise."

"We did have a very nice time," he acknowledged. Before she could sit down at the tea table, he stepped closer to her. "I was very concerned about your welfare, however, my dear. You have a tender heart, and I know you felt you should be with that dog… but you should not have gone away alone with Hartcliffe."

"I appreciate your concern, but you should know that I disdain the rules restricting the movements of females, as if we were too feather-witted to set our own standards of conduct." Emeline patted his hand. "If I had just left the schoolroom, it might be different, but I am three-and-twenty, my lord."

Tobias blinked. "But surely you don't mean to go on alone indefinitely."

"At this moment, yes, I do." *Charting my own course, even if it is unconventional.*

Tobias took her hand and fixed her with his warm gaze. "You are headstrong, and I find that charming." He stepped closer until they were almost touching, and she inhaled his spicy shaving lotion. "Your spirit attracted me from the moment we first met… that and your rare beauty, of course. But rest assured that I see beyond your beauty." His face grew ruddy as he set a big hand against her cheek. "My dear Emeline, I have something important to say to you and I hope you will listen…"

CHAPTER 17

By the time Hart closed the door on his brother's departing figure, his thoughts were disordered. Glancing again at the tall-case clock, he made up his mind that he would go immediately to Chesterfield Street to speak to Emeline.

And say what, *exactly?*

Monte followed close at his heels, clearly intending to be included in his master's plans. "No, you are not going with me," he informed the dog. "You will remain here with William… That is, if he has the consideration to ever return from his errand."

Just then, the garden door could be heard closing, and Hart's pulse quickened. When William came into the stair hall, he looked surprised to see both Hart and Monte waiting for him.

"Is anything amiss, my lord?"

He couldn't help himself. "You were able to deliver Miss St. Briac safely to her door?"

"I was," replied William, brows aloft.

Remembering Emeline's cool demeanor when they parted, Hart wanted to know more. Had she betrayed any emotion during the carriage ride to Chesterfield Street? Anger? Hurt? But if he pursued this line of questioning with William, who had known him since he was in short coats, he would be revealing too much.

"Fine. Thank you," Hart said, avoiding the older man's keen gaze. "And now, I need you to wait here, with Monte, while I see to some…business."

"Of course, my lord." William nodded, still watchful. "And you will recall that many of the new furnishings will be delivered within the hour, so I was already planning to remain here to receive them." He paused. "You will return to advise where you would like the items placed?"

Bloody hell. This entire situation, which of course included Emeline, began to feel like a runaway horse. "Yes. I'll return, but I can't give you a time."

With that, Hart left through the rear door. The last thing he wanted today was to encounter anyone else on the street outside his new home.

He had walked a short distance before he realized he had neglected to pick up not only gloves and walking stick, but also his hat. With each breath, it felt as if a steel band was squeezing his chest, and his thoughts were conflicted. A part of him wanted to go to Emeline and not only ask her forgiveness for losing control that day in the library…but also tell her—*what?* That his existence had not been the same since she rushed into it and now, he couldn't live without her?

This made his mouth go dry as dust.

Lost in his own jumbled thoughts, Hart narrowly missed colliding with an old woman selling apples.

"Watch yerself, son!" she cried.

He drew out some coins and gave them to her without even looking at them. Overjoyed, the old woman pressed an apple into his hands. "Bless ye!"

Hart was too preoccupied to thank her. Passing a young boy in tattered clothes, he gave him the apple and continued on. His mind seemed at last to clear as he thought about the house he had so impulsively purchased. Was he going to lie to himself about the reason? Better to face facts. It hadn't been for Monte, but for Emeline. And for *him,* with her! Some mad part of him had begun to dream of a life he had never allowed himself to imagine.

But then, no sooner had Hart brought her through the door, than he had succumbed to lust and ravished her. His body felt hot at the memory of those stolen moments, of her unashamed passion, of how damned close he had come to stealing her innocence forever.

Surely the alternative was impossible. Emeline deserved a proper courtship, but her father would never accept him as a suitor, let alone a son-in-law! And even if St. Briac should agree, it would mean that Hart must change his entire way of life. Scrub away the stains of the past and emerge a different man.

He gave a cynical laugh. *Absurd!*

And yet…in the deepest recess of his soul, he yearned to believe.

He saw Emeline's radiant face, gazing up at him in the shadows, and her parting words came back to him: "Perhaps when next we meet, you will be saner."

Turning onto Chesterfield Street, Hart paused, leaning against a railing of a wrought-iron fence. He drew a deep breath, imagining himself telling her the truth of how he felt. *Truth.* A cold chill ran down his back, and suddenly nearly three decades fell away. It was the twins' fifth birthday, and he was standing next to Austell in Caversham Castle's gothic library, facing their father, the duke.

"It's time you boys knew the truth," intoned His Grace, even more impassive than usual. "Yes, you are twins, but Austell came into the world first, and he will inherit the dukedom." Something akin to a smile had caused his thin lips to twitch as he patted the smaller twin's shoulder. "Austell, you shall henceforth be known as the Marquess of Hartcliffe and be expected to comport yourself accordingly."

Turning to Hart, the duke had raised his quizzing glass, waiting. "Nothing to say to it, Jasper?" His father gave a low snort of amusement, and Hart hadn't been able to speak. As the duke stared at him, his words seemed to freeze in his throat. "Perhaps it is fortunate that Austell is the heir!" sneered his father. "It wouldn't do to have a silent duke."

Damn him. Up until that day, the brothers had somehow assumed that Hart, who was taller, stronger, and bolder, must be the first born. The future duke.

After the old duke's announcement that day, Austell had waited until the two of them were alone, outside in the woods, before he burst out, "Why didn't they tell us sooner, Jasper? Why was it kept a secret?"

But Hart's younger self could only shrug, his eyes stinging, unable to utter a reply to his brother's question. It wasn't that, even at five years of age, he wanted to be the *one*, but it hadn't felt right. Something cold in the duke's eyes had made it seem he had chosen Austell...and rejected Hart. Of course, that couldn't be. They were twins! Austell simply must have been born first.

Drawing a painful breath, Hart closed his eyes for a long moment and shoved the past back into the mental cave that he had long endeavored to block off.

The creamy ivory façade of the house on Chesterfield Street was only a few yards away. Straightening, Hart envisioned Emeline's face, her shining eyes searching his face, her lips parted to welcome his kiss, and he went forward.

It wasn't until he was in front of the house that he recognized Viscount Melford's elegant carriage. No surprise, of course. Perhaps Emeline had left something behind during her hasty departure with Hart, and Melford was returning it.

Hart turned toward the house, but before he could start down the walk, a movement in the bow window caught his eye. He stopped, and his heart jumped. Inside the parlor, two figures were clearly visible.

Viscount Tobias Melford and Emeline.

They were standing close together, smiling at one another. As Hart watched, Melford gently put a hand on Emeline's cheek. She covered his hand with hers. *God, how right they look together.* A memory flared: watching as Louise wrote *Viscount Tobias Melford* at the top of Emeline's Bridegroom List.

Hart's gut clenched as he grappled with another kind of truth: *That is the sort of man she deserves.* Kind, titled, intelligent, wealthy, respectable. A solid pillar among the ton, not an outcast like Hart. And although Melford might lust after Emeline, he behaved as a gentleman. Of course, she would deny that she wanted such respectful treatment, but clearly her judgement was impaired. Another snippet of conversation came back to him: *We are both rather misfits in London society, don't you think so?*

Hart shook his dark head. Emeline didn't understand that she was above him. She deserved so much more.

Turning away from the house before he was noticed, Hart took a few steps in the opposite direction and paused. How close he had come to doing something mad, to taking Emeline's hand and leading her down a road that was certain to bring her pain in the future.

Even if Melford did not court and marry her, it was clear now that someone else with the same fine attributes would. Hart just needed to get out of the way.

As he retraced his steps back to Wigmore Street, he felt the storm inside him begin to calm…then go blessedly silent. He had spent years practicing ways to flatten those turbulent emotions, and it was a relief to know it was still possible.

Hart knew a second surge of relief as he realized he didn't need the blasted house after all. He would go to Lisbon, as planned! Once there, he could find myriad ways to forget about this London debacle. It was a lesson, after all, not to allow himself to become embroiled in the lives of others. If he hadn't surrendered to an urge to help Austell, which led to the agreement to help St. Briac with his captivating daughter, none of this would have happened.

The misplaced key was *distance*—and had been since Jasper the little boy withheld his words for a full year to remain at a distance from his father.

Think of Lisbon, he told himself, seeking distraction. He waited for the familiar rush of anticipation that always accompanied the move to a completely different place, with new ways to sin, yet even as Hart quickened his pace, he felt nothing.

* * *

"I KNOW you hesitate to invite the attentions of a gentleman," Tobias said earnestly. As he spoke, he brought one hand to her cheek. "But I beg you to consider. I admire your intelligence and ingenuity. I will give you the freedom you need to pursue your own interests."

As Emeline listened to him, it came to her that the Bride-groom List was more than a ruse to fool Papa. It involved real people, with real feelings. Tobias didn't know her well enough to truly be in love, but still, the tenderness in his eyes made her feel guilty for involving him in her game.

Softly, she covered his hand with her own, grateful that he hadn't uttered the word *marriage*. "I like you so very much. Can we be friends for now?"

He looked hopeful. "Yes. Of course!"

Just then, the sound of footsteps on the stairs reached Emeline and she brought Tobias's hand down from her cheek. "Ah, here is Louise." She turned to greet her cousin, who was looking flushed and pretty in a new dress of leaf-green silk. "I am eager to hear what parts of Kew Gardens you visited after I left you today. Let us sit down for tea and Dora's first attempt at baking seed cake." With a mischievous smile, she added, "The girl is not a gifted cook, I fear, but she never stops trying."

* * *

It wasn't until Tobias took his leave and Louise curled up on the settee with a purring Bartholomew that Emeline was finally able to steal a few minutes alone. Hearing the clock strike half past three, her heart sank. Hart had not come after all…did not mean to come.

Again, his harsh words echoed in her heart: *Curse it, this is who I am.*

Emeline felt an overwhelming need to get out of the house, to walk, perhaps to lose herself and not find the way home. Quickly, she donned a straw bonnet, wrapped herself in a blue shawl, scrawled a note for Louise, and went out through the front door.

Her heart ached as she walked. If only Anthony, who lived only a short distance away, was at home. She could confide in him, or Frederica! They understood the struggles one endured when in love. But they were still with the Darwin family at their new country home.

Vehicles of every description passed to and fro on Chesterfield Street amid the shouts of drivers. Emeline pressed on, walking as quickly as she could in her skirts and narrow shoes. She had just reached South Audley Street when a voice broke through her reverie.

"Emeline! *Emmie!*"

Whirling around, she saw her mother waving from an open landau. Tears sprang to Emeline's eyes. "Mama!"

Helivet, who had been the family's coachman as long as Emeline could remember, hastily maneuvered the horses over to the edge of the walkway. Moments later, the Frenchman sprang down, opened the door for her, and helped her into the carriage.

"How fortuitous! We were just coming to fetch you," Mouette announced as Emeline settled gratefully into the seat opposite her. "It is a fine afternoon, and we hoped you might join us for a drive in the park."

It was then that Emeline focused on the diminutive figure seated next to her mother. "Grandmama!" She leaned forward to embrace first her grandmother, Devon Raveneau, then Mouette. "How did you know that I needed you both today?"

The two older women exchanged glances. "We have not had time with you to simply talk, Emmie," said her mother. "We miss you."

"And we love you," Grandmama chimed in.

"Oh, I cannot express how wonderful it is to be with you both." She knew an urge to sob. "You see, my heart may be breaking."

"Perfectly normal, I assure you," came Devon's calm assurance. "I wish I had had someone to confide in openly when I was young…and falling in love with your grandfather."

Emeline looked from her grandmother, whose winsome beauty belied her age, to her lovely, albeit worried-looking mother. "Will you both promise not to tell Papa anything I share with you today?"

"Of course!" they cried in unison.

The landau slowed as it approached Hyde Park corner, and Emeline impulsively rose and came across to squeeze herself between the two other women. Looking from one to the other, she declared, "I have fallen in love with a rake."

To her consternation, her mother and grandmother exchanged glances and began to laugh. Emeline stiffened between them. "May I ask what you both find so amusing?"

Devon leaned over and kissed her cheek. "My dear, perhaps you have forgotten because we are no longer young ourselves, but your mama and I also fell in love with rakes!"

"Do you mean Grandpère and Papa? Were they both *truly* rakes?" she asked, doubtful.

"Not only rakes, but pirates," confirmed Devon.

"Hmm." Emeline considered this for a long moment. "I suppose I did know this, but how much credence can one give such tales when the men in question are one's own father and grandfather?"

This frank speech elicited another peal of laughter from her companions.

"I assume this rake of yours is Lord Jasper Hartcliffe?" asked Mouette.

Emeline gasped. "How did you know?"

"It is not hard to guess. He is the most wicked libertine to appear in London in a long time, and he has hired *you* to help with his archaeological research. I must confess, I felt a feminine twinge myself when I met him." She wore a playful smile. "How does he feel about this romance?"

"Oh, Hart doesn't realize it is a romance at all! It is quite unbearable, Mama. You will both be shocked to hear this, but one moment he is kissing me quite…um, ardently, and the next he tells me he wants nothing more to do with me."

"Yes, we could have predicted that," Devon murmured, her blue eyes twinkling.

"Let us not forget that this man has a long list of conquests to his name," Mouette said dryly. "Why do you think you are different, my darling? Are there other signs that love is brewing between you?"

Emeline glanced down at her lap as the landau rolled past other riders and carriages on Rotten Row. "When we are together, I feel so much more alive than ever before. Even the colors are more intense. And, this might sound mad, but I feel understood in a way I've never known before. For the first time in my life, I don't have to explain myself or what I am thinking. Hart just *knows*." She drew a ragged sigh and rushed on, "And even when he is pushing himself away from me, saying we can never be together in that way again, I can see in his eyes that he… cares very much."

"That means more than you know." Her mother was nodding

more seriously now. "And I must ask…what do you mean by 'together in that way'?"

Emeline's face grew hot. "We have not…lain together, if that is what worries you."

To her surprise, Grandmama said, "We would not condemn you for it, I assure you. How can one resist with such a man? But there can be…"

"Consequences," finished Mouette as she reached for Emeline's hand. "Do have a care, my bold daughter."

"And have the courage to follow your heart." Grandmama took her other hand. "It sounds as if your rake is falling in love as well…but the question is, how far will he allow it to go?"

"Thank you both for your wise counsel." Emeline sat up straighter, dry eyed and determined. "I do have the courage! I shall speak honestly to Hart…and contend with the outcome."

CHAPTER 18

$\mathcal{A}$s the landau started back from Hyde Park, dark clouds crowded the sky, and the air turned chilly. Helivet halted the carriage and instructed the groom to put up the folding top.

"It has been an exceptionally lovely October," remarked Mouette when they were closed inside, "but I fear our golden autumn is ending at last."

Outside her little house on Chesterfield Street, Emeline embraced the two women she loved so much. Raindrops were pelting the walkway as Helivet came to hand her down.

"Wait." Mouette reached out and caught Emeline's gloved hand.

Hearing the note of urgency in her mother's voice, she looked back. "What is it?"

"I wish I did not have to say it, but as your mama, I must." Mouette sighed. "The truth is, even if Hartcliffe loves you…you cannot expect him to change. You must accept him as he is."

Emeline felt a pang at her words, yet deep inside she knew it was true. Drawing a fortifying breath, she waved and went into the house. Perhaps she would find Hart waiting for her in the little parlor at that very moment.

* * *

HE WAS NOT THERE, however, and by noon the next day there was still no sign of him. Not even a note! What could it mean? It seemed he must truly regret their interlude in his library, but if he now meant to keep her at a distance, she would not submit.

After picking at her midday meal, Emeline joined Louise in their study, where she found her studying the sketch of Hart's ancient sword.

"Oh, good, there you are!" Louise paused to polish her gold-rimmed spectacles. "Don't you want to delve back into our research? Just because his lordship hasn't asked recently how we are coming along, that doesn't mean we can stop what we've been doing. I confess I live in fear that our monthly income from him will cease if we cannot show more results." She replaced the glasses over her slim nose and blinked. "Besides, I find that I am more intrigued than ever since your outing to Amity Park. Aren't you?"

Emeline couldn't begin to explain to her cousin what she was really thinking about, but she did see an opening. "Yes, you are right! And Hart may have brought other relics from Woodcroft Priory. I am feeling a bit restless, so I will walk over to see him now and ask."

"On a day like this?" Louise looked out the window at the gathering clouds. "You don't wish to drive with me to the Reading Room instead?"

"Oh, no, you know me. I don't mind the rain!" For good measure, she added, "And in addition to asking about the arti-facts, I would like to see Monte."

Louise's sighed. "Dear Monte! I should love to visit him too. Do you think—"

"No." Emeline leaned down and looked at her cousin. "Let me be plain. I must see Hart alone, speak to him alone. About a personal matter."

"Why didn't you say so? Do you imagine that I am oblivious to what has been happening between you?" Louise patted her hand. "I can assure you, I am not."

Her face felt warm. "Well then, if you don't mind, I will leave you to your work."

With that, heart pounding with excitement, Emeline stopped in the kitchen to ask Dora to heat water for a small bath, then hurried upstairs to dress. Of course, it was quite possible that Hart wouldn't even be at his new home, if *home* was the right word for it. But she meant to be prepared, just in case.

A half-hour later, after bathing in a few inches of steaming, lavender scented water, Emeline let Dora help her into her demi-corset and layers of petticoats. She chose a new gown of soft, patterned lilac and cream foulard, belted at the waist and set off by a white silk bonnet with lilac ribbons.

As Dora set the bonnet on Emeline's upswept raven curls, she gave a sigh of appreciation. "Oh, ma'am, you are a vision."

Emeline scrutinized her reflection in the mirror. "Do you think so? Excellent!" Her appearance had never mattered much to her, but today she checked each detail: the rosy color that washed her cheekbones, the appealing tint of her lips, the black lashes that set off her striking violet eyes.

Dora looked on, eyes wide with curiosity. "Will you be attending a party, ma'am?"

"Perhaps. I do hope so," Emeline replied enigmatically. Reaching for her reticule, she added, "If I do not return this evening, please tell my cousin not to worry. And now I must summon a hackney."

* * *

A RAIN SHOWER was in progress when Emeline arrived at the handsome brick house on Wigmore Street. She was relieved to see that lamps burned in some of the windows. No doubt Hart was unpacking. Perhaps he had meant to come to talk to her but had simply lost track of time.

Holding her umbrella in one hand, Emeline used the brass knocker to rap at the door. Only a minute passed before the heavy portal swung open and William stood before her, clearly startled.

"Miss St. Briac! How nice to see you."

When he didn't immediately invite her in, she smiled warmly. "Thank you, William. May I come in? A storm is brewing."

"Oh, yes, of course." Even as he ushered her into the stair hall, Emeline could see that he wasn't certain how to proceed.

"You must be wondering if his lordship is expecting me," she said helpfully.

He blinked. "Is he?"

"No. But surely, he won't mind. Is he in the library?" Removing her mantelet, she handed it to him along with her wet umbrella and went into the library. This evening, a cozy fire was burning there, and several lamps were lit around the room. A magnificent desk now stood before the tall windows and a pair of wing chairs flanked the fireplace. Emeline scanned the rows of burnished walnut bookshelves that were only partially filled, until her gaze fell upon Mrs. Peachey standing next to one of the boxes.

"Oh, Mrs. Peachey, how lovely to see you again!" Crossing to the older woman, Emeline warmly clasped her hand. "How I envy you, unpacking all of his lordship's wonderful books. If I were in your place, I fear I would spend weeks, for I should want to peruse every one of them."

Although Mrs. Peachey seemed genuinely glad to see her, she was pale, and Emeline saw the worry lines in her brow.

"What brings you to this house, Miss St. Briac?" The housekeeper cast an uneasy glance toward the staircase that led up to the next floor. "Lord Jasper did not tell me you might visit."

"I have come to speak to him about…an important matter," she confided. "I know it is very improper for me to come here alone, but I hope after spending years with his lordship, you are not horribly shocked."

Mrs. Peachey twisted her hands together. "And Lord Jasper is expecting you?"

"No!" Her tone was tinged with charm. "But I mean to see him all the same. Is he upstairs?"

"He is, but I think William should announce you. I mean, it might be…" Her voice trailed off.

Something in the housekeeper's nervous manner added to Emeline's lurking sense of disquiet, but she smiled all the same. "Please don't worry, ma'am, or trouble William. Just go on with your unpacking and pay no attention to me."

In spite of her show of bravado, Emeline's heart pounded like a drum as she climbed the broad stairs. Suddenly it came to her that Hart might have another woman in his bed.

No. She straightened her shoulders. *That could not be.*

The stairway opened onto a spacious landing, and the corridor that extended in both directions was quite dark. All the doors appeared to be closed. *Now what?* Emeline knew a moment's panic. Somehow, she had expected to discover his room immediately, even with the door standing ajar. Perhaps she should have asked William to go ahead after all.

As she stood there in the shadows, a soft "woof" reached her ears. She broke into a wide smile. *Monte!*

Emeline followed the sound to the end of the darkened corridor where a thin bar of golden light shone under the last door. She heard Hart speaking in a muted, ironic tone but could not make out the words. *Woof!* came a canine reply. The notion that Hart had Monte with him and the two of them were having a conversation made her heart swell.

Her hand was shaking as she prepared to knock, but then she heard Hart's voice again. "Now what do you want? More dinner?"

Woof, woof!

"You are a four-legged tyrant, you know. Go downstairs and appeal to Peachey."

A moment later, as Emeline stood there, poised to knock, the door flew open.

Her heart was in her throat as she confronted Hart's tall, imposing figure, silhouetted against the firelit bedchamber. His silver-flecked hair was in disarray, he wore no coat or neckcloth, and his snowy shirt was open at the neck.

Blinking, he gave his head a quick shake. "Are you some sort of cursed mirage?"

She put up her chin. "That is not a very civil greeting."

"What the devil are you doing here?"

"May I come in?"

He drew a harsh breath. "In *here*?"

"You are a trifle slow tonight, my lord. Have I disturbed your nap?" Sailing past him, she looked around the room until her eyes fell on the decanter of brandy and nearly empty glass that stood on a table near the fire. "Or perhaps strong spirits are to blame for your muddled wits."

"My wits are *not* muddled!"

Monte now hurried toward her, emitting little yips of joy, and Emeline crouched down to receive his affectionate kisses. When the dog seemed satisfied, she whispered to him, "There is a treat waiting for you downstairs."

Watching as Monte raced from the room, Hart closed the door behind him. "I'm not going to ask how you were admitted and came to find my bedchamber," he said, frowning. "Let us go straight to the part where you bid me goodbye and go on your way. No one need know you were here, alone with me. Again."

The emphasis he placed on the last word made her smile as she rose to her feet. Removing her bonnet, she set it on a velvet-upholstered chair.

"Nonsense," she said, and went to stand before him. "However, I will be plain with you. Two days ago, when we were interrupted by your brother's arrival, forcing me to depart so abruptly, I expected you to come to me later so we might discuss our…situation."

A rather poignant shadow seemed to pass over his features before they hardened again. Was it her imagination? She longed to reach for his hand, but he seemed to be erecting an invisible wall between them.

"I have already told you," he said roughly. "We cannot have any sort of *situation*. My brother arrived here at precisely the right moment to save you from ruin at my hands."

Something was very wrong. Emeline looked around the shadowed bedchamber. On a table, she saw the small chest marked Woodcroft Priory, the same one she had seen before in the library. Tonight, there was a key in the lock. Nearby, stacks of clothing filled an open portmanteau. Almost hopefully she murmured, "I see that I have disturbed your unpacking."

"No, not unpacking. *Packing*." With that, Hart turned away and returned to his task.

"I don't understand." She followed him, tried to catch his sleeve.

"I was always planning to leave. Perhaps you chose not to believe it, but I told you I would be gone by the end of October, before the last leaves are stripped from the trees."

"But you just purchased this house!" Her chest hurt when she tried to breathe.

"I have come to my senses. I am not the sort of man who has a *home*."

"I thought…" She faltered.

"Whatever you thought was born of a dream, my girl." Hart turned back to face her, his eyes stormy. "I have told you, *warned* you, that I am broken. I can never be worthy of you, Emeline. It is best for both of us that I leave as planned for Lisbon. Believe me, I cannot be the husband you deserve." His mouth twisted as he added, "In fact, I doubt that I could be any sort of husband."

"But that is…balderdash!" she exclaimed. "Perhaps you were not listening when I told you that I do not *want* a husband, especially in this world where men have all the power. I mean to chart my own course in life, not take directions from a husband." Taking a step closer, until she could feel the energy of his body, she added, "But that does not mean I intend to be celibate."

"Don't say things you will regret," he growled. "Clearly, you do not know what is best. Your innocence should not be stolen by the likes of me."

"Oh, how dare you?" It was a relief to feel outrage replace her shock and grief. "I am a grown woman, and I am the only one in charge of my own blasted innocence! Perhaps I want to surrender it. At this age, it has become a burden."

"Emeline," he warned roughly.

"Please listen! Hart, if you must go, do not leave me unsatisfied," she said, and closed the distance between them. Stripping off her gloves, she slid her hands under his loosened shirt and caressed his smooth-muscled back and the hard, warm breadth of his chest. She felt him tense as a smoldering ember of arousal flared inside her. "Give me a memory to hold in my heart, for the years to come."

Hart winced slightly and he caught her shoulders as if to put her from him. "I may be mad, but not *that* mad."

"I want you," she said boldly. Rising up on tiptoe, she pressed herself against him as heat coursed through her body. Even through her boned bodice and corset, her breasts awoke, tingling with need. "I want the first time to be with you, Hart."

"No." He seized her then and groaned, "God, *no.*"

However, it seemed that *No* meant *Yes*, for in the next moment, Emeline was being kissed. Tenderly, ruthlessly, in a way that told her there was no turning back. She clung to his broad shoulders, drinking in his kiss, and it felt so right she could have wept.

When Hart broke the kiss, it was to lift her into his arms and carry her to the big four-poster bed. With his usual careless grace, he swept back the covers and straightened, looking into Emeline's eyes.

"Tell me again," he demanded.

"I want you," she whispered. "I want…this." She nearly said *Us* but caught herself.

"It cannot be undone in the light of day."

Her only reply was to reach up, open his shirt, and press her face to his chest, aching with needs she understood only dimly. His scent was intoxicating. She nuzzled him, loving the tickle of crisp, soft hair against her nose. She wanted to push him back onto the bed and discover every secret of his splendid body.

His fingers moved to the fastenings at the back of her gown. "I swore this would never happen."

Deftly, he flicked open the tiny buttons, and it came to her that he must have had a great deal of practice. None of that mattered. This was different. Emeline watched his strong, elegant hands as he removed her dress and spread it over a chair back.

"Now *you* must remove something," she challenged.

Hart glanced up in surprise, then gave a low laugh, a sound she had come to adore. "You are a minx."

"Indeed, I do hope so," she replied, beaming. Reaching up, Emeline drew off his shirt and drew in her breath at the sight of his bare torso, broad shoulders, and hard-muscled arms.

Hart laughed again. "You have never seen a man…undressed?"

A memory flashed of a man's naked chest, momentarily bathed in moonlight. The stranger in the bedroom where she had taken refuge from Lord Fulham so long ago! His touch, his kisses. The shock of her involuntary arousal.

"No, not like this." *Not someone I know, a man I have come to want so very much.* Impetuously, she leaned forward and touched her tongue to one of his nipples, tasting. The flat disc stiffened, and Hart made a sound in his throat.

"You are playing a dangerous game," he warned.

"It is not a game." It seemed that a locked door gave way inside her, releasing a tide of desire. Even her blood felt heated.

He lifted her onto the edge of the bed and kissed a fiery trail down from her throat to the swell of her breasts above the corset bodice. She sank her fingers into his hair, loving its rich texture, the intimacy of touching him this way. Just then, to Emeline's shock, he lightly bit at her nipple through the sateen fabric, and an electric shock seemed to radiate to her intimate core. Already aroused, she now felt an urgency she had never imagined, and between her thighs she was wet.

"Please. More," she managed to gasp. How crazy it was to feel so much when her body was still mostly covered!

His long fingers were unlacing her corset, more deftly than any maid ever could, and he stripped away the garment, tossing it to the floor. "The devil," he swore, confronting her chemise.

"I hate the thing," she encouraged him, and in the next moment, he had rent it in two and cast it aside.

Her breasts were so tender, yearning for him. Even as Hart knelt before her, Emeline reached for him, bringing her nipple into his mouth. Minutes passed in a blur of blinding sensual pleasure.

As he suckled and worked magic with his tongue, Emeline's head lolled back, and she moaned. Finally, lifting his face, Hart uttered, "That's right, love. Let go." With both hands, he molded her breasts and kissed each one, licking, nipping, as they swelled against his palms. With fingertips and lips he traced the outline of her ribcage, her slender waist, the graceful swell of her hips.

He kissed the insides of her wrists, her palms, her fingertips, until it seemed that every inch of her body was aflame for him.

Emeline knew a powerful urge to open her legs to him, to discover what he might dare to do, but she wanted more. "You are still clothed," she managed to protest, and reached for the waistband of his trousers.

Hart rose and quickly doffed the last of his garments. She stared at the shadowy outline of his male member, fully erect above a nest of black curls. Following her gaze, he laughed again. "Not only a minx, but a wanton."

"Do you think so?" she teased hopefully, moving back onto his bed. "Please, Hart…lie with me."

For a moment, she saw stark conflict in his handsome face, and it seemed he might refuse. It came to her that he had hoped to take her sitting on the edge of the bed, keeping his own body somewhat removed. If they lay together, it would bring him a step closer to surrender. But then he was joining her, drawing her soft form fully in contact with his long, powerful body. Emeline drank in every sensation. She reached up to invite his kiss, and as his mouth covered hers, his questing hand found its way between her thighs. This time, she opened to him, pushing against his palm, gasping when one finger, then two, found their way inside her. All the while, he touched her in the most delicious ways, the pad of his thumb stroked her aching sex, driving her mad with pleasure. Her hips seemed to respond of their own accord, and as she began to spiral higher, Hart's mouth found her breast again, his tongue swirling, heightening every carnal sensation in her body.

His free hand clasped her bottom as she tipped over the edge, seeing stars, nearly weeping with the keen, shuddering pleasure of her release. Hart turned on his side then and gathered her into his arms. As he kissed her, she felt him throb, hard and hot, against her soft thigh.

Uncertainly, Emeline drew back slightly and looked down,

seeking. When she reached out to touch him, he made a low sound, like a jungle cat. She caressed him experimentally, watching his face, until his hand covered hers and showed her how to stroke up and down.

"Yes, love," Hart muttered hoarsely. "Just like that. Don't stop."

This brought a new, thrilling element of excitement, and Emeline loved the thought of giving him a magnificent climax as he had done for her. But...what about the rest of it? Did he hope to fob her off with these...half measures?

"Oh, no, wait..." Angling her naked body, she hooked her leg over his hip until her swollen womanhood brushed against his shaft. "Please."

She moved her hips so that her slickness caressed him, and as she grew wetter, he thickened more. "Emeline, for God's sake." A plea perhaps, but more likely a warning.

"Don't deny me this." Had she spoken aloud? Pressing her breasts against his broad chest, she reached down and brought him to her entrance. Nudged herself closer, fit herself to him, pushed until he was partially inside. She could feel Hart shaking his head even as he made an incoherent sound of surrender.

He was cupping her bottom, easing himself further inside her taut, slick channel. "I will hurt you."

But any pain Emeline felt was overridden by the fiery desire that drove her to fuse their connection. "I want you," she whispered again. "Hart."

He eased her back against the pillows then, kissing her, fitting himself into the cradle of her hips, and she wrapped her arms around his back. Once fully inside her, he moved slowly, as if he feared she might break. Emeline bent her knees and arched up to meet his increasingly urgent thrusts. She could smell their mingled perspiration and feel their hearts beating in unison. But then, confusingly, it seemed that he was drawing back, leaving her, and she instinctively lifted her hips to keep him inside. An instant later, Hart gave a rough groan and buried his face in her neck, their bodies fully joined.

The world seemed to stop as Emeline savored the feeling of Hart throbbing, deep within her. *It feels,* she thought dreamily, *as if we are connected forever.*

CHAPTER 19

A storm of emotions swept over Hart as he lay in the big bed with Emeline in his arms. When she sighed, guilt tore a ragged gash in his heart. Looking down at her long spill of raven curls and her creamy limbs entwined with his, he thought that she was the most exquisite woman alive. He adored her.

And he'd ruined her.

All of Emeline's earlier pleas and protests echoed now in his mind, but he should have been strong enough to hold her at bay, to do the right thing even if she didn't realize what that meant. And if St. Briac ever found out, he could wreak vengeance not only on Hart, but Austell as well.

He surveyed the place where their bodies remained joined. She enveloped him, so snug and warm that his sex stirred and began to stiffen again inside her. Damn it, she was like a drug.

Yet every moment that Hart stayed inside her like this only intensified his villainy. How he wanted to start again, to pleasure her in other delicious ways, to test the limits of her passion, to let her push him to his.

But it could not be.

Slowly, he disengaged from her and withdrew, trying to smile when she glanced up in disappointment.

"Must you?" she whispered.

"I fear so." He touched a forefinger to her cheek. "Are you all right?"

Emeline gave a wry little grimace and nuzzled his chest.

I should be shot, he thought, but said gently, "Let me get a damp cloth."

Castigating himself every moment, Hart padded naked over to the basin and soon returned with a cloth. While submitting to his efforts to blot away the streaks of blood, Emeline reached out to twine her fingers in his wild hair.

"I'm fine, truly. I can promise you that there was far more pleasure than pain for me." With one of her unguarded smiles, she added, "And it is a relief to be free of my horrid *virginity*. Isn't that the most detestable word?"

Hart shook his head. "I wish I could share your amusement, but it's impossible."

"You didn't enjoy yourself?" Emeline reached for his hands and drew him back onto the bed. "Do not say so, for I know otherwise. And I feel...transformed."

He held her, unable to meet her eyes, and heard her yawn. "Go to sleep, love. You've had an eventful night."

Emeline clung to him as she dropped off to sleep, utterly at ease in her nakedness, in hearing the word *love* on his lips. He watched her, and for one stinging moment, glimpsed a life that might have been.

* * *

HOURS LATER, Emeline dreamed that she awoke to the sound of wind and rain rattling the windowpanes. In the pitch blackness, she imagined Hart's dark form standing near the bed, gazing down at her. Reaching out, she touched his sleeve, and dimly it came to her that he had dressed.

"Go back to sleep," he murmured.

As his long fingers pushed the tangle of curls from her face, then tenderly caressed her brow, sleep pulled her back under.

Dawn, harsh and gray, came soon enough.

The instant Emeline opened her eyes and found herself alone in the big four-poster bed, she was gripped by a sense of unease. She became aware of a mild burning sensation between her legs, reminding her that her coupling with Hart, in this bed, had not been a dream. How she had wanted him to make love to her and had reveled in every moment in his arms! And yet, in the light of a new day, last night's blissful joy was disturbed by doubt.

Where was Hart?

Her mind suggested that perhaps he had gone to fetch breakfast for her, but her aching heart knew better. Tentatively, she sat up and looked around the room. The portmanteau, filled with his neatly folded clothes, no longer sat open on the low chest.

I was always planning to leave, though perhaps you chose not to believe it.

Her throat swelled with tears. Spying her torn chemise, tossed into a chair, she got up and put it on. Numbly, she picked up her corset and tried not to remember the erotic sensation of his mouth, teasing her through the fabric. It wasn't possible to lace it herself, so Emeline stuffed it into one of Hart's drawers. She never wanted to see it again.

After struggling into her gown, she hastily pinned up her hair and surveyed the bedchamber again. The small chest labeled *Woodcroft Priory* remained on the table. But no sooner had she gone over to it and touched the key, longing to look inside, than something else caught her eye. On the velvet chair nearby, propped against her bonnet, was an envelope addressed: EMELINE. She wanted to be sick.

Her fingers trembled as she broke the seal and read the message, written in Hart's bold hand:

> *Darling minx, I tried to tell you the truth, but in the end, it didn't matter because I took you. I never wanted to hurt you, but as you now know, I am selfish.*
>
> *Last night's dream, fragile at best, is over. The light of day brings honesty. Eventually you will understand it is for the best. No one ever needs to know what occurred between us.*
>
> *As I have told you, I am bound to Lisbon with William.*
>
> *I hope one day you can forgive me.*
>
> *H.*

Emeline's heart was a stone in her breast. Tears burned at the backs of her eyes, but she could not cry. In a daze, she cast her bonnet aside and sat down on the velvet chair, unable to reconcile this terse note with the man she had loved in the rumpled bed a short distance away.

Time passed. Eventually she looked around. Now what? Feeling disoriented, she rose and wandered back to the little red chest that occupied one corner of Hart's writing desk. Had he meant to leave it behind? It was tempting to turn the key and look inside, but Emeline decided against doing so, at least not yet.

She was just about to back away and leave this room, this house, when her eyes fell on a crumpled, discarded paper lying under the writing desk. Something compelled her to reach down and pick it up. Perhaps Hart had read the missive, then balled it up in his fist and thrown it down. Her heart began to pound as she carefully unfolded the many creases until the remaining wax seal became visible. There, embedded in familiar midnight-blue wax, was the St. Briac coat of arms.

Emeline stared at it as if it were a viper. Smoothing out the sheet of vellum, she forced herself to read. The sentences were a blur, but their meaning struck her in a series of blows.

> *Safe travels, Hartcliffe... Our bargain is complete... My daughter will never know who was truly behind her employment... In return for your service, I have sent a new accounting to His Grace...erasing his debt and showing him a profit.*

And finally, if there could possibly be any doubt, she beheld the striking signature she knew so well: *J. St. Briac.*

Emeline began to tremble as she tried to take it in. *Bargain?* Her memory spun backward to the day Papa had arrived at the house in Chesterfield Street with Lord Jasper Hartcliffe. The notion that Hart would actually employ her and Louise to search for information about his ancient sword had always seemed fantastic, but exhilaration had overpowered her doubts. And then, gradually, he had become woven into the fabric of her life...to the point that Emeline went to sleep thinking of him and awoke in the morning elated by the prospect that she might see him that day.

Fool. *Fool!* It was as if her father and her lover had taken up the knife together and wielded it against her. Heartbreak boiled over into fury as Emeline stuffed both notes into her reticule, donned her bonnet, and strode to the door. Opening it, she resisted the urge to look back one more time at the bed.

I have told you, warned you, that I am broken, Hart had said, only last night. *I can never be worthy of you.* If only she had listened!

As she descended the stairs, Mrs. Peachey appeared at the bottom and exclaimed, "Oh, my dear Miss St. Briac. Here you are at last!"

How could she speak to this kind lady—or to anyone, for that matter? "Yes," she managed, avoiding the housekeeper's concerned gaze. "Here I am, but I must be on my way immediately. Is there anyone here who might hail a hackney for me?"

"Yes! I will summon a driver." Mrs. Peachey looked relieved to have a task to perform. "We have hired servants for the new house…although, as you may have heard, it might not be for long."

"So it's true. His lordship has changed his mind about this house!" Emeline was grateful that her rage had obliterated the tearful emotions she had felt earlier. In fact, her tone was almost scornful. "How upsetting it must be to go to all the trouble of helping to move and then have it all undone before the last box is unpacked."

"You are angry…" Mrs. Peachey moved aside to let Emeline stride past her, then followed anxiously into the stair hall. "With good cause, I suppose! But miss, if you knew Lord Jasper as I do, I believe you might find—"

"Please, say no more." Emeline turned back, drawing on her gloves, and suddenly hot tears blurred her vision. "Where will you go, Mrs. Peachey?"

"I will stay behind for now, to await Lord Jasper's instructions about the house. Then I must travel to Woodcroft Priory to discover how things go on there. One doesn't want to leave the staff unsupervised for too long, after all."

Suddenly it came to Emeline that Monte had not appeared to greet her, and she looked around, expecting to hear his nails clicking on the stone floor. "Where is Monte?"

"Oh, he has gone with Lord Jasper!" The housekeeper's wrinkled face broke into a broad smile. "When his lordship and William made to leave before dawn, Monte cast himself down before Lord Jasper and moaned as if he were stricken. Still, I couldn't have been more surprised when his lordship ordered the little dog to be made ready to travel."

Emeline banished a sting of envy and straightened her shoulders. "I really must go now."

"No need for a hackney, Miss St. Briac. I'll summon Bertram, the new groom, to drive you in his lordship's chaise."

* * *

EMELINE SAT silent as the young groom drove them along Oxford Street. Turning south into Mayfair, they passed tradesmen delivering supplies to the servants' entrances of grand homes, lamplighters extinguishing the last of the night's streetlamps, and crossing sweepers who cleared away the manure that had accumulated in the streets overnight.

"I've changed my mind," she said abruptly. "I don't want to go to Chesterfield Street. Take me to Grosvenor Square instead."

Soon enough, Emeline was marching up to her parents' stately brick home, pausing only to wave to Bertram, who was climbing back into the chaise. Then, without knocking, she opened the heavy door and entered. Mouette's lovely morning room opened off the stair hall and, looking in, she saw her mother seated at her graceful desk, writing.

"Mama." She entered and approached the desk.

"Oh!" Mouette clasped a hand to her bodice and blinked. "Goodness, you startled me!"

"I didn't bother to knock, so Baptiste does not know I am here." Emeline caught a glimpse of her reflection in a gilt-edged oval mirror on the wall and winced. "I look terrible, but don't worry. I simply haven't had time to make myself presentable."

Mouette rose, came around the desk, and clasped Emeline's shoulders, studying her. "You've done it, then."

"Indeed." How wonderful to feel perfectly understood, and not to see condemnation or judgment in her mother's loving gaze. "I had to."

Just then her brother Charles appeared in the doorway. "What's this?" He came forward and looked her up and down. "The prodigal daughter returns?"

"I am only paying a short visit."

"Come and sit down, darling," her mother said, drawing

Emeline down next to her on a settee upholstered in delphinium-blue silk. "Charles, perhaps you should leave us."

"As a matter of fact, I was just on my way out." He glanced in a nearby mirror and adjusted his black silk cravat. "I'm going by shortly to visit Hartcliffe. I understand he has purchased Lady Valencia Brook's house in Wigmore Street." He flicked up his brows for one suggestive instant.

Before she could think, Emeline said, "You won't find him at home. He..." She was shocked to feel her throat constrict with emotion. "I believe he has gone to Lisbon."

"Has he indeed!" Charles quickly crossed the room and took a chair facing the settee. "What's afoot?"

Feeling overwhelmed, she turned to her mother. "I have come to speak to Papa. Is he at home?"

Mouette's eyes widened. "No. He had an early meeting at his office...but I believe he will return here afterward."

"I shall wait."

Charles looked back and forth between his mother and sister. "Fascinating! Clearly Justin has done something underhanded—again. Please don't keep us in suspense."

"Really, Charles," Mouette protested. "You are speaking of your stepfather. And furthermore, you are probing into matters that don't concern you."

"If they have to do with Lord Jasper Hartcliffe, with whom I hope to do business, they may very well concern me."

Unable to hold back another moment, Emeline blurted, "I have reason to believe that Papa struck some sort of bargain with Hart and that he was secretly funding the so-called work Louise and I have been doing here in London." Her heart was racing. "In fact, I think Papa arranged for Hart to *pretend* to hire us."

Mouette looked aghast while Charles jumped to his feet, exclaiming, "He has certainly been guilty of duplicity before!"

"*Sangdieu!*" A deep, sardonic voice interjected from the doorway. "I hope you are not speaking of me."

"Justin!" exclaimed Mouette. Rising, she went toward him with outstretched hands. "You have come just in time."

"Just in time to bid my stepson au revoir." With a cool smile, he glanced toward Charles. "I do not want to waste your time with a matter that does not concern you."

Emeline watched as her half-brother flushed, made his farewells, and left the room. Already Justin was taking back control of the scene, but she knew him well. And she was very angry.

She rose but as he came toward her, she stepped back from his proffered embrace. "Sit down, please," she said sternly.

Justin arched a brow above his silk eyepatch but went to sit beside Mouette. Cocking his head, he inquired with a hint of amusement, "Am I on trial, petite?"

For an instant, Emeline saw the roguishly irresistible father whom she had adored all her life. A part of her wished he might beguile her one more time, but then she remembered the note she had read that morning.

"This is serious, Papa," she said. "I have reason to believe that my new life here in London has been a sham. Louise and I were not *employed* by Hart at all! Instead you manipulated us, making us believe that we were truly independent, making our own way, doing valuable work—" Her voice broke, which only made her angrier.

Mouette broke in then. "Darling...why do think your father has done this?"

Really, she thought, there was no point in trying to whitewash the truth. "I was at Hart's new house today, and—"

"Alone?" Justin shouted. "At this hour of the morning? That blackguard—"

"I am speaking!" Emeline pointed a finger at him, and he closed his mouth. "After Hart left for Lisbon, I saw a note that he had crumpled up and discarded. Imagine my shock to discover it was from you, Papa! You mentioned your *bargain* and said that I would never know who was truly behind Louise's and my employment."

Her mother turned to stare at him. "Oh, Justin, how could you?"

He looked as if he was about to stand and proclaim his innocence but instead sank back against the settee and ran a hand over his face. "I felt I had to do it. Emmie was wasting her life with that Anning female, traipsing around in the rocks at Lyme Regis, when she could have been taking London by storm!"

"But that was not what I wanted," Emeline said in a tight voice.

"*Eh bien*, and so I gave you what you *did* want! A house of your own. Meaningful employment. Independence!"

"But, Papa," she cried, "can't you see? It was all counterfeit! And now that I know the truth, Louise and I will give up the house."

"You are very harsh toward your papa," he protested. "Perhaps I can redeem myself when you are living here again, with us."

"Indeed, I am harsh today, with good cause." Emeline stiffened her spine. "You can no longer cajole me as if I were still a child. And I certainly will not return to live under your roof!"

Looking offended, he protested, "You may not believe it today, but I did all of it for your own good."

Mouette spoke again. "Justin, can't you see that you have deceived and manipulated your own daughter, just as your mother did to you? Have you forgotten how incensed you were with Cerise?"

"How dare you compare me to Maman!" he shouted. "She perpetrated deceptions simply to fulfill her own notions of what was best for me! She—" He broke off then as Emeline lifted both brows and nodded at him.

"Grandmère taught you all her tricks," she said evenly. "Beginning with your letter persuading Louise and me to return to

London because you knew a gentleman who needed us to do research for him."

Grimacing as if he had detected a bad smell, Justin swore, "*Mon Dieu*. It did not occur to me that I might be following in Maman's footsteps." He paused. "But still, *ma fille*, why can you not live here with us? Where else would you go?"

Emeline softened a bit toward him, but there was no time for more than that. "I am not certain what I will do next. I must think about it."

Her mother broke in gently. "I perceive that you have feelings for Lord Jasper." She patted the space between her and Justin. "Come and sit down and tell us about it."

Emeline wasn't ready to sit that close to her father, but she took a chair nearby and leaned forward. "I do have feelings for Hart, but I now feel confused and betrayed by him as well. Also, I think we might say that he left England to get away from me, so it has been a double blow." She blinked back tears. "This has been a very emotional morning."

Her mother turned to look at Justin. "You have made a big mistake in your dealings with your daughter. Will you begin to mend it by telling her the truth?"

"I am the villain," he said reluctantly. "The entire plot was my idea. Hartcliffe only agreed to help his brother, the duke. His Grace had borrowed from me to make a big investment in my new steamship, and he was about to lose it all due to an accident at sea. Hartcliffe tried to simply give me the money, but I had a better idea. His lordship could redeem his brother's debt by posing as your employer." He paused. "I didn't imagine he would cause you to fall in love with him."

"Hart didn't *cause* it. It happened…very naturally." She felt a tear escape and burn a trail down her cheek.

"Ah, ma petite." Justin stretched out his arms in invitation, but she couldn't go to him. Not yet. "It's for the best that he has gone.

Hartcliffe is not only too old for you, but also an outcast from society *and* a notorious libertine!"

"Fiddle." Emeline rose to her feet. "I am very tired of men deciding what is best for me. I am the only one who can make that decision. Perhaps I *want* a libertine!"

CHAPTER 20

*A*fter the scene with her parents, Emeline went upstairs to her old bedroom and undressed. The lavender foulard gown she had chosen the day before now held too many memories. Hart holding her in his arms, deftly opening the fastenings… And now, when she pressed her face to the bodice, she inhaled his stirring scent.

Face facts, she chided herself. *Hart is gone.*

A search through one of her trunks turned up a corset and a simple, if somewhat outmoded, brown-striped day dress that she could wear. Once she had changed, Emeline rolled up the voluminous lavender gown, stuffed it into the trunk, and closed the heavy lid.

Thunk!

If only it were so easy to pack away her memories of last night.

Standing in front of the cheval mirror, she pinned her ebony locks atop her head. With the addition of a plain tan bonnet, she was ready. Just as she picked up her reticule and turned to go, Mouette appeared in the doorway holding a tray.

"Oh…you are leaving."

"Yes." In her mother's embrace, Emeline felt a sense of release. "Oh, Mama, I don't know what will happen next, but I have to make a change."

"You are determined to leave the house on Chesterfield Street?" She set down the tray of tea and brioches. "Your papa wants you to know that he owns the house, so if you change your mind…"

"I won't stay there, now that I know the truth, and Louise will agree with me."

"Darling, promise that you won't leave London without sending word to us."

For one sweet moment, Emeline let herself lean on her mother's shoulder. "I promise."

* * *

To Emeline's surprise, she found that Bertram was waiting outside the St. Briac home, walking the two horses around Grosvenor Square. When she stepped out of the front door, he brought the gig around to fetch her.

Once again, Emeline was ruled by intuition. "How kind you were to wait for me. I shall return with you to Wigmore Street."

The thicker traffic was a welcome distraction as they wound their way back to Hart's new house. She really didn't know what she expected to learn there but hoped that a frank conversation with Mrs. Peachey might prove enlightening. Earlier that morning, when the housekeeper had tried to talk to her about Hart, Emeline had been in a state of shock, but now her mind was clearer. It felt as if her life was a puzzle at that moment, with many of the pieces missing. Perhaps Mrs. Peachey could help her.

"Oh, Miss St. Briac!" exclaimed the older woman when Emeline appeared unannounced on the library threshold. Today the draperies were open, and sunlight, freshened by the night's rain, streamed into the room. "You've come back."

"I had to talk to you. I hope you don't mind." Emeline approached her with a tentative smile. "You tried to tell me about Lord Jasper this morning, but I could not listen then."

Mrs. Peachey's worried expression softened. "I don't mind a bit. Are you hungry?"

She managed a smile. "Thank you, but I have eaten."

"Tea, then?"

Without waiting for a reply, the housekeeper poured a fresh cup for Emeline. They sat facing one another in a pair of wing chairs that flanked the fireplace where a fire burned low.

"As you may know," Mrs. Peachey began, "I have known Lord Jasper since he was a babe. When William and I first came to Caversham Castle, I oversaw the kitchen staff and William was being trained as a groom. We watched the boys grow up." She paused. "You knew, of course, that they are twins?"

"Yes, I did know that. But his lordship has told me very little else."

Mrs. Peachey was twisting her hands in her lap. "They were very different lads, not only in looks but in nature as well. From an early age, Lord Austell was quite stiff. Always keen to please their father, the duke."

"Well, I suppose he understood all along that he was heir to the dukedom," remarked Emeline.

"Perhaps, though I never heard anyone speak of it until the occasion of their lordships' fifth birthday. It was all very odd! I heard that the duke was waiting for the boys to grow up a bit before he talked seriously about his heir."

"Odd indeed," mused Emeline.

Mrs. Peachey leaned closer. "Some of the other servants whispered that His Grace was holding back the heir's identity in case one of them proved sickly or slow-witted. Then he would have a choice." She reached for her own teacup and drank the small amount remaining. "I must say, we always expected it to be Lord

Jasper. He was the handsome one. Black curls, the bluest eyes you've ever seen, and such charm!"

"He sounds like he was a compelling character from the first," said Emeline. "I wonder then why the duke was so hard on him?"

"His lordship has told you that, then." The housekeeper nodded slowly. "I can't really answer, except to say that Lord Jasper was a bold lad. Never afraid of anything or anyone, not even the duke. There was talk belowstairs that the boy would not submit to his father's strict authority. So many rules! And..." She paused, sighing. "I suspect that in time, His Grace began to turn against his little son."

Emeline's heart ached for that little boy. "How sad. And yet, knowing Hart now, it does not surprise me that he stood up to his father, even at a young age."

"After the duke announced that Lord Austell was the first-born twin, inheriting the title and estates, His Grace focused on training Lord Austell for his future. I felt that Lord Jasper was ignored. Made to feel as if he didn't matter, wasn't good enough. The duke was very cool to him, and the spirited child I had known seemed to turn inside himself. Indeed, he stopped speaking for nearly a year! What saved him was a stray dog he found one day on the road. He announced that the dog would be called Felix, and from that moment on, Lord Jasper began to smile again, at least with some of us." Mrs. Peachey's expression was poignant. "He just learned to plow his own furrow, so to speak. Lord Jasper has led an exciting, adventurous life, but at the same time, he's always been wary of attachments. No doubt those early years, when he was rejected at every turn, took a toll."

"I see." Even as Emeline felt a swell of compassion for Hart, she tried to quash it. "Thank you for telling me this. It does help to explain some of his lordship's actions, but I must be grateful that he has left London." Tears blurred her vision. "I was...beginning to have feelings for him."

"I understand." Mrs. Peachey bit her thin lower lip. "I could throttle him for doing this to you."

Their eyes met. Of course Mrs. Peachey must have guessed! After all, Emeline had spent the night under this roof. In Hart's own bedchamber. Heat climbed up her cheeks. "You...know?"

"I had to take the sheets off before anyone else saw...the signs."

Emeline turned her face away for a moment, then drew a breath and met the older woman's soft gaze. "I hoped that he loved me, but even now I wouldn't take it back, Mrs. Peachey. You see, I mean to live an independent life. Unmarried. And so, I wanted to have that one time...with Hart."

"I see." There was deep compassion in her thin, weathered face.

"I love him, and I hate him, at the same time," Emeline said despairingly.

"It is just as well that he has gone to Lisbon, I think. I care for Lord Jasper almost as if he were my own son. I didn't agree with the treatment he received from his father, the duke. That's why I chose to leave Caversham Castle and serve Lord Jasper when he reached his majority and left university." Mrs. Peachey stared into the distance for a long moment. "However, I know his lordship very well and I fear he isn't capable of giving you...what you deserve."

"That's just what he said!"

She nodded. "Lord Jasper may be a rake, but I have never known him to lie." Patting Emeline's hand, she asked, "And why did you return here today, miss? Simply to speak to me?"

"Actually, I would like to see the chest that Hart left behind in his bedchamber. The small, red one labeled Woodcroft Priory." Emeline leaned forward. "You see, I am still fascinated by the antiquities I've been learning about at the British Museum. Before I leave here forever, I would like to have a look in that chest in case there are artifacts inside!"

Mrs. Peachey nodded slowly. "Lord Jasper did leave it behind…"

"With a key in the lock!" confirmed Emeline.

"Yes, he may have intended that you should examine the contents. I will fetch the chest."

"Thank you, Mrs. Peachey." She was grateful to be spared a return to Hart's bedchamber with all its memories of last night.

After the housekeeper had left the library and started up the stairs, Emeline rose and began to peruse the volumes that remained on the shelves. To her surprise, she found herself looking at many of the same books she had studied during her days in the Reading Room at the British Museum. It was one more reminder that Hart hadn't needed her help at all. It seemed it had all been a ruse, from the first time Papa had brought Hart to meet them.

Disillusionment pricked her as she leaned against the polished bookshelves. Had every moment of connection between them been false?

Just as she had made up her mind to go home and forget about Hart and his artifacts, Mrs. Peachey reentered the library, carrying the little red chest. She set it down on the side table near Emeline and waited expectantly.

"I hope you don't mind if I watch as you open it," said the housekeeper. "I suppose it is my duty."

"Of course. But I must tell you, I have been thinking about it, and it is best if I end my involvement after today. I must face reality and continue on with my own life."

Mrs. Peachey's expectant expression faded. "Oh, I see."

"But before I go, do let us take a look in the chest," said Emeline. "Perhaps it doesn't contain anything of interest at all."

With that, she turned the key and opened the lid. Inside lay a cloth of royal blue velvet, the corners folded in on themselves. The two women exchanged a look, then Emeline opened the layers of velvet.

"Oh!" Emeline exclaimed softly. It felt as if she were looking back in time, perhaps to a small group of treasured possessions from someone who had lived a thousand years ago.

Nestled among the velvet furrows was a triangular gold belt buckle. It was a stunning piece, for it was rare to find a buckle made of real gold.

Her heartbeat accelerated. Moving the velvet aside, Emeline beheld a delicate, gold lady's ring, crowned with a setting that resembled a flower. Garnets and emeralds were inserted in the tiny petals, while a larger garnet was mounted at the center. Next to the ring was a small note, written in what appeared to be a youthful hand.

Emeline read: *Private – Do not touch! Secret treasure discovered by myself, Miss Theodora Fenwick, on this tenth day of June 1799, while digging my kitten's grave near the ruins. If Found, Return at Once to Miss Theodora Fenwick, Woodcroft Priory, Boyton, Suffolk.*

Again, Emeline was transported to another time and place. Vividly she imagined Hart's mother as a little girl, accidentally coming upon these artifacts, centuries after they were first placed in the ground. The buckle seemed to signify grave goods, buried with the remains of a prominent male leader. But what did the woman's ring mean?

A soft voice brought her back to the present moment. "It is fascinating! And that reminds me, Miss St. Briac...a letter was delivered today from the priory, barely an hour after Lord Jasper departed for Lisbon. It is from the gardener, Cyril Ackerman..." Crossing to Hart's desk, Mrs. Peachey picked up a thick envelope and brought it to Emeline. "Perhaps it's important."

She shook her head. "In that case, you should read it, not I."

The housekeeper looked doubtful but broke the seal. As she opened the heavy sheet of parchment, a smaller piece of paper, folded several times around a flat object, fell out. Emeline retrieved it and waited. Her pulse accelerated as she watched Mrs. Peachey scan the scrawled note from Hart's gardener.

"Cyril writes that they have not touched the site since Lord Jasper was there last month, as he instructed." She glanced up, sensing Emeline's surprise. "Perhaps you did not know? When we traveled back from Florence, Lord Jasper wanted to visit the priory before we continued on to London. I think Cyril and Peter, the old gamekeeper, had discovered pieces of the sword by then. And while we were there, Lord Jasper, Cyril, and William uncovered the jeweled hilt."

"I see!" Emeline felt a pang as she realized how much he had never shared with her.

Mrs. Peachey returned to the letter.

"It seems that, although Lord Jasper had instructed that a barrier be erected around the excavation site, one rainy day Cyril glimpsed something shining in the ground. He encloses it here and asks that his lordship come to the priory as soon as may be, so that the explorations can continue before the weather worsens."

They both stared at the folded packet in Emeline's hands. Her fingers shook slightly as she opened it and spread the parchment out on the desk. In the middle was a small, ancient gold coin, with carving on both sides. Her pulse raced, for she knew that the coin might be the key to the treasure's date and origins.

"This little coin may have an important story to tell," she said softly.

"November approaches, and Cyril is eager to begin digging again before the rains come," mused Mrs. Peachey. "But Lord Jasper may be in Lisbon by the time word reaches him!"

"The gardener cannot carry on alone, even if he has some knowledge. He must be supervised. It's very important that such work be done properly, or the artifacts could be damaged! Do you think...I might go to Woodcroft Priory, to assist Mr. Ackerman? I could ask my cousin Louise, who has spent years unearthing rare fossils, to accompany me. And I know of a male antiquarian who might come as well."

"Oh, miss, I think that is a splendid idea!" The housekeeper's cheeks colored as she reached out a hand to Emeline. "And no matter what has happened between you and Lord Jasper, I know he would trust you to oversee this matter in his absence."

"Yes." Her eyes stung. "It could be a last gift between us."

* * *

EMELINE ARRIVED home to discover Louise working in their converted study, papers spread before her on the long table.

"Where have you been?" Louise looked her up and down. "I know you didn't return here last night. How did you manage to change your gown?"

"Such a lot of questions!" Emeline gestured indifferently toward her striped dress. "I changed my attire at my parents' house this morning."

"Oh!" Louise looked slightly disappointed. "I had a notion that you were with Hart last night..." Her voice trailed off suggestively.

To Emeline's chagrin, her face grew hot. "I shan't lie to you. I *was* with Hart. It's a rather long story."

Her cousin pushed the papers aside. "Oh, my dear, do sit down. Shall I ring for refreshments?"

"No. I'm not hungry." Drawing her chair close to Louise, Emeline divulged most of what had happened since her departure from Chesterfield Street the day before. She was grateful to feel rather numb, so that when she reached the part about Hart leaving for Lisbon, there were no more tears. "And then...just when it seemed the situation couldn't get worse, I found a message from Papa to Hart. Oh, Louise, it has all been a *hoax*! Papa made a bargain with Hart. Apparently, the Duke of Caversham owed a large sum to Papa over some failed steamship investment, and Hart pretended to hire us in exchange for Papa cancelling his brother's debts. Hart wanted to keep it secret from the duke."

Louise sat for a moment, shaking her head. "So much makes sense now. I always thought the situation was too good to be true, but we were so happy to think we were making our own way in the world."

"Instead, Papa was behind the curtain, directing the entire play! It is infuriating!" Emeline jumped up and paced the length of the long table. "I had to go there this morning to confront him. And thankfully, Mama was there to support me."

"Uncle Justin has always been bigger than life, I think. He doubtless believed he was doing it all for our benefit."

"Exactly!" cried Emeline. "But I told him, now that we know the truth, we cannot remain in this house. We will find a way to live independently, just as we always planned…before he secretly interfered."

Although Louise looked taken aback at this news, she slowly began to nod. "Of course. Perhaps we can find employment at the British Museum."

"Everyone warns that they would not hire women to do more than scrub the floors, but of course *we* must find a way to breach the museum's defenses." Returning to her chair, Emeline leaned forward. "But first, we are going to enjoy an adventure. We must travel to Woodcroft Priory to uncover ancient treasures!"

"Wh-what?"

"I was just thinking that we should keep the house for now, because of Bartholomew. Dora can stay here to look after him. When we return from Suffolk, we will all find a new living situation."

"Clearly you have done a lot of planning!"

Before Emeline could respond, the knocker sounded at the front door and Louise rose. "I believe that may be Tobias." She flushed. "I mean, Viscount Melford. He was planning to drop by for a chat."

Emeline looked on curiously as her cousin went to the door and received Tobias. He came into the study and took a chair on the other side of the table. In spite of their rather awkward last meeting, he gave no sign of discomfort when Emeline greeted him. On the contrary, he seemed utterly at ease, especially when he looked at Louise.

"I believe Dora will be serving a light luncheon," Louise was saying, her cheeks still pink. "I wanted to thank Lord Melford for taking us to Kew Gardens."

"Of course!" said Emeline, nodding, a hint of mischief in her tone. "How lovely."

"Your cousin was kind enough to invite me here to discuss the progress of the excavations at Amity Park," said Tobias. "You may remember that I hoped both of us might be involved. However, it is going very slowly, and there isn't much for us to do at this juncture."

"That is excellent!" proclaimed Emeline. "I have just been telling Louise that I must travel to Suffolk to look into an archaeological discovery at Woodcroft Priory, and I would like her to accompany me."

"Isn't that the name of Hart's estate?" queried Tobias.

"It is, but he has departed for the Continent." She lifted her brows ever so slightly. "Perhaps you would care to join us?"

"Indeed I would!" The viscount looked between them, clearly delighted, then pointed toward himself. "You will need male protection during this adventure. In fact, I propose that we journey in comfort in my traveling coach!"

This, of course, was exactly what Emeline had hoped he would say. "My lord, we are honored to accept your generous offer."

"Yes," Louise chimed in. "It is exceedingly kind of you."

"Splendid!" Tobias reached one large hand toward Louise, then seemed to remember that they were not alone. "Now that we have settled those matters, I hope you will tell me more about this priory and its antiquities."

Dora was wheeling a cart laden with covered dishes toward them, and Emeline realized she was ravenous.

"Certainly! I will enlighten you both over lunch," she said, her spirits rising by the moment. "But first, a question! Is it possible that we might depart for Suffolk without delay?"

"What date did you have in mind?" Tobias inquired cautiously.

Emeline beamed. "Would tomorrow be too soon?"

*I*n the end, Emeline was forced to wait two days for their departure to Suffolk. There was so much to do, and everything took longer than she imagined. A visit had to be paid to Grosvenor Square to tell her parents and grandparents that she and Louise were off to Woodcroft Priory for an indefinite time. Fortunately, all the family embraced her and wished them well, even her difficult Papa.

Next, Emeline visited the British Museum to look for information about Viking coins. After two hours of poring over various texts, she was about to give up when Antonio Panizzi came to her rescue. Hearing of her plight, the Keeper of Printed Books, who had originally tried to bar her from the Reading Room, went out into a private room and returned with a small leatherbound volume.

"This rare, handmade book is from my personal collection. It has fine drawings and paintings of ancient coins, with descriptions, to aid in your archaeological endeavors, Miss St. Briac," he murmured, and put the book in her hands. "You may take it along with you, and I hope it provides you with the information you seek."

She had beamed back at him, gratified to realize how their relationship had evolved to one of trust and respect. "I shall return it to you in the same condition as soon as I can."

That evening, Emeline paused in the midst of packing her portmanteau to sit and scan the detailed, hand-painted illustrations of fantastic-looking coins. How wonderful it would be to show the amazing little book to Hart! When something excited her, Hart always understood, even without an explanation.

But those days were in the past. Grief swept over her at the realization that it had all been a dream, and now it was ended.

The journey to Suffolk, on England's east coast, was accomplished in stages over two days. Tobias, Emeline, and Louise traveled together in a fine coach, while Bertram drove Mrs. Peachey in Hart's phaeton.

By the afternoon of the second day, they were well into Suffolk, and Emeline stared out the carriage window in wonder. "How flat and open it is! So different from Cornwall." She thought of the dramatic cliff paths she walked near Polruan and the picturesque coves where smugglers had for decades hidden their ill-gotten gains. By contrast, the Suffolk landscape was like a vast plain, stretching into the distance, and the land eased down to the pale sea amidst sleepy marshes and reed beds.

"Yes," agreed Louise, "so different, yet quite peaceful and lovely."

Emeline was thinking of Hart's mother, who had left her Suffolk roots to become the Duchess of Caversham and live among the ton in London. He had made it sound as if he rarely came here and was only interested in Woodcroft Priory because of its archaeological possibilities. But as she well knew, he was a master at distancing himself from the people and places that most tempted him to care.

As the carriage jounced over a sandy, poorly tended road, the coachman gestured to an ancient-looking sign that pointed into a grove of alder trees. *WOODCROFT PRIORY.*

Tobias leaned forward and nodded to the driver. As they turned down a narrow, rutted lane with trees on either side, a startled pheasant flew out of the bracken.

"I'll say one thing," he remarked with a wry smile, "I've known Hartcliffe since university, and none of this seems like a place where he would care to live. No wonder, as we arrive, we find him gone to Lisbon."

A few minutes later, the coach emerged from the woods and Emeline beheld Woodcroft Priory. She thought she remembered Hart saying once, "It isn't much," and of course compared to the grand estates near London, that was the case.

The rambling brick manor house was relatively modest in size, with a stable and other outbuildings to the west. Not far away, on the brow of a gentle hill, the ruins of the original priory were visible, while the River Alde undulated lazily in the distance.

"No doubt this house was built on a section of those ruins," remarked Tobias as the coach rolled to a standstill on the sandy drive. "Very common, of course, after the dissolution of the monasteries under Henry VIII."

As he spoke, a stout middle-aged woman wearing a long apron emerged from the manor house. Regarding the travelers with frank curiosity, she called, "Good day. I am Mrs. Dawson, the housekeeper. Mrs. Peachey arrived a short while ago and told us to expect you folk. My son, Robbie, will help with your things."

A tall, fair adolescent boy appeared and began to assist Tobias's young driver as he clambered up to take the luggage strapped to the roof of the coach.

Tobias made their introductions to Mrs. Dawson, explaining their connections to Hart. Emeline watched the woman for any sign of her feelings about the owner of Woodcroft Priory, but she only said, "Lord Jasper is seldom in residence, so we were not aware of his plans. However, Mrs. Peachey claims his lordship would want this and that's good enough for me."

As they moved toward the heavy arched doorway, Tobias remarked, "I am pleased that the others arrived ahead of us, since you are already acquainted with Mrs. Peachey."

Emeline smiled, remembering how happy the young groom had been to drive her to Grosvenor Square. No doubt Bertram could not resist testing his skill as a coachman.

"Good day, Miss St. Briac!" called a voice just before she stepped through the door.

Looking around, Emeline saw Bertram striding toward her. "Why, Bertram, I was just thinking about you. You certainly made good time on these bad roads."

"Indeed." He doffed his cap and nodded to the three travelers. "And now I am off again."

"Really!" said Tobias in surprise. "Where are you going?"

The young man touched his coat pocket. "Mrs. Peachey has sent me on an important errand," he said proudly. "I am charged with delivering a letter for her."

"I hope you don't have far to go after these two long days of travel," said Emeline.

His face went ruddy. "Aye. Quite far, it may be! But I don't mind."

Mrs. Dawson cleared her throat. "Then be off with you, lad!" She turned to Tobias. "Kindly follow me inside, your lordship. I've ordered food, and my daughter Sarah has already begun preparing your bedchambers. Fresh sheets on the beds!"

As they crossed the broad, flagstone entry hall, Emeline looked around, intrigued. "Can you tell us when Woodcroft Priory was built?"

"Of course I can, miss," she said proudly. "The oldest ruins are said to date back to the 7th century, founded by Clement, a Benedictine monk. It was the early days of Christianity in Britain, I'm told. Later, in about the year 1100, the larger priory was built on the same spot. This house took its place after the Catholic Church was ended in Britain."

Tobias turned to stare at her in surprise. "You are quite a scholar, Mrs. Dawson."

"And why not?" She sent him a quick glance. "I live here. I ought to know the history."

"Indeed," he hastened to add. "And we are very interested in hearing about it."

As they continued on toward the broad staircase, they passed the arched entry to a room where a fire was lit. Emeline couldn't resist pausing to look inside. The dark shelves built into the walls were only partly filled with threadbare volumes. "Is this the library, Mrs. Dawson?"

"Yes, but you can see that most of the books belonging to the duchess's father, Baron Fenwick, have been packed away. It's the coziest room during colder weather, so when we learned you were coming, Mr. Ackerman laid the fire there."

Emeline's ears perked up. "Mr. Ackerman...the gardener?"

"Indeed, miss. Because his lordship resides elsewhere, Mr. Ackerman and I, along with my children Robbie and Sarah, are the only house staff living here."

"We understand that Mr. Ackerman has discovered some artifacts near the ruins," interjected Tobias, "and that he is conducting an excavation of sorts?"

"Calling it an excavation sounds too fancy. I do believe he has accidentally come upon a few items while clearing ground for a new garden, and now he's become quite curious." Mrs. Dawson paused. "Mrs. Peachey told me that was what brought you here, but you'll be disappointed if you think he knows what he's doing."

"That's why we are here," Tobias replied, nodding. "As it happens, I have some experience with such excavations. One is underway on my own property."

"We are most eager to meet Mr. Ackerman," Louise added.

"I see. I'll show you to your rooms, then, and perhaps after you've rested and taken refreshment…" The housekeeper started off toward the stairway, and they had no choice but to follow.

Emeline was about to protest that she would rather speak to Mr. Ackerman first, but Tobias and Louise both sent quelling glances her way. Instead she said nicely, "Thank you, Mrs. Dawson."

Upstairs, the housekeeper showed Tobias into a shadowy and faintly musty bedchamber, assuring him that the sheets were fresh that very hour. From the threshold, Emeline could see that his portmanteau waited on a low bench near the four-poster bed. When Mrs. Dawson frowned and crossed to thrust open the heavy draperies, soft light streamed in.

"That's better! My daughter Sarah isn't used to acting as a proper maid," she explained. "And because we rarely have anyone else in residence, she forgets."

"There is no need to apologize," Tobias assured her. "We three are actually quite capable of looking after ourselves."

They left him then and continued down the corridor to the bedrooms Mrs. Dawson had chosen for Louise and Emeline. The first one, for Louise, had leaf-green walls and a pretty corner desk, and Mrs. Dawson directed Emeline through a connecting door to her own room. She found it surprisingly lovely, painted dusty blue, with two windows that looked out over the ruins to the distant River Alde.

From the bedside, Sarah had just smoothed the last crease on the counterpane of dull gold brocade. "Oh, I beg your pardon, my lady," she murmured.

Mrs. Dawson shook her head at the fragile, fair young woman who looked to be close to Emeline's age. "This is Miss St. Briac."

Sarah smiled at Emeline. "If I can help in any way, miss, please ring."

"Thank you, Sarah. I will!"

Mrs. Dawson made a shooing motion at her daughter. "Go on then. Mrs. Peachey will need your help in the kitchen."

The knowledge that Mrs. Peachey was present in the house, perhaps even preparing their meal, felt deeply reassuring. She could hardly wait to seek out the older woman and ask her a score of questions.

Before long, Mrs. Dawson had gone away, and Emeline was alone for the first time since leaving Chesterfield Street. It was rather a relief to see that the connecting door was closed, and she guessed Louise was resting. Opening her portmanteau, she found the book about ancient coins loaned to her by Antonio Panizzi and sat with it in a chair near the window where the light was best.

The drawings were all so small and minutely detailed, however, that Emeline's attention soon wandered. It was a task for another day, she realized. Standing, she leaned against the casement and looked out at the ruins of the priory. Only a crumbling series of arches remained of the ancient structures Mrs. Dawson had described.

Emeline felt insignificant as she thought of the people who had spent their lives here over the centuries, now lost in the shifting sands of history. What had happened to the original priory that dated back to Anglo-Saxon times? Could Hart's Viking sword, discovered near the ruins, tell a story of an attack? Remembering the terrible Viking raid on Lindisfarne Priory that was carefully recorded in history books, a shiver ran down her back.

Just then, a movement caught her eye from behind one of the arches and a very tall man with the look of a cadaver came into sight, carrying a shovel. He wore a wool cap, pulled low over his brow. Remembering that only a handful of servants lived at Woodcroft Priory, she straightened. Surely this was Cyril Ackerman, the gardener who had discovered the artifacts! Suddenly, all the uncertainty she had felt since arriving at the priory melted away. It seemed the adventure had truly begun.

Without pausing to consider the wisdom of her actions, Emeline hurried out into the corridor, determined to present herself to Mr. Ackerman. However, as she rounded the doorway, she nearly collided with Sarah, who was carrying a stack of towels that tumbled toward the floor.

Emeline caught them in mid-air and handed them back to Sarah. "I am so sorry. I was in a hurry, and I wasn't thinking!"

"Is anything wrong? Did you need help?"

"I think I saw Mr. Ackerman outside and I was rushing down to speak to him, that's all." Emeline gave a wry laugh. "I can be impetuous."

A warm smile lit Sarah's face. "We need a bit of that here, miss."

"May I ask you a question?" Emeline met the maid's brown eyes. "Have you lived here all your life? Did you know the late duchess?"

Sarah nodded. "My mum was born here, too, when Her Grace was just a little girl. My pa was the stable master, but he died." She swallowed. "I did know the duchess, a little. She came here to live for a year or more before she died."

Did that mean that Hart's mother had left his father, and they lived apart? Somehow, having heard about the duke, this did not surprise her. "What was she like?"

"I was no more than twelve when Her Grace passed. Before that she spent most of her time in her rooms." After a pause, Sarah added, "Her Grace certainly doted on Lord Jasper."

"Yes, I imagine so," Emeline murmured, reflecting on the lengths Hart's mother must have gone to in order to keep this property separate from her marriage—and then, later, bequeath it to her second son. Such arrangements were virtually unheard of. "May I ask which bedchamber belonged to the duchess?"

Sarah turned to look down the corridor. "The last door leads to Her Grace's rooms. Since her death, no one is permitted to enter or disturb any of her possessions."

"Not even…Lord Jasper?"

"'Twas his lordship who gave the order," whispered Sarah. "No one goes in except my mum to occasionally dust and tidy up."

"I see." Emeline felt a chill.

"I should get on with my chores before I am missed."

"Yes, and I must go in search of Mr. Ackerman." She reached out to touch Sarah's sleeve. "Thank you! You've been very helpful."

The maid flushed. "It's a pleasure to have someone to talk to, miss."

"For me as well." The words caused Emeline's heart to ache anew for her lost love. "Everything is very different here."

With one last smile and nod, Emeline hurried away down the corridor. On the landing at the top of the stairs, there was a large window that afforded an even better view of the ruins.

Mr. Ackerman was still there, leaning on his shovel. Now she could see that he was staring down into what might be a trench, a smaller version of the one Mr. Cartwright made at Amity Park! Had the gardener begun excavating in earnest, on his own? And if so, what else had he discovered?

Emeline lifted her skirts and fairly flew down the stairs.

CHAPTER 22

As Emeline came down the stairs, she was relieved to find that no one else was about. Retracing her steps to the entry, she emerged onto the gravel drive and made her way around the corner of the manor house to the arched ruins, now silhouetted against the rosy, late afternoon sky.

Spying the tall man partially bent over behind a crumbling stone wall, Emeline called, "Hello! Are you Mr. Ackerman, the gardener?"

He straightened, shading his heavy brow with one canvas-gloved hand. "I am."

She went forward, smiling, and introduced herself, adding, "I am a friend of Lord Hartcliffe, and I have come with my two learned associates to assist with the excavation of this site."

"Assist?" The word rang in the air. "How do I know you are competent, or that you can be trusted?"

"We are antiquarians. Lord Melford has even been conducting an extensive dig on his own estate! And my cousin Louise and I have been assisting Lord Hartcliffe in London, researching the possible origin of the sword discovered here." Then, taking a chance, she added softly, "And I have seen the coin that you sent to London."

Ackerman pushed back his cap, considering. "I see."

"His lordship is traveling on the Continent, but since you are eager to begin digging again before the weather changes, I know he would want us to assist you." Seeing that the gardener remained uncertain, Emeline remembered her secret weapon. "It was Mrs. Peachey's idea for us to come here!"

His gaunt face seemed to relax. "Why didn't you mention Peachey straight away? If she approves, so do I." He pulled off one dirty glove and shook her hand. "It's good to meet you, miss."

"We've just arrived, so my friends are still getting settled, but I cannot rest until I know more," Emeline said, smiling up at him. "Will you enlighten me about your discoveries up to this point?"

"Yes, miss. I'd be glad to."

As she followed him around the corner of the ruins, she was relieved to see that the trench she had glimpsed from the window extended only a few feet into the hillside.

"It all started last spring, when I had a notion to plant some berries here, along the ruins, where they could get the morning sun," Mr. Ackerman explained, pointing toward the River Alde to the east. "The very first day, I came upon corroded pieces of an ancient sword. I felt a chill, miss, and because Lord Jasper was far away in Rome or some such place, I decided to wait for him to return. But I did write a letter."

"His lordship has shown me sketches of the sword."

Ackerman nodded approvingly. "When he returned later this past summer, we dug together a bit more and discovered part of an ancient sword hilt, with markings I'd never seen! His lordship seemed to remember hearing some talk of ancient relics when he was a lad. So, he began looking around in the library and the late duchess's bedchamber, hoping to find a clue. He came upon a little red chest, with a buckle and ring, hidden in the back of her armoire."

"Oh, yes! I have seen it," Emeline exclaimed. "In fact, Mrs. Peachey and I brought it with us from London."

Ackerman nodded and lowered his voice. "We knew then that ours was not the first discovery on this site. Lord Jasper had to travel to London to visit his brother, the duke, but promised, while there, to study the emerging science of archaeology, and determine the best way to proceed." The gardener paused, sighing heavily. "I was surprised to hear that he had departed for the Continent without returning here."

"Never fear, we have come in his place," Emeline assured him, trying to sound more confident than she felt. Kneeling next to the long trough, she touched the sandy soil. "I gather this is the place where you discovered the pieces of the sword. It is a very good thing that you didn't dig deeper. We have special methods and tools to excavate without destroying any of the artifacts, but first there must be real digging. Do you know any young men who would like to help with that stage?"

"Aye, I have two nephews living at the next farm over. I will ask them."

Emeline rose to her feet, tingling with anticipation for the grand adventure that lay ahead. "Excellent! Mrs. Peachey has the funds to pay them." Reaching out, she shook Ackerman's callused hand again. "We shall begin tomorrow morning at first light."

* * *

THE NEXT MORNING, Emeline walked with Louise and Tobias in the hazy glow of dawn, carrying their tools to the excavation site. All three of them were wearing trousers, woolen shirts, suspenders, and sturdy boots.

"I am so excited!" Emeline declared, for perhaps the dozenth time.

Louise reached out to take her hand. "We all are! I haven't felt like this since the day we uncovered that winged pterosaur with Mary Anning. That seems like another lifetime."

"Oh, yes, that was a magical summer. Can you imagine, I was only nine years old! I called it a flying dragon…"

"You were always very precocious, Emmie," Louise said affectionately. "It is no wonder that you have brought us to the brink of an entirely new ancient discovery."

"We mustn't get ahead of ourselves," said Tobias, looking serious. "It may be that others have been here before us, and the best artifacts were looted centuries ago. I am concerned that the belt buckle and ring were found so close to the surface."

He clambered down to take a closer look inside the trench, which only extended a few feet into the hillside.

"What do you think?" Emeline called when she couldn't bear another moment's suspense. "Can we work with this existing trench?"

"I think so." Tobias looked up, shading his eyes. "I wonder if this area might have once been a barrow—one of the burial mounds the Vikings favored for those of high status." He studied the sloping landscape. "Perhaps, over time, it became incorporated into a broader hill. I consulted with Mr. Cartwright before we departed, and he informed me that mound burials were customary in East Anglia centuries ago."

Emeline knew that Suffolk was just one part of the Anglo-Saxon kingdom of East Anglia, which was the stuff of legends and fairy stories. "Isn't it wonderful?"

Even as she spoke voices came to them, and she looked toward the priory to see a pair of young men approaching, each holding a shovel.

"Just in time," Tobias said approvingly. "Come closer, lads. We must dig a trench, searching for the edge of a pit…what we hope will be a grave, or even a burial chamber. You must take care not to dig too forcefully, so as not to cause damage." He paused.

"There may be more than one grave, it's impossible to say at this point."

As the young men began to work, Emeline turned to Tobias. "If we haven't found the burial chamber yet, how have the sword and other artifacts been discovered?"

"I think we cannot know what may have disturbed the remains over the centuries," Tobias said. "Badgers and foxes have doubtless burrowed here. And rabbits cause all manner of chaos in burial mounds, I'm told. Also, robbers could have been here, but we must hope that they did not go far enough."

Louise spoke at last. "Emeline and I have been reading about stratigraphy, wherein the layers of soil and rock are recorded to determine the location of artifacts, or even an ancient grave. If that is possible, it will help to narrow our search."

"Yes, that is excellent." Tobias sent her a warm gaze. "Louise, I think you might be just the person to document the details of our excavation. I brought a journal just for that purpose. What do you say?"

"Oh, yes!" She flushed becomingly. "I should like that very much."

"As you doubtless know from your years with Miss Anning, it is imperative to capture every detail: the exact location, depth, and description of each discovery."

Emeline put an arm around her cousin. "Louise will do a splendid job! And I hope that, once we reach a place where we can work more closely, I can use the archaeological tools you gave me to uncover some of the hidden treasures."

"Of course!" Tobias was pensive as he watched the men dig. "We are only extending Mr. Ackerman's existing trench because some relics have already been discovered there. However, Mr. Cartwright advised me that we may have to dig a second trench into the side of the hill, or even a third, to be certain we are really in the right place. Otherwise, we might completely miss the actual burial chamber." He paused. "If it exists."

Ackerman pursed his dry lips, appearing unimpressed by this line of reasoning. "Oh, there'll be no need for that, my lord. I can feel that this is the right place. And be assured that Lord Jasper agrees."

Emeline's pulse quickened at the mention of Hart. If only he were there, standing beside her with easy assurance in the mellow dawn light. She could easily imagine Hart's crisp blue gaze fixed on the proceedings. But then, a moment later, he would flash a lazy smile her way or offer a remark that would be exactly what she needed to hear. A potent mixture of longing and grief stirred in her heart.

Emeline was roused by the sound of a soft, familiar voice speaking behind her.

"If this one trench is what Lord Jasper would want," said Mrs. Peachey, "I believe that is the course you must follow."

"Certainly." Tobias folded both arms over his burly chest. "For the time being, at least."

* * *

THREE DAYS LATER, Emeline lay wide awake in her bed, too excited by the events of the day to sleep. Her mind went round and round, reliving every moment of work in the trench, from the first scoop of a shovel to the last, when the sun had been setting and young Sam Ackerman came upon a dark rectangle under his feet.

"Something's different!" called the boy.

A ladder had been placed at one end of the deepening trench, and when Tobias climbed down and saw the darker rectangle of soil, he drew a sharp breath. "There could be a burial chamber below us…or perhaps it's just a place where dirt was backfilled from the robbers. We'll find out tomorrow, when the light is better."

Now, as the clock struck twelve midnight, Emeline imagined

the thrilling events the next day might hold. Imagined herself using her tools, gently troweling around a half-buried artifact… losing herself in the painstaking unveiling of layers of history.

She told herself to close her eyes. *Go to sleep, or you won't be of any use tomorrow!*

Moonbeams crept ghostlike through gaps in the curtains. As one streamed across Emeline's pillow, it seemed that she might reach out to find Hart lying next to her. She ached to be in his arms again, but nearly as powerful was the longing to share with him every single thing that had happened at Woodcroft Priory.

Pain squeezed her heart and one hot tear spilled onto the pillow. At least, if she never saw Hart again, she would have the vivid memories of their lovemaking to carry with her. She would live an independent, celibate life, for no one else could ever take his place.

A muted tap sounded at the connecting door. "Emmie?"

"I'm awake," she called softly. "Come and join me!"

A moment later, Louise was crossing the room, slim and ethereal in her white nightgown. "I can't sleep," she confessed as she sat down on the edge of the bed. "You, too?"

Emeline sat up, nodding, and they embraced. "My mind is in a whirl."

"Are you thinking of the excavation?" Louise looked directly into her eyes. "Or…of Hart?"

"Both." Tears threatened, yet it was liberating to share her feelings with someone she could trust. "This is his mother's family property, and I yearn to tell him everything that is happening."

"Perhaps you miss him in…other ways as well," Louise suggested gently.

"It is a kind of grief," she admitted, drawing a painful breath. "But of course, Hart is alive somewhere in the world. So I will confess that my grief is tinged with something I should not properly speak of."

"Of course you can say the word to me, Emmie."

Emeline raised her eyes, smiling as her cheeks grew warm. "*Lust.*"

"You are a minx," laughed Louise.

"That's just what Hart calls me!" Feeling better, she dried her eyes on the sheet's embroidered hem and looked at Louise. "It's so confusing. Part of me hates him for letting me fall in love with him and then leaving me with only a note. But then I remember how many times Hart warned me to stay away. Even that last night! I thought I could change his mind…" She shook her head and sighed. "Let us talk of you instead, dear cousin. Is it only the excitement of the dig that keeps you awake?"

"No." Color stained her cheeks. "Other thoughts do intrude."

Unable to help herself, Emeline prompted, "Perhaps you feel drawn to Tobias?"

"I do have those moments, I confess. But my heart has been otherwise engaged for more than two decades, and those tender feelings cannot be abandoned overnight."

Drat! She badly wanted to urge Louise to forget about Charles. It wouldn't do, though. It came to Emeline that her shy cousin might use her unrequited love for Charles as a shield, allowing her to avoid the attentions of other men, but Emeline couldn't say any of this aloud.

Instead she murmured, "No, I can see that it would be diffi-cult to change the direction of one's heart."

Louise sighed. "We both must try to sleep. If there is a discovery behind that rectangle of dark earth, tomorrow will prove to be a very exciting day!"

"Yes," Emeline agreed with a wry smile. "We should be thinking about archaeology, not men."

"Well said, cousin."

After Louise returned to her own room, Emeline lay back and closed her eyes. *Sleep.* But Hart's arrogantly handsome face would not be banished from her mind…or her aching heart.

Where are you tonight, my love?

* * *

SEATED in the coffee room of his favorite inn on the Left Bank, Hart distractedly broke off one more piece of warm baguette, spread butter, and ate it with a hot cup of *café au lait*. Outside, the River Seine glowed pink in the dawn light.

"Woof," came Monte's muffled reminder from under the table.

"You have already devoured a boiled egg and two chicken hearts," he told the dog. "I suppose you think you should have my baguette as well!"

Monte replied by laying a paw on Hart's boot.

"No. Learn to be content with what you have." He seemed unable to keep the harsh edge from his voice. "You should be grateful I let you accompany us at all."

William watched him from across the table. "Your lordship does not seem to be quite yourself," he ventured.

"Indeed?" He tried to smile but felt his mouth twist in mockery. "Who exactly do I seem to be?"

The manservant was not put off. "A discontented sort of nobleman, I suppose."

"But that is just who I have always been."

"My lord," William dared to persevere, "these past few weeks in London, my sister and I watched you undergo a change."

"I have no time for this conversation." Hart pushed back from the table. "We have lingered in Paris long enough. If we are ever to reach Lisbon, we must depart. As it is, unless we travel at a breakneck pace, we may not arrive for another fortnight."

William opened his mouth, then, thankfully, shut it again. "As you wish, Lord Jasper."

Rising from his chair, Hart froze at the sound of a familiar English-speaking voice. "Do you hear that? The boy who is with the landlord—"

Before William could reply, Bertram, the groom who had recently been hired at the Wigmore Street house, burst into the coffee room.

"Milord! I've *found* you at last!" cried the boy, seemingly on the verge of tears.

"You have indeed—but how? And what the devil are you doing here?" Even as Hart spoke, he realized that there was only one person who had knowledge of his preferred lodging places between London and Lisbon.

Peachey.

"I've pursued you from the priory, across the channel to France just to deliver this letter, milord!" exclaimed Bertram, hurrying forward to place the somewhat crumpled envelope in his hand.

His heart clenched as he broke the seal and began to read.

CHAPTER 23

Hart would have recognized Peachey's neat, cramped hand if he'd glimpsed the letter from across the room, for he'd been reading messages from her since he was in short coats.

Lord Jasper, I regret to write to you in this manner, but Miss St. Briac's welfare is too important...

For a moment, Hart couldn't breathe. Something had happened to Emeline, curse it, and he was to blame!

Pardon my plain speaking, my lord, but did you give no thought to the implications when you took the girl's innocence and then rode away in the night?

A black wave of guilt and anger swamped him. Never in all the years since he'd left Oxford had Peachey dared to raise the subject of his amorous encounters, not even when he brought a woman home to his own bed and he knew she must have heard them. Why *now*, when he hadn't wanted Emeline there at all, had warned her repeatedly that only heartbreak could come of it? Somehow, he expected Peachey to understand that he had only gone away to spare Emeline from any further pain at his hands.

Perhaps, before you decamped to the Continent, you did not consider that this young lady might find herself in a delicate condition? I suggest that you consider it now, my lord! And you should further be aware that Miss St. Briac and her cousin have come with me to Woodcroft Priory. In your absence, they kindly volunteered to assist Mr. Ackerman with the dig.

Hart barely saw Peachey's signature at the bottom of the brief missive. The room seemed to tilt as he sank back down into his chair.

"Lord Jasper, has something happened?" A hand touched his arm, and he looked up into William's anxious gray eyes.

"No one has been injured, if that's what you're asking."

"But—something is clearly amiss. Must we return to England?"

Feeling as if his head was in a vise, Hart closed his eyes and groaned. "Possibly." The bloody priory was the last place he wanted to be, especially with Emeline. She didn't belong there with all his family ghosts. "I need a few minutes to think. Bring me a brandy."

William drew back and blinked. "Really, my lord, the sun has not fully risen yet."

"Perhaps you did not hear me correctly." Hart sent him a dangerous look.

Turning to Bertram, who stood quaking near the door, William ordered, "Fetch a brandy for his lordship!"

Monte added three sharp barks to the conversation, jumped onto Hart's lap, and boldly licked his cheek.

* * *

The digging at Woodcroft Priory proceeded at a snail's pace, or so it seemed to Emeline.

"I had forgotten how many long hours we spent with Miss Anning as she patiently revealed fossils encased in rock for millennia," she remarked to Louise as the excavation entered its second week. The two of them sat at a small table placed under an elm tree so those who labored in the nearby trench might enjoy a respite.

"When one is lost in the work, time becomes a blur, but this initial stage is always trying," agreed Louise. "I hope that soon enough we shall uncover some real artifacts, not just the bits of pottery and glass we've come across so far."

Mrs. Peachey was walking across the grass holding a tea tray that looked enormous against her tiny frame. "I see I am just in time," she called.

Emeline gladly ate a biscuit and drank the strong, hot tea with milk that Mrs. Peachey prepared for her, but then she gave up her chair to Tobias and went back to work. The first dark rectangle of earth they'd discovered days ago had yielded only a few shards of bone and some bits of colored glass, causing Tobias to warn that it was another sign that robbers had beaten them there long ago. "It is said that Henry VII sent men to explore the mounds along this stretch of coastline, and Queen Elizabeth's astrologer visited as well."

"That doesn't mean they located a burial chamber, or even all the graves," Emeline had insisted.

Now, she climbed back down the ladder into the trench, which was so deep now that she had to stand on tiptoe to see over the edge. After the men finished digging each day, it was Emeline's practice to spend time gently troweling the far edges of the trench to check for any important new signs. First one place, then another, working her way up and down with the edge of her trowel, looking for anything that didn't quite fit with the surrounding area.

The work had an almost hypnotic effect on Emeline. She could lose herself in it, imagining the moment when she might come upon...

"Oh!" she gasped softly. The edge of her trowel had caught on an object, and her heart kicked up. In the distance, she could hear Tobias and Louise talking, occasionally laughing.

Scrape, scrape. The odors of rotted wood and soil filled her nostrils. After a few minutes, Emeline realized that her great find seemed to be bits of decayed timber. This felt anti-climactic, and yet it quickly came to her that the wood could be the remains of a casket or...even something more substantial.

"Tobias! Can you please come here?" Emeline heard the slight tremor in her voice.

When Tobias descended into the trench and crossed to look over her shoulder, he let out a low whistle. "By Jove," he muttered. "You may have discovered the burial chamber itself."

Her heart was thumping now. "How thrilling!"

"What is it?" Louise's pale face appeared above them, peering over the edge of the trench.

"Your cousin is a proper archaeologist!" declared Tobias. "Look at this!" He pointed to the place where the soil was stained in the shape of a beam. "The wood itself has decomposed, but it left a mark behind."

"I'm coming down," cried Louise, waving her journal in the air. "I must record the event and the description of the find."

He shook his big head. "The light is going. Let us call it a day and begin early tomorrow." Smiling up at her, he added, "You can write down the details you know up to this point."

"I can't imagine how I will sleep tonight," Emeline murmured.

Once the trio were standing together again on the lawn, and Mrs. Peachey came to join them, Emeline thought of Hart.

"We must get word to his lordship, as quickly as possible," she said to the older woman. "It's possible that we have found the burial chamber!"

After all that Mrs. Peachey had done to get them to come to Woodcroft Priory, Emeline expected a stronger reaction to this news. "That's good to know," Mrs. Peachey said, pursing her lips. "But we do not know quite where Lord Jasper might be, and even if we did, he cannot return so easily."

Her heart sank. "But if there is a burial chamber, I feel certain he would want to know! It wouldn't be right to open it without him."

Mrs. Peachey would not meet her eyes. "If that was truly what he wanted, miss, he would not have gone to Lisbon."

The full import of her words surged through her. Hart had made a choice to travel thousands of miles away, to take his pick of beautiful, willing women along the way, to pursue a life without *her*. Perhaps he didn't feel worthy of Emeline's love, but that didn't change the fact that he had left her.

"So…you are saying that we should carry on without him," she whispered.

"I am." Mrs. Peachey reached out to clasp her hand, and now she was looking directly into Emeline's eyes. "It's just that…I happen to know, it will take more than an archaeological discovery to bring Lord Jasper back to Woodcroft Priory."

* * *

"I DIDN'T EXPECT it to progress quite so slowly," Emeline said to Mr. Ackerman on the third morning after she had uncovered evidence of wood in the trench. But even as she stood with the gardener, drinking a cup of coffee before climbing down the ladder, she knew that it had to be this way. If they rushed to reveal too much too quickly, the few fragments of wood might crumble to dust.

"I've a feelin' about today, miss," said Ackerman in his flat Suffolk accent. A smile flickered at his mouth.

"Do you? I'd better get at it, then!"

The entire shape of the trench had changed, widening considerably at one end as Tobias and Emeline, with help from Cyril Ackerman and his nephews Sam and Tom, had carefully followed the outline stained on the soil from a wooden structure. Now it was time for the more detailed work of troweling and sieving.

As the morning stretched on, the hazy chill of dawn was broken by intervals of sun. Emeline wore a tweed cap over her thick ebony locks that she had pinned up in a coil atop her head. Gloves protected her hands, but there was always dirt under her fingernails when she bathed each night.

Tobias had decided that they might begin to search deeper into what appeared to be the burial chamber. None of them dared to hope they would find anything, however. Even if robbers hadn't gotten there first, there might not have ever been anything of value in the chamber. Perhaps it had all turned to dust, even the body.

Then Tobias gave a yell and Emeline looked over to see him holding up a large, corroded iron hook. "It must have been attached to the inner wall!" He pointed then to what appeared to be the edge of a vessel peeping from the dirt. It would take time to reveal the entire piece without causing any damage.

"It's so exciting," called Emeline. "And it certainly tells us we are on course."

Louise went to join Tobias, all the while writing in her book about the time and exact location of each find and adding sketches. She pointed to the piece Tobias was uncovering with his trowel. "Perhaps that will be a hanging bowl or a flagon."

They were smiling at each other, heads bent close together. Emeline stayed where she was, leaving them the space to share the thrill of this initial discovery. The bond between Louise and Tobias was clear, forged quietly over time rather than in a few moments of heady romance. She was happy for them, of course she was! Yet Emeline's heart stung at the realization that her own love was lost to her.

It was a relief to turn back to her work on the other side of the pit. Time passed in a blur, and Emeline barely noticed when Sarah appeared to say that luncheon would be served in a quarter hour. Soon after, Louise tapped Emeline on the shoulder.

"Tobias and I are going in to wash and eat."

"I'll stay here for a bit," Emeline said. "I think I am close to a discovery of my own."

Louise smiled and reached out to brush some dirt from her nose. "Don't forget, my dear, you must eat, too."

When they had gone off and Emeline was alone, a sudden wave of melancholy washed over her. The time was coming to plan the future. When her task here was ended, she would return to London and find real work so that she might craft a life for herself. If the British Museum would not grant her employment, perhaps she might tutor young women in the sciences—and if a way forward did not present itself, Emeline would carve one out herself.

Tears stung her eyes, and she wiped them away. It seemed she had been right all along...life was so much simpler without the confusion and heartache of men.

Giving her head a shake, she returned to her troweling. There was an area at her feet where the dirt seemed a bit softer, and as she worked at it with the flat edge of the blade, a rim of greenish glass appeared. Her first thought was that it was a bottle, dropped in recent decades, but more troweling revealed that the piece was more elaborate. A conical beaker or goblet, with claw-shaped blobs around the circumference, and smaller ones encircling the base! Each green glass claw was edged with tiny ridges. No sooner did Emeline release the first beaker from the soil and begin brushing away the dirt, than she glimpsed a second one peeking out nearby.

Her senses swam, and again she felt as if she were looking through a window in time. Who were the people who had lived here? She imagined a man and woman drinking together from these colorful, intricately made goblets. How long ago had their fingers touched the same places as hers? It tore at Emeline's heart that the one person she longed to share this moment with was far away, making a new life without her.

Dimly, she became aware of the sound of hoofbeats. After replacing the goblet and covering it with a layer of soil, Emeline got to her feet and looked out above the edge of the trench. A tall, dark man with wide shoulders was riding toward her on a fine chestnut stallion.

"It is an illusion," she whispered to herself and closed her eyes. When she opened them, she saw Hart swinging gracefully down from the horse's back and striding toward her, even more splendid than she remembered. *It cannot be...*

CHAPTER 24

No matter how many times Hart rode up to Woodcroft Priory, the same tangle of emotions waged war inside him. And today, once again, he struggled to suppress an urge to turn back.

There were too damned many memories.

His mother, bringing him here with Austell when he was barely five years old, tucking him into bed, and suddenly beginning to weep. *Darling, no matter what happens, this place will belong to you.* She had rushed from the room, leaving him alone in the dark, surrounded by strange shadows and sounds, to wonder why Mama was crying.

Hart narrowed his eyes and surveyed the sprawling brick manor house. How many times over his lifetime had he witnessed her tears? It seemed she always saved them for their visits, just the two of them, to the priory. *They have taken everything from you, but you'll always have Woodcroft,* she had whispered on her deathbed.

He'd wanted to shake his head. No. Bloody hell, no thank you! She'd found a way to leave him a portion of her own inheritance, and that he could use, but not this place with its ghosts and veil of sadness.

And now *Emeline* was here! Peachey's letter seemed to be burning through his pocket. The sun was low over the River Alde as Hart rounded the drive, compelled by a force he didn't understand to see the ruins where the new excavation must be in progress.

To his shock, he saw that the shallow trough that had existed in August was now a deep trench, with a much wider opening at one end. Just as Hart reined in and swung down from the saddle, an all too familiar face peeped above the edge of the pit.

His heart wrenched at the sight of her, smudged with dirt and utterly captivating. A tweed cap was pulled low over her hair, and for an instant Hart's memory inhaled the fragrance of her gleaming locks, flowing over his pillow.

Emeline blinked, shaking her head, as if she doubted that he could be real. She glanced around, seemingly trapped, but Hart was at the edge of the trench and then he jumped easily down to stand before her.

"I thought," she faltered, "I might never see you again."

"I was trying to do the right thing for you," he said roughly, pulling her into his arms.

Before he could cover her mouth with his, she came up on her toes to meet him halfway. *Oh, God.* She was ambrosia. Salty, dirty, so delicious he could barely stand it. Opening to his questing tongue, tasting him in return, pressing against him as if she could meld their bodies.

"Oh...I missed you so," Emeline confessed when at last they broke the kiss.

All his long-honed instincts flared, warning him that this was very thin ice. He glanced away. "You are a bit mad, my sweet minx."

She was watching him. "There is so much to tell you, to show you! Hart, we have discovered the burial chamber. I wanted to send word immediately, but Mrs. Peachey seemed to think that was not enough to bring you home."

"Peachey never gives away her hand," he said with a twisted smile. "She told you that because she had already summoned me with urgent news I could not ignore."

Emeline took a step back toward the wall of earth. Her breasts pressed against the rough cotton of the shirt that tucked into her trousers. He took in her suspenders and sturdy mud-caked shoes. "I see you are a proper antiquarian, my dear."

"I already had these clothes. Sometimes I wore them while at Lyme Regis, with Miss Anning." Her chin went up in a way he recognized, her gaze fixed on his face. "What did Mrs. Peachey write to you that was so compelling?"

"She merely told me what I should have already suspected." The words seemed jammed in his throat. "I have come to…do the right thing."

"What can you mean?" Her violet eyes were wide, as if he was speaking a foreign language.

"Surely you can guess?" Hart coughed. "I mean to marry you."

Devil take it, now she looked as if she was going to cry but not tears of joy. "Do the right thing…and marry me? For what reason?"

"Peachey has made me realize that there could be consequences to our—" He broke off. "Uh, interlude back in London, and of course she is right. If we are going to be…parents, then there is nothing for it." Every awkward word sounded as if it was wrung from him by force.

Emeline seemed to grow paler as she took another step back, away from him. "My lord, to receive such a heartfelt proposal of marriage, in this romantic setting… It is the stuff of a girl's dreams."

She narrowed her eyes as she spoke, and he heard the slight razor's edge beneath her words. "Emeline," he coaxed.

"Oh, no, please, you have said quite enough!" Now she

marched back up to him and poked one grimy finger into his chest. "Clearly you are suffering, but you must not fret about doing the *right thing*! Since our interlude, as you so tenderly call it, I have had my monthly flow, so your great sacrifice is no longer needed."

Oddly enough, her words did not bring the surge of relief he might have expected. "Now see here! Do you mean to castigate me for coming back in what I believed was your hour of need?"

Emeline was trembling. "No, I castigate you because you are just like other men and I was a fool to hope otherwise! You took it upon yourself to decide what was best for me without any regard for my own wishes or feelings." Her voice shook with fury. "Furthermore, you are just like Papa, who secretly enlisted your help managing *my* life— because clearly I was incapable of making my own decisions!"

Good God. His heart seemed to stop beating. "You know about that."

"Indeed." Unshed tears shone in her eyes. "Now you may breathe easy, my lord, since there is no need for a forced wedding. You are truly free! Goodbye."

Hart stared as she walked to the ladder, her back straight, and climbed out of the trench, leaving him to stand alone in the gathering darkness.

* * *

Emeline was pacing back and forth in her bedroom when a tentative knock sounded at the connecting door. A moment later, Louise peeked in.

"Hello! Sorry to push in, but I couldn't wait to speak to you." She came across the room and reached for Emeline's cold hands. "Am I going mad, or did I see Hart outside on the lawn a few minutes ago? Someone who looked exactly like him was walking a horse toward the stables."

"You aren't going mad, but I think I may be," Emeline said, her voice shaking. "Oh, Louise, we had the most hideous scene! He came down into the trench and announced that he had come back from Europe to *do the right thing* and marry me!"

"What!" After pulling Emeline over to sit beside her on the edge of the bed, Louise embraced her. "Is he saying this because he feels guilty for…taking your innocence?"

"Oh, no! It's because Mrs. Peachey seems to have written to him and implied that I am with child!" She laughed a trifle hysterically. "You should have seen his face. One would think that he was being pressured to go into battle, facing torture and certain death."

Louise looked thoughtful. "At least he didn't ignore her letter. At least he came back."

"Next *you* will say that he was doing the right thing!" She jumped to her feet and began to pace in front of her cousin.

"I take it that you refused his proposal?" Louise murmured cautiously.

"Of course I did, especially since he only offered it because he thought I was pregnant! Don't you see, he is just like all the rest, telling me what is best for me without one moment's consideration for what *I* want. Men like that are the very reason we have sworn to remain unmarried."

"But, Emmie, you love him."

"Yes." She squeezed her eyes closed against the sting of tears. "That's what makes my choice so clear. If I grasped at this proposal, knowing that he only asked out of a sense of guilty obligation, I would always suspect that Hart felt trapped and wished he were free again."

* * *

HART SAT ALONE, brooding, at the long, scrubbed table in the kitchen while Peachey made the preparations for the household's supper.

"You must eat, Lord Jasper." She set a plate of roasted chicken, potatoes, and green beans in front of him. "You've had a long journey."

"I'll have brandy," Hart said roughly. "Give this to William—or Monte!"

"My lord, I must insist." She sent him one of the warning looks that had always worked when he was a boy. Next, she'd be cutting the chicken and trying to feed it to him.

He pushed the plate away. "I've seen Emeline. What made you think that she was with child?"

"Did I say that she was? I think not. Only that it was possible."

"You know perfectly well that you implied it!" His voice rose. "In such a way that I assumed she must have *told* you!"

In spite of his outrage, the housekeeper remained maddeningly calm. "I wanted to bring you home to deal with the situation like the man I know you to be. When I considered the matter, it seemed that was the only thing I could write that would definitely achieve my goal."

"I see. But it was a trick." Hart wanted to add that he'd made an ass of himself that day with Emeline and now there was no repairing it.

"Not really. For all I knew, it was true. And if it had been true, you needed to come home." She paused. "In any case, I didn't think you would want to leave Lord Melford in charge on your estate."

"Melford!" he flared, remembering the tender moment he had witnessed between Tobias and Emeline. "What the deuce is he doing here?"

Peachey was unruffled. "His lordship kindly offered to assist the two young women with the excavation." She paused. "I can see that you suspect him of making overtures toward Miss

Emeline, but I have seen no sign of that. Only friendship between the two of them."

Hart snorted. "I suppose you advise me not to call him out."

"Indeed, unless you wish to put the lady off completely." Peachey nudged the plate closer again just as Monte came prancing into the kitchen. "Now eat your dinner, Lord Jasper, and I'll order you a hot bath. You'll need to be at your best in the days ahead."

Hart stared after her, wondering what the devil she meant by that.

* * *

THE NEXT MORNING, when Emeline went out to the excavation site, Hart was already there, chatting with Tobias, Louise, and Mr. Ackerman. In spite of herself, she felt her heart skip a beat at the sight of him standing near the arched ruins, bathed in hazy dawn light. He looked travel-worn, yet more appealing than ever. His tousled dark hair glinted with more silver than she remembered, and there were worry lines about his eyes.

"I've just brought Hart up to date on all that we've discovered here," Tobias announced as Emeline drew near. "We are about to go down into the pit so he can see for himself."

"Ah. Good morning, Miss St. Briac," Hart said, his blue eyes lingering on her face.

"Good morning." She gave him a prim nod and looked at Tobias. "I have something of my own to show you when you are free."

Tobias blinked, smiling. "Splendid! Let us go down then."

Emeline and Louise descended the ladder first, and as the two men followed them, she heard Hart say, "This trench is deeper than I realized, and the Suffolk soil is sandy. There should be wooden supports, especially at this end, where the passage is so narrow."

"Yes," Tobias agreed. "You are quite right. Ackerman can set his nephews on it as soon as we finish here."

"The sooner the better," Hart said. "I'll speak to him myself."

They crossed to the more open area where the excavation of the burial chamber was in progress, and Tobias began relating to Hart the story of Emeline's first discovery of the stained soil, and then the iron hook and the copper flagon still being uncovered. Next to them, Louise made notes in her book.

Emeline stood apart, feeling torn. Since they first arrived at the priory, she had ached to have Hart there as well, yet this new reality was bittersweet. It seemed that she had idealized him, dreaming of him at night, remembering each exquisite moment of their lovemaking, imagining that only Hart, who was lost to her, could understand her completely.

But now, in the wake of his return and the terrible moments when he had announced that he would marry her if *there is nothing for it*, her love for him seemed tarnished. Emeline shivered in the damp cold and wrapped both arms around herself. She should have faced facts upon discovering that Hart was helping her father to manipulate her! Hadn't she always sworn that she would never marry a man like Papa?

"Emeline?" Tobias's voice broke into her revery, and she looked up to find the others watching her. "What was it you wanted to show us?"

"Oh, yes." Sternly, she reminded herself of the serious work that had so absorbed her just before Hart appeared yesterday to upend her world. "I found something important."

Emeline led them over to the place where she had uncovered the green glass beaker. Before leaving the trench, she had tucked it back into the space where it had originally been and patted a thin layer of dirt over the top to keep it safe.

"It's really quite amazing," Emeline said, glancing up before she brushed the soil away and held up the glass goblet with its claw decorations.

"Goodness!" exclaimed Louise. "I never imagined that the brutish Vikings could be so artistic."

Hart held out his hand, and Emeline found herself setting the goblet in his palm. The barest brush of his fingers against hers sent a warning tingle through her body.

Holding the piece to the light, he blew away more of the dirt that was caked into each tiny crevice. Sunlight shone dimly through tiny bubbles within the pale green glass.

"What does this mean?" wondered Tobias. "Could the grave be Roman? Or medieval, perhaps?

"When did glassblowing even come along?" asked Louise.

After a moment, Hart said, "I once saw a similar claw beaker in Germany. It was said to be more than a thousand years old." He paused. "Seventh century, in fact."

"But that would mean the Dark Ages!" protested Tobias. "We all know that British civilization took a massive step backward after the Romans packed up and left."

Emeline spoke up. "Perhaps we don't understand the Dark Ages as well as we thought! Meanwhile, there is more." With that, she pointed to the edge of the second goblet that protruded from the dirt.

"By Jove, another one!" Tobias blinked in amazement. Out came his trowel and he went to work with the fine edge of the blade, wedging away bits of soil to gradually reveal the matching beaker. Louise perched on a small step carved into the side of the trench, watching him as she recorded the details in her book.

Hart reached into Emeline's case of tools, availed himself of her pastry brush, and began cleaning the first green glass beaker. She walked over and tapped his shoulder.

"Excuse me, but I would like a private word with you." She glanced up, toward the ground above the trench.

One of his dark brows flicked up. "Of course."

Emeline went ahead of him up the ladder. When they were

both standing next to the crumbling arches of the old priory, Hart turned to face her.

"It's amazing what you have uncovered," he said. "You've done excellent work."

"Thank you." Trying to resist the powerful tug of his attraction, Emeline stepped backward. "Now that you see how well it is going here, you may feel free to return to Lisbon."

He gave a short laugh. "Is that what you wanted to say? You are dismissing me? Perhaps you have forgotten that this estate, including the excavation site, are my property."

Her entire body felt alive in a way she knew to be dangerous. "If you intend to remain, working on the dig, I must return to London. I have plans, you see, and it's just as well that I get on with them before winter descends."

"Are you really this angry with me?" His dark hand reached out to grasp her arm. In spite of the chilly air, Emeline felt the heat of his touch through her tweed jacket. "Fine. If you insist on ending even our friendship, so be it."

Their *friendship*? "I thought you had already done that when you rode off to Lisbon in the dead of night, while I was asleep in your bed!"

"*Touché.*" Pain flashed in his eyes. "Perhaps I can never make you understand."

"I assure you, I have come to understand all too well."

"Then, you are right, one of us should go, and of course it should be me. You've done such fine work on the dig, I hope that the three of you will carry on as long as you care to remain." Releasing her arm, Hart added, "I will tell William to pack our things."

Emeline turned away to hide her own tears and hurried back toward the trench. Thankful that Louise and Tobias were still busy at the other end of the site, she set her boots against the ladder rungs and descended blindly. Once safely hidden from

Hart's view, she pressed her face against the cold wall of earth. Would this grief twisting her heart ever end?

Opening her eyes, she glimpsed what appeared to be a row of four amber and lapis beads protruding slightly from the dirt in front of her. No sooner had she lifted her hand to touch them than a sound like thunder filled her senses.

Emeline was swept by a chilling sense of doom. She glanced up toward the sky just as the steep walls of the trench gave way. The world went black as a massive, rumbling cascade of sand, chalk, and loam buried her alive.

CHAPTER 25

*H*art turned to see the trench wall shudder and collapse, pouring down over the ladder and every-thing in its path. *Please God, not Emeline...* His heart threatened to burst as he dashed to the edge of the pit, which was now a raw wound in the earth.

Dropping to his knees, Hart scanned the site, praying to see her safe. Tobias and Louise were scrambling over from the other side, but there was no sign of Emeline. *She's under there. Buried!* No sound, no cry or movement, could be heard from the giant pile of rubble below, only a soft hiss of the settling soil. *She is smothering!*

"Emeline!" His voice was wracked with pain and fear.

In the next instant, Hart jumped into the pit, heedless of any danger that there could be a second collapse. Tobias came up beside him, holding a spade. Moments later, Ackerman and his nephews were scrambling down to join them, everyone shouting.

"Careful with the spades!" ordered Hart. "And no shovels! Use your hands if possible. There is a live woman under there!"

The woman I love, cried his heart.

He plunged his own fingers into the wet soil and began

digging. Each second that ticked by seemed an eternity. How long had Emeline been buried, deprived of oxygen, crushed under the weight of the damp, ancient earth?

With a fury born of terror, Hart clawed at the shockingly heavy, chalky soil. His arms burned, but he could not slow his pace. Someone was shouting Emeline's name, and it came to him that the voice was his own.

"Don't give up! Emeline, I love you!"

Behind him, Louise's voice broke through the melee. "She knows, Hart. She knows that you love her."

Just then a bloodless, mud-caked white fingertip appeared, and Hart gave a ragged sob. "We're coming, my darling! Hang on!"

Tobias was beside him, carefully moving the soil with a trowel, while Hart used his bare hands to gradually uncover first Emeline's limp arm, and then her shoulder. At last he saw the line of her jaw emerge from the earth and then he used his fingers to carefully reveal her mouth, nose, eyes. The sight of her, white and still as a corpse, compounded his fear.

"Emeline, it's me, Hart. Please, open your eyes. Breathe for me." It seemed that her skin took on a bluish cast even as he spoke. There was no time to reveal more of her, not yet. Hart lightly pinched her chin with his thumb and forefinger to open her mouth. Covering her gritty lips with his own mouth, he exhaled, then paused to press with both hands on her cold sternum. Again. Finally, breathing for a second time into her mouth, he felt her chest shudder.

"She's alive," he managed to choke, giving way at last to tears. "Alive!"

As Emeline's eyelashes fluttered open at last, she coughed and soil came to her lips. Other voices were exclaiming in joy and relief, but as Emeline gazed up at Hart, it seemed they were alone in all the world.

* * *

WHEN EMELINE OPENED her eyes again later that afternoon, she was wearing a soft cotton nightgown and tucked in under a dull gold counterpane. Before she could get her bearings, a hand squeezed hers. For a moment, she dared to hope it might be Hart.

"You're awake." It was Louise, sitting at the bedside.

"How…" She looked down at her clean body and the nightgown covering it.

"Sarah and I bathed you with a sponge and a basin and then dressed you for bed. You seemed to be somewhat awake, yet not really aware of what was happening."

"Oh, yes, I think I do remember now." She tried to smile. "A little."

"You must rest." Louise reached out to smooth her brow. "As Hart said, you've been through hell."

"I hope I never go there again," Emeline murmured ruefully. "I thought I had died."

"I know. But don't worry, you are very much alive! You only need rest. Sleep."

She wanted to ask about Hart but couldn't seem to keep her eyes open.

* * *

EMELINE NEXT AWOKE to find evening shadowing her bedroom in shades of plum and gray. A comforting fire crackled in the grate. Hearing a male voice speaking from the direction of the doorway, she turned her head on the pillow. Her pulse quickened. Could it be Hart?

"I am putting new safety rules into place for the dig site." He was standing in the corridor, only a sliver of his back visible through the partially open bedroom door.

"No one must be down in the pit alone," Hart was continuing.

"Last night, when I arrived at dusk, Emeline was there alone, presumably discovering her green glass beaker. If the walls had collapsed then, she would doubtless be dead today."

"You're right of course." It was Tobias, sounding a trifle defensive. "But Louise and I were simply going inside to prepare for dinner. It was Emeline's idea to stay on a while longer. She can be stubborn."

"I can assure you, I shall inform her of the new rules as well." He paused. "In addition, I noticed that the 'spoil heaps' were very near the far end of the trench, where the collapse occurred, and I suspect that weight nearby put even more stress on the trench wall. Going forward, when more digging occurs, I want those piles of discarded soil to be moved further away from the site." He paused. "There is more, but I'll save it for tomorrow."

Muffled words of parting, then she heard the door click.

When Emeline next opened her eyes, the room was dark except for a cozy fire burning in the grate and an oil lamp flickering beside her bed.

A deep male voice murmured, "Ah, there she is."

Her heart soared. "Oh! It's you…" Hart stood above her like a vision, reaching out to smooth stray curls from her brow. Perhaps she *was* dreaming.

There was no trace of cynicism in his smile. "Of course it's me."

"I thought…" Their last harsh conversation echoed in her memory. "You are leaving soon."

"Leave? Nonsense." His expression was so tender, Emeline wondered if she were dreaming. "How do you feel? Hungry?"

Something smelled very good. Her mouth watered. "Yes."

"Splendid. I've brought your dinner." Hart was watching her. "Can you sit up? I'll help you."

Emeline felt weak, as if her body belonged to someone else, but once he had propped pillows behind her and lifted her up against them, she was better. Moments later, he placed a dinner tray on her lap. The gold-edged plate held a savory roasted partridge, buttered noodles, and some glazed carrots. On the bedside table, Hart pointed out a small glass of wine and another of water.

"Peachey insisted on the noodles, even though Mrs. Dawson wanted to make rice for you. I predict a battle for control of the kitchen."

"That should be interesting." She couldn't help smiling. The food tasted so good, and Hart had perched on the edge of the bed rather like a concerned lover, casually chatting as she ate. Could this be real? No doubt he was just being kind to her because of the accident. "Thank you for dinner. And, of course, for saving me." She paused, savoring a last bite of carrots. "At least, I assume you must have done. I really don't remember anything after we… exchanged harsh words and I went down the ladder."

His face looked more serious than she could ever remember. "I must say something to you."

Emeline put down her fork. Suddenly the last thing she wanted to do was sleep, and even the last vestiges of her hunger receded to the background. "I am listening."

"You were nearly killed today when the walls of the trench collapsed on you."

She nodded. "I felt that. Perhaps it was a dream, but at some point, I think I was leaving my body."

"Oh, God." Hart flinched, as if in pain, before wrapping his warm hand around hers. "Emeline, I thought I had lost you, and I knew regret beyond anything I could imagine. Regret for every cynical word I ever spoke to you, for every time I pushed you away!" He raked his free hand through disheveled hair. "But thank God, you are alive and I have been given a second chance. I just pray it's not too late."

Tears blurred her vision as all her own conflicted feelings stirred to life. "Too late for what?"

"To say that I was a fool, telling you that you are better off without me. That I don't deserve you. I was *afraid*. God only knows where it comes from, but I've spent a lifetime pretending I don't give a damn about loving other people."

"Afraid…" Emeline whispered the word, amazed that he was exposing himself this way.

"It's a terrible skill I've perfected, hiding behind the mask of a libertine." The familiar mocking smile twisted his mouth, then it was gone. "But I am done with that now. When you were buried under the weight of all that earth, I swore that if you lived, I would not push you away again." He drew a harsh breath. "The question is, will you still have me?"

Emeline felt tears on her cheeks. "But your freedom—"

"I don't want my bloody *freedom*! Once I left London, nothing was as it used to be. All I could think of was you, my darling. When Peachey's letter reached me in Paris, I was secretly relieved to have an excuse to return to England and marry you, but I was too cowardly to admit the truth, even to myself." After a brief pause, he added, "That's why I talked like an ass when I saw you last night and said I had returned to do the *right thing*."

Her incandescent joy was tempered by caution. What if the shock of her accident was causing him to say these things? Later he might well have second thoughts. "I am almost afraid to hope this is real," she whispered.

With that, Hart lifted the tray away and set it on the table. Then, leaning forward, he took both of Emeline's hands in his and looked into her eyes. "I may never fully deserve you, Emeline, but I want to be with you more than anything in this world. If you'll have me…"

"But…what exactly are you suggesting? You have insisted that you could never be a husband or have a real home." She held her breath.

"I have said a lot of devilish idiotic things, haven't I?" Hart cocked his head. "Can we forget them after tonight?" With that, he dropped to one knee at the bedside, still holding her hand.

"You see, Emeline, I love you. I mean to marry you. I want us to make a real home and raise children together. I want us to make love for the rest of our lives…and search for artifacts in our spare moments." He cocked his head in a way she found irresistible. "Will that do?"

"Oh, yes, that was quite wonderful. I accept!" She was weeping and smiling at the same time, her chin quivering. "Now then, do get up, Hart. Come and lie down here next to me and hold me."

Quickly, he rose, pulled off his boots, and joined her on the bed, but maddeningly he remained on top of the counterpane.

"But what's the point if we are separated by covers?"

"What are you suggesting?" He feigned shock. "The entire household would have my head if they thought I was trying to have my way with you after what you have endured today." Caressing her cheek with the edge of his warm, strong hand, he asked, "How are you feeling? Do you have pain when you breathe? Do you notice any changes when you move your arms or legs?"

"I feel fine. Just a bit tired, as if I've been on a long journey."

"That's one way of putting it." Hart stared into the distance just long enough to remind her how close they had come to being separated forever. "You must sleep," he murmured at length, kissing her so tenderly, it only made her crave more. "We will talk about our future tomorrow. Perhaps you'll have second thoughts? My involvement with your father…"

"Papa admitted all to me, Hart. He said he was to blame, and you were only doing it to save your brother."

He looked relieved, but only for a moment. "Yet weren't you just as adamant as I was about never marrying?"

"That's true, I was." Emeline nodded. "But deep inside I didn't really mean it, once I knew you."

Hart drew back and arched a brow. "In that case, what about your Bridegroom List?"

"Oh, thank you for reminding me." Adapting a concerned expression, she pointed to the low chest beside her bed. "Will you please look in there for a folded paper?"

He did as she asked, opening the top drawer and removing the sheet of vellum that she had folded into thirds. "But—wait." Hart held the paper away, just out of her reach. "Is this going to disqualify me?"

"Give it to me." Emeline tried to sound stern. When the list was in her hands, she opened it and pretended to ponder the contents. Then, unable to suppress a smile, she brandished it in front of him. At the top, were the words: THE BRIDEGROOM LIST.

Emeline watched as Hart scanned the names that Louise and she had added over the weeks: a few random noblemen they thought handsome, Sir Giles Peyton, Viscount Tobias Melford. Finally, at the very top, one name was written in bold letters: LORD JASPER HARTCLIFFE.

Hart laughed in disbelief. "This is a *jest*! You added me a few minutes ago, when you were alone."

She put down the list and wrapped her arms around his broad shoulders. "How could I? You saw the state I was in when you brought dinner, and I didn't begin to revive until I'd eaten, and you favored me with the...stimulation of your company." Her smile widened. "Besides, I had no way of knowing you actually meant to offer for me."

"But..." He glanced over at the list again and then met her gaze.

Emeline fitted one of her hands to the side of his jaw. "I've been in love with you for so long. The rest of this list was a farce. Only your name was genuine." She leaned closer, aching for him as her body awoke again to desire. "Part of the reason I continued to swear I would never marry was the realization that no other man would do."

"Not even...Melford?"

"What?" She shook her head in surprise. "Tobias? Of course not."

"Well, then, thank God I declared myself."

She smiled at him dreamily. "Now please, do come here and hold me properly, not sitting on top of the counterpane! I promise to behave."

Hart gave a low snort of laughter as she drew back the covers for him to join her. "This is mad. If your cousin should come in through that connecting door and discover us..."

"But you're fully clothed, darling. Besides, even if we were both completely naked, I think Louise would be delighted!"

"If you say the word 'naked' again, I can't be responsible for my actions." He gathered her into his arms. "But you must close your eyes. What you need right now is rest."

She smiled to herself. The feeling of Hart close to her, holding her against his warm, hard-muscled body, was pure bliss. Emeline felt not only his calming heartbeat, but also the depth of his love. He wanted her, but he could wait.

Just before surrendering to sleep, she murmured, "I think I must be nearly recovered from the accident because I'm having some...feelings." Her hand drifted over his chest, concealed beneath a fine cotton shirt. When she dared to trail her fingers lower, Hart caught her wrist.

"I assure you, I am having the same feelings, but we *cannot...* not until I know you haven't suffered any worse injuries."

"Tomorrow?" Emeline persevered a bit groggily.

"My incorrigible minx, go to sleep."

CHAPTER 26

Standing in the excavation site beside Tobias, Hart paused to lean on his shovel and glance up at Emeline's bedroom window. Behind them, Ackerman and his nephews were digging out the cave-in and preparing to shore up the trench with planks of wood, while Tobias and Hart uncovered more cooking utensils and other grave goods at their end of the site.

Was she awake yet? Although he had asked Sarah to take breakfast to her, what if the maid had forgotten? Perhaps he should go up and check.

"You didn't have to come down here at all," Tobias remarked. His breath was visible in the November morning air as he brushed centuries of dirt from a drinking horn with a decorated metal rim. "I know you have other concerns today."

"I believe Emeline is fine." Hart frowned. "She seemed herself earlier, when I—" He broke off, realizing that he couldn't say he'd last seen her in bed at dawn, curled up like a kitten in his arms.

"Yes…?"

"When I was keeping an eye on her—to be certain there were no lingering effects from the cave-in."

"A very *close* eye, no doubt."

"And what of it?" he flared. "I love her." Hearing his own voice saying those words was a bit of a shock.

"Oh, I know that." Tobias grinned. "I suspect the only person who didn't know it was you, my friend."

Hart blinked at that, realizing that his days of being heartless and uncaring were over. *Thank God.*

Just then, the garden doors opened and Emeline emerged, arm-in-arm with Louise, with Monte capering along beside them. Mrs. Peachey brought up the rear, pushing a tea cart laden with breakfast rolls and a steaming pot of coffee.

Although the ladder had been lost during yesterday's cave-in, Hart found a foothold in the trench and climbed up onto the lawn. Walking toward Emeline, his blood thrummed, and again it came to him how easily she could have been killed. Every moment of life now felt like a precious gift, one he would never take for granted again.

Reaching out to him with both hands as they met, Emeline stood on tiptoe and murmured against his neck, "Thank you for staying with me last night."

"I mean to make a habit of it, very soon." He managed to resist the urge to catch her up in his arms and indulge in a long kiss. Casting an appraising eye over her sky-blue gown, cape, and bonnet, he added, "I'm glad to see that you have dressed warmly. How are you feeling?"

"Quite well." Color touched her cheeks as she added, "When I awoke and remembered everything you said last night, I thought perhaps it had all been a dream."

"It was no dream." He held her closer for one sweet moment. "I love you, Emeline."

Before she could reply, they were interrupted by Monte who began leaping about at their feet. "Won't you pick him up? He is longing to be with both of us, I think."

"He is a tyrant," Hart said with mock severity, even as he

crouched to lift up the scruffy dog, and Monte happily made himself comfortable in the crook of his arm. Straightening, Hart saw that all the men in the trench had stopped working to stare at them.

"Good morning!" called Emeline, waving. "Thank you all for helping to rescue me yesterday. I'm doing quite well!"

With that, Hart wrapped his free arm around her waist. "We all have a lot to do," he announced to the others, smiling. "I hope you'll join me in working harder to unearth the artifacts so that we will be free to begin preparations for a wedding."

"A *wedding*!" Tobias echoed loudly.

"Miss St. Briac has done me the honor of agreeing to be my wife," Hart replied. Emeline leaned her cheek against his shoulder, and it was the best feeling in the world. "We both would like to be wed as soon as possible."

"Congratulations!" exclaimed Tobias, and the other men joined in. When the cheers had died down, he added, "As for uncovering more artifacts, you'll be glad to know I've just found something new and quite astonishing."

Monte was quickly set back on his feet while Hart moved a chair from their rest area for Emeline to sit on. He placed it at the edge of the pit, where all the recent items had been discovered, and Sarah brought her coffee and toast from Mrs. Peachey's cart.

When Emeline was properly settled, Hart rejoined Tobias in the trench. "Show us."

"I believe it may be the place where the coffin lay," he said, pointing to a dark stain in the soil, perhaps two feet wide, not far from where they had found the hanging bowl and the drinking horn. "I think the wood of the coffin has dissolved, just like the frame of the burial chamber itself, but it left behind a mark."

"Yet, there are no bones..." mused Louise, who was back in the trench near Tobias, writing in her notebook.

"It's rather a mystery, isn't it, why some ancient graves hold complete skeletons and others nothing at all," said Emeline from her chair, looking down over the others.

"I suspect it has to do with the degree of acidity in the earth surrounding the grave. But we will sieve every bit of this soil," said Hart. "There may well be evidence of a body. Teeth, or bone fragments."

Suddenly Emeline leaned forward, pointing. "I just saw something, glinting in the sunlight. Oh, I want to come down and join the rest of you!"

"You'll get dirt on your pretty gown," warned Louise.

"Devil take my gown," she exclaimed. "Hart, do help me!"

He obeyed, reaching up to catch her as she jumped from the edge. Once on her feet beside him, Emeline removed her bonnet and cape.

"Won't you be cold?" whispered Hart.

"No. Though when it is time for luncheon, I shall change into my trousers and wool coat." She gave him an irresistible smile. "I am just fine! And I need to be here, working alongside the rest of you." Her gaze returned to the wood-stained area that might have marked part of the coffin.

"What do you think you saw a few moments ago?" Hart asked.

"It looked like a bit of gold, but now it's gone. Perhaps I imagined it…"

The morning slipped away. More grave goods were uncovered around the periphery of the chamber: an iron spur, a pot, the remains of a wooden bucket with iron hoops. Hart was completely engrossed in his work, troweling carefully down in the coffin area, when Emeline gasped.

"There it is again, do you see?" She pointed over Hart's shoulder to a tiny glint of metal.

When Emeline pushed her skirts aside and crouched beside him, Hart handed her his small, soft brush. Slowly, as she brushed, a paper-thin gold foil cross emerged into the daylight, no more than one inch in length.

"It's in the shape of a Latin cross!" she whispered. "But what can it mean? The Vikings were pagan, weren't they?"

"I suspect there is a great deal we don't understand yet," he replied, turning to meet her gaze. Their faces were just inches apart, and deep love swelled in Hart for this woman who seemed to be created just for him. "Beginning with your glass beakers that may pre-date the Vikings by centuries."

"But if the grave is Anglo-Saxon rather than Viking, it's equally confusing, because weren't they pagan as well?"

"Not necessarily." Tobias, hovering in the background spoke at last. "There were certainly pilgrims, newly converted to Christianity, who traveled through Britain after the Romans left. Perhaps they converted the fellow buried here?"

Emeline's eyes lit up. "I have just recalled what Mrs. Dawson told us about the history of Woodcroft Priory, shortly after we arrived." She looked at Tobias and Louise. "Don't you remember? She said that the oldest ruins are said to date back to the 7th century, founded by Clement, a Benedictine monk. Those were the early days of Christianity in Britain. Can you imagine? Perhaps Clement himself is here!"

"Slow down." Hart put a hand up. "I think we should do more research before we rush to conclusions."

"But isn't it exciting?" Emeline had returned to brushing the dirt near the gold foil cross, and soon a second, virtually identical cross emerged, perhaps four inches to one side of the first. What could it mean?

"If this is the head of the coffin, and the bones have disappeared with time," Emeline mused, "perhaps these crosses were placed over the eyes? They are exactly oriented where the eyes would be..."

"Brilliant." Hart longed to kiss her.

"I can't stop wondering who these people were, when they lived here, what they believed." Smiling, she shivered slightly.

"Are you ready to go inside for a bit to warm up and eat something?" he asked.

"Just a bit longer. Please!"

Tobias used tweezers to gently remove the foil crosses, marking the spots where they had been with two pebbles. When excavation continued, everyone agreed that if this was truly where the body had lain, they must be as painstaking as possible, so trowels were set aside. Hart and Emeline took turns carefully brushing away at the dirt, moving down from where the crosses had been. After another hour, Hart's breath caught at another glimpse of gold.

The excitement was palpable as they gradually revealed a small, irregularly shaped, inscribed gold coin, in approximately the place where the body's heart would have been.

"This could be just the clue we've been waiting for," said Hart.

Emeline looked up at him, a hint of color in her cheeks. "There is something I must talk to you about, regarding this coin…and some others."

"Let us go inside then," he replied. Privately, Hart wanted to get her alone, to hold her in his arms, to feel the lush curves of her body beneath his hands and soak up her response. "We'll have lunch and…" Catching her eye, he flicked up one brow. "*Talk.*"

Emeline blushed but continued to meet his blue gaze.

Ackerman had located another ladder and now one of the nephews lowered it into the pit. As Hart and Emeline climbed out, Louise called, "Emmie, do take care and rest! You have just come through a terrible ordeal."

"Nonsense!" she replied. "I have never felt more wonderfully alive than I do today."

* * *

"I am ravenous," Hart said as they came into the house.

"For food?" Emeline teased.

296

"Naughty minx." He lifted his brows, smiling.

They were passing through the flagstone entry hall when Mrs. Peachey appeared, as if she had been waiting for them. After offering her good wishes for their betrothal, she said, "I feel that the time has come to speak to you about an important matter. Might we meet in the dowager duchess's bedchamber?"

Hart blinked. "What the devil can you possibly have to say to me there?"

"My lord, please trust me when I say I have a good reason. I promise to be brief, for I know you both must be eager to have luncheon."

"Peachey, you know I hate that place."

Her smile brooked no refusal. "Shall we say…ten minutes?"

"Fine." He scowled.

As they walked slowly up the broad staircase and along the passageway, Emeline marveled at how quickly Hart's old barriers had risen. Hoping to distract him, she said, "Before we go back downstairs to the dining room, I must get the book I brought from London about ancient coins." Briefly, she explained about Panizzi loaning her a volume from his private collection. "It will be invaluable, helping us to pinpoint the date of the coins in the grave!"

"Yes." His tone was distant. "That's an excellent notion." Had he heard a word she'd spoken?

At the end of the corridor, the door to the Dowager Duchess of Caversham's bedchamber loomed up before them. Emeline recalled all too well how Sarah had told her that no one ever went inside that room except Mrs. Dawson, to tidy up.

Today, there was a key inserted in the lock. "Apparently Peachey has been planning this," Hart muttered as he unlocked the door and they entered.

* * *

HART FELT as if he were entering a tomb, scented with the stale remnants of his mother's expensive perfume. The cavernous bedchamber had windows overlooking both the long avenue in front and the ruins in back. However, the views were obscured by heavy draperies, and the room was chilly, damp, and cluttered with the dowager duchess's eccentric possessions. Nothing had been touched since her death a decade ago. Certainly Hart hadn't wanted to go through her things, and it was easier just to lock the door and stay away completely.

"God, it's freezing in here," he muttered.

Emeline touched his shoulder, clearly waiting for more, but he couldn't look at her. He walked away, over to an ornate writing desk. It was still littered with his mother's notes and papers, as if she might return at any moment.

"I wish I could pretend none of my family existed, but it's impossible in this house," he said, picking up a letter opener. "You surprised me, turning up here, and now I have no choice about it."

"But if we are to be married, you cannot keep your family and your past locked away. You have told me a bit about your father… and your brother. It sounded as if you had an unhappy childhood…"

"It's in the past." His heart felt like it was folding in on itself. "I can't change it, so why dwell on it? That's why I rarely come to the priory or, for that matter, even see my brother."

Just then, Mrs. Peachey appeared in the doorway. "Ah, there you are." She walked briskly to the tall windows overlooking the drive and opened the drapes. Soft, late autumn light shone in, lifting some of the gloom. "There now! Isn't that better?"

"I would prefer to not be here at all, Peachey," he replied in a hard voice.

"Of course I know you'd like to go, my lord, but I cannot allow that." The housekeeper crossed to stand next to him. "Your mother entrusted me with a series of tasks before she left this world."

He sent her a skeptical look. "You are having me on."

"Not a bit. You see, Lord Jasper, it was the duchess who asked me, along with William, to leave the duke's employ and go with you when the time came for you to leave university."

"But Mama died before I completed my studies." Hart stared at her. "Devil take it, Peachey, are you telling me she made these arrangements with you in advance—when all these years, I believed that you and William came with me simply because you...preferred me to Father and Austell?"

"Have I ruffled your feelings? Of course, we preferred you to them, Lord Jasper. We came to you because we *cared*." Peachey touched his arm, and Hart felt a stab of old pain before she continued, "But we were also with you in service of the duchess. When she left Caversham Castle and returned here to live, she wrote to me very clearly about her wishes. And now that we have gotten you safely to this juncture in your life, I believe you are ready for the next step."

Hart mutely turned toward Emeline. She came to his side, reached out to him, and squeezed his hand.

"What juncture do you mean?" he asked.

"Today you announced your betrothal." The older woman beamed at them. "Now you are no longer alone, Lord Jasper, and although it won't be easy, it is time for you to learn the truth."

Hart couldn't decide if he was glad or not for Emeline's presence. He spoke through clenched teeth. "Go on then."

"You have already discovered the little red chest your mother kept in the back of her armoire. Those were artifacts that she discovered on her own, near the ruins when she was a child. But there is something more, hidden in plain sight, for years."

As Hart and Emeline watched, the housekeeper pointed to an ugly footstool in front of his mother's favorite chair by the window. He snorted. "If you mean that hideous thing, in my opinion it should remain hidden. Or better yet, disposed of."

Peachey gave him a cryptic smile. "You say that now." She perched on the edge of the duchess's chair and regarded the footstool, which consisted of a cushioned tapestry top, frayed and soiled, over a flat-bottomed wooden base, intricately painted with crimson and gold flowers against a pale green background. The entire thing was a monstrosity.

Glancing over at Emeline, Hart shrugged slightly. "Perhaps she's gone mad."

But when Peachey reached out to press a hidden catch beneath the cushioned surface, the top sprang open to reveal an interior that resembled a large jewelry box. Hart felt a chill. Inside were four hinged, covered sections, and one by one Peachey opened them. Soon the entire footstool appeared to be filled with glittering pieces of jewelry, many of which Hart recognized.

"Her Grace desired that all of these should to go to you, Lord Jasper, or should I say…to your bride? She knew your father or even your brother might come here one day and poke around, but no one would suspect this old footstool could conceal the dowager duchess's private jewels."

He was stunned. "But the current duchess has the Caversham jewels. I've seen Margaret wearing some of them."

"These were pieces your mother accumulated separately during her lifetime. She had no way of knowing that you would amass a fortune on your own, and so this was her way of providing for you once you married," Mrs. Peachey explained.

"Right. But I don't bloody need my mother's jewelry." Hart felt his mouth twist in a cynical smile. "Have I shocked you?" He shrugged. "All of this is entwined with a past I want no part of."

Even before Hart finished speaking, he felt Emeline's light touch on his back. "You and I may find a way to use this added fortune for good," she said softly.

Peachey raised a hand. "Let me assure you, Lord Jasper, the real treasure for you cannot be measured in shillings and pounds. It is in this secret drawer." Pointing to a thin, wide drawer tucked into one of the compartments, she brought a fragile key out of her pocket and handed it to him. "Her Grace gave this into my keeping shortly before her death and I've been waiting ten years to put it in your hand."

Hart sent her a dark look. "You're killing me, Peachey." But he took the key, sat back on his heels, and inserted it in the tiny lock. More of the musty perfume assailed him as the drawer slid open. Inside, like a ticking bomb, was a letter.

His heart froze as he read the inscription in his mother's familiar curving hand.

To my son, Jasper: His Grace, the rightful Duke of Caversham.

CHAPTER 27

The air in the bedchamber felt too thick to breathe. Emeline watched Hart, waiting until he finally broke the seal and unfolded the letter. It was a single page, covered with more of his mother's writing.

"I'm not at all certain I want to read this." He looked down at her, and she saw the conflict in his eyes. "Can't we go back to London and forget all about Woodcroft Priory?"

"I don't think so."

Mrs. Peachey spoke up. "Lord Jasper, I know you. There's no need to fear this. Deep inside, you have craved this knowledge."

"I am not *afraid*." With that, he sat down on the edge of the duchess's bed and Emeline perched next to him. Together they read the letter. There was a passage professing her love for him, explaining that she could not reveal the truth until he was old enough, strong enough to deal with it. It was better too, that his father was already dead, for she feared her wild son might kill the duke if he knew what he had done. Finally, came the heart of the letter:

It was an ordeal, giving birth to twins, but I knew in my heart

303

from the first that you were the first born. Your papa suggested we not speak of this to you and Austell until you were older, so that you could enjoy being little boys. I believe now that Richard wanted to wait so that he could choose an heir who was more biddable and acquiescent to his wishes. You, my darling Jasper, were never biddable. You always questioned rules and craved adventure.

The day of your fifth birthday, when Richard announced that Austell would be the next Duke of Caversham, I was aghast! We had quarreled about it once before, but I believed that when the time came, he would do the right thing. And when I confronted him, he claimed that I had been out of my mind during the terrible birth, that I almost died, and thus only he knew which baby had been born first.

The old midwife was dead. I searched for Julie Lamb, Austell's and your nurse who was also at your birth, but she had left the county. When your father learned of my inquiries, he found ways to punish me...and you as well, constantly disparaging you, reminding you that Austell would be the duke and you would have nothing. All I could do was make a plan for your future, to ensure that you would have property and means of your own.

Thank God for dear Mrs. Peachey. When you went up to Oxford, I couldn't bear to live at the castle another day, and so I returned here to be with my parents at the priory. She agreed to carry out my wishes, to look after you as I could not.

I love you and Austell equally, but I cannot help having a special, protective love for you, my darling. You were cheated out of your dukedom by your scheming, manipulative father. He chose Austell because he could manage him in a way you would never have allowed.

Now that you know the truth, I pray that it will be salve for the confusion and wounds you suffered, especially during your childhood. With my dearest love, Mama

Emeline glanced over and saw that Hart had closed his eyes,

the letter lying slack against his leg. She touched his hand and murmured, "Perhaps this helps you to reconcile some of your feelings?"

He swiveled to look at her. His blue eyes were stormy. "You have a happy family. People who love one another and showed you love your entire life. You cannot imagine what it feels like to be trapped in this sort of madness. All I want to do is forget about it, put it away, move on. The last thing I want is to be sitting here in this airless room, receiving yet another visit from my suffocating mother." A muscle moved in his jaw. "Only Mama could find a way to torment me this way a full decade after her death."

Mrs. Peachey had been waiting near the door, and now she approached Hart. "My lord, may I be frank?"

"You will do so in any case," he said, with a dismissive movement of his hand.

"Speaking thus about your departed mother may give you some relief in this moment, but the time will come when you regret it. The dowager duchess was not a perfect person, but who among us is? If she was a bit mad, perhaps she suffered in the same way you did."

"There is no proof of anything that she says except for her very questionable word," Hart snapped. "What I will allow is that Mama obviously *pitied* me once Austell had been anointed and I was shunted aside. No doubt she wrote this letter to console me, but I don't need her pity any more than these jewels."

"I believe I do have proof, Lord Jasper."

"I've heard enough for one day." He glared at her, clearly wishing he'd never entered this room. "Emeline and I are hungry."

Peachey pretended not to hear him. "The nurse who was present at your birth, Julie Lamb, was pensioned off by your father, the duke, when you were two years old. He provided a cottage and gave her £20,000 to remain silent for the rest of her life."

"£20,000?" Hart scoffed. "Is this some sort of fairy story?"

"Not a bit, my lord." Peachey gave him one of the quelling looks that made him feel twelve years old again. "Julie and I were friends, growing up in the nearby village of Boyton. Our parents worked here at the priory, and when your mother married the duke, she was comforted to have familiar faces come with her in her new life." She paused to let this sink in. "Caversham Castle is far away in Gloucestershire, but Julie returned to Boyton, to live in the cottage the duke gave her." Another pause. "I could take you to her."

"Absolutely not," he said flatly. "I would rather be stoned by a mob."

Emeline intervened. "Mrs. Peachey, you have given his lordship a great deal to think about. Perhaps it would be best if he and I take our luncheon in his rooms, where we can talk."

Hart rose to his feet and gave an absent nod. It felt to Emeline as if he stood alone on one side of a wide gulf and she was on the other...along with the rest of the world.

* * *

NONE OF EMELINE'S daydreams about her first visit to Hart's rooms at the priory were like this. She had imagined a romantic setting, perhaps the two of them stealing away after a long day of excavating. Sharing a sensuous bath...a glass of wine...and at last being together in Hart's bed, with no further impediments to their love.

Instead, the grimly handsome man who sat across from her could have been a stranger. Or even Satan himself, with his brilliant eyes and silvery hair glinting in the occasional shaft of sunlight. William had delivered their luncheon tray, watching his master out of the corner of one eye. Once the small table near the window had been set for them, the manservant disappeared and Emeline was alone with Hart and his invisible armor.

They ate in silence for several minutes. There was lamb, roasted carrots, spinach soufflé, and fresh buttery rolls, but Emeline couldn't taste any of it. Hart drank two glasses of crimson wine, ate everything on his plate, and set down his napkin.

"You should reconsider your decision to marry me," he said. "We both ought to reconsider. I was a fool to think I might be capable—"

Abruptly overcome with frustration, she stood. "I won't have this."

His mask slipped for a brief moment. "What?"

"I understand that you have been hurt by the very people who should have taught you how to love. But you are grown now, and I am here with you! You may tell me as many times as you like that you don't want to be loved, but it is too late. I already love you and I'm not going to stop."

"I've made a mistake," he persisted, pushing back from the table and rising to his feet.

"Yes! You made a mistake when you said you began to reconsider letting me in to your life. No, not *letting*, welcoming! If you think you can go hot and cold with me from one day to the next, you are mistaken indeed."

"That's what I'm trying to tell you! Get out, now, while you still can. Before you grow to despise me the way my own parents despised one another." He raked long fingers through his hair in a gesture of despair. "My God, can't you see—it's bloody inevitable."

Emeline heard the throb of pain in his voice, and that was all the confirmation she needed. Crossing to stand in front of him, she began to unfasten the delicate pearl buttons that marched down her bodice. Her fingers were shaking slightly but it didn't matter. Let him see! She was finished with hiding her true feelings.

"What the deuce are you doing?" he demanded as she drew off the sleeves and let the gown fall to her waist.

"Surely a man with as much experience as you, my lord, must know what it means when a woman begins to undress in front of you." As she felt the long-suppressed tide of desire rise within her, the tops of her breasts swelled above the simple corset, and her nipples tingled with need. "I am going to make love to you. Perhaps that is the only language you can understand at this moment?"

"*Emeline.*" His voice was a low growl. A warning, even as his gaze singed her breasts.

She pulled the pins from her mass of ebony hair, and it fell around her shoulders. "Touch me."

Hart couldn't take his eyes off her, but he stepped back. Emeline stepped closer. "I want you," she breathed. "Desperately."

He stood rooted to the spot but turned his face away as she began to unfasten his woolen shirt. When she had opened it to expose his broad, lean-muscled chest, she gave a little sigh and pressed her mouth to his heart, then moved slightly to brush her lips against one taut male nipple. The scent of him, mingling in crisp chest hair, was one more aphrodisiac.

"Mad." He shook his head again, but his voice faltered. "Save yourself, my darling, before it's too late."

"But it's already too late. Far too late." Rising up on her toes, Emeline wrapped her arms around his shoulders and pressed her body, aching with need, to his. "I want you to take me. Do all the things you've dreamed of, because I've dreamed of them, too."

With that, Hart scooped her up into his arms and carried her to the massive four-poster bed with its spread of claret velvet. Reaching out with one dark hand, he tossed back the covers and set her down.

"Damn it," he muttered hopelessly, dragging off his own clothing. "I want you too much."

Emeline stared up at him, saw the glint of tears, and felt her own eyes burn. She wanted to reassure him but knew better than that with Hart. "Take me, then," she repeated. "I'm yours." And she opened her legs, in spite of the petticoat and drawers that hid her intimate secrets from his gaze.

"Witch." He knew exactly how to quickly undress her, and it came to Emeline that he had more practice at this than she cared to imagine.

"You must mean *wife*," she gasped. "Soon, I will be your wife."

Hart shook his head, but then he stripped away the rest of her clothes and his burning gaze raked over her. In the next moment, he was kneeling over her, covering her slim, pale form with his powerful male body. His flesh was so warm, and when she felt him, hard and hot, nudge between her thighs she wanted to welcome him in right then.

Instead, he took her in his arms and kissed her deeply, letting his sex pulsate against her thigh as he invaded her sweet mouth with his tongue. Emeline was drunk with joy and pleasure. She soaked up every sensation, every emotion that thrummed between their two bodies. After running her fingers lightly down the sides of his back, she explored the rock-hard curve of his buttocks, felt his muscles flexing against her soft hands as he moved over her.

"Vixen," he uttered, burning a trail of kisses down to her breasts.

"Yours," Emeline urged. "Completely...yours."

His mouth closed over her aching nipple, and she made an unintelligible sound. His tongue stroked the sensitive peak before suckling in a way that made her feel she might climax then and there. Her legs opened again, seeking, and Hart trailed one hand slowly down the curve of her belly, waiting a moment or two before he touched her there at last. Emeline was pulsing, throbbing. She pushed back against his hand and whimpered slightly.

"I want…" she begged.

Still, he took his time, lingering at her breasts, kneading, suckling, drawing a series of soft cries from her, while his fingers explored the slick, delicate folds that wanted more, so much more. At last, Hart began to kiss the feminine curve of her hip, her sensitive inner thighs, and she nearly begged him aloud to find the swollen bud that was at that moment the center of her being. And yet, simultaneously, Emeline feared that very thing, for surely it would be *too much*. Like a bolt of lightning, it might kill her.

As if he could read her mind, Hart caught her wrists and pinned them at her sides. His tongue, hot and deft, found her apex and Emeline whimpered. He knew just what to do. How, how? She writhed against him as the sensations became so blissfully intense her legs trembled, and then it seemed she was plunging off a cliff. Still he persisted, as more fire trailed in the wake of her climax.

Damp with perspiration, Emeline lifted her head and smiled helplessly. "I… I…"

Hart gave a short laugh before rising up to kiss her again. "Harlot."

"Yes, thank you." She smiled. "Now, you." Her hands found him, hard, warm, and shockingly large. "Hmm. I perceive that you want me."

He had never looked more irresistible than at that moment. "God help us both."

"Tell me…you surrender." Her small hand was wrapped around him, gently stroking.

"Of course. By Lucifer, I surrender." He pushed her glossy hair back onto the pillow and kissed his way along her neck, scorching her tender flesh. "For today, at least."

Emeline knew it was true. There could be no easy victory for

Hart's battered soul, but she trusted now that they would fight together.

"I want you, Hart," she murmured again, guiding him to her entrance. "Here."

Their eyes met as he began to push slowly inside her. "If I hurt you—"

Her eyes closed for a moment as he filled her. "No." She arched up to bring him deeper still. "Yes! Oh, *please.*"

And then Emeline was clinging to his broad shoulders, finding his mouth with hers, and one of his hands reached down to cup her bottom as she matched his pace. Dimly she realized it was a different sort of rapture: the connection, the mating, the utter yielding of one's own will. Their hearts beat in unison, faster, faster. When at last he plunged deep and paused, shuddering in his own moment of release, Emeline saw the unguarded face of the man she loved.

And in that moment, it came to her that this was the man whose bed she had stumbled into long ago, whose touch and kisses had first awakened her as a woman…and caused her to flee to Lyme Regis, trying to deny her needs.

"It was you, wasn't it," she breathed.

And of course, Hart understood. "Yes."

"How long have you known?"

Their eyes met with a glimmer of shared memory. "Always."

As they held each other, she drank in the thud of his heart against her warm, damp breasts and reveled in the scent of their passion. Was it possible that anyone else had ever felt quite this way?

"Emeline…" Lifting his head, he gazed into her eyes. "I love you."

"I know." She beamed up at him and lifted a hand to brush back a lock of his silver-flecked hair. Their bodies were still fused. "And I love you. We were meant to be."

* * *

THREE DAYS LATER, Hart sat next to Emeline at the big, scarred desk in the library as the two of them inspected the rare coin book Panizzi had loaned her. It was open before them, next to the two small gold coins. One had been recently found by Ackerman and sent by post to London. The second coin was the newest one, discovered in the grave along with the paper-thin gold crosses. The pieces of the sword Ackerman and Hart had uncovered last spring were also there, set out on a pristine linen cloth for further examination.

Outside, it was raining. The excavation site was covered by a series of tarpaulins, produced by Ackerman just as dark clouds blew in from the sea and the first raindrops began to fall.

It would have been difficult for Hart to say so aloud, but sitting there with Emeline brought a feeling of peace he had never experienced. A fire blazed in the hearth, and they were immersed in a project together, contented in their silence. With every passing day, he was beset by fewer impulses to ride away to some distant land like India. Or Mongolia.

"Oh, my!" Emeline gasped, gesturing with her magnifying glass. "Look at this!"

He gladly moved his chair over until it touched hers. "Show me."

The page, in the middle of a chapter titled *Merovingian: 7th Century,* was covered with tiny, intricate drawings of odd little coins. Emeline pointed to a coin crudely inscribed on one side with a draped bust wearing a diadem, in the Roman style. On the other side, a cross was encircled by other markings. It nearly matched one of their coins.

"So much for any lingering theories about the Vikings," she said.

"We know that East Anglia didn't have a coin-based system until at least 900 A.D.," Hart mused with a frown. "From this, are we to assume that the graves date back three or four centuries earlier?"

"Yes! According to the book, this coin was minted around 625 A.D.," Emeline proclaimed, glowing. "And I further postulate that the people who lived here and dug these graves had traveled abroad and acquired these coins in Merovingian Gaul—what is now France."

"Yes." Hart stared at the book, the coins, and felt Emeline take his hand. "I think that's it. You're brilliant."

Her radiant smile widened. "Well, I had the book. It could have easily been the other way around."

"So we are to assume, from the coins and the crosses, that the early Christian pilgrims passed this way from Ireland," he mused.

"Yes!"

"It doesn't mean that they had both feet in the Christian boat, so to speak. I've seen plenty of objects in that grave that lean pagan, but it does offer a glimpse into the changes that were happening."

"And how much more civilized the Dark Ages were than we could have known. Oh, Hart, isn't it fascinating? Let us go and tell Tobias and Louise. They are playing chess in the Hall!"

However, no sooner had they risen than Hart glimpsed a small, closed carriage pulled by a pair of grays coming up the lane toward the manor house. "Who can that be? Perhaps someone from your family. Do you recognize the equipage?"

She shook her head. "No, I don't know who it can be."

Already there was a commotion in the entry hall. Hearing Peachey's voice, Hart knew a sense of foreboding. "I believe I will go upstairs for a bit."

Emeline caught his hand before he could make good his escape. The look she gave him was more eloquent than any words.

"Lord Jasper," Peachey called gently from the doorway. "You

have a guest. Shall I show her in?" Behind her, he glimpsed a tall, thin older woman peeping over the housekeeper's head.

Hell, no, he wanted to bark. But when Emeline squeezed his hand, he frowned and nodded. "Yes. Of course."

The two females came into the library and Peachey led the intruder over to stand before him. She wore a large, black bonnet and a black cloak. "This is Miss Julie Lamb." After performing introductions all around, she continued, "My lord, as I told you recently, Miss Lamb was your nurse, assisting at the births of you and your brother, and caring for you during the first two years of your life."

He couldn't believe that Peachey had summoned this person here behind his back. "It's kind of you to stop, madam, but as it happens I must—"

"I am afraid I cannot stay more than a few minutes," the woman interjected in a clear voice. Although her long face was pale and rigid, Hart realized with a shock that tears shone in her eyes. "My brother died last night, and so I was passing by on my way to be with his family." She exchanged a glance with Peachey. "I understand that you have been dealing with some difficult news, my lord. I only came to tell you that all of it is quite true."

Emeline took charge then, directing the four of them to chairs and suggesting that they ring for tea. Miss Lamb shook her head. She truly could not stay, she insisted.

Hart wanted to say that he would have brandy. An entire bottle, please. The woman was gazing at him in a way that stirred up memories that must be far too ancient for him to access. The sound of her voice, clear yet gentle, was like a hot poker in his heart. Why the devil did he have to endure this torture?

Just then, Emeline took his hand again and sent him a meaningful gaze that told him exactly why. If he didn't clear out the poison that festered inside, he could never be the husband she deserved.

"I'm listening, Miss Lamb," he managed to say.

"Oh, Lord Jasper… When you first learned to talk, you called me Lambie," she said fondly. "But of course, you couldn't remember that." She spared him from replying by continuing, "I would have known you anywhere, my lord. So handsome, just as you always were even as a babe. Handsome and fearless, much to the displeasure of the duke."

Hart couldn't stand another moment of this. "I find it hard to believe that my father could have perpetrated the sort of hoax Mrs. Peachey described to me recently. More plausible would be the notion of my mother hatching this entire story out of pity for me…and resentment toward the duke."

"Oh, no, my lord," Miss Lamb said, apparently unfazed by his harsh words. "The duke did it, just as you have heard. The duchess had a terrible birth with the two of you. Of course, no one guessed there could be two babes! She nearly died from the pain alone, I think, and they gave her so much laudanum she didn't remember a thing. But I was there, a witness! You were born first, then ten minutes later, young Austell surprised us all."

Hart dug in. "But don't new babies look just the same at birth? Perhaps it's you who has it wrong. And in any case, why should my father play this trick? It makes no sense."

"You did not look the same, not a bit! You were always stronger, the one who cried more, demanded more. And the duke wanted to…bring you to heel. Break your spirit, if you will, so he might begin to train you. But you wouldn't be broken. No mention was made about an heir during those years when you and your brother were so tiny."

As the story continued to pour out, Hart's fists clenched until his nails cut into his palms. Miss Lamb leaned forward now, confidingly. "I began to suspect that His Grace was watching the pair of you so that he might choose for himself who would be the heir and the spare, if you will. One day, I was passing in the corridor, and I overheard an argument between the duke and duchess. He was telling her that she could not know which child was born first because she was out of her senses. He said, and I will never forget it… 'Only I know the truth of it. It was Austell!' And then as he stormed out of her bedchamber, he saw me standing there, dumbstruck."

Hart wanted to put his hands over his ears, but Emeline was wide-eyed, listening with rapt attention. "My God. How terrible! What happened then?

Pale as death in her black bonnet, Miss Lamb sat back in her chair and folded her trembling hands. "The very next morning, the duke called me to his library and closed the door. He told me that I would have to leave his employ, but I needn't fear being without employment or lodging. He asked me where I would like to live and of course I said the village of Boyton, to be with my family again. I was given a nice cottage…and £20,000 to 'live a quiet life' as he put it. It was a fortune to someone like me, enough to see my own ma and pa through their last years in comfort."

"And why are you breaking your silence now?" asked Emeline.

"My friend Madge here came to see me and explained all that happened since the day I left the castle." Miss Lamb looked over at Peachey, who reached out to pat the woman's cheek. "My conscience has always been troubled, not that I think I could have done much to stop His Grace, even if I tried. But now he and the duchess are both gone, and I wanted to make it right." She looked at Hart. "Will you challenge the dukedom, my lord?"

Hart blinked. "What? Oh, God, no." He gave a harsh laugh. "It's the last thing I want. But I will admit, I'm glad to know the truth. It explains a lot of the madness I've witnessed."

Miss Lamb made to rise from her chair. "I must be going now. My nephew is waiting with the carriage." They all stood together.

"Thank you for coming," said Emeline.

He extended a hand to the older woman, even as the dark past swirled inside him. "I'm very grateful to you…Lambie."

A smile lit her thin face, and she held fast to his hand. "You know the truth now, Your Grace. That's what matters."

EPILOGUE

"$\mathcal{I}$ am incredibly jealous," Anthony said to Emeline as he stood shoulder-deep in the excavation site and watched Hart brush dense layers of soil from a thousand-year-old gold shoulder clasp. "You two could have included me sooner, you know!"

She gave her brother a little push. "Don't be nonsensical. I did tell you about Hart's project before you and Freddie went off to help the Darwins settle into their new home, but you had more important things on your mind. Besides, you are here now."

"It's the next great frontier, you know," he said, picking up a trowel. "Archaeology."

"You are welcome to stay and work on the dig as long as you like. You know, I have a feeling that there is another grave nearby...perhaps this man's wife! Just before the cave-in, I thought I saw some amber and lapis beads. Of course, now they are hopelessly buried."

"Excellent!" her brother said. "It sounds as if we'll be at it here for weeks or months to come."

As Anthony set off to work in his own corner of the trench,

Emeline exchanged a smile with Hart. He came to stand close to her.

"Remind me again, how many days until the wedding…when we can go away together?" he asked in a low, suggestive voice. "*Alone.*"

"Three." She caressed his hard cheek. "But no doubt my parents and others who travel here from London will stay on for a bit—and we cannot go on a proper honeymoon until the dig is finished."

"Perhaps not a proper one, but I mean to take you away all the same. I like the notion of returning to the empty house on Wigmore Street where we can spend our time in bed and wander down in our nightclothes to cook for ourselves."

Hart's wicked smile made her tingle all over. "Yes, and if we must go out, we might don disguises."

"I like the way you think, your ladyship." His breath was warm and stirring against her cheek.

"I'm not a ladyship yet…"

Sliding one strong hand around her waist, he brought her close enough to feel the heat of his body. "In every way that matters, you are."

Tobias's deep voice boomed behind them, breaking the spell. "Excuse me, lovebirds! Do you know where Louise has gone? I have unearthed a silver spoon, Byzantine I reckon!" He brandished the blackened spoon with its long, thin handle. "The details must be entered in the record."

"Amazing," said Hart as he released Emeline. "More signs of travel to the Continent."

"I believe Louise went inside a few minutes ago." As Emeline spoke, she realized that her brother Charles was also in the priory. He had arrived the day before, with the rest of her family, and several times she'd seen him bent over the artifacts labeled and displayed in the library. "Also, I am hungry! I believe Mrs. Dawson has made apple tarts. I'll bring some back with me."

With that, she climbed up the new ladder and strode across the lawn in her trousers and boots. Her father was standing on the terrace, drinking coffee and watching her with one brow quirked above his eyepatch.

"Ma petite, are you certain you are planning a wedding in a mere three days?"

"You needn't fret, Papa. I am fully capable of doing more than one thing at once." She paused close to him, smiling. "In any event, the wedding will be small and intimate. To be honest, I am more focused on the dig right now. Every day it gets colder and there is more risk that hard rains could damage our work."

He pretended to frown. "It is just as important that you are properly wed, before that libertine Hartcliffe attempts to compromise your virtue."

"One might imagine you *believe* that nonsense!" Emeline laughed and patted his cheek. "I, however, know who you really are."

"Of course you do," St. Briac said gruffly. "You share my blood."

"Indeed. I learned the secrets of life at the knee of my pirate father." She kissed him, excused herself, and went on into the manor house.

Muffled voices reached her from the stairway, and she glimpsed Mouette and Frederica ascending the steps with little Oliver between them, doubtless to put him down for a nap. More conversation drifted from the dining room, where her Raveneau grandparents lingered over their luncheon. The approaching wedding afforded her a rare opportunity to have time with much of her family together, and she paused to absorb the sense of deep contentment. After years of claiming bridependence, she realized that a new chapter had truly begun in her life. Ahead lay strengthened bonds with family, present and future...

Out of the corner of her eye, Emeline perceived movement in the library and heard her brother Charles speak in a low, intimate voice. "You know, I have missed you, Louise." There was a pause, some murmurs, then, "You have grown prettier with each passing year."

She held her breath, listening, edging her way toward the arched doorway in case her cousin needed her. Charles and Louise were standing next to the table where the artifacts were laid out to be cleaned and catalogued. Her fair-haired brother remained angelically handsome, while Louise gazed up at him, especially lovely in delicate profile.

"Oh…I never thought I would hear you say things like that," Louise murmured. She looked up at Charles in wonder, and Emeline could see that he had reawakened all her cousin's old, hopeless longings.

"It's true, my dear. We are both getting older, and I've realized that no other female could take your place or love me as you do." He reached out to gather her into his arms, and Louise did not resist. "I would like to show you the world! Let me take you to Italy. If you are able to persuade his lordship to let me sell some of these pieces to worthy collectors, all of us can profit…"

Emeline waited, her heart in her throat. She had hesitated about inviting Charles to the wedding, and now she was furious with him for being so selfish. A part of her wanted to interrupt them and tell Charles off, but she forced herself to remain silent. Although Louise might falter, she had come a long way toward severing her connection to a man who had proven himself unworthy, time and time again.

"That jeweled brooch, for example…" Charles glanced over toward the table and seemed to shiver with excitement. "Oh, my sweet, I know of a wealthy collector of antiquities who would pay an immense sum for that piece alone."

Louise looked torn. "I really don't think…"

"You have been thinking too long, my darling. It is time to begin enjoying life more *passionately*."

As Charles leaned down to kiss Louise, Emeline held her breath. Surely this was what Louise had waited and prayed for since she was a young girl, when the seeds were planted for her attachment to Charles.

"I don't think so," Louise said softly. She took a step back, away from him, and her voice became more determined. "In fact, I *cannot*, Charles. I have an important role to play, right here, in this excavation. I am part of a team."

Footsteps sounded behind Emeline, and Tobias's stocky form loomed up and strode past her, into the library. "Furthermore, Brandreth, the lady is in love with *me*," he announced.

Upon Tobias's appearance on the scene, Louise hurried forward to meet him, cheeks pink. "Oh, Tobias," she whispered.

He held her at arm's length and searched her face. "I should have told you sooner, Louise. I love you. I was only waiting for this wedding to be over before declaring myself."

"This is"—her face shone with joy as she received his embrace —"most welcome news."

Looking rather baffled, Charles made his way toward the doorway, and Emeline stepped out of the shadows to head him off.

"Really!" she frowned, pulling him out into the entry hall. "How could you?"

"You wouldn't speak to me that way if we were truly siblings," he accused. "You and Anthony are the genuine St. Briac offspring, and I am merely an afterthought from Mother's first marriage. You all doubtless wish that I would return to Italy and never return!"

Emeline looked out onto the terrace and was relieved to see that her father was walking away with Monte, down toward the slowly winding River Alde.

"Come with me." She drew Charles out of the house, away from other listeners, and stopped by a brick wall. "Do you think I want to feel this way toward you?" Emeline demanded, lightly tapping his shirtfront with one forefinger. "On the contrary, Charles, we could all enjoy being part of the *same* family if you would cease being pretentious, vain, and devious! Why not remain here in England and embark on a life of honest effort and accomplishment rather than running off to Italy and scheming to enrich yourself at the expense of others?"

Charles bristled. "Oh, so now that you're about to be Lady Hartcliffe, you imagine you can issue commands to me? You and Anthony don't care a fig if I'm part of this family or not."

"That is not true." Emeline knew she must not give up on him, no matter how he pushed her to do so. "You are our brother. But I know you, Charles, and it upsets me that you would try to use others, like Louise, for your own gain. There is another way, if only you would trust in your own talent! You could use your architecture degree and achieve great things."

Her brother sniffed doubtfully, but now his eyes gleamed with real emotion. "I don't know…"

"It's not too late to find real happiness," Emeline said softly. "Perhaps you'd like to live in the empty house on Chesterfield Street until you settle on a plan? Louise and I won't be there any longer and I don't believe Papa means to sell it."

"I will think about it." Squeezing her hand, Charles whispered, "Thank you, Em."

* * *

HART WANTED to rush the events of his wedding day in order to reach the end, when Emeline would openly come to his bed and sleep there every single night. It took all his powers of restraint to appear relaxed as the day unfolded.

Fortunately, he and Emeline had agreed that the entire affair should be as simple as possible due to the relative urgency of the dig. Just yesterday, Anthony St. Briac had uncovered three of the amber and lapis beads Emeline had glimpsed just before the trench walls collapsed on her. She and Louise were now convinced that they were on the verge of discovering a second, female grave, and Emeline hesitated to take time away even for her own wedding.

Hart had felt obliged to write and invite Austell and Margaret, but perhaps the letter had arrived too late for them to make travel arrangements. Privately, he was relieved to be spared the presence of his twin. It would feel deuced unsettling to be at Woodcroft Priory at the same time as Austell. Hart still hadn't quite worked out what to do with the knowledge about their birth order, and this hardly seemed the time to focus on it. Today was meant for Emeline.

As Hart allowed William to arrange his starched white cravat, he scanned his clothing. Would Emeline approve of his charcoal-gray frock coat and waistcoat of midnight blue silk? He glanced at his reflection, and a smile touched his mouth. Yes, she would definitely approve.

Hart looked around the room. "Kindly remind Mrs. Dawson to bring a few small vases of flowers." He straightened his cuffs. "Also, her ladyship and I will have dinner served here, with wine." Hart opened a drawer and took out the two green glass goblets they had uncovered in the dig. Now carefully cleaned, they glowed in a ray of sunlight when he set them on the table. "I will turn them over to the British Museum along with everything else, but first I can't resist toasting our marriage with these tonight."

William beamed. "May I be so bold to say, my lord, that I could not be happier for you and her ladyship today. I'd begun to worry that you might never take a wife...especially not in an arrangement like this..."

"Do you mean a love match?" He flashed a smile. "To tell you the truth, it didn't seem possible for me, either...until Emeline."

As the clock on the mantle chimed, the two men went out

into the corridor. Nearby, the door to his mother's rooms was unlocked and ajar for the first time in years. Hart paused to look in. Some of her clutter had now been packed away, but her scent still lingered. He was gradually coming to terms with a new image of his mother now that he understood the reasons behind her fretful, overprotective attitude toward him. Peachey's words continued to ease the moments of old pain: *The dowager duchess was not a perfect person, but who among us is? If she was a bit mad, perhaps she suffered in the same way you did.*

They all had suffered at the hands of his autocratic father and continued to bear the scars. Just then, the clouds parted outside and sent a shaft of sunlight streaming into his mother's bedchamber, and Hart drew a deep breath. Thank God he didn't have to live that way another day.

"We must go, my lord," William murmured from the doorway. "Your bride will be on her way to the church, and you must be waiting there."

"God, yes." Joy swept through him. As they started down the stairway, Hart saw that the massive front door stood open and he glimpsed the carriage outside.

Monte came scampering out of the library, trailed by a beaming Mrs. Peachey, to meet him at the foot of the stairs.

"How splendid you look, Lord Jasper," she said. "This might be the happiest day of my life, for I feared it might never happen."

He went forward and captured her slight form in a warm embrace. "Allow me to express my gratitude and deep affection, Peachey. I never would have reached this day without you and William."

Monte danced on his hind legs for a moment and yipped.

"I suppose you think you had a part in this, disreputable mongrel?" Hart said with a laugh. He was bending to pet the dog when a shadow lengthened in the doorway.

"By Jupiter, so it is true after all!" declared a voice he knew as well as his own.

Monte began to bark madly as Hart straightened to see the Duke and Duchess of Caversham entering the house.

"Silence," Hart ordered Monte, and the dog instantly closed his mouth and sat down on the cold flagstones. Going forward, Hart greeted Austell and Margaret with as much pleasure as he could muster. "This is a welcome surprise!"

"Accept my apologies for our last moment arrival," Austell said. "Estate business, you know. But couldn't miss my little brother's marriage!"

Hart could feel Peachey watching him. "Well, I am glad. I feared the only guests on my side would be Peachey and William, but now our simple wedding will be graced by the presence of a duke and duchess." Drawing on his gloves, he added, "Sorry to ask you to turn around and get back into your coach, but we are due at the church. I hope you don't mind."

"Not a bit!" Austell took Margaret's arm and they started back outside. "Won't you drive over with us?"

"Yes, thank you." To William, he said, "Why don't you and Peachey use my carriage to travel to the church?"

When they were settled inside and the liveried groom had closed the door with its ducal crest, the magnificent team of grays started forward.

Austell met Hart's eyes. "I brought a small gift for you." Reaching into his coat pocket, he brought out a small oval miniature and set it in Hart's hand. "Something…personal."

"My God." He stared at the exquisitely rendered image of their mother, painted perhaps about the time the twins were born. She wore a serene, kind smile that was quite different from the fretful woman Hart remembered.

"Father insisted I keep it after Mama left and returned here to live…about the time you went up to Oxford. She had it made for him early in their marriage, but when she left us, Father said he couldn't bear to see her face again." Austell looked on wistfully as Hart put the miniature in an inner pocket of his coat. "You must have it, Jasper, not I. And now Mama is present, in a way, for your wedding."

Surprisingly, Hart did not find this concept as appalling as he would have a few days ago. "Yes, I suppose so."

"It's only right," Austell assured him. "No matter what I did, Mama always favored you. I suspect she wished you had been firstborn, heir to the dukedom, so that cast a shadow over our bond."

Hart drew a painful breath. "If that's true, Mama was wrong. Not only are you a splendid duke, but we both know I would fail dismally at it." Smiling at his sister-in-law, he added, "And Margaret was born to be your duchess."

As they approached the small Norman church near the village, Austell replied, "You are kind to say so, yet Margaret and I are both keenly aware that we have not produced an heir in our five years of marriage." Leaning forward, he gripped Hart's forearm. "I must admit, this wedding is a great relief, for I'd begun to fear the dukedom might die with me. I am reassured to know that, if you have a son, *he* will one day be Duke of Caversham."

Before Hart could acknowledge this truth, the door to the coach opened and he had a view into the flower-bedecked church. Soon he would be at the altar, exchanging vows with the woman whose love had transformed his life. A warm tide of joy swept through him, carrying off every other concern.

As the groom put down the steps and handed Margaret out, Hart clasped his brother's hand. "Our past is over; the future awaits."

* * *

MY HEART IS FULL, Emeline thought as she and her father alit from their carriage and entered the ancient church, waiting just inside the doorway. Ahead were gathered the people she loved most.

At the altar, Hart stood waiting for her, still sinfully handsome yet no longer showing signs that he might be about to bolt.

Among the small party of guests were Mama, Charles, Anthony, Frederica, and little Oliver, who lifted his pudgy hand and waved. Her Raveneau grandparents turned in their seats to look at her, and she was filled with gratitude that they were able to be there. Grandpère was more than ninety, yet he continued daily to walk his dog around Grosvenor Square and work at his study desk. When Emeline lifted her simple bouquet of autumn wildflowers and mouthed, "I love you," he touched his fingertips to his heart, and she glimpsed the rakish privateer captain who had captivated her grandmother sixty years ago in New London, Connecticut.

The elderly organist commenced, somewhat unsteadily, to play a prelude, and Emeline saw Louise sitting with Tobias, across from a couple she didn't recognize at first.

"Goodness," she whispered after a moment, looking up at her father. "The Duke and Duchess of Caversham are here."

Justin St. Briac nodded, apparently unsurprised. "As they should be. And all eyes are on the utterly exquisite bride." Leaning down, he kissed her brow. "I have never been prouder that you are my daughter."

"Papa…I know this wasn't the man you would have chosen for me—"

"But you are wrong, ma petite." He gave her an enigmatic smile. "You and Hart were each utterly determined never to marry. Yet how is it possible you two arrived at this moment?" As Emeline stared back in disbelief, he nodded and tucked her hand into his arm. "Only someone as cunning as your papa could have managed to herd you both along, all the while claiming to disapprove of the match."

Before Emeline could react to this outrageous revelation, the organist launched into Handel's joyous "Arrival of the Queen of Sheba" and everyone rose, watching them. As her father escorted her down the aisle with his usual assurance, she couldn't take her eyes off Hart, the most effortlessly compelling man she had ever beheld. At the altar, when he took her hand, she felt dizzy with anticipation.

"At last," Hart murmured, his breath warm on her cheek. "Our life begins."

I am honored that you've read my book, and I sincerely hope you enjoyed it!

Would you like to be the first to know when I have a new release, a contest, sale, or a giveaway? You can sign up here for my occasional newsletter: www.cynthiawrightauthor.com.

You're invited to join my private "Cynthia Wright's Rakes & Readers Group" on Facebook. You'll be the first to see my coziest posts and "Behind the Book" tidbits. You'll also be included in special previews and giveaways and have a chance to interact with me—and with new friends who enjoy reading historical romances. I hope you'll come by now to join us—just click HERE.

You can also follow me on Instagram @CynthiaWrightAuthor.

In response to reader requests for a family tree, you can now access one on my website, under "Extras"! It shows all the connections between the characters in my books, most of whom are related in one way or another. I'd love to know what you think.

If you enjoyed reading this book, please consider posting a

brief review. It's the very best way to say thank you to an author, and your review will help other readers make a choice

Members of the irresistible St. Briac and Raveneau families reappear throughout the Rakes & Rebels series:

The St. Briac Family:
    1 – HIS MAKE-BELIEVE BRIDE (Justin & Mouette)
    2 – HER IMPOSSIBLE HUSBAND (Justin & Mouette)
    3 – HER SECRET ROGUE (Anthony & Frederica)
    4 – HIS FIERY ANGEL (Benedict & Camille)
    5 – HER BRIDEGROOM LIST (Hart & Emeline)

The Raveneau Family:
1 – SILVER STORM (André & Devon)
2 – HER HUSBAND, THE RAKE a sequel novella (André & Devon)
3 – SMUGGLER'S MOON (Sebastian & Julia)
4 – THE SECRET OF LOVE (Gabriel & Isabella)
5 – SURRENDER THE STARS (Ryan & Lindsay)
6 – HIS RECKLESS BARGAIN (Nathan & Adrienne)
7 – TEMPEST (Adam & Cathy)

The Beauvisage Family:
1 – STOLEN BY A PIRATE: a novella prequel to RESCUED BY A ROGUE (Jean-Philippe & Antonia)
2 – RESCUED BY A ROGUE (Alec & Caro)
3 – TOUCH THE SUN (Lion & Meagan)
4 – SPRING FIRES (Nicholai & Lisette)
5 – HER DANGEROUS VISCOUNT (Grey & Natalya)

Do you love audiobooks as much as I do? Most of my titles are now available in audio format, with special prices on Chirp-books.com.

A special excerpt of a related book is just ahead! And if you haven't yet read SILVER STORM, the bestselling romance of André and Devon Raveneau that started it all, you can download your copy now.

Once again, my heartfelt thanks for your support, interest, and encouragement for my books. I welcome your comments and suggestions, and I hope that you'll write to me at Cynthia@ CynthiaWrightAuthor.com. I promise to reply!

Warmest wishes,
~ Cynthia

~AUTHOR'S NOTE~

I hope you enjoyed traveling the twisty road to love with Emeline and Hart!

This series, set during the time in England when the natural sciences were growing at a fast pace, has been fascinating for me to write. Each book features a subject that initially interested me but which I had to learn *much* more about as I wrote the story.

Perhaps this is truer of HER BRIDEGROOM LIST than any other book. I was fascinated by the little I knew about artifacts and graves being discovered under parking lots and in people's gardens, but the more I learned, the clearer it became that I needed to learn even more.

In 2022, I was in England with my family and we spent a day at the British Museum, where I saw the stunning collection from Sutton Hoo (a story vividly dramatized in the film The Dig). Later, when I decided to feature an Anglo-Saxon archaeological dig in Her Bridegroom List, I read countless books and also perused fantastic scholarly papers on the website Academia.edu. Finding the material I needed was like assembling a jigsaw puzzle that wouldn't end. I also watched at least a dozen episodes of

Time Team, the fun and informative British archaeology TV series, and listened to all the podcasts I could find on this subject.

Some of the ideas for the burial chamber at Woodcroft Priory were inspired by a real-life excavation at Prittlewell, Southend-on-Sea. The "princely burial" discovered there in 2003 is of great significance, and it provided me with the idea to include the foil crosses, among other items. If you are interested in learning more about the "Prittlewell Prince", more information is available online.

A real person included in Her Bridegroom List was Antonio Panizzi. In 1842, he was the Keeper of Printed Books and oversaw the Reading Room that Emeline was so determined to infiltrate. However, it wasn't long before Panizzi championed the construction of a magnificent round Reading Room. In 1856, Panizzi became the museum's Principal Librarian.

If you'd like to see more of the images "behind the book" for Her Bridegroom List, I hope you'll visit its Pinterest page.

If you page ahead, you'll find an excerpt of HIS MAKE-BELIEVE BRIDE, the tempestuous 1818-set romance of Emeline's parents, Justin and Mouette. It's a favorite of all the books I've written. In it, you'll also meet many now-familiar characters at an earlier age.

Thank you, as always, for your friendship and support!

Warmest regards,
Cynthia

EXCERPT: HIS MAKE-BELIEVE BRIDE

RAKES & REBELS: THE ST. BRIAC FAMILY, BOOK 5

CHAPTER 1

POLPERRO, CORNWALL, APRIL 1818

*I*t didn't help Justin St. Briac's mood when the gray sky began to spit cold raindrops at him. His knees ached, curse them, as he climbed the steep hillside path to his brother's manor house. Shielding his face with one hand as the rain fell harder, he looked ahead with his good eye and saw Izzie's painting cottage nearby, just as his brother Gabriel had imagined it a decade ago, on the eve of his wedding.

As that long ago night had worn on, the St. Briac brothers imbibed more and more cognac. Eventually, Gabriel had brought out a sheaf of sketches, enthusiastically describing his plans for a hilltop estate above Polperro, including a light-filled atelier where Izzie could paint. Justin had pretended to listen while silently scoffing at his brother's dreams. Even now, seeing the handsome manor house come into view, framed in an archway of rhododendrons, he thought that appearances were usually deceiving.

"M'sieur, how fine a home your brother has made," remarked his manservant, Baptiste.

Justin was so deep in thought he'd nearly forgotten Baptiste was walking beside him. "Fine enough, I suppose."

"But of course," Baptiste amended quickly, "it pales beside your mansion in Saint-Malo."

"Do not attempt to placate me as if I were an ill-tempered old man."

"Certainly not, m'sieur." The rail-thin Frenchman fell back into his habitual state of silence.

Built of mellow Cornish stone, the home Gabriel and Isabella called Elysium was simple yet handsome, lined with windows and fronted by neatly trimmed boxwood hedges. Parkland and gardens spread as far as the eye could see. Justin found it odd to think of his younger brother as a prosperous landowner. Odder still was the notion of Gabriel as a contented husband and father who no longer cared for adventure.

It was Justin's experience that people didn't change. At least, not in ways that really mattered.

Reaching the house, they were greeted by a plump, ginger-haired housemaid who took Justin's greatcoat and Baptiste's hat. Unlike most servants who kept their eyes averted as if they weren't permitted to be human, this girl gave them bright, welcoming smiles. She was even bold enough to announce that her name was Claire.

Justin saw that the entrance hall was spacious, with a tile floor and walls paneled in carved walnut. Although the atmosphere was homey rather than impressive, he had to admit that the effect was not unpleasant. And there were tantalizing smells wafting toward them from a kitchen at the back of the house.

"*Mon Dieu*," Justin said, inhaling appreciatively. "It smells like *Bretagne*."

"Aye, sir," said Claire. "That be Madame Kerjean's fine onion tarte, made with onions brought from Roscoff." She turned her friendly gaze to Baptiste. "I'll ask that you wait here, please, while I take M'sieur St. Briac to my master. Then I'll bring you a large piece of Madame's tart!"

Baptiste, who was used to discreetly running a very grand

household, bit his lip but allowed Claire to put him in a chair before she led Justin to a door at the back of the house. At first, as she opened it, it seemed they were returning outside, but quickly he realized that he was in a sprawling, open room with floor-to-ceiling windows on three side and a high, vaulted ceiling. Seeing rows of dwarf citrus trees in pots, Justin realized this must be his brother Gabriel's conservatory.

"There you are!" called a familiar voice, and he turned to find his brother, standing at a long, rustic table with two little girls. All three of them wore long aprons, doeskin gloves, and were clearly in the midst of transplanting what appeared to be an exotic cactus.

"Are you Uncle Justin?" asked the younger child, pronouncing his name with a flawless French accent. She walked right over and extended a gloved hand. "My name is Camille St. Briac. Louise and I have been waiting for you for the *longest* time."

Justin was instantly captivated. The child couldn't have been more than four years of age. Blessed with huge eyes of Parisian blue and gleaming tawny ringlets, Camille was already a great beauty.

"*Ma belle,*" he said softly. "It is an honor to meet you."

Gabriel had put down his trowel, removed his apron and gloves, and now he took the hand of Camille's older sister. As they drew near, Justin saw that the other girl was a delicate, serious brunette, perhaps eight years of age, who wore spectacles like her mother. She regarded him with some uncertainty.

"How good it is to see you, *mon frère,*" said Gabriel. Releasing Louise's hand, he embraced Justin, who tried not to stiffen. It had been a long time since anyone had touched him with genuine affection.

As greetings were exchanged and Louise bobbed a reserved curtsy, Justin observed that his brother was still fit and lean at forty-two, with only glints of silver in his chestnut hair.

"Grandmère says you are a wicked pirate," Camille declared,

staring at Justin with frank curiosity. "It must be true. You wear an eye-patch!"

Gabriel shook his head. "Enough of that, *ma poulette*. It is midday and you two must be hungry." He gestured to Claire. "Go and see Madame in the kitchen."

Watching the girls leave the conservatory, Justin felt a momentary pang of regret that they didn't know him.

"I'm sorry that it took Maman's illness to bring you to our home at last," Gabriel said, as if guessing his thoughts. "I trust your Channel crossing was uneventful. Did you hire a conveyance?"

"No. Baptiste and I walked up from the harbor." The pain in his knee intensified as he spoke.

"Ah. I suppose I should have warned you about the steep lane leading up here from the village. Actually, there is a less precipitous drive that leads over to the main road, but no doubt my intrepid brother could climb a dozen hills like this one."

Justin looked around for a chair. "What sort of conservatory is this, without any seating areas for guests?"

"I like to keep it just for myself and the plants. It's much more convenient to be able to move in and out of the house, rather than working in an outdoor greenhouse. What's wrong? Do you need to sit down after your exertions?"

Before Justin could make a sardonic reply, Gabriel took his arm and led him back into the house.

They soon came into a library filled with books of every size and color, ranged along the floor-to-ceiling shelves and precariously stacked on a worn desk near the window. A cheerful blaze beckoned from the fireplace, where a pair of worn leather wing chairs waited for them.

"You'd doubtless like a bit of fortification before going up to see Maman." Gabriel said, pouring cognac into two crystal glasses. "Shall I order food?"

"Later, perhaps." As Justin settled into one of the unfashionable chairs, he found that it was surprisingly comfortable compared to those in his own magnificent, immaculate library. He was beginning to relax when his brother spoke again.

"What has happened to your eye?"

Justin wanted to flinch but managed instead to shrug lightly. "Ah, just a misstep during a duel. I never think of it now." Deftly, he changed the subject. "Where is your beautiful wife? I would much rather greet Izzie than our mother."

He was gratified to see Gabriel's body tense. "Isabella is in London for a few days. She's gone to visit her friend Mouette Raveneau Brandreth. Perhaps you remember her from our wedding?"

"I believe I do." To Justin's surprise, a hot tide of memory swept over him at the mention of Lady Brandreth. He'd nearly forgotten her – until that very moment. "She is well?"

"Unfortunately, Mouette has fallen on hard times - but that's another conversation." Taking a drink of cognac, Gabriel added, "Isabella was happy that you were coming to see Maman and looks forward to seeing you when she returns."

"Unfortunately, I will not be here. I must return to France as soon as possible."

"You have just arrived but you are leaving?" Gabriel murmured dryly.

"Correct." Unable to resist dangling a reminder of what his married brother was missing, Justin added, "A beautiful woman awaits my return, quite possibly in my bed."

"Indeed?" Gabriel showed no sign of envy. "Is it Azelma Marchand?"

Justin blinked at the mention of the woman he had dallied with years ago. "Are you in jest? Azelma is far too old for my taste."

"How fortunate that you alone, at forty-eight, have remained unmarked by age," Gabriel said dryly. "In view of your crowded social calendar, we are grateful you could travel to Cornwall, even for the briefest of visits."

Justin frowned. Was Gabriel mocking him? "If you imagine that I want to be with Maman any longer than necessary, you are mistaken."

"I trust you don't plan to tell *her* that."

"Do you blame me for feeling manipulated to make this journey? I have a busy life, as you know, with a great many responsibilities." Drinking his brother's fine cognac, Justin was relieved to feel the pain ease in his knee. "I came because you informed me I must, but after I see our parents, Baptiste and I will return to sleep on *Deux Frères* and set sail for France with the morning tide."

"I see." Gabriel leaned back in his chair and nodded in a way that Justin found extremely annoying. "You feel nothing when you consider the prospect that Maman may soon pass from this world?"

Justin couldn't suppress a harsh laugh. "Do you expect me to believe that she is truly at death's door? For God's sake, since the moment of my birth, I have been forced to watch her play out her little dramas and call the tune while our father danced – and you and I foolishly joined in. I vowed long ago never to join in her games when I was old enough to have a choice in the matter." Waiting in vain for his brother to agree with him, Justin reached for his snuffbox. "I will tell you plainly that I felt liberated when Maman and Papa decided to move their household to Cornwall after your marriage."

"Indeed?" Gabriel sounded unconvinced. "You could have come to visit. After you returned from your adventures with Surcouf in the Indian Ocean, our parents expected you to appear. Have you even seen their little home? It's quite charming."

"Leaving France was their choice. Can you blame me for being relieved that Maman would no longer be turning up on my doorstep, claiming to have run away from Papa?"

Gabriel's tone was maddeningly calm. "No matter their faults, they are still our parents. And it does appear that Maman is desperately ill. Before Isabella left for London, she insisted that they come here to stay, so that we could look after them."

"Maman is plotting something," Justin insisted.

"Ah yes, plotting. Perhaps a pastime that you yourself learned at her knee?" came his wry response. "Can you not suspend your judgment until you assess how ill she appears to be?"

"You seem to have fallen under Maman's spell, just like our father." When Gabriel only shrugged in response, Justin marveled again at the change in his brother. Arching a dark brow, he murmured, "Are you really happy, confined here in this conventional existence? Can you possibly enjoy – what, raising plants? – as much as planning a dangerous smuggling venture?"

Finally, he saw Gabriel's blue eyes flash. "You don't understand the first thing about botany, or the challenge of growing something new." He leaned forward. "As for this *conventional* existence, my days are filled with a treasure you have never known and could never gain through smuggling or any other reckless escapade." With soft emphasis he added, "Love."

Justin felt his nostrils flare. "Oh, please… spare me."

Gabriel pushed gracefully to his feet without any sign of aching knees. "Shall we go upstairs to see Maman? Clearly you are in a hurry to be on your way."

* * *

As GABRIEL LED the way down the wide upstairs corridor, Justin noticed the exquisite paintings that lined the walls and guessed they were the creations of his sister-in-law. One watercolor perfectly evoked his favorite view in Saint-Malo, of the isle of Petit Bé, as seen from the ramparts. A few were delightful portraits of his nieces, capturing them at the various ages he had missed, while one larger painting portrayed a family he didn't immediately recognize, seated on the wildflower-strewn Cornwall cliffs.

"That is Isabella's brother, Sebastian, with his family," Gabriel supplied, following Justin's gaze. "No doubt you remember him from his days as a smuggler? There is his wife, Julia, and their children, Cassandra and Lucas. They hosted our wedding, on their estate overlooking the River Fowey."

"But of course I remember the daring Lord Sebastian. I am very surprised that he continues to resist indulging his craving for adventure. Perhaps age and another decade of marriage have made him dull."

Gabriel seemed not to notice the bait Justin had cast before him. Instead, he continued down the corridor, inclining his head at a framed sketch as they passed by. "Isabella framed a likeness of you as well."

Justin paused before the informal portrait made so long ago. In it, he was lounging in an elegant Sheraton chair, impeccably dressed, his favorite agate snuffbox in one hand as he flicked it open with his thumb. Seeing the faintly predatory expression on his face, Justin felt a pang. Was that the way he'd appeared to Izzie? Perhaps he had rather tricked her into being alone with him, but he hadn't truly meant any harm.

Gabriel, who had gone ahead, stopped before a paneled door and knocked. After a long moment, during which Justin came up beside him, the door opened a few inches to reveal their father's face.

"By all the saints," Xavier breathed, "it is you, Justin. You have come!"

It was a shock to see his father looking considerably older, his strong shoulders slightly bent, his weathered face careworn. Justin felt himself soften just a bit. "Of course I have come, Papa. What do you take me for, an ogre?"

Before Xavier could reply, his mother's quavering voice arose from the bed. "Justin? Can it be?"

A wave of emotion engulfed Justin, catching him off-guard. For a moment, he felt physically ill. "Papa, will you swear to me that this is not a trick?" he demanded in a harsh whisper.

Xavier recoiled. "Truly, you shock me. Age and hard living have made you more cynical than ever!"

Was that an answer? Justin supposed it would have to do. His heart was in his throat as he went forward, so preoccupied with the scene in the bedchamber and his mother's pale countenance that he forgot about his own quite drastically altered appearance.

"Oh, Justin, how I have dreamed of this moment," Cerise St. Briac began, extending a shaky hand in his direction. "My first-born son. So magnificent - "

As his mother spoke, she looked up at him, focusing in disbelief. Justin watched as the rest of the blood drained from her face. He looked past her, into a mirror on a stand near the bedside, and saw the reason for her shock.

No longer was he the daring, irresistible corsair who seemed only to grow more attractive with each passing year. No, the man who stared back at Justin in the mirror was dissipated from too much wild living, too many reckless brushes with death and, a soft voice whispered inside him, an aversion to love. His black hair was now streaked with silver, lines bracketed his hard mouth, and even his waist had thickened.

Worst of all, under the black eye-patch, his arresting face was now marred by a thin white scar that slashed down from his brow, continued through his left eye – or the place where it had once been - and ended below his cheekbone. Even the duel that had cost him his eye now seemed a taunt that he was no longer invincible.

Justin's heart pounded as he saw the questions in his mother's eyes. Dying she might be, but she was as shrewd as ever, her gaze peeling back his defenses until he was utterly exposed.

"What have you done to yourself?" she asked in a ragged voice.

Reflexively, he raised a hand to touch his eye-patch. It was fashioned of black silk, edged in the same dark plum as his waist-coat. As soon as the physician had told him that he could not save his eye, Justin had decided to turn it to his advantage. He would make every man in France want to wear a rakish patch over one eye.

"'Twas but a twist of fate, Maman," he replied, adding more jauntily, "Do you not find me more dashing than ever?"

"Pray do not waste our time." Cerise patted the bed. "Sit down beside me. Each moment is precious, for there may not be many left to us."

Although Justin longed to resist, he obeyed, searching her face for signs of impending death. True, she was paler than usual, and appeared to be very tired, but if she only sat up and pinched her cheeks, wouldn't that make a difference? "Maman, I think that you may only need a nice bath, some good food, and your maid to dress your hair properly. What about a glass of champagne? I have seen that raise your spirits more than once."

She swatted at him weakly. "Pah. You are nonsensical, Justin. I am an old woman and my life is ebbing away as surely as the tide."

"Get up and walk with me. I will help you." He started to motion to his father and brother to join in his efforts, but Cerise gave him a sharp look.

"It is too late for that, don't you see?"

"Maman…" he protested. "There must be something I can do."

"You have come," she whispered. "That is a… beginning."

Justin was still absorbing her pronouncement when his father rushed over. Gently, Xavier lifted Cerise up from the pillow and held a crystal glass of water to her parched lips. Justin felt a sense of profound disbelief as he watched her attempt to sip the water, managing only a few drops before turning her face away. *Sangdieu*, how could he have allowed a full decade to pass without visiting his parents? Was it possible that his vibrant, maddening mother might actually die before he could mend things between them?

"Show me," she was saying now, watching him under her lids.

"What do you mean?" he asked warily.

"Show me your eye, *mon fils*."

She was like a cat, he thought, seemingly somnolent yet fully capable of tormenting her prey. "I would rather not."

"I am your mother. I washed your private parts long before you knew what to do with them, so I can certainly view your injured eye. You must show me now."

This interview was excruciating. Better to get it over with! He leaned closer and slowly lifted his eye-patch so that she alone could see the wound – a wound that replaced an expressive black eye nearly identical to Cerise's own.

Just when he thought this ordeal couldn't get any worse, at the moment he was about to replace the covering and retreat to safety, his mother unexpectedly reached up and touched her fingertips to his scarred eyelid. To his further horror, she began to weep.

"Justin, do you not see that this is but a sign of your broken life? You are at an age when other men have raised their children and are enjoying their homes and families."

"I am not other men," he growled. "My life is not broken! On the contrary, it is what all men secretly aspire to."

"You are speaking to your mother," she said softly, staring at him in a way that made him feel like a child again. "I will not be fooled. It is time for you to put aside your games of adventure and take up the challenges of real manhood."

"Maman! Are you delirious?" He felt his brother and father watching them with interest but forced himself to ignore them.

"If you want me to die a happy woman, a fulfilled mother, you must grant my last wish."

"Last wish?" What the devil was she talking about?

"You must take a wife...before it is too late, Justin! I cannot leave this world in peace unless I know you've taken a bride and are endeavoring to make a happy marriage." Glancing over toward Gabriel, Cerise turned the knife as only she could, "As your brother has done so *magnificently.*"

For a moment, Justin couldn't breathe. A black curtain closed around him, but he fought it off. He wasn't about to let his mother of all people perceive how deeply he dreaded being trapped in the prison of marriage, without any avenue of escape.

Breathing slowly, he felt his head clear. His relationship with his mother had been disastrous over the years, Justin realized, and now it was nearly too late. If he could win bloody battles against pirates and the British Navy, could he not find a way to grant his own mother's dying wish?

On his own terms, of course.

"*Eh bien.* If that is what you want, Maman," Justin said in a low voice, reaching for her hand, "consider it done."

She blinked. "Oh, *mon fils,* you love me after all! Will you divulge the identity of your future bride?"

"Patience, Maman, patience."

Gabriel came up beside him and spoke to their mother. "You have had enough excitement for one day, and Justin must have food after his long journey."

As they left the oppressively warm bedchamber and emerged into the corridor, Justin inhaled the fresh air of freedom.

"Thank God you rescued me just now," he said.

"For the moment," his brother replied. "Come downstairs and have a large piece of Madame's onion tart. I can't wait to hear more about the stunning plans for your marriage."

"Oh, I'm not *really* getting married." Justin gave a derisory laugh, arching a brow as he added, "But what harm can it do to pretend to grant Maman's wish? I shall fool her into believing that she alone had the power to make me take a wife, when in truth I shall remain as untethered as ever."

CHAPTER 2

LONDON, ENGLAND, APRIL 1818

ouette Raveneau Brandreth sat at a small writing desk in the window of her morning room, facing Bedford Square. Holding a quill pen poised above an inkpot, she waited for inspiration.

She was making a list of ideas for possible employment.

Governess, wrote Mouette. Seconds later, she crossed it out. How could she become a governess, living in someone else's home, when she had two sons? It might be slightly feasible if they were either adorably young or nearly adult, but Charles and Anthony were at the rather horrid ages of thirteen and nine.

Teacher, Mouette wrote more tentatively. Hadn't she been tutoring her own boys? Was it possible that anyone might actually employ her to educate their daughters? It seemed unlikely, for such positions were usually filled by men.

Mouette put down the pen and looked around the room. Although very sparsely furnished, it was not as empty as the rest of the townhouse. Piece by piece, she'd sold off the stylish furnishings chosen with painstaking care during her decade-long marriage to Sir Harry Brandreth. She'd been comfortably ensconced in the *ton* during those years, but it had all come crashing down when Harry betrayed the trust of Mouette's father, André Raveneau, and even tried to kill him. Only a few months later, he had hanged himself in prison.

It seemed a lifetime ago rather than four years. Her parents had lovingly rescued her and the boys and taken them away to their other home in Connecticut, where they'd remained as the wars between England, France, and America raged on. But Mouette couldn't be satisfied hiding from life forever.

Although her entire adult life had been spent in England, now that she had returned, she found herself struggling to craft a future. Harry had left her debts rather than a fortune. All that remained were the lavish possessions accumulated during her years of striving to become a society hostess. She'd returned from America to find trunks of exquisite, if rather dated, gowns. Storerooms were filled with furnishings in the most recent Empire style, sets of china, paintings, and other treasured valuables.

Mouette had taken this perfectly respectable home in Bedford Square, hired a

staff, and waited for something to happen, for surely something *must* happen.

And yet, her circumstances had taken a turn for the worse.

Why had she imagined her old friends would welcome her back into their midst? Instead, Mouette felt tainted by events she'd been powerless to control. Her former friends held routs but did not invite her, or they pretended to not see her in a crowd. When Mouette did attend a social gathering, she began to notice the subtle cues sent her way: the angling of shoulders to shut her out, the glances that were exchanged when she approached. Was she to be ostracized for the rest of her life because her handsome, ambitious, charming husband had turned out to be the worst sort of villain?

Apparently so.

Staring down at the sheet of foolscap, Mouette picked up her pen and forced herself to write, *Seek out a protector.* It was the one option that had a real chance of success. However not only did her spirit rebel against such a notion, but the thought of giving her body to another man was abhorrent. Even with Harry, her own husband, she had had to force herself to submit to his desires.

Just then, the bell jangled inside her front door. She'd dismissed her servants one by one over the last year, and now only one kind-hearted housemaid came to assist her when she had guests. Mouette had learned to always plan well in advance for those occasions.

Gracefully, she rose from her satin-upholstered side chair and smoothed her skirts. Her heart raced as she glanced in the gilded mirror above the mantel. She'd hung the looking-glass here just last week, to replace a family treasure she had been forced to sell, a portrait of Mouette herself. Painted by Élisabeth Vigée Le Brun, it had been made to celebrate her engagement to Harry in 1804.

Now, instead of viewing her likeness in the portrait, made at a moment when she had been young and filled with hope, she saw her older reflection in the mirror. True, she was thirty-six years of age, but was she not still lovely? If one didn't look too closely, her gleaming ebony curls, azure-blue eyes, creamy skin, and fine figure, remained relatively unchanged.

The knock came again at the door and Mouette continued on toward the entryhall. Who could possibly be calling unannounced? If it was another bill collector, she would pretend to be her own servant and say that Lady Brandreth was away for the afternoon.

Opening the door, Mouette was utterly shocked to see her younger sister, Lindsay, standing on the front step next to her childhood friend, Isabella. Could they hear the pounding of her heart?

"Goodness! Whatever are you two doing here in London?" Surely they were wondering why she was answering her own door instead of a butler. Since she had been forced to let Steele go months ago, Mouette couldn't invite anyone to come to her home. "I – I'm quite unprepared for guests!"

"Unprepared?" echoed Lindsay Coleraine with a laugh. "We have come to surprise you, darling sister! Aren't you pleased?"

With a rising tide of panic, Mouette watched them enter uninvited. "Perhaps you were surprised that I opened the door to you myself!" She wanted to press her hands to her flushed cheeks. "Steele, you see, has gone to – to visit his aunt, who is very ill!"

"Surprised? It never entered my mind," Lindsay replied with a quizzical glance. Removing her bonnet to reveal upswept strawberry-blonde curls, she added, "Whatever is the matter? You're very flushed. Do you have a fever?"

Mouette quickly recovered her composure. "Of course not. I simply was not expecting guests. Do come into the sitting room and I will order refreshments."

With a flourish, she threw open the doors leading into her sitting room. This one room remained a vision of sheer perfection, the place where Mouette had fully exercised her talent for creating an artistic living space. She'd had the walls painted the warm, inviting color of beeswax and discovered just the right Axminster carpet. Its muted shades of blue and gold perfectly accentuated the upholstery. Every candlestick, every piece of art, every small ornament that graced the polished tabletops, had been carefully chosen and placed by Mouette.

"Oh my dear, what a beautiful room!" exclaimed Isabella St. Briac, her eyes shining behind her spectacles as she turned in a circle, staring. "Where is the portrait of you by Madame Le Brun? I have dreamed of seeing it again."

A wave of shame washed over Mouette. Her friend Izzie was an artist and Madame Le Brun had been her mentor. While the Frenchwoman executed the portrait, Izzie had practiced at her own easel, while Mouette's mother, Devon, poured tea. The memory of that long-ago, convivial day in Madame's light-filled

London home, when the future held only promise, made her heart ache.

And she couldn't possibly tell her friend the truth, that she had sold the portrait to pay a particularly nasty bill collector. "I – I - " Wildly, Mouette searched her mind for a plausible explanation for the portrait's absence. "I loaned it to an artist friend who wanted to study Madame Le Brun's technique."

"Oh!" Isabella nodded, looking rather perplexed. "Well, your home is simply lovely. Clearly, your situation must be more agreeable than I had imagined."

"Izzie, don't you know that it's very bad taste to allude to one's financial resources?" Mouette scolded. They had been close friends for so long that she could speak to Isabella like a sister. "Is that why you are here? Because you two thought I might I need rescuing from dire circumstances?"

Having taken seats in a lovely pair of Adam chairs, Lindsay and Isabella exchanged guilty looks. "As it happens," Lindsay said, "I have been wanting to visit again, ever since our brief reunion when you and the boys first returned from America. However, one can't simply pop in from Oxford – and I've been very occupied with baby Bridget."

Mouette knew a moment's shame that she hadn't made a real effort to meet her new niece. "I understand completely. I've been longing to see Bridget for myself – and of course, you and Ryan. The year has flown by since I returned to London."

"You will adore Bridget! She has my hair and Ryan's blue eyes and she is already a flirt."

"It sounds like Bridget is the image of our mother. I'm rather surprised that you didn't bring her with you today." As she spoke, Mouette watched her younger sister. It wasn't easy to be with Lindsay again, remembering the way their lives had been entangled during the weeks of Harry's descent into ruin. Once, Mouette had enjoyed a feeling of superiority. She had been a member of London society, with a grand home, two beautiful children, and a handsome husband.

Now, her flush deepened as she remembered how she had held herself up as a role model for Lindsay, assuming that her sister would covet her status and apparent wealth. It was humiliating to consider how their situations had become reversed, with Lindsay enjoying a rewarding life, married to her great love who was now a professor of astronomy at Oxford University. Mouette was alone and penniless, her pride in tatters.

Lindsay spoke, bringing Mouette back to the present. "You are right, Bridget does have Mama's coloring, even more than I do."

"Speaking of our mother," Mouette said very casually, "I was just thinking today of her ruby necklace. Do you remember it? It fit around her neck like a collar." Her heart began to race. "She never cared for it because it was incompatible with her reddish hair. Do you think she left it behind in the Grosvenor Square house?"

"Of course I remember it! But I believe Mama took all her jewels back to Connecticut." Lindsay leaned forward in her chair, pinning Mouette with her gray eyes. "What's wrong? You've gone a bit pale."

"I forgot to eat at midday. Tea will help," said Mouette quickly as she rose from her chair. "And some little cakes."

"Let me help you," exclaimed Isabella. She was beside her in an instant.

"No! My maid will prepare it. We will return in just a few moments." Of course, there was no maid, and surely they must suspect something was amiss, but Mouette turned away and hurried blindly from the room.

Traversing the corridor, she paused to close the doors to the now-empty dining room and library. It was a relief to reach the kitchen at the back of the house. Shame flooded her as she remembered her mother's necklace and the expression on Lindsay's face when Mouette had mentioned it. Did her sister guess that she had sunk so low she would consider selling some of their mother's jewelry to keep a roof over the heads of her little family?

She had just filled a kettle and put it over the fire when the sound of footsteps reached her ears, accompanied by the sound of doors opening along the corridor.

"Mouette? Where are you?"

With a shock, she realized it was Isabella, following her, looking into all the rooms she had emptied of their contents in recent weeks.

Mouette's stomach churned with panic. She wanted to open the back door and run out into the garden, but just then her best friend appeared in the doorway. Looking around the kitchen, she clearly saw that there was no maid, just as the rest of the house had been nearly bare of furnishings.

"I am worried about you," Isabella said solemnly. "Please, let me help you."

To Mouette's further shame, hot tears welled up in her eyes and spilled onto her cheeks. "Help me? Why, nothing is wrong." As she spoke, her voice became a sob and she covered her face with her hands.

"Oh, darling," exclaimed Isabella. She was beside her in an instant, gathering her near. "Whatever is troubling you, you must not be afraid to tell me."

Mouette wept on her friend's shoulder for a full, blessed minute before finally she could speak. She was older than Isabella by two years and had always held the balance of power in their relationship. Mouette's parents, André and Devon Raveneau had taken Izzie in when she had been orphaned. Mouette had blossomed into a swan, making an impressive marriage, while Izzie long remained a duckling, ill-at-ease with men.

Yet now the tables were turned. Isabella was a self-assured artist, married to a charming, handsome Frenchman who treated her like a princess. It was Mouette who no longer fit in. She was six-and-thirty, for pity's sake, with awkwardly adolescent sons. Those impediments, combined with the lingering stench of Harry's scandal, rendered her virtually unmarriageable. For a woman in this world, there were few options.

Even carrying on as a respectable widow seemed virtually impossible. As an American by birth who had infiltrated London society with beauty, charm, and connections, Mouette had to realize there was no place for her now that her titled husband had died in utter disgrace.

"I perceive that you are in difficulty," Isabella was saying, patting Mouette's curls, "and I know that you have a great deal of pride. But pride must go out the window now, darling."

"I've been trying desperately to keep up appearances," Mouette admitted tearfully.

"I can see that." There was an undercurrent of gentle irony in her voice. "How are the boys? Do they realize the truth of your situation?"

Mouette straightened and wiped her eyes with a napkin. "Perhaps. A bit. Especially when I began to remove their bedchamber furniture to be sold." In spite of her misery, she laughed a little, overcome with relief to be telling someone the truth.

"Clearly you were running out of things to sell. Was your mother's necklace going to be next?" Her tone was loving rather than judgmental.

Just then, Lindsay appeared in the doorway. "I grew tired of waiting and I confess I'm rather peckish. Where are those pretty little cakes you promised?"

Mouette's chin began to tremble again. "Oh, Lindsay, I have no pretty cakes. Nor is there milk for your tea. Your sister is a *fraud!*"

* * *

ISABELLA AND LINDSAY put Mouette in a chair as they made tea. Upon discovering some eggs in the larder, Isabella cooked them with a little cheese. Once Mouette had eaten, the two women led her into the sitting room and all three of them sat together on the beautiful blue-and-gold striped settee.

Mouette felt surrounded, yet it was a relief to be forced to address her problems head-on. She had no more energy for grappling with them alone.

"I don't really understand why you are struggling this way," said Lindsay. "You know that our parents will provide a home for you and the boys, forever if necessary."

Mouette frowned. "You don't understand. We spent three years living with Mama and Papa in Connecticut. At first, it felt wonderful to be safely in their care, given all that had happened – with Harry, you know." It hurt just to say his name. "But as time passed, I realized I had to make a life for myself. A future!"

"I see." Lindsay nodded slowly. "And I can imagine that it would be daunting to be in the company of our parents every day. They are so much in love, even after all these years…"

"Yes! In truth, I gave up long ago on any dream of achieving that sort of marriage for myself. If I could make my own way in the world, I would be quite content to manage without a husband. In fact, after Harry, I would prefer it."

Isabella was staring off into space. "There must be a way for you to support yourself, without selling your possessions…"

"Or Mama's jewels," Lindsay interjected.

Mouette felt her cheeks flame. Did they have to sit so close to her, watching her every reaction? "I only thought of it in passing since Mama was never fond of rubies." When Lindsay did not reply, she admitted, "But of course, you are quite right. I suppose I have become desperate."

"It is a shame you don't have a talent," said Isabella. "Like painting."

"Or teaching," added Lindsay, who had been a schoolteacher in Connecticut before coming to England four years ago.

"I have been making a list of possible professions," Mouette told them a trifle defensively.

"Our friend Natalya Beauvisage became a successful author," said Lindsay. "Even now, as Lady Hartford, she continues to write. Her novels are nearly as popular as those of Jane Austen!"

"I'm quite sure I haven't any talent for writing, and even if I did, the thought of turning my imagination toward *romance* makes me feel ill." Sinking back against the graceful settee, Mouette added with a sigh, "The only talent I have is for furnishing a home."

After a long moment of silence, Isabella sat up straight, her eyes sparkling. "Of course! That's it! Why can you not offer your services to wealthy aristocrats who need help with artistic home decoration?"

"Izzie, you may have hit on a solution," Lindsay said, tapping a finger to her cheek.

"It's very far-fetched." Even as she resisted, Mouette felt a little twinge of excitement. "How could I do such a thing? Knock on all the doors of the very people who have shunned me since my return to London? They would surely scoff at me."

"Wait." Isabella held up a silencing hand, smiling warmly. "I have a wonderful idea! Come home with me to Cornwall for a few weeks. I know you have always found it dreadfully provincial, but it is also a place of peace and beauty where you can rest and recover from this ordeal. We can go for long walks and make better plans for your new endeavor, and when you and the boys return to London, you'll be ready to plunge right in!"

Mouette's heart spun like a top as she remembered her last journey to Cornwall, on the occasion of Isabella & Gabriel's wedding a decade ago. An unexpected wave of anxiety swept over her. Although her friend's plan sounded inviting, she wasn't a bit sure she could bear to return.

Just then, through the wide bow window, Mouette saw Charles and Anthony walking across Bedford Square, accompanied by their fencing master who doubtless expected to be paid. The sight of her sons made her straighten her shoulders. More and more often, she had regrets about the sort of mother she'd been. She wanted her boys to have a proper future, to be educated as gentlemen, and to be proud of their mother.

It came to her that she couldn't go on this way. She must put her own reservations aside and do what was best for them.

"Yes." She looked first toward her concerned younger sister and then met Isabella's eyes. "I shall come with you to Cornwall and devise a new plan going forward. I owe it to my boys to do everything in my power to make a new life."

* * *

Download HIS MAKE BELIEVE BRIDE on AMAZON!

Cynthia Wright is the *New York Times* and *USA Today* bestselling author of the three *Rakes & Rebels* series, 17 intertwining historical romances starring the irresistible Raveneau, St. Briac, and Beauvisage families. She has also written beloved series set during the Renaissance in France, England, and Scotland, and in the 19th century American West. Cynthia has won numerous awards over the years, and Romantic Times Magazine hails her novels as "Romance the way it was meant to be."

Cynthia lives in northern California. She enjoys riding a tandem bike and taking road trips in an airstream trailer with her Colombian-born husband, Alvaro and their two dogs, Watson and Halsey. She is also a devoted Gaga to her two teenage grandsons who live nearby.

You are invited to visit Cynthia's website (where you can sign up for her newsletter and peruse the Books Page):

http://cynthiawrightauthor.com/

You can join Cynthia's Facebook Reader's Group here: https://
www.facebook.com/cynthiawrightauthor/

View her "Behind the Books" boards on Pinterest:
http://pinterest.com/cynthiawright77/

* * *

RAKES & REBELS: THE BEAUVISAGE FAMILY 2

(Touch the Sun, Spring Fires, Her Dangerous Viscount)

CROWNS & KILTS: COLLECTION 1 – CROWNS

(You and No Other, Of One Heart)

CROWNS & KILTS: COLLECTION 2 – KILTS

(Abducted at the Altar, Return of the Lost Bride, Quest of the
Highlander)

ROGUES GO WEST

(Brighter than Gold, In a Renegade's Embrace, The Duke and the
Cowgirl)

OLIVERHEBERBOOKS

A small press bound by the belief that every voice matters.

Sign up for our newsletter to learn about new releases and more.
https://oliver-heberbooks.com/subscribe/

Follow us on social media:

facebook.com/oliverheberbooks
instagram.com/oliverheberbooks
amazon.com/oliverheberbooks
youtube.com/@OliverHeberBooksPublisher